LETO'S CHILDREN

THE LETO TRILOGY
BOOK 1

WILLOW DAWN BECKER

LETO'S CHILDREN

This book is a work of fiction. The characters, incidents, and dialogue are drrawn from the author's imagination an dare not to be construed as real. Any resemblance to actual events or persons, living or dead, is entirely coincidental.

Paperback Edition
ISBN: 978-1-7378918-3-3

Published by Weird Little Worlds, LLC, Cedar Hills, UT 84062
http://www.weirdlittleworlds.com

Cover art by Stefan Keller ©2022
Cover design and additional design by Willow Dawn Becker

LETO'S CHILDREN

BOOK I OF THE LETO TRILOGY

WILLOW DAWN BECKER

To Abigail and Elyse.
Can I tell you a story?

Shall I sing how at the first Leto bare you to be the joy of men,
—the lord Apollo and Artemis who delights in arrows;
her in Ortygia, and him in rocky Delos—

as she rested against Mount Cynthus in that rocky isle
—while on either hand a dark wave rolled on,
landwards driven by shrill winds —
whence arising, you rule over all mortal men?

All mountain-peaks and high headlands of lofty hills
and rivers flowing out to the deep
and beaches sloping seawards
and havens of the sea are your delight.

Rejoice, blessed Leto, for you bare glorious children.

Anonymous. The Homeric Hymns and Homerica.
Translation by Hugh G. Evelyn-White. 1914.

PROLOGUE

Portland City, *Earth*

April 2077

It was nice to take a taxi alone, usually. It was a chance to get out of her trailer, with its bags of debris and collection of used parts scattered across the floor. And there was something other than screens to look at. Ezrie's eyes didn't love the light (years of late night coding will do that to you), and it had taken two taxis and a walk to the transit station for them to stop watering.

But Ezrie didn't love *this* ride. And it was one of the few times she could remember in years that she was scared to be alone.

She wasn't from Portland City, and the green of the downtown trees was a brilliant change from her sandy patch of the Texas Territories. But the driverless vehicle had snaked through the city, down along the long-dead Columbia River, and into what could only be described as the ass-crack of the city.

Broken windows gazed out over the dusty concrete wasteland, matched by the gaping front window of abandoned gas station nearby. The light from the setting sun turned the few fragmented and stunted trees—relics from the city's prime—into shadows, their leaves charred from too much sun and not enough water.

The car arrived at the location, the AI stating that she was at the address she had double-checked a million times. Fare was deducted from one of her fake accounts as she stepped through the ion field door scanner, pausing only to tap the screen that told the car to wait.

A man passed, shirtless, and muttering, and Ezrie tucked her hand into her pocket, touching the weapon there like a talisman.

"Relax, Z," she muttered. "Don't make it weird."

As Ezrie walked to the building, she glimpsed a pair of leggy girls leaning against it, shrouded in shadows. But they didn't see her or care. They stood together beneath a street lamp, staring into their trace devices. Zooming is what the Gen kids called it. They giggled, their eyes focused on the visions the biometric device in their brains offered them. Ezrie was lucky she'd been smarter than that. God knew where or who she might be if she'd still had a trace fused to her brain stem like these poor idiots.

Ezrie buzzed the door of the three-story building, her guts in knots. She gripped the laster—an uparmored taser she'd gotten as payment a few years back. It had belonged to a police officer, at least that's what she'd figured from the serial number that had been hastily scratched out. She was more of a runner than a shooter, so she'd never had a reason to pull the trigger. At least not on any real person.

Am I even meeting a real person, she wondered? She half hoped it was a weird prank. Usually her business associates were more than happy to stay unseen. But this one had been insistent they meet IRL. And she couldn't afford to blow this deal. Not when they had exactly what she needed. What Marcus deserved.

A voice muttered something from the buzzer box. The door lock snicked open and Ezrie assumed it had been an invitation.

The building was a relic from a time long past. No ion field doors here, that was for damn sure. A large overhead light had been smashed, and pieces of glass crunched beneath Ezrie's feet as she bypassed the decaying elevator for the stairs. She trudged up dirt-caked steps and past forlorn condom wrappers and Happy Meal boxes to the fourth floor, the location for the exchange. It wasn't as dark up here—pale streetlight and a stale breeze wafted through gaping windows—but it didn't help much. She walked beneath rust-eaten beams and over chemical stains. The whole deal rankled on her nerves, but Ezrie had the laster. If the deal was a trick or a setup, Ezrie would unload 400,000 volts into someone's brains.

Hey, there was a first time for everything.

When she reached the third-floor landing, however, she was surprised to find a shiny titanium door nestled between two massive beams. As she came close, the door slid open, and a slight figure greeted her. A woman with blonde hair and green eyes.

"Come in." The woman's voice was dark, but crisp. Her smile was gracious, but there was calculation behind her lips. "So, you're Ezrie Collings. Quite a celebrity. I've looked you up."

Ezrie shifted uncomfortably. She hated when people knew her.

She glanced around the room, half-expecting the black armored goons from ICET—the International Communications Enforcement Team—to pop up from behind the wood-inlaid armoire or low-slung Winchester chairs. That wasn't this place at all. This place was a lot of chick-lit chic and money. Not Ezrie's typical customer.

Over the woman's shoulder, behind a pair of tall French doors, she could see perfectly polished metallic tables and stands of rolling carts. From the steel-beamed ceilings nearly thirty feet overhead, she could see what looked like bodies strung up. But no. They glinted metallic in the setting sun through the tall banks of windows that overlooked the city. On a table, there was an android, it's head open and attached to something pink and fleshy.

"What is this place?"

The woman smiled. "My private lab. I like to keep it off the radar. You understand, I'm sure."

Ezrie nodded. A chill floated over her skin.

"Come back to the sitting room," the woman said, pausing to close the door to the lab as she went. Ezrie strained to see more, but only caught a glimpse of surgical instruments and android parts. The woman led her to a small room that adjoined a meticulous kitchenette. She sat down on an overstuffed couch the color of bone adorned with a plush turquoise blanket and two chevron-patterned pillows. She motioned Ezrie to the matching chair.

The woman poured two glasses of water and handed one to Ezrie before curling up on the couch. Ezrie took it, dipping a fingernail surreptitiously into the drink. After a minute, when the polish didn't turn red, she took a sip. It was delicious. Not like the desal and reclaimed water she had to make do with back at her trailer in Texas. She drank it too fast, giving herself a headache.

"Good, isn't it?"

"Amazing," Ezrie said, too overcome to pretend otherwise. She wiped her face with the corner of her radiation jacket and burped. The woman gave her a look. Something like a teacher grading a test.

"The Black Door," the woman said, sipping her water. "An interesting thing. A lot of people told me it wasn't real. The same people who told me *you* weren't real."

"It's real." Ezrie finished the drink. "As soon as you give me what I came for."

The woman laughed again, and shook her head. There was something strange about her eyes. Green colored contacts. "Relax, Ezrie. I'm not here to con you. You could change the world with tech like this, you really could. Consider that. All the people who could instantly get to where they need to go. Space travel. I have some connections—"

"I'll stick to what I know, thanks."

The woman smiled. "Well, maybe you'll change your mind. There's a lot of money out there. A lot of need for people who think big. People like you and I."

Ezrie considered the lab she'd glimpsed. She was some kind of scientist maybe. Tech was probably very much in this woman's wheelhouse, considering that she'd tracked Ezrie down all on her own. Ezrie made a note to be harder to find.

The woman smiled. "Only people who are willing to make the sacrifices for progress ever change the world, Ezrie."

Ezrie snorted. "My father sacrificed everything for progress. Not interested."

Not today. Not ever.

Ezrie brought out the drive—a small red item that reminded Ezrie of the tiny flags that they sometimes put in sandwiches. Except that this one had a flag made up of several hundred circuits. "Where are your doors?"

The woman took her through a door and into another room that looked like some kind of study. A large bookshelf lined one full wall. In place of a window, a large retina screen played scenes from an impossibly green location.

From the shadows, another woman rose.

"Intruder," the woman's voice stated.

Ezrie's hand went to her laster. "What the—"

"Hold," her host commanded. The woman paused.

"Jesus," Ezrie breathed. Not a woman. But it was so close it was hard to tell otherwise. The android had flawless skin, and its hair was the same color as the woman's before her. It was one of the most realistic androids she'd ever seen. The two looked as though they could be twins.

"What the hell is going on?" Ezrie snarled. "I never signed up for—"

"It's not personal," the woman interrupted. "I always have one or two around when I do business. It's safer for everyone."

Ezrie wondered. Despite her stasis, the androids' eyes clicked over her, perhaps recording her. Android lore wasn't Ezrie's specialty, but even she knew that it was probably new on the market or even a prototype. She held her questions, though. If she asked questions, the woman might ask her own. There was no place here to make friends.

They entered a large open room which seemed to be nearly half a football field long. In the middle was an ancient production line, complete with a conveyor belt and a graveyard of rusting machinery.

"It used to be a thread factory," the woman said. "They boiled and wove it here. A fascinating history, if you ever have a minute to look into it. A lot of children lost a lot of fingers in this room."

Several large refrigerators lined the walls of the room, interspersed with what Ezrie could only imagine to be large threading mills and defunct boiling vats. Several metallic tables had been pushed against the far wall. On each side of the room a porter had been erected. Ezrie inspected them thoroughly, looking for all the same flaws and misalignments that she was in the habit for looking for. But the scanners were clean, the mainframe was fully integrated. The woman had installed a port log. Ezrie fiddled with it, ensuring that it accurately tracked the same information that ICET was tracking.

"Have you used these before?" Ezrie asked.

The woman shook her head. "It would defeat the purpose to put them on the radar, wouldn't it?" She smiled. "They're functional, though. I printed them myself. The goal is to make sure they stay hidden."

Ezrie flipped the access panel open, pulled out a small penlight, and installed the flag-like drive from her backpack directly into the main motherboard. The ion field flickered. She walked the long distance to the other side, painfully aware of the woman and her android watching as she tripped over a pile of dusty detritus on the other side of the great hall. Ezrie cursed herself, then dropped and installed the match.

The all-seeing eye of the oculus flashed green. Ezrie stepped on the platform before the great titanium door—a door for a giant, over twelve feet tall and girded by supports that had been driven at least a foot into the concrete floor of the warehouse. The oculus summed her up, scanning her from both the top and from the daughter oculi on each of the door's sides. They tallied her molecules even as they were in motion. They created a shadow version of her, in some reality where ones and zeros were like mountains and spacetime was set on its edge like a sheet of paper. Each ion of the unseen Ezrie entangled with her own.

From behind the woman, the android watched. Its eyes flicked in and out of focus.

Ezrie paused before stepping through, even though she felt the woman's eyes boring into her back. Even now, at nearly twenty-nine years old, stepping beneath the watchful eye of the porter oculus shrunk her down, making her thirteen again. Making her the girl who wanted to destroy the machine because it had destroyed her life.

Ezrie took a breath and closed her eyes. There was this moment, at the instant you stepped through the porter, when it felt as though you would tear apart into nothingness and be eaten by the infinite distance of what you were and what you were about to be. A second later, she was breathless and on the other side of the room.

Don't think about it. Don't think about what's inside the dark. Don't think—

The woman smiled at her. "Incredible," the woman said, shaking her head at the port alert readout. "It doesn't even register with ICET at all." She clapped her hands together, her eyes bright, her cheeks flushed and high. "It's perfect. Range? A thousand miles? A hundred thousand?"

"Infinite. At least that was always the original plan." Ezrie's memory flashed. Her father had been adamant. *There is no limit to what we can do, Z,* he'd said. *We can travel the universe.*

Ezrie cleared her throat. "There's no limit. Anywhere. But it's not as stable as the ones ICET tracks. You can't port less than 0% transmitter strength. Ever."

The woman lips curled. That calculated look was back in her eyes. "Of course. Very faze. Isn't that what the kids say?"

Ezrie shrugged. "I wouldn't know. About the payment—"

"Patience, Ezrie. You'll get what you came for." The woman blinked into her trace, her eyes going slightly distant. Ezrie resisted the urge to sneer. It was impolite to tell someone that they were a brainwashed idiot when they were about to help you settle a lifelong score.

The door to the abandoned factory opened and yet another woman with the same face entered. Ezrie thought of the silver and gold bodies hanging in the great room. If they were anything like the androids she had already seen, this was the cutting edge of technology. Not only did every android represent billions of quan, but, if they were all activated at once, they were strong enough to tear down a city block in a few hours.

The android offered a small silver tray with a black box the size of a deck of cards. The woman placed her finger on box's black glass top. A blue light flashed from beneath the shiny exterior and the box unfurled, revealing infinitesimal cracks along geometric lines that widened to gashes. The box segmented into diamond-cut shapes, then settled into a petal formation around a velvet bet.

Lying inside was a shining black pearl. Ezrie leaned in, her fingers itching to touch it.

This is what death looks like, Ezrie thought. *It's a lot smaller than I imagined.* "How do I know it will work?" she asked.

The woman plucked the pearl delicately, revealing a short metal prong that made the device look like an earring. She reached over to the android and pushed its blonde hair back from its neck. The woman pushed it into the android's small cortical control unit.

The android eye's flickered, flashed.

"Warning," it said. "Warning, malfunction. Critical failure."

The legs and arms shook, dropping the box. Ezrie took a step backwards as the android shuddered and jittered, its eyelids fluttering spasmodically.

"Error. Error. Critical failure," the voice box crackled.

The android dropped to the ground with a crash. There was a hiss and a series of soft pops. A greasy yellow fluid ran from the ears and nose. The eyes flickered and went dark.

The woman stooped down and plucked the small device from the android's brain, snagging the box as well. She wiped it off and handed both to Ezrie. When Ezrie's hand placed the pin back in the box, the blue light blinked on and it closed the way it had opened, like an ocean of glass shards coming to rest on a mirrored shore.

There was a coppery taste in Ezrie's mouth. Even though she had no great love for androids, it took a special kind of sociopath to let such a piece of artistry be destroyed to make a point. Whoever this woman was, she wasn't someone to toy with.

"I better be on my way." Ezrie said, coughing the words out of what felt like sun-bleached vocal cords. "Thanks."

"Of course," the woman said, her green eyes blazing. "Thank you for everything. If there's a problem with Black Door, not that there will be—" Her voice had a slight edge. "Maybe I could have you help me again. It's always good to have someone who knows the Olet Porter inside and out."

The woman's eyes were flat, but the smile was broad. It was unnerving. She wondered if the woman had looked up some of the old interviews. There were a few that had avoided being erased, saved by people who'd believed her back when she was still trying to set things right.

"Maybe," Ezrie said.

Ezrie slid out the door as fast as she could. She sped down the steps so fast she almost tripped. *Slow down, Ezrie,* she told herself. *Relax. Don't drop the damned thing because you're in a panic.*

She slipped into the waiting car, the box clutched to her stomach like a talisman, feeling that she'd done something wrong. No. She was always doing something wrong. This time, she felt like she'd made a mistake, and she didn't even know why.

Ezrie went back to Texas the long way, boosting Fords that hadn't gotten the 2055 security update. She hacked the nav, rode them until she found something new, and kept driving. Always making sure the box was safe. Waiting until dark to watch the shell open like a rose to reveal the poisoned pearl within.

When she got home, she placed the box beneath her bed, pushing it to the wall where it would collect dust for nearly two years, out of sight but never quite out of mind. When the time came for her to take care of Marcus, she had the means. The perfect solution. But she had nightmares sometimes of the android shaking, buckling, the yellow fluid leaking. And she'd see it wasn't an android at all, but her own father drowning in cerebral lubricant.

She burned up the online feed that the woman had tracked her down on. Ezrie killed any accounts or avatars that the woman might have touched. But she worried for a long time that the android-killer might somehow try to find her again. But she was a ghost already, she figured. What did she have to lose?

PART 1
RED IS FOR REVENGE

"You begin simply, by learning how to divert systems. It only takes a bad piece of code or a carefully placed comma to confuse the machine. Diverting systems is about reorganizing the brains of the machine to follow a set of commands that will take it down the rabbit hole while you sneak up behind it and steal what you need."

The BlackBook, Last Accessed 2072

I

New Texas Territory, *Earth*

January 2080

IMPOSSIBLE TO KILL. That's what the package said when it arrived. Ezrie opened it up with an undue amount of excitement, red dust fluttering from her fingers as they tore at the tape. She had it inside the trailer even before the postal drone had fully disappeared back into the sky.

"Impossible to *open* is more like it," she muttered, picking at the tape with broken fingernails, then slicing it open with a butter-covered knife. It was two weeks late, but beggars couldn't be choosers when you wanted to find an undocumented, untraceable delivery drone service. Her heart squeezed with an excitement that she knew wouldn't last. But, at least for today, it made her feel something.

Ezrie pulled out her prize, pricking her finger only once on the jagged needles of the cactus. Of course, it was risky to have anything delivered to her. But she couldn't help it. No matter what kind of danger it put her in, she had to have something alive. Even if she knew that eventually—no matter what the packaging said—she would end up killing it.

Ezrie introduced the cactus around the tiny trailer, showing it her computer and the room where her teleporter sat, unplugged and unused for almost six months, before depositing it with the others—nearly 20 ceramic pots with plants in variable states of decay.

She sighed heavily. "It's the water, you know. Not a lot to go around," she said to the cactus, half imagining its shock at the rampant vegicide. It was a lie. They usually died because Ezrie forgot that they were there. But at least she was only hurting a cactus this time.

Despite the blackout curtains, the trailer was already starting to warm up. She called the air conditioning on, then took a quick peek from behind her front window.

She could see the dusty, sunbaked earth frying beneath the January sun. Deadly hot. At the edge of her property (which she got for a steal because no one wanted to live in the No Man's Land of the Texas Territories) her counter-intelligence drones buzzed, setting up the shielding that kept her invisible. There were several more potted plants that had long-since died lying against the trash heap which was now two months high. She shook her head at their corpses.

Impossible to kill, my ass, she thought. *I should write a scathing Nets review*. But honestly, it said more about Ezrie than the plants, didn't it? Ezrie could kill the unkillable.

Ezrie linked into the Nets over breakfast and called on the news, smiling at the new cactus—the centerpiece of her coffee table. From the holoprojector, the political garbage, celebrity gossip, and riot footage poured over her as she gnawed a bone. She washed it down with the last of her reclaimed water so as not to taste it.

All the Nets boards were quiet this morning except for a message from a contact she had in Pakistan about finding a weak patch for RocketForce, and could she create a crowbar program by next week? She tapped her response, half-listening to the news, scrounging a couple jobs she could do for water money. It was all easy code cracking and simple tech builds. Nothing big, but worth a few thousand yuan in total. A good week's work.

A message flickered across the screen. She scanned it, her eyes snagging on the name at the bottom.

Marcus Olet.

Everything went hot and cold at the same time. Her hands were shaking as she flicked off the projected screen. It couldn't be him, it couldn't...

She wanted to scream. She wanted to smash something. But she felt numb and frozen. She was suddenly so cold.

Ezrie fumbled to the shower, not bothering to take off her tank top and underwear. She turned the water to scalding, knowing it was burning her, but not caring, not even bothering to wipe the stinging blue chemical scrub from her eyes. She tried not to think, but there were too many thoughts and memories crowding, drowning her.

It had been a long time since she'd seen Marcus. How many years? Fifteen?

So much had happened since then. Too much.

She thought she felt the shadow of that old hatred, the rage that had driven her in the first, desperate years. The places she had searched for him that barely existed except for dog-eared maps and whispered clues.

Newton, Pennsylvania.

Orchard Grove, Utah.

Liberty, Mississippi.

Ezrie had driven that last one herself, brazen, unafraid of being tracked by the patrol drones that flitted above the dry, baked-earth riverbeds that served as the state's unofficial highway. That had been nearly five years ago now.

When she had arrived, the house ha d been another dummy—an empty lot with a "For Sale" sign. The trace integration chip that would have allowed her to hear the price and number of bathrooms (if she'd had a trace herself, that is) had been long since stolen. She had been more disappointed in that, actually. At least the chip would have bought her a night in a skeezy hotel. A dead end with no Marcus was one thing. Another night spent half-awake, jamming the truck's signal so that the trollers passed by was like salt in the wound.

Ezrie came out of the shower, commanding the air dryer on. As she sat on a pile of dirty laundry, her blue footsteps dried to nothing. Like she'd never even been here at all.

She could forget the past, let it dry up and blow away. None of it mattered any more. Marcus had won. She had lost. The only ones who cared were dead, anyway.

But then she remembered sitting, small and scared in the plastic hospital chair, defending him—even as Marcus jockeyed to put his name on the teleporter prototype that her father had died to complete.

The case worker who had been assigned to her asked questions that Ezrie refused to answer.

How long ago did your father die?

Were you the only one caring for him?

How long has it been since you've been to school?

Where is your mother?

Ezrie could only tell her one thing: *Marcus will come. Marcus will take care of me.*

It had taken time to realize that he was a liar. But she'd only been thirteen. And she had wanted to believe him. But when she'd seen the porter in the news for the first time—The Olet Porter—that's when she knew.

He was never coming for her. And he was her enemy.

Ezrie went back to the holoscreen and opened the message. The location was real. Sent through the trace security program Ouros. If anyone knew how unhackable that was, it was Ezrie.

It had to be a hoax. Yet the teleporter location pin included as a footnote looked real enough. The DNA-generated sequence included the same tagged characters she had tracked him with all these years.

After all this time, he'd finally come to her.

Breathe Ezrie, she thought. *It's a trap.*

"No shit," she muttered. She tapped the message open, anyway.

```
Ezrie,

    I am sorry for all that has happened
between us. I have found a way to make
things right. This pin will bring you where
you need to be. I don't have much time. I
can understand if you leave me here to die.
You should after what I've done.
```

Marcus

Marcus' message ignored the years but struck the right notes. Apologetic. Contrite. He knew what she wanted to hear.

Once a liar, always a liar.

But he had finally answered her messages. He had finally come to repair what he'd broken.

It's probably death if you go, a quiet, small voice in her head whispered. *How can you trust him?*

She smiled. "I don't."

Ezrie backtracked Marcus' message, opening up the hidden coding and using a custom tracking program to map its progress. She removed the security code, a few lines of logic that needed to be redirected. Then she visualized the data on her projector screen. It called up a map of Earth, the Mars and moon colonies, and a few outlying mining stations on Titan—every place that a message might be coming from.

The map blinked a single light, of course, her own location in Texas. After a breathless moment, additional lights blinked on the screen tracking the path of the message. Locations lit up in California, El Salvador, Nigeria, and Mars South.

"Someone doesn't want to be followed," she mumbled.

ERROR. LOCATION UNKNOWN.

Ezrie ran the location again through all her maps and location programs, this time including off-shore sites, private mining databases and personal properties on the lunar surface and Jupiter's colonized moons, Io and Europa. Nothing.

"He's sending me into the goddamn nothing of space," she muttered.

So, the Marcus train ended in Texas and began somewhere unknown. On principal, she refused to go where he wanted her to go. But if she could get ahead of him a step, she might be able to gather some intel. Figure out what he wanted before she took the last leg of the trip.

The signal was protected, high level. Mars. She'd been out there before. Mining country was always a little like the wild west. The only law there was paid for by the mines. Everything else was survival of the fittest.

"This is crazy," she muttered. "I can't." Her things were here: her screens. Her drones. The components and parts that she used to build and hawk porter hacks. But, somewhere, there were magazines with Marcus' face on them, the eyes torn out.

You promised. You promised to make it right.

She felt that old ember burning now. Yes, she still hated Marcus. She had business to finish with him.

The porter loomed, a shoddy-looking thing that stood nearly fifteen feet tall in the shed at the back of the trailer. The two legs that supported the oculus beam were made of scraps, which gave it a patchwork color. She touched one of the rough welds, shaking her head at her own haphazard work.

She revved the generator on, the sound ear-splitting, and plugged the porter in. It began its own hum, the oculus light blinking red as it warmed up. She hadn't powered it on for months now, maybe even a year. Not that ICET could track her ports—the Black Door frequency made her incognito wherever she went. But the police drones sometimes made rounds, even out here, and the kind of energy that the porter needed had aroused suspicion before.

The empty door frame of the porter sizzled to life, and a sizzling, popping field of light filled the empty space where a door should be.

There was a *ker-chunk* from the generator, and the light flickered twice before resettling as a smooth panel of yellow ions. She swallowed hard. It was probably fine.

Her father's image flashed in her mind, his skin sloughing, his eyes bleeding yellow gore.

I won't think of that. Not today.

As the sound of the porter's hum increased, she dug out her radiation suit from a pile of dirty clothes and stuffed essentials into her "go" bag. A manual screen and computer board, a few personal items, a few weapons (just in case) and her laster. It had been partial payment for a crack job she had done for some weapons dealers a long time before. She'd still never used it, but it always made her feel safer to have it with her. She flicked it on, relishing the hum and warm vibration in her hand.

The last thing was the virus. She took the earring from its box beneath her bed, wiping the dust gently. It unfolded in diamond brilliance, the black pearl stud like a jewel against the velvet. Ezrie put it on carefully. Even though she knew it couldn't hurt her, she had seen what it could do. She was counting on it.

On impulse, she grabbed the dog-eared photo from beside her bed. It had been taken at the ocean on a vacation. Her mother hadn't wanted to pay for a picture. But her father had insisted, and he'd paid the man with the acne and moustache almost twice what he'd asked to take as many pictures as it took to get a good one.

In it, the light of the setting sun filtered through her father's thinning hair and highlighted her mother's short, round nose. Molly was looking up at Richard, as if she might kiss him. Ezrie looked up at them, smiling, her black hair pinned back with plastic barettes. It had been taken so long ago that Ezrie now resembled her mother more than herself. They had the same pale skin and black hair. But her boxy jaw and her eyes were her father's. The combination had always confused people. "You're Japanese?" she'd had a teacher once ask incredulously. "I don't believe it."

"Neither do I," Ezrie had said. But her looks gave people the impression that she was something that she was not. Throughout her life, strangers had spoken to her in different languages—Japanese, Chinese, even Spanish —assuming she could understand. But she understood them about as well as she had understood her own mother, who never spoke a single word of Japanese. No, Molly's language was English, but she was as closed and coded and unknowable as if she were speaking an alien tongue.

Ezrie gave one last scan of the trailer. Was there anything she was forgetting? The cactus sat on the coffee table as if to answer. Impossible to kill. Maybe she would be back soon. Maybe this time her little plant would stay alive long enough to greet her when she returned.

Ezrie wanted to believe it was true, but she knew better. Nothing that she cared about ever lasted. Like that poem her father had read her when she was little: *Nothing gold can stay.*

By now, the generator roared like a diesel engine and the porter read the signal strength at ninety-one percent. The oculus eye was steady green, ready to send her into the unknown. She felt small. Scared. But the shimmer of the ion field was patient. It hummed in her father's voice.

She inputted the location manually, her stomach queasy and greasy. Then Ezrie placed her hand on the porter panel. It took her DNA and made that shadow copy of her. Somewhere she was already there. Somewhere on Mars, not quite where Marcus wanted her to be. But close enough to take matters into her own hands.

Because I can kill anything, she thought. *Even Marcus.*

The door shimmered, the ions speeding up, becoming a yellow frenzy of motion. Ezrie gripped the laster tightly in one hand, the strap of her pack in the mesh glove of the other. She held her breath and stepped through.

II

PanGen Headquarters, Marwth Vallis, *Mars*

January 2080

PURPLE WAS BRAINED, full on. He'd been awake near twenty-four hours and he was flagging hard. The code swirled in front of him, numbers and letters that dodged and skittered when he tried to understand what they were saying. Naught but abnormal algorithms and abortive executions.

TRANSMISSION ATTEMPT…LINKING…TRANSMISSION FAIL.

TRANSMISSION ATTEMPT…LINKING…TRANSMISSION FAIL.

It was a gobby mess, is what it was. The error codes that covered the visual display from his trace made it virtually impossible to see the porter beyond—the porter where every engineer and coder on the PanGen campus reamed sideways about the Apollo team not porting back from the planet Leto.

They were late. And late back from an interplanetary port was a bloody nightmare.

He connected to the diagnostic team chat, and every virtual voice seemed to fill up his field of vision. He blinked the display to minimal so that he didn't feel like he was choked out before serving up a new slice of the failure logs.

ANYBODY. I NEED ANYTHING, he sent. WHAT CAN YOU TELL ME?

THEPACMAN##: I'VE RUN DIAG FROM EVERY DIRECTION. THIS THING IS STICKY, BRUH.

PRAYDOLLZ: YOU NEED A CIPHER. IT'S DEFINITELY SOME KIND OF CRYPTO. HAVE YOU CHECKED CRYPTKREEPZNET?

DONE IT, Purple sent, sighing. No new solutions. Just circles running his head raw. If anyone should be able to fix this, it was himself.

FRIDD225: YOU'RE UP A CREEK, MAN

JIMINEZSEAN10: HAVE YOU TRIED TURNING IT OFF AND TURNING IT BACK ON AGAIN?

Purple chuckled, but it caught in his throat as Rand barreled into the control room. He sheared through the frantic bodies of porter technicians and engineers like a shark through a school of fish. Rand was the Captain of the PanGen Artemis team and a walking cliché—all hard jaw and buzzed hair. His face was constantly disappointed, as if someone had dredged him up from an old military movie and then told him the war was over. Rand, of course, refused to believe it.

"Are we able to send anything through?" Rand clipped.

"A plant, maybe," Purple hedged. "One that nobody liked."

The glare Rand gave him made Purple's balls sweat.

"Sorry. Um, not really. Everyone on the code team is stumped. We've never seen anything like it. It says we are not approved to port to the planet."

"Under whose authority?"

"I don't know. All I know is that it's coming *from* Leto."

"You're sure?"

"Whatever code is breaking the system is coming from up there," Purple explained. "I've never seen it before. Also, one of the transmitters is offline." Purple took a deep breath, "And so is the Mountain porter."

Rand rubbed a hand across the salt-and-pepper stubble on his chin. "Why the hell are we missing transmitters and porters? Jesus—"

"We've rerouted so that we can use the two working parts together, going through the Mountain transmitter and the Ocean porter—"

"Reroute through goddamn Angola if you have to," Rand snapped. "Whatever you have to do to get us back on the planet."

"I'll keep trying, sir."

Rand stalked off, blinking something silent on his trace to people Purple couldn't see. Purple never had a hard-on for leadership, but it had crossed his mind. Still, he was glad he wasn't in charge today.

Alex sidled up next to Purple at the console. Alex was Russian, and huge, and was what Purple privately considered "disastrously confident." According to Alex, he had slept with two of the three stars of Pitaña Gang, and sometimes went drinking with Kevin Garner's assistant. He was the fazest person Purple knew. His easy manner belied only a fraction of the anxiety that Purple knew he must be feeling. As the head Safety Officer, Alex was the one that everything would land on if someone at HQ had messed up.

"I hear you're the guy to talk to if we want a plant murdered," Alex said, his voice strained but jovial. His accent always thickened when he was stressed out. Even though he seemed faze, Purple noticed the extra thickening around the word "murdered." It sounds like "more-dirt."

Purple's smile felt thin on his face. "Superfaze. I'm running a special on making things die painfully, cut into little pieces, and shot into space. Supplies are limited."

Alex chuckled, clapping Purple on the back so hard that the wind was knocked from him. "You'll get it figured out. Besides," he nodded towards Rand, "getting all cranky will only make it worse."

Except Alex's thickened accent turned it into "make it wars." That's exactly how it felt. *Rand should be happy about that,* Purple thought. *The war is back on, don't you know, and I'm in the line of fire.*

"Aye," he said with what felt like plastic optimism. "I'll figure it out."

"Good kid," Alex said, ruffling Purple's hair. Purple yanked his head away, scowling. He hated being called kid.

As soon as Alex was gone, Purple blinked his trace into the diagnostic team chat.

PURPLE: I NEED SOME ANSWERS. WHAT DO YOU HAVE?

The chat feed froze as his team scrambled to come up with more lame excuses for why no one could fix the one thing they were paid to fix. Purple could see Samantha walking towards him.

"Shite," he muttered. *Lord Jesus, don't let her talk to me now.*

Sam was the Artemis team psychologist, but she was also Rand's wife. And the owner of the nicest pair of boobs Purple had ever seen in real life. All things that made her very, very dangerous.

"How are you feeling, Purple?" Sam beamed. Her cleavage winked at him and Purple felt his face go red.

Dammit, Purple thought. *As I suspected, God does not exist.*

"Uh," he tried to refocus away from Sam's cleavage. "Um, fine. I've found at least one porter and one transmitter, so hypothetically, they should be able to port back home."

"And how about you? You look like you've been up for a while. When's the last time you slept?"

He groaned inwardly. She was always doing this "professional concern" thing that felt so much like having a second, uncomfortably attractive, mother. At nineteen, he was the youngest member of the Leto team, and Sam was always calling him into her office to make sure he was acclimated and asking lots of questions about his mom and sisters. She gave him advice about girls. Stuff that he supposed was normal from any therapist, but he was ninety-nine percent sure this is how Oedipal complexes were born.

"Fine as rain." *Mostly because I've eaten enough caffeine tablets to choke a horse.* "I'm tougher than I look."

"Of course," she said, giving him a small squeeze on the arm. "We all know you're tough. The smartest of us all."

A private message opened on his trace from one of the lead diagnostic specialists.

PRAYDOLLZ: I CHECKED AROUND ON THE BLACKNET AND FOUND SOMETHING. THAT TRANSMISSION FAILURE? IT HAS A CASKADE LOCK SIGNATURE AT THE VERY END.

PURPLE: WHOSE DNA IS THE LOCK SET TO?

PRAYDOLLZ: NO ONE WE KNOW.

"Dreck it," Purple hissed.

"What?" Sam folded her arms, flipping from mom-mode to professional mode. "What's going on?"

PRAYDOLLZ: THERE'S ONE MORE THING YOU SHOULD KNOW. ONCE THE RIGHT PERSON, WHOEVER THAT IS, PORTS TO OR FROM LETO? THAT DOOR WILL START A SHUTDOWN SEQUENCE. THERE IS NO WAY TO STOP THAT. IT'S A ONE-WAY TRIP.

Purple shook his head. "It looks like someone on the planet closed the porter on purpose. The code on Leto's signal has a Lock on it."

"What does that mean?"

Jesus, Mary, and Joseph. It felt like his whole life was he was telling fairy stories to children. "A Lock is a timed virus that eats away the integrity of the porter code kernels. Very specified and very blacker. It's attached to a DNA sequence, so only one person can unlock it. From what I'm seeing it was set *on the planet*."

She paused, a blank look on her face. Purple wondered how much of her brain had just burned out.

"But our porter works fine, right?" Sam said, pushing a long curl back from her moon-shaped face. "They couldn't shut our porter down...."

"Our porter is fine. It's the porter on the planet that's the problem." He rubbed his eyes, thinking of a way to explain that didn't make him look like a technical freak show.

"So, the porter works kind of like an elevator, right?" He put his hands in the air for effect, as if he were telling it to his kid sisters. "You go in on one floor—here—and then travel through space to the next floor—Leto. We can open our door, but the elevator is still on the Leto floor."

"So if we go through," she said, slowly, "we're basically walking into an empty elevator shaft."

"Bingo," he said. "That is a door we should *definitely* not step into."

There was a rustle amongst the techs. A burst of energy from the porter diagnostics. The room filled with the unmistakable hum of the porter receiving DNA sequencing data. Purple dropped to his console, scanning the incoming porter log on the holoscreen. The titanium doorway of the porter came to life, the yellow field of ions shimmering as they gathered and recreated whoever had found a way to come through.

INCOMING PORT. INCOMING PORT.

"It's them," someone shouted. "They're coming back!"

"That's not them, lad," Purple muttered. "That's someone else."

What's going on? He sent on the trace emergency all-call line. Who gave outside access to the port?

PrayDollz: It's not us. They're riding a direct line. Somewhere on the mainland.

There was a shudder of the field, and then a figure came through. There was a moment where the engineering room was oddly quiet. The figure paused, then flipped down their mask.

But it wasn't Chuck or Jenny or Cassie. It was Ezrie Collings, a laster in hand, and looking even fazer in real life than she did online.

III

THERE WAS THE TEARING, rending feeling of the port. Ezrie stepped through into a large domed room. There were gasps, and people were staring. She brought the weapon up on instinct.

Whatever this was, it was not good.

"She has a weapon!" someone yelled.

"Who the hell is that?" A man in fatigues snapped. "How did she get through?"

Ezrie had figured that this was a trap, but coming up short on the coordinates—one stop shy of wherever Marcus' highway to hell actually led—was supposed to have given her some kind of advantage. The element of surprise, as they said on all those old-timey Nets movies.

"Surprise." Ezrie said with a thin laugh.

Before she could say more, her body exploded in pain.

She dropped like brick, shuddering and convulsing on the polished steel floor. Every part of Ezrie was buzzing, tearing itself apart as the electricity continued to vibrate to her very bones. She felt like tiny saws were going through her cells, violent spasms in her spine and legs dropping her to the ground like a brick.

Then, there was a woman over her, her muscled arms holding an uparmored laster. She was in jet black fatigues. On her arm was a snake tattoo with the ICET logo behind.

Ezrie had enough brains that weren't on fire to know that she was in deep shit.

"Lookie here," the woman said, her voice gravelly and sharp. The woman cuffed Ezrie deftly, the snake on her arm rippling over muscle "Looks like someone made a bad decision."

There were too many to choose from.

Ezrie frantically fought against the broken meat of her mouth. *I'm not supposed to be here,* she tried to mutter through slack lips. *This is all a mistake.*

The woman dragged her, her body still twitching, into a concrete cell with soundproof panels pasted to the walls. A large black one-way window dominated the room. The guard sat Ezrie into a vise chair at the table in the center of the room, clipping her cuffs in so that her arms were locked behind her back. Not that she would move them. Every touch sent another burst of pain straight to Ezrie's skull. She bit her lip to keep from crying out again.

What had she been expecting? Ezrie cursed herself for being so stupid, so myopic. Of course ICET had tracked her down. It was only a matter of time, wasn't it? And they had somehow pulled Marcus in, the man who always knew where she was going to be next. She felt tears threatening in her throat. She had been so stupid.

"So, sweetheart," the woman said, not even bothering to look at Ezrie, and definitely not sweet. "What's your name?"

The woman rifled through Ezrie's bag carelessly, pulling out several small porter boxes, a knife, and an explosive device that had gotten Ezrie out of more than one scrape. Ezrie half hoped the woman would accidentally turn them both into hamburger.

"Where am I?"

The woman blinked and Ezrie felt a surge of pain into her wrists and arms. She grunted, whimpered. The chair she was strapped to was wired.

"Oh no, honey. I'm the one who asks the questions around here."

The woman roughly pulled out the small, faded picture. It was the only personal thing Ezrie had. A rare picture of her mother and father together, a pink-and-yellow silk scarf in Molly's hair. Richard's glasses catching the glare from the sun. They were both young and stupid. Happy.

"Who's this?" the woman asked.

"Leave my shit alone." Ezrie's voice grated through raw vocal cords. Her skin felt like it was made of fire.

"Or what? You'll cry?" She dropped the picture on the small pile of contraband, then sat back into the other metal chair in the room. She looked like she was measuring Ezrie up, and the sneer on her face meant that she didn't like what she saw.

"What are you doing at PanGen, girlie?"

PanGen was one of the Big Six, with water mines across the globe and half ownership in the Stackton Lunar well. What did Marcus have to do with water mining?

Ezrie kept her mouth shut. In situations where you didn't know how much trouble telling the truth would get you, silence was the easiest way to stay alive.

The woman sniffed at her. "Okay, so you want to play dumb."

She pulled out Ezrie's control screen from the pile of items. The woman tapped it on the table before dropping it. Ezrie flinched as it dropped. Next to the specially designed earring it was the most expensive thing she owned. All her custom programs, her specialized hacks. Everything was on it.

"You're trespassing on private property and carrying illicit technology. Blacker tech." Ezrie recalled the snake tattoo. Yes. This woman *would* be ex-ICET, a Snake. A hired security goon with a history of tracking and finding blackers. "Funny enough, we've had some bad code giving us some trouble. Strange you would show up at the same time."

Ezrie stonewalled.

"I promise you that if you don't start talking, that blast you took when you showed up will feel like a bee sting to what you're about to experience." The woman's eyes, too wide, had a maniacal glee in them, as if she were anticipating this. Ezrie decided not to call her bluff.

"I don't know anything about your code. I was sent this location."

"By who?"

"I don't know," Ezrie lied.

"Bullshit," the woman snorted. "Only a brainhole would ride a protected line like this unless they knew what was on the other side." The woman scrutinized her face. "I actually could almost believe it, looking at you. You sure as hell weren't prepared for me, that's for damn sure. Give me one reason why I shouldn't take you into ICET custody right now?"

The woman leaned over the metal table, and Ezrie could see the snake tattoo peeking from beneath the sleeve of her leather jumpsuit. Below it, "LeeAnn" had been tattooed in graffiti calligraphy.

"You won't take me to ICET," Ezrie snapped. "because you're not really ICET." The woman scowled, and Ezrie felt a thin satisfaction. "You're a glorified rent-a-cop, probably some ICET dropout who's slumming for dope money. Legally, you can't do shit to me, *LeeAnn*."

The woman moved impossibly fast, grabbing Ezrie by the hair. There was a moment when Ezrie was sure that LeeAnn recognized the obsidian earring in her left ear. The virus that was her most precious piece of technology. The thing that all of this was about, really.

"You better watch whose name you put in your mouth, girlie," LeeAnn growled. Ezrie winced as the woman clutched her hair harder, feeling it rip from her scalp. "No trace, huh? We'll figure out who you are."

The woman ripped a snatch of her hair, and Ezrie yelped. "What the hell is wrong with—"

"Before you shoot your load, hun, take a look around." The woman's voice was dark and deadly. She deftly pulled out a small plastic baggie and dropped the hair inside. "No cameras. No recordings—" The woman smiled. "And you don't have no trace to record any of it. As far as the law is concerned, you don't exist. I can make that happen without even breaking a sweat."

Ezrie felt her stomach go cold. Whoever this woman was, whoever she worked for, it was clear that Ezrie was outmaneuvered.

The woman dumped the contents back in the bag and stalked out with it.

Ezrie felt the pang of loss. Her shit was expensive and without it, she was a prisoner. But more importantly, she was powerless. Expendable.

But what had she really expected to happen?

She didn't know, but it hadn't been this.

Ezrie sat, staring at the black two-way glass, wondering if LeeAnn was hiding behind it, talking to Marcus even now. Would he be here, somewhere?

But how had Marcus known that she wouldn't follow his directions? How had he known she would end up here? Or had he? What fresh, fun hell had she accidentally dropped herself into?

They said they were having code issues. Someone blacking their water system. She wracked her brain for a connection. Marcus could code, sure, but she had never taken him for a blacker. If he had that skill set, it would make sense, though. He had always managed to stay one step ahead of her. Even after she'd gone off the grid, he always seemed to know where she was—or rather, where she would be looking for him next.

She groaned, pulling against the cuffs at her back. She was so, so stupid. Those should be the words on her tombstone: Here lies Ezrie Ann Collings, too stupid to live.

But it wasn't all her fault, a small little-girl voice in her head complained. If only Marcus had simply done what he said he would do. If only he'd taken care of her the way he had promised. The images flashed through her mind, threatening to take shape. All the things she had done to survive. All the things that had broken her and stolen what she could have been.

The streets. The men. The running. The fighting.

But never killing. That wasn't Ezrie's style. She was a piece of human trash, but she wasn't a monster. She had reserved that last act for Marcus himself.

She thought of the virus in her ear. An eternal error-loop that dissolved any information it touched. It was specially designed to move across the mechanical-biological wall, a feat that was amazing considering there was still no real way to hack a trace. To have access to a trace, you had to be given access. Even this highly expensive marvel of technology couldn't *steal* information. All it could do was destroy. But that's all she needed.

If everything worked, she would place it in Marcus' biological trace interface and then the code would jump the mech-bio wall and begin eating him. He might go crazy. He might go brain dead. Either way, it would be a fitting, final note to his place in history, she thought.

The prettiest disguise of death you could buy with twenty-first century cash on hand, no receipt.

But you bought that with trade, not cash.

She didn't know why that thought was so threatening. Why it made her stomach turn. She was scared. Really scared.

"Who cares," she whispered to the concrete walls. "Today, I jacked his plan, that's all that matters."

There was some satisfaction there. No matter what happened next, she had done something he hadn't anticipated. And that meant that she was ahead of him for once, as crazy and stupid as it seemed. Being in this concrete cell was no different than being trapped in the Texas trailer waiting for her life to change. But at least here, she was one step closer to finishing him the way he deserved.

IV

RAND SOMETIMES FOUND himself on the wrong side of the desk. The side that took orders instead of giving them. Sitting across from him was Zenzui Zhong, PanGen's Operations Director. Beside the Director was Aris, the Board's android Liaison.

He did not like the side he was on today.

"The board is adamant." Zhong looked collected, the knot of red silk at his neck was perfectly placed to contrast with his pale skin and grey suit. "Ezrie goes to Leto."

Zhong was on the right side of the desk, of course. The side that got to make decisions. There was a pitcher of clear, natural water on the desk. Zhong hadn't even touched it, nor offered any to him. From Rand's perspective, that made him an asshole.

"We've been running missions for more than two years," Rand retorted, his patience running on fumes alone. "My team and Byrion's team—we all know each other. Adding in a loose cannon like Ezrie goes against every safety protocol that we have. And we're already behind because goddamned Living Waters refuses to budge without the ecological survey—"

"Ezrie is the only one who can get through the Lock," Zhong said, his voice impassive. "Correct?"

"Yes." Rand rubbed his chin. He was two days without sleep and had hashed and rehashed this information to every level of management. Now, the top of the iceberg needed it again, only more bureaucratic, and he was at the end of his patience. "It's called Caskade. It's a DNA encoded lock, usually timed, and built for one person to go through. For whatever reason, Ezrie is the one that can go through it. We think that whoever sent the signal to her made a mistake on the coordinates and accidentally sent her to us."

"Lucky for us," Zhong said coolly. "She can get us back onto Leto. It seems like a simple solution."

Rand resisted the urge to smash something. Working with civilian leadership was nothing like working in the services, and there were times like these when it was so crystal clear that he was in the wrong place. Of course, the pay was better. But the costs were so high.

"The lock is meant for one person," Rand clipped. "Trying to send the team behind is incredibly dangerous. It would mean shutting off the porter safety protocols. I can't risk that."

Aris stepped forward, her carefully collected appearance serene. Objectively, she had been designed to be a lovely woman. Red hair, green eyes. She smiled at the right parts of the conversation. But the lack of emotion behind those eyes gave Rand the creeps. It was too easy to forget that any decision she made was a leveraging of risk and reward, the combination of algorithms. He wondered how long this one would last on Leto before she became a pile of parts fit only for research.

"Captain Everton," Aris said sweetly, "Leto represents one of many investments. You have been to five different installments, correct?"

"Yes."

"Each has had its share of difficulties, is this not correct?"

Rand considered the mining operations he had led teams on. On Io, he had navigated the success of the mine despite near-disastrous issues with radiation shielding. On Enceladus, they'd had to find creative ways to get the drills through hundreds of feet of rock-hard ice, not to mention reprinting the bits almost every day. And then, of course, the fire at the Stackton mine on the lunar surface.

"Yes. Every outland mine has issues." He sighed. "But this isn't an equipment failure. This isn't a chipped bit or a torn radiation reflector. This is sabotage. Are we really going to trust this nobody? A confirmed top-tier blacker? She probably set this whole scheme up in the first place—"

"No." Zhong adjusted the silk at his throat. "I do not believe that Ms. Collings is capable of the ingenuity and skill it would take to hack through our systems. It is more logical that it is someone who knows our systems. Someone on the inside. I'm sure you're aware of those rumors."

"Yes, sir. Most of us are."

Was this an interrogation? Was he being set up for something?

He felt his heart pick up pace. He knew that Captain Byrion had accused him once of sharing administration codes. Despite his assurances that he could never have done that, even if he wanted to, she had been adamant.

The truth was, Byrion herself seemed a more likely candidate. She had been on the Apollo team longer than anyone and had full access to the kinds of materials that had gone missing over and over again. And wasn't it on her watch that the porter had started that five-minute glitch? For some reason, there had begun to be a constant lag between port times. It wasn't until Purple started working on it with Jenny that it got all fixed up.

He felt his throat constrict.

"The Board believes that this may be our best chance at finding who is behind all of this," Zhong said, seemingly unaware of Rand's discomfort. "Whoever it is has set Ezrie up as the only way to get back to Leto. I believe our best course of action is to send her through and find out who it is. You know, of course, that her father and Marcus worked together on the porters"

A file blinked into Rand's trace view. He flicked through it—records, police reports. A snippet from an old interview with Ezrie red-faced, young, and angry.

"He stole my father's work," she said. "There has to be justice for that."

"This doesn't make sense." His head was reeling. "This says that Marcus put a restraining order on her code over a decade ago. She's not supposed to be within fifty miles of him. Why would he lock us out and bring her?"

But he knew Marcus. Marcus was slimy and narcissistic. He could do anything and it wouldn't surprise Rand.

"We don't know," Zhong said. "And when you find him, you'll find out. *After* we know for sure that the mine is secure."

"Using that door is a one-way trip," Rand argued, his finger emphasizing the point on the desktop. "Purple said it's not meant for piggy-backing, and it will force a shutdown of the system once she's ported through. If we can't figure out a way to wedge the port open for long enough, we're talking about potential genetic deterioration of anyone who ports through after her."

"How many people know this?"

"I do, Purple does, and the diagnostic team. Ezrie is a blacker, for God's sake. She probably knows better than all of us."

"Still," Zhong said quietly, "could Purple be persuaded to keep this information private?"

The words hit Rand between the eyes, his jaw going slack. "You want me to make the kid *lie* about our chances of getting home? About the danger of porting to Leto?"

"Not lie," Zhong said. "Simply restrain himself."

"And put my entire team in jeopardy?" Rand snapped. "Hell no. I will not do that, sir."

"If I may." Aris' voice was honeyed and cloying. "As the captain of the Artemis team, your responsibility is to the final success of the company. The mine is important, of course, but it represents only a segment of our market."

"What does that have to do with putting my entire crew in—"

"There are trillions of dollars at stake on Leto alone," Zhong said. "But the more important issue is that Marcus is actively working to bring down PanGen from the inside." His voice took on an edge that Rand had never heard before. "We need someone to go down there and find out what's really going on before he takes the entire company down with him."

"So, you're asking me to put my crew in danger, put this blacker on Leto, knowing that every one of them might die to protect your bottom line?"

"Mr. Everton," Zhong said, his voice too smooth. "This mission is much larger than your team."

"Ezrie Collings has never been on an interplanetary mission," Rand exploded. "She is not even a registered citizen on the trace—

"But she can get us on Leto."

Rand stopped, his heart racing, his blood pounding. How could Zhong ask him to do this? How could he himself do this? When he spoke again, his voice grated against his own ears like diamond on glass. "Yes. She can."

"Then she will go. And the rest of the team will follow."

"I won't put my team at risk for her. Or for you."

He clenched his jaw, daring Zhong to fight back. His fists were balled tight, itching for a chance to swing.

When he'd led a squadron in the Southern War, Rand had made some bad calls. One of the worst was a live area in Louisiana called Ville Platte. He thought about it sometimes when everything was quiet. Sometimes he dreamed about it, slinking through the streets while children with guns shot through his armor.

He'd split the team into striking groups to protect a small group of kids trapped inside their school. What he hadn't known was that the building was empty, and that the intel had been bait. The child militia had gunned down nearly all of them but him and Lee. He still woke from nightmares where he was shooting back. The head of a ten-year-old disintegrating into blood and brain.

"Rand," Zhong said quietly. "If you don't head this mission, Aris will, under the Board's direction. Whether you are there or not, Ezrie is taking us to Leto."

"Do you know what you're asking me to do?" Rand said, slamming his hand on the desk. It rattled the glass of water and a teardrop slipped down to make a spot on the mahogany. "You're asking me to risk their lives."

Zhong's gaze never faltered. "Can you really tell me that your integrity is so unimpeachable?"

Rand met Zhong's gaze. A thread of guilt snaked through his stomach.

"I know you, Rand," Zhong said. "I know that you're a person who can make the tough choices."

This was not a negotiation. This was a brick wrapped in a velvet glove.

"Fine." Rand snapped. "Ezrie can come. As long as she's traced."

"I thought you might feel that way," Zhong said with a careful smile. "And Aris will go with you, in case there are any...issues."

Zhong stood, blinking the ion doors open.

A small security retinue was waiting outside to escort them. Zhong waved as they left.

Rand wished he could twist the cravat around the man's neck until his head popped like a wine cork.

As the lift sunk down into the belly of the PanGen complex, Rand could hear the android's eyes flicking in and out, documenting and saving everything. He could not trust the safety of his team to her calculating anode brain. The safety of himself. His wife. His lover.

He didn't dare even think her name.

SAM, he sent. WE'RE GOING TO HAVE ANOTHER PERSON ON THE TEAM.

SURE, his wife replied. THAT'S A HILARIOUS JOKE. TELL ME ANOTHER ONE.

He closed the line. Dammit. He was in over his head on this whole thing.

But there was more, wasn't there? No matter how loud he yelled, he wanted to get back on Leto as desperately as Zhong did. Not for money or position, but for the people that were trapped there. He had to face it: Leto wasn't just another mission. It wasn't just another mine. The team was out there. Maybe hurt.

The guilt of what he'd done sat on him, sinking him down. He wished he could walk away, but the person that mattered most to him was down there on Leto. Despite his misgivings, Rand would do whatever it took to get back to the planet, even if it meant using Ezrie to get there.

V

THE WATER GLASS was sweating a ring on the metal table. Ezrie was tempted to drink it, but she wouldn't give in. Even though she'd screamed herself hoarse and her throat felt like it was on fire. Not when there were so many questions still to answer.

LeeAnn materialized through the ion door, breaking Ezrie's thoughts like so much glass. She still looked as mean-ass as when she left.

"So, *LeeAnn*," Ezrie said, "When are the real cops showing up?"

The woman moved quickly, towering over Ezrie, her wiry body tall and lean. Her eyes were too wide for her face, her chin too sharp. She could have been a model, maybe, if it weren't for how ugly all the mean had turned her.

"You say my name like that again, girlie, and I'll break you in half like a cracker. My name is Lee."

Lee grabbed Ezrie's cuffs and released her from the chair, pulling her to her feet roughly. She dropped Ezrie's pack on the table.

Ezrie looked up at her, totally confused.

"We have a water mine on a planet called Leto," Lee said. "A pretty big one, pretty far out. About eight light years from here."

Ezrie shuddered inwardly. That was a long port. Much further than she'd ever ported before.

"Yeah," Ezrie said shortly, grabbing her pack. "What does that have to do with me?"

"Every twenty-eight days, we have a window to port. We sent a team out there on the last window—our first long stay. The Apollo Team was supposed to come back here sixteen hours ago, but no one showed up." The woman scowled at her. "Except you."

Ezrie knew that her face made some people angry. Some kind of "attitude" is what she'd been told by countless teachers and foster parents. Lee looked like one of those kind of people.

"From what you say," Lee said, "someone sent a transmission signal from the planet to bring you here. From what we can tell, the same person locked the planet porter and made your DNA the key. And since you and Marcus are such good old friends, he's our best bet."

"I don't know—"

"Save it," Lee chipped. "We know who you are and we know your record, so don't lie. From what I've heard, you're smarter than that."

Ezrie clapped her lips shut. Of course they knew. They'd taken her DNA and now they knew everything. But why would Marcus send her to a distant planet without telling any of his crew? And why now?

"I don't know why you're involved in all this," Lee said, "and I sure as hell don't want you here. But I'm not the one making the rules."

She uncuffed Ezrie. With a blink from Lee, the ion field of the security door disappeared. Lee put the laster in her holster. She handed Ezrie her backpack and the screen. On the face was a small sticky note with a hand-drawn map that showed a porter a floor down and a few hundred yards away.

"That's how you get home, Betty," Lee said. "If you are smart, you'll leave now."

"Wait, what—"

"Leto isn't a play area. It's deadly. No one who cared about you would bring you there without you knowing what it was." Her jaw softened. "And Marcus...He's never been the best person, I know you know that. You're not cut out for whatever is going on here. And if you go, there's a real good chance you won't come home. Leave while you still can."

There was something more than hardness in this. A slight tremble of Lee's eyes that flashed and was gone in an instant.

She was scared.

Lee turned on her heel, stalking out the door. She glanced back only once before she disappeared around the corner.

Ezrie listened to Lee's feet on the tiled floor. She shouldered her backpack and looked at the notes on the paper. Down the stairs, a right and a left. She could go back to Texas and pretend that none of this had ever happened.

I can go home now, she thought. *Leave him to die wherever he is.*

But Marcus had sent her here. He'd called for her. He'd said he had a way to make things right. And that wasn't her home anyway.

But he's a liar, Ezrie, the cold voice of her logic explained. *He lied about taking care of you. He lied about the porter. He's lying now. You can't trust him.*

But what if she could? What if she did?

Then you're as stupid as Lee thinks you are, the cold voice said.

She could hear Lee's footsteps fading into the distance. Lee was an asshole, but she'd given Ezrie a choice. Something that she hadn't always had.

She jogged to the access door on the map and tested it. No alarms. Just a stairwell.

Then a right, then a left.

But what about Marcus?

Why do you care? You've never cared about anyone else before.

That was a lie. She had cared about people. But it always got her hurt. Besides, she had a promise to keep. That was all. Whatever it took to face Marcus one last time, she would do it.

When she caught up with Lee, the woman didn't even look at her.

"Welcome to the team, Ezrie," Lee said, a strange smile at the corner of her mouth. "I guess you're stupider than I thought."

Ezrie struggled to keep up with Lee's long, strong legs as she tunneled deeper into the PanGen complex. They passed through a white-washed section flooded with UV lights, then past a large room with huge glass windows. It looked huge from the outside, but it was packed with life: colorful plants bursting from behind hundreds of feet of plastic sheeting and growing beneath tables as long as swimming pools, lit from above by orange-colored UV bar strips. There were workers inside wearing tight-fitting suits and masks. Only one was not, a skinny black woman with frothy hair that was barely contained by the ponytail on top of her head.

The woman caught sight of them and rushed out of the room, barely stopping beneath what Ezrie could only guess was a decontamination sprayer.

"Lee," the woman gushed, misty droplets forming on her hair and face. "Have you seen Rand? I really need to talk to him about the analytics running on the phlax samples, and he's not answering my ping."

The woman's eyes seemed too large for her face, the intensity pouring out of them like lasers. "The program here isn't calibrating with the Leto lab, and every time I run water analyses, I'm getting error messages in gibberish—"

"Birdy, no one can talk to the planet. We're all in the dark," Lee snapped, pushing past her. "Get out of the way—"

"—possible that something in the water itself is skewing the data…"

Birdy paused, as if she'd just noticed Ezrie was there.

"Hello, I'm sorry." Birdy smiled sincerely. "You're Ezrie, aren't you? Purple mentioned that you were a celebrity of some sort? Something about your father being a friend of Marcus'?"

"This is Ezrie," Lee snapped, clearly annoyed. "She'll be working with us on the surface as a porter engineering consult. I'm keeping her safe."

"That is Lee's specialty," Birdy said with a smile. "Don't worry, you're in good hands." She offered her hand. "My name is Meeshel Arnold, but most people call me Birdy. I work as the co-lead for the biology unit. We're doing some amazing science, finding incredible things—"

"Water," Lee interrupted, glaring. "We're finding water. Birdy is doing the ecological survey, which is a huge pain in my ass."

Birdy waved her hand, as if sweeping the comment away. "It has been slow going, and I am sure we'll be done any time now. What about you, Ezrie? What is your background?"

She looked at Ezrie expectantly.

"Systems. Porter systems."

"How long have you been doing that?"

"A long time."

There was a moment of awkward tension, and Birdy filled it with a fluttery laugh. "Well, we'll have time to talk when we're there, I suppose. But, Really. Lee, please have Purple or one of the technical specialists look at those readings. If I can't read data, I can't make sure the data—" she paused. "I really need the data to ensure that the water we're pulling is safe. I know Zhong would agree that it is a top priority."

"I'll be sure to do that," Lee said, dryly, already striding towards the door at the end of the hallway. Ezrie scrambled to follow.

"So nice to meet you, Ezrie," Birdy called after them, "and, Lee. When you talk to Purple, can you find out why I still can't control the biological settings from the main lab console—"

Lee slammed a hard-shell steel door behind them, cutting off Birdy's sentence. They were in a small office foyer. On all sides of the oblong room, there were smaller offices. A set of double-doors swung open, and a balding black man with a salt-and-pepper beard came through, smiled warmly. As the door swung back, Ezrie could see an operating table beyond.

Her heart sank.

"Ezrie," the man said. He was tall, with broad shoulders that strained against the white lab coat. "I'm James. I'm the Leto Artemis team doctor. We'll need to update your hardware before you can port."

"Hardware?" Ezrie's throat felt sticky. Her hand involuntarily went to the back of her head.

"Well," Lee said offhandedly, "You wanna come to Leto? You gotta be on the trace."

Ezrie remembered the pain of having it removed, looking up to see

Robyn standing over her. Thinking of her made Ezrie a little heartsick. It had been so long ago—over a decade since she'd been connected to the network. To anyone, really. The thought of connecting again made her feel queasy. All those voices, all the time. How could she stand it after all these years of being alone?

"Is it safe?" She had never heard of someone getting a trace as an adult, unless they were going to prison.

"It's not ideal. There's a reason that we usually implant at five or six." The doctor smiled warmly. "The brain is more malleable and pubescent hormones haven't usually begun influencing brain chemistry. But at, what? Thirty—"

"Twenty-eight," Ezrie retorted, "actually."

"Sorry, sorry. No offense meant. I should know better than to guess a woman's age." He laughed, and the sound was kind. "At twenty-eight, your brain is stable. It should only take a couple of weeks to heal."

Ezrie couldn't help the pure revulsion she felt at the thought of having her trace reinstalled. She thought of her mother, her perfect, glazed eyes staring up at nothing and everything. Zooming.

What do they see in there? she had asked her father once when they were at a hardware store. The boy behind the counter had been zooming, not even realizing that they were there.

They see what they don't have, he said, *which makes it impossible to see what they do.*

"I've done it many times," James said, his face gentle. "Even on people who have had them removed. You're safe with me."

Lee looked at James for a moment, and Ezrie realized they were talking on the trace, probably about her. James balked. "I don't feel comfortable doing that."

"It doesn't matter," Lee spat. "Those are Zhong's orders, not Rand's."

Lee stalked through the door, the slam of the steel resounding in the pristine silence of the waiting room. Lee struck an imposing figure, the laster clipped to her belt, her muscled arms flexing beneath the black jacket.

"What do you want to do, Ezrie?" James pulled a chair over and sat on it. He was a wide-faced man with serious eyes. His voice was warm and round, and it reminded her a little of her grandpa Pete, her dad's dad who had died when she was very little. "This doesn't have to be a permanent change. We can always remove it when you come back."

What do I want? I want to run away, she thought.

But if this was the only way to get to Leto, she would do it. She'd had her traced removed once. She could get it removed again. As long as the doctor didn't render her brain dead in the process.

"Fine. But just for now."

"Of course," he said. "This way."

Ezrie followed James through the double-doors to where the white surgical table was already prepped.

He positioned her on the table, stomach down and face fitting into a little cradle like at a massage parlor. Below her lay a screen in the floor. She flinched at the feel of the alcohol swab on her head.

"You'll feel a little pinch, then take a nap until we're done."

There was the prick of a needle, and Ezrie winced.

I don't want to do this. I don't want to do this.

The last time she'd had a surgery like this, Robyn had been there. She had at least had that. This time, it was like jumping out a ten-story window without a parachute. Who the hell knew what was waiting at the bottom to smash her into a bloody pulp?

"Ezrie, go ahead and count backwards from twenty."

"Twenty. Nineteen. Eighteeeee—"

But the world was too hazy and slow and warm. The numbers were lost, rolling away like marbles or moons into the blackness of space.

VI

Oceanside, California, *Earth*

January 2080

KENNER DIDN'T LIKE the city. It had a carnival atmosphere, nothing like the solitude of the mountains. He loved his little oasis in Alabama—a tiny self-sustaining farm on a hidden hill beside an anemic, but stocked lake. The city made him feel like he was walking into an invisible snare. He shifted restlessly despite the plush leather of the car's seat.

He scanned the walkways as a distraction from the tension in his chest. Clutches of tourists in scant clothing took pictures of the Grand Lodge archway, or stood in lines beside the carts of exotic food. The grounds of the Marquis de Slade hosted some kind of expo, and Kenner could see hundreds of men and women in business suits through the glass of the thirty-seven-story building, its overhanging swimming pool with crystal clear water seeming to hover above the freeway more than a hundred feet above.

Below it, a trace-integrated billboard was blank. As Kenner glanced at it, it connected to the device implanted in his brain, and an attractive, brown-skinned girl with a wild halo of black hair smiled at him.

Birdy.

"Welcome to Oceanview, Kenner. It's a sunny 112 degrees, and that's the way we like it."

The advertisement had even gotten her voice right, though the cadence was wrong. It had none of her energy or passion. But Kenner felt his pulse quicken, nonetheless. Even though he knew it was a trick of the trace, he couldn't help smiling back at her. Birdy.

Birdy smiled down from the billboard. To see her delicate jaw, the chocolate cream skin larger than life…it made him sad and self-conscious. If the trace could pull her from his brain, anyone could.

He would have to be careful of that.

Kenner's Trace murmured the general low white noise of interactive ads. He muted them with a flick of his eye. The billboard went back to being a blank slate.

The car stopped at a towering building in the city's center. At the base of the building, several trees grew—taller and greener than anything Kenner had ever seen—other than Leto, of course. He was almost used to it. The water, the life of that place. He watched a group of dark-skinned tourists gathered in front of one of the trees. A teenage girl accidentally bumped into the protective ion shield, giving her a jolt that stunned her and dropped her. Her friends laughed uproariously, their mouths too wide, their voices too loud. In front of the Living Waters building, skinny protesters screamed and waved signs.

He would be glad to be rid of this world.

The car pulled up to the front door, and a service android with a beautiful face and a thick head of auburn hair opened the door for him. She was dressed like an old-fashioned flight attendant, in a light blue jacket and skirt that rose high enough to reveal perfectly tanned thighs. He imagined sliding his hand between them, if only to release some of the tension…

Kenner chastised himself silently. *Not the time or place, boy,* as Grandam had been fond of saying—a phrase usually followed by the lightning lash of an electrical cord on his back.

Not the time or place.

"Sir, please." A man in a ragged jacket holding a sign blocked his way. He had a thin, watery-eyed woman with him. "Take a minute and read this before you go in." The man pushed a yellowed pamphlet into Kenner's hand. *The Truth About Your Water,* slithered across the front flap, with a picture of Reverend Andrews smiling in front of the very building they stood at.

Kenner pushed the pamphlet back at the man.

"No, thank you."

He walked through huge glass doors and a large holographic greeting board welcomed him by name. "Join the Family," it said, and showed a picture of Kenner standing happily with a group of diverse, happy people holding crystalline bottles of water with the Living Waters logo. Next to himself, he saw the CEO and president, Colton Andrews. Seeing the Reverend, even as a hologram, made the tension in his chest ease.

"Kenner," a familiar voice called. "How's my favorite son?"

Kenner turned to see Reverend Andrews coming down the steps. He was wearing a smart powder-blue suit with a black tie. His greying hair meticulously cut. The Reverend clasped him in a handshake bearhug, then fixed his wide, kind eyes on Kenner.

"Reverend." Kenner bowed in respect, his eyes to the ground.

"Let's talk downstairs, shall we, son?"

They walked down a series of staircases and elevators, his trace going thankfully quiet. The walls below the compound were full of mitrium—a dampening material that blocked out electronic signal.

They descended until he almost couldn't tell how deep below the ground he was. But he could feel the weight of at least a hundred feet of earth over his head. When the guards opened the door at the bottom of the stairway, he felt a specter of fear in his belly. The only thing inside the room was two chairs, a table with a green folder lying on it, and a wide, curtained screen. There was a small drain in the corner. The smell of old blood.

The Reverend preceded him, sitting in a well-used leather chair. He motioned Kenner to sit. He glanced at the folder, reading own name at its top. The door behind him clanged close, locking in the sound like a vault.

Kenner took a deep breath. He could kill a struggling animal with his bare hands, dress a deer in less than twenty minutes, mix poison from fertilizer and cleaning supplies. He had nothing to fear. Still, he clenched the arms of the fancy black chair as if it were a life raft to a drowning man. His stomach, already churning with excitement and fear, shifted tenuously.

"I appreciate you coming. Did you enjoy the car ride?

"A little much for me, sir," Kenner said, allowing his southern drawl to roll a bit. If he sounded relaxed, he might start believing it. "I'm used to the quiet."

"That's what I love about you," the Reverend laughed. "One hundred percent honesty, all the time." His face fell, and he sat back in his chair. Kenner noted the spareness of the room. The concrete walls. He had been here before, but it had never seemed so stark. As if everything had been stripped down. Hadn't the drain been covered by a rug before? He felt his testicles squeeze up towards his chest.

The Reverend smiled again, and Kenner saw how his eyes stayed flat. It reminded Kenner of a wolf.

"Now, Kenner, I'm going to need you to be one hundred percent honest with me right now. What is going on with Leto?"

"Yes, sir," Kenner said, his heart quickening. No one liked a bearer of bad news. Grandam had said that, too. Kenner looked at the dark splotches near the drain.

Must have faith. Must be strong.

"A lot of things went right," Kenner said, keeping his pace leveled despite his anxiety. He found it put people at ease, even people in important places. "The first crew is quiet, the planet porters were managed. We had at least 500,000 gallons pumped and shipped through."

"But..." the Reverend prodded.

Kenner took a measured breath. "I don't know, sir. The Ark door went silent after the distress calls went out. We haven't been able to get any other information than that."

"And the PanGen people?"

"No indication that the Ark has been discovered."

"Hmmm." The gold ring on his finger tapped on the edge of the desk. Kenner thought of all the concrete between him and the outside world. The guards outside the door. If the Reverend wasn't happy with him, he might mete out justice. He tried not to glance at the drain in the corner, the chrome recently cleaned.

"Another good thing," Kenner said. "The backup plan is in motion."

"And she'll come?"

Despite how much he didn't want to be here, he was able to present himself at ease in this tomblike room. He wished he were in the quiet, dark cover of the forest, hidden in the smell of mushrooms and wet earth. He felt his racing heart slow.

"She didn't follow the rules. Not surprising, I suppose. So she's…" he hesitated, hating himself for the fear that wormed its way into his blood. "She's at PanGen as we speak."

After a moment of tense silence, the Reverend rocked back in his chair. "I have to admit I'm disappointed. Hopefully, you have some ideas on how we can salvage this. I would hate to think that the church's time and money has been wasted." He leaned forward, templing his fingers below his chin. Kenner could feel the concrete on all sides pressing down.

"I have a lot of faith in that, sir. We'll be on the planet within twenty-four hours. And I'll make sure that everything gets back on track. Personally."

The Reverend seemed to ponder this. Then he nodded, smiling.

Kenner took a breath, not realized he'd been holding it in. He would live. For now. But it had always been this way. He could do the thing that no one else had the balls or stomach to, to say it coarsely. So the Reverend could trust him.

Reverend Andrews called out a command and the wall shifted into light and color. The concrete melted, revealing a wall-length screen covered in green trees at the edge of a mirror lake. Kenner knew this place. The lake by Mountain Base on Leto. He had gone there once to protect Birdy while she gathered samples. He counted those short hours as one of his favorite memories. If he looked closely, he could imagine her there on other side of the lake with a specimen jar or bag, some plastic gloves, wading in the red water, strands of wild hair falling out of her ponytail. She would be talking about the creatures with a transcendent joy. She would laugh, and he would feel human.

After the first time he'd gone with her, he had laid in his bunk at the PanGen HQ, poring over the Book of Genesis on his trace. It had been a small crisis of faith. Of passion.

In the beginning, the book said, *Adam named the animals.*

But watching her, seeing the spark of her under the alien technicolor sky of Leto as she named the fish, Kenner knew better.

Eve had been the one who named them all along.

Even here, deep below Living Waters, the thought of her made the fear melt for a moment.

"This is the new world," the Reverend said, touching the wall gently. "This is the real world, the world we have been working so tirelessly to restore. But it requires sacrifice. Hard work. Faith." He turned to Kenner. "Since you came to us as a boy, I have always believed those are attributes you possess."

"I've learned a lot since then." Kenner still remembered coming to the Happy Home. He had been convinced he was chosen for some higher plan. How else could he have survived living with Grandam? "I know that God chooses leaders and that the rest of us mostly end up following."

"True," Andrews said thoughtfully. "But leadership isn't the real power, Kenner. People who do the things that really change the world? They work behind the scenes. In the shadows. Men like you." He turned to Kenner.

Kenner looked up to see the Reverend's eyes boring into his own.

"We live in a fallen world," the Reverend said. "It is dying. Killing itself, really. Do you know what the root of that destruction is?"

"Sin, sir?"

"Yes, but even more than that. The root of human destruction, human evil, is selfishness. People only care as much as it affects them. Do you think those people out there who are spreading lies about God's church, do you think that they really want to change the world? No. They want a free handout. They want to be given a lifetime supply of water and be on their way. Do you think any one of them would turn their nose up at that offer, even if it meant that their "great cause" would be forgotten? No. They only care that they get their share."

The Reverend stared at him with those piercing eyes, and Kenner felt his soul's selfishness illuminated, hung out to bleed like a dead rabbit.

"Our goal, God's goal, is to make of this world something better. And if we can't, to find a better world. You understand, this is the only way to save humanity from suicide. In order to save the living tissue, the cancer must be cut away. Or in the case of the righteous few, we must leave the wicked to the world they've created and build our own. Do you understand?"

The Revered made the question a pronouncement—an edict from on high.

"Yes, sir."

The Reverend smiled, placing a comforting hand on Kenner's shoulder. "I knew you would. Still, our situation is precarious. We can't have outsiders taking control of what God has set aside for his children."

"Yes, sir."

"You are in a position to prepare the way for the new era, a new way of life. But to do it, we have to have a safe place for our people. That means consecrating Leto for ourselves and protecting it from selfish interest. And it means protecting our people. With blood, if necessary."

The reality of the request dawned on him.

"All of them?"

Birdy. Her skin like rich earth. Her smile rare as a red thrush.

The Reverend's eyes went soft, his voice sotto. "The greatest good demands the greatest sacrifice." He placed a heavy hand on Kenner's shoulder. His touch exuded power. Control. "We can't allow anyone who is not worthy to remain on Leto."

Birdy is worthy, I know she is, she *may not know it yet, but she is, I know.*

"I trust you, Kenner. And God trusts you. Leto has been set apart for only the worthy. You are God's righteous arm, do you understand?"

Kenner nodded. "I understand."

"But," the Reverend added, "If you ever forget why you're doing what you're doing..." He tucked a small envelope into Kenner's hand. "Remember that the greatest cause demands the greatest sacrifice. And earns the greatest rewards."

Kenner walked up the stairs and out the front doors, moving trancelike past the image of him beside the Reverend. He passed the protesters, barely hearing their slurs.

When he reached the car, he got a trace notification that he had received money from a private donor. It noted, "For Religious Services."

"Oceanview International Launchport," he told the car, his voice cracking. The vehicle signaled and merged into the tourist traffic.

Everything had gone wrong. If it hadn't, he wouldn't be on his way to Leto. On his way to see Birdy one last time.

Mistakes must be fixed. Now, there would be blood on his hands.

Birdy.

From the side of the highway, Oceanview slid past. From his trace, he heard the advertisements, the music, the sounds of the city. On every billboard, he saw her face.

He did not look away.

VII

Santa Monica, California, *Earth*

June, 2065

EZRIE DOES eighth grade algebra and tries to pretend her father isn't dying. She tries to occupy herself as the screen blares some comedy that he can't even see. But every so often she catches herself staring at the bones of his skull. He has a soft spot that rises and falls with each breath as if he were an infant.

The equations given by the teacher are too simple, and she adds to them, trying to ignore the soft spot that breathes with him, creating more and more complex questions for herself. Gravity, energy, quantum fields. Like an artist, she carefully crafts each function and segment, placing each in relation to its corollary as he has taught her. She looks over to show him, but he is asleep.

She cleans the room up, removing the soup bowl and spoon, turning the screen to sleep. She sees that there have been calls from the college and the doctor's office, but she deletes them with a command.

During the day, when he sleeps, Ezrie cleans as best she can. She wears the pink dishwashing gloves her mother left behind and picks up pieces of skin that have fallen off her father's arms and thighs—spongy stuff that makes her sick. She buries it in the sandy soil of the back yard, like a seed. She half wonders what will grow from it. Then she goes to work.

The rest of the time, she is in the workshop with the machine, stopping only for water and sometimes the packaged food from their emergency supplies. She fixes the holes in the safety protocols. She finds the weaknesses in the code. She reads her father's notes and the Black Book. It becomes her bible—grown-up blackers telling her about how they made things right by doing the wrong things.

When the truant officers come, she hides in the neighbor's yard behind the storage shed.

"You can't keep working on it," her father says to her in his wet, rasping cough. It is rare for him to speak now. "I don't want this to happen to you," he says. He doesn't need to say more. There are abscesses of pus that have begun to grow on his jaw and down his neck. "Destroy it, Z. Promise."

She lies to him. She hugs him, feeling the crackle of the bones beneath her hands, feeling guilty and sick as the bloody bruise pools up where her hands have touched his skin.

Ezrie feels her thirteen years like stones, as if each one were an epoch where her father is devolving from man into some primordial slime. She works faster, racing the softness of his bones and the blood that pools at the bottoms of his feet.

At night, she comes in exhausted and sweat-stained. Her father sits in the Barcalounger in front of the screen, his face a mask that fits wrong. His breath smells like copper and rotting fruit. She tucks a blanket around him and changes the colostomy bag that is full of black.

Ezrie finds a fatal error in the original program. A problem of the frequency. In her head, she knows that it has turned the teleporter into a cancer, a Black Door from which he will never step back through. She should destroy it before anyone else can be eaten.

Instead, she buys three different radios with the last bills from the shoebox, patches them together, and begins the new experiment. The White Door. It will be better. It will work.

When she is sure it is finished, she sends her neighbor's cat through.

It comes out on the mirror door at the other side of the garage (*the workshop*, her father says, *Call it the workshop*), hissing and yowling. It claws when she tries to pick it up.

She watches it for a day and a half, taking notes on an old yellow pad and feeding it hamburger helper that her father won't touch. It does not die. Not right away.

She reads and re-reads her father's last notes. She asks him questions, though his answers more and more focus on her mother, Molly. He thinks she is her mother more than once, and begs forgiveness.

Ezrie stops making him food. The smell of sweetness is overpowering, and she comes in the last time somehow knowing that she is saying goodbye.

"Did you get rid of it? They'll be coming for it."

She lies to him and he closes his eyes.

"Tell her I'm sorry," he says. Ezrie knows that he is not talking to her. Her mother's face is a ghost between them.

That night, she is too numb to cry. Instead, she closes the door and goes to the garage. It is a mess of tools and trash, and she feels a scream building inside her head. She grabs the hammer from the top of the aging refrigerator where she stores her milk and cereal. The machine is a monster.

But as she comes closer, she sets the hammer down. The lights at the top of the doorway blink green.

She steps through the machine.

She is broken and split, the emptiness so infinite for that instant that she is sure she is lost. She is sure that she hears his voice in the darkness.

Then she is huddled on the floor—fear and pain and the taste of oil and concrete. But mostly relief. Now she will die, too. She can be with him, wherever he is going. Now she can destroy it.

Because the machine is her father. Her family. All the hours in that garage, smelling cedar beard oil and ozone and solder. The stories about Oma and Opa, his own great-grandma and great-grandpa. It is the times he stopped and looked out the small window into the sky or her mother came in with food and that distant, choleric laugh. And when her mother died, the machine was how they grieved her.

The work had been the weld. The machine had been the tool that bound them all.

The next months are a black blur. She closes the room with the screen and the Barcalounger and pounds boards around the outside. She sleeps in the garage and eats sparingly. Her birthday comes and goes, and she decides to pretend it doesn't exist. People knock at the door—neighbors, local cops—trying to get through the security systems to find whatever the smell is that taints the suburban street. Ezrie hides and works.

She walks through the teleporter—ten, twelve times a day—but does not die.

In the end, it is Marcus who she opens the door for.

Marcus is tall and brave, the prize student of her father's and an assistant at the college. He has been the prince in her little-girl fantasies, when she had room for such things. She has lain in bed, listening to Marcus and her father talk deep into the night, soaking in their conjecture and conceptualizations, adding in her own thoughts in a notebook she keeps by the bed.

Marcus' eyes meet hers and she feels the sadness that she has been running from. She falls into his arms and drowns in loneliness.

"Ezrie." He glances at the boards closing off the television room, and she shuts her eyes tight. "What are you doing here? Everyone has been so scared."

"I don't want to do it anymore," she weeps. "I don't want to do it."

He hugs her to him, and she notes how the canvas of his jacket swallows up her tears as if it is thirsty for them. He lets her cry for a while, and when she pulls away, his face is firm.

"Ezrie, where is the machine?" He holds her at arms' length, his face showing an intensity she's never seen on him. "Please. It's important."

She shakes her head. "He...he wanted me to break it."

Marcus holds her shoulders, kneels, and looks intently into her eyes. She is suddenly very aware of how big he is.

"It is very important that you tell me where it is," Marcus says. "When your father was sick, he might have said things. Things he didn't mean." His eyes search hers. "It's going to change the world, Z. You know that, don't you?" He states this, as if he has known all along. "That's why you were helping him. So that whatever happened to your dad never happens again."

And so, when he asks her if she knows how to turn it on, she tells the truth. Because he remembers Richard Collings the way Ezrie does—alive, brilliant, and unafraid. Because she has no one else to turn to. Because she is not strong enough to give up the last piece of herself by her own hand.

She shows him the code errors. The changes to the teleportation frequency to make it foolproof. The jury-rigged frequency shifter. When he asks her how she knows it works, she tells him she has tested it herself.

"You need to go to the doctor." Marcus shakes, pale as he holds the blueprints. "We need to make sure you're okay—"

Her father's voice echoes at this: *They'll cut me open, Z. They'll want to know how it happened, and then the secret will be out. You understand?*

She says she will go. Only with Marcus, but she will go. In the car, he holds her hand.

"It's for the best," Marcus says. "Don't worry about your dad. What's important now is that you're safe."

And the machine. She has not ignored that he is glad the machine is safe.

It isn't safe, Z, her father's ghost whispers. *It will climb inside you and crush your cells one by one. It will destroy you from the inside out.*

What the ghost of her father doesn't know is that the porter can't destroy her. There is nothing left inside of her to destroy but a series of numbers and letters. Variables. Unsolved equations.

VIII

EZRIE AWOKE and in her mind's eye, a red cursor blinked. She had been dreaming about her father. About the porter. About Marcus.

But she must still be dreaming, because her trace overlay had returned. She hadn't woken up to that in...how many years? She went to touch her throbbing head, but found that her arms were strapped. She was staring at a screen.

INITIALIZING. INITIALIZING.

"Welcome back, Ezrie"

She could see legs, but could not remember where she was, or why she was looking down through a hole. A man was speaking to her, and she noted that he was wearing black running shoes. It struck her as odd, somehow. Where were they running?

Ezrie tried to push herself up, but the straps immobilized her.

"We need to initialize your trace and then you can get up."

Ezrie groaned. Everything came back to her in a rush of information. Leto. Mining mission. Marcus. Trace.

Ezrie felt a pinprick in her arm.

"What's that?" Ezrie croaked. She felt something like a shiver in her blood. Her throat hurt so badly.

"The activators connecting with your neural cells," the doctor said.

Ezrie struggled to remember his name. Jason. Jeremiah. J-something. "They mimic your brain patterns and share that information with the trace. When they learn your thought patterns, you can communicate without saying anything."

"I don't want a trace." Her voice was petulant, but she had no way to control it. The dream seemed to cling to her, and she felt the thirteen-year-old part of her scrambling to the surface. *Everything is so unfair,* it clambered. *Why me? Why this?*

"Remember, this is temporary," the doctor said kindly. "Once we're back from Leto, I'll make sure it's removed. That's a promise."

The cursor inside her mind blinked a new message.

TRACE INITIALIZED.

For a moment, all she could see was the overlay. Although she could still see the simple medical room, she also could see icons and folders. She groaned. She remembered all of this too well.

"You're doing a great job," the doctor said. "Soon, you should be seeing your personal storage from the device," James said. "We didn't have backup files from your previous trace, so it's empty. But even if you go offline, you'll still be able to see what you save here."

The words were muddy in her head. But she vaguely remembered that. There had been times when she and her friend, Robyn, had disappeared into the concrete bunker below the high school theater—a props storage area—to get away from the icon that meant she was connected to the network. Anything to get rid of that watchful eye.

As if on cue, the small round icon blinked on.

TRACE RELAY CONNECTED.

The information began to pour in. The running dialogue of the chat populated, full of names she didn't know. Information about the room temperature, the depth they were below Mars' surface. Then avatars blinked across her field of vision. She read the list:

RAND

LEE

ALEX

KENNER

SAMANTHA

PURPLE

JAMES

BIRDY

ARIS

The avatars filled with outlines of red bodies, each with a name and image. She saw her own red avatar added to the list, its little heartbeat in rhythm with her own, a ticker of data flowing over its head.

From inside her mind, she saw a line of text, but also heard it, too. As if it were being spoken very faintly in her ear.

"Think of your own name," James said. On her screen, she saw the words.

JAMES: THINK OF YOUR OWN NAME.

Ezrie hated the feel of the thing in her head, the stream of information dominating her mind. But this was the price of revenge, wasn't it? She took a deep breath and thought her name:

Ezrie. On the overlay, her small avatar parroted.

EZRIE: EZRIE

"Excellent."

He waved his hand over the restraints and they retracted from her arms and legs. She pushed herself up, feeling shaky. Ezrie rubbed at her wrists, which still felt raw. From one set of cuffs to another. They really knew how to make a girl feel welcome.

The doctor was a balding black man with a salt-and-pepper beard and broad shoulders that strained against the white lab coat.

James. That was it. The same as her ninth grade gym teacher. Mr. James.

On the tray beside the bed, James set a cup of something pink. How long had it been since she'd had a drink? It felt like an eternity. But her throat hurt too much to not drink it now. She shot it back, some dribbling down her chin. Had she ever had such clean water before? It had a metallic taste to it, as if pennies had been sitting in it.

"It's an an acquired taste," James said. "Brought over from Leto. It's good to get used to it a little before you go."

Ezrie croaked her thanks, putting the empty glass on one of the silver trays near the bed.

A woman came through the operating room doors. She had a soft face featuring coffee-colored eyes framed by wavy long brown hair. She had a stack of clothes which she set on the bedside table. Ezrie might have called her beautiful under different circumstances, but her brain was pounding and refused to function.

"Hi, Ezrie," the woman said. "My name is Sam. I'm the team psychologist. I brought you some things." She laid them out one by one. "I had to guess at your size but I think they should work. The skinpants run a little small, but you get used to it."

Ezrie glared. As the woman spoke, Ezrie's trace identified her as Samantha Everton. It scrolled a handful of prestigious degrees from expensive colleges. Ezrie loathed the incessant stream of data, the deluge of information, entertainment, and chatter that came with the trace. She hadn't missed it.

She seemed not to notice, or, if she did, didn't let Ezrie's truculence faze her. "Not as fashionable as your radiation jumpsuit, but much safer for where we're going." She sat on the rolling chair and looked at James. The two paused, sharing some private trace-only discussion. Ezrie considered how nice it must be for people to be able to talk shit behind her back when they were literally in the same room with her. What a time-saver.

When they turned their attention back to her, James looked disappointed.

"I'll be watching." He tapped his head. There's a shower through there." James said, pointing to a small room beyond the surgical area. "Whenever you feel up to it."

The lock clicked heavily behind him. Ezrie thought longingly of her trailer. Her pile of chicken bones. She wanted to take it all back, make the other choice. She could be eating take-out and watching the world burn.

"How are you feeling, Ezrie? This has been quite a big day, I'm sure."

NAH, Ezrie thought, ALMOST TASERED TO DEATH AND THEN HAD SOME OF MY BRAIN REMOVED? TYPICAL MONDAY.

Sam laughed, and Ezrie realized that her thoughts had broadcast over the trace without her even knowing it. She'd have to work on that.

"You're funny." Sam said. "A good sense of humor is a great asset. Especially when things are hard." Sam's tone shifted, the smile transitioning to determination. Mrs. Peterson had looked almost the same way before giving her particularly hurtful pieces of "advice." *It's for your own good,* she'd say. Ezrie bristled.

"I know this may not be the time, but I'm afraid that time is something we don't have." Sam seemed to struggle for the right words. "It's PanGen's policy to do a comprehensive psychological evaluation of all its employees, but under the circumstances..." Her voice trailed off, and a flash of skepticism flitted across the woman's eyes. Sam stopped herself, shifted her ample hips in the chair. "The point being that all I really know of you is from your historical file, which, you can agree, is very thick for a girl who disappeared at fifteen. I need to ask you some questions, specifically about your relationship with Marcus Olet."

Ezrie struggled up, finding the muscles in her arms and stomach watery. She didn't want to talk about Marcus, especially not now and especially not with a PanGen shrink. Sam put a hand on her arm, which Ezrie pushed off with a shaking hand.

"Don't." Ezrie muttered, focusing her throbbing gaze on the tiles of the floor.

"Ezrie, I'm on your side." Sam gave her an empathetic glance. "I believe that you are as much a victim in this as the rest of us." She paused. "It's better if you're as honest as possible. If you withhold information, it might be dangerous for all of us, especially you. Why do you think that Marcus sent you that message?"

"I don't know." Maybe because I've been looking for him my whole life. Maybe because he owes me. But it would be something else, wouldn't it? Marcus wanted something from her. Something only she had.

"From your file, I get the impression that you had a difficult relationship with Marcus. He was a friend of your father's, wasn't he? He found you after your father died?"

"Leave me the hell alone."

"Listen," Sam said kindly, "We need to know about any underlying tensions that might impact the outcome of the mission—"

"Let me tell you something, Dr. Collings," Ezrie spat, "everyone is broken. But not everyone knows how to walk over the pieces to get what we want. Now, if you excuse me, I'd like to take a shower. Alone."

Sam's eyebrows knitted for a moment, then she smiled and rose. "Of course. I can respect that." She stood, smoothing her pencil skirt with a beautifully manicured hand. Ezrie balled her own broken and uneven nails into fists.

"It is my responsibility to ensure the psychological safety of the team." Sam's words were measured. Calm. "If I feel like you might harm anyone on this mission, including yourself, it is my responsibility to keep us all safe."

"Thanks," Ezrie said, "I'll keep that in mind."

"Of course. I'll be here to take you to the launch room when you're finished." Sam said. She pushed through the steel double doors, her eyes blinking some trace message that Ezrie couldn't see.

Ezrie stepped into the shower, stripped off the few clothes she had on, and prostrated herself beneath the soapy blue sludge of the chemical spray. She winced at the weight of her body on her feet, the burning in her eyes and fingers—remnants of the laster blast. She touched her raw throat and the gauzy soreness at the back of her head, tenderly trying the new trace installed there.

Across the screen in her mind, information rained down as thick and caustic as the blue chemical water replacement. Schematics of the base, the control room outlined in red. The chattered thoughts of every human on the PanGen base clamoring to be given a piece of her mind.

She closed her eyes against it, trying to disconnect herself from their madness. But when she did, she could only see her mother, zooming through the window or up at the sky, her eyes vacant. Molly had left them long before she had ever gone, trapped in the trace, too busy looking inside to see the life she was missing.

Tears ran down her cheeks, mixing with the chemical shower to make a watercolor blue on her fingers as she rubbed them clean. She felt her parents both so close now, ghosts whispering of promises she had not kept.

They could have her, she decided. Her thoughts, her mind, her soul. All that she had been for so long, all husk and hate. If there was a place she could put them to rest, a place to fill her up or hollow her out forever, Leto was as good as anywhere else.

IX

BIRDY BELIEVED that biological systems were magical, and that the magic was made more so by being quantifiable. The fine attachments of muscle to bone that withstood enormous pressure was the alchemy that defined strength, size, and sex of a creature. The intricacies of skin in response to the pressures of the environment explained the movement of the seasons, the resilience or weakness of an animal who, at its most fundamental, had created the organ as protection against specific dangers. At this moment, though, she had a primal hate for her biology.

She gave a rasping wheeze, and took a hit of albuterol.

"Why?" Cy's shoulders dropped, his ever-present smile fading. "You told me yourself that it was dangerous—"

"You are my world, you are, but I have to go. I can't let them lie about Leto any more. It's not right."

He said nothing, which is usually what Birdy loved most about Cy. He didn't mind that she filled the silence with words. He seemed to soak up her stories, facts, and analyses as if he were a desert and her voice was a river running through it.

Now, the silence felt like famine.

"I thought I might be able to get out of this another way, but I can't." She felt her voice waver, and wished she was in Costa Rica, in his arms instead of the belly of PanGen's labs. The white plastic sheeting draped over the plants felt suddenly sterile, like ghosts. "But, not now. Leto is where I need to be. Whether you approve or not."

"Maybe it is better to not pretend, Birdy." He looked at her, his eyes far away and sad. "You will always choose them over me. I hoped it would change, but I know now."

"Them?" she sputtered. "You mean Zhong and Rand—"

"No," Cy said sadly. "Your creatures. Your animals. As if they were more important than the people who love you. You love them most. I get what's left over."

"No," she interrupted. "Listen—"

"I don't understand how you can go, after everything you have seen. All the things you told me, about the water, the phlax, the lycants—You told me yourself it wasn't safe."

His face, usually so relaxed, was sharp with emotion. He was rarely angry, but his passion was Cy's most endearing quality. His intensity radiated through the holographic display, making her want to kiss him.

She had a sudden, desperate regret that she had shared the truth with him. She nervously looked over her shoulder, even though she knew the lab was empty.

Purple says the porter will be open in less than an hour, Rand sent on the team channel. We need to be ready to go. Response is required.

The team chimed in with acknowledgement.

On my way, Birdy sent.

"The team needs me," Birdy said emphatically. "I have to go to the planet. That's the only way to prove to Zhong how dangerous it is. I have to get the experiments and bring them back."

"They have others, don't they?" His face hardened. "Have Purple bring them back. They don't need you to risk your life—"

"I'm the only one who can do this, Cy," Birdy said, her voice too shrill, too fast. "If I don't bring the samples home, there is no telling what could happen."

"Zhong won't listen." Cy's eyes blazed. "He doesn't care if the water hurts people. He cares about his company, nothing more."

Her chest tightened. It was dangerous that he knew so much. She took the inhaler from her chest pocket and took another deep hit. But Cy could never understand. Zhong needed Birdy to make sure that the water was good enough, but Birdy needed Leto, too. She needed to be there, to see it grow, to be a part of it. She loved Cy. But Leto was an entire world. A world that needed her more.

"Then I'll show the world," Birdy said. "They'll have to believe me."

"Birdy, I love you," he said quietly. "No matter where you are, you have to know that." He looked at her, his face softening. "Be safe."

She nodded, then blew him a kiss. "I'll be back, I promise. When this is finished, we can talk again."

He nodded and flicked off the transmission. She sat at her desk, staring at the empty holographic display, then put her head into her hands. After a few moments, she blinked into the test results of the samples they had taken before the Apollo crew had gone. The readings were iffy, at best. Birdy changed some parameters, reordering the data enough to make the water fit the requirements the Water Safety Commission had set. It was the only way to keep her cover. To continue the lie for now.

The fraction of difference was so small. Statistically insignificant, at least, when she contrived the reports in the right way.

But the reality was that the unknown compound was evaporated, it left a microscopic sheen on the petri dish. Charleston and she had discussed the potential ramifications at length, finally bringing their concerns to Zhong.

"But is the water safe?" Zhong had asked.

"Well, we can't know for sure," Charleston said. He and Birdy had been over it a thousand times, with Birdy anxiously sounding the warning bell. To her, the unknown particle constituted a shiny red flag. The kind that should stop the entire mission and send them all out to look for another planet.

"Mr. Director, Particle R may have impacts on biology that we can't account for. We really can't take any chance at this point bringing in biology to Earth that simply isn't meant to be—"

"But we can filter it."

"Yes," Birdy said, "but the R particle is very small. Smaller than the common cold virus by a hundred times, down to .012 microns wide. If it were a virus, we could assume that it would be attached to something that would spread it, something larger that we could filter—"

"Particle R is attached to the hydrogen of the water molecule," Charleston said, his voice slow. He didn't mean to be condescending, but there was an "I'm a man, and this is the real truth," kind of tone in his voice. "Whatever the stage of the water—ice, rain, fog—the R particles go with it."

"We have attempted to remove the R particles through electrolosis, but they don't split," Birdy interjected. "Instead, they bond to the molecule itself, instigating a growth reaction."

"What does that mean?"

"It means that electricity is a catalyst for R particles," Birdy blurted out. "The R particles are inert until they are exposed to electrolosis. Then they become phlax. That's why they are growing on the transmitters and around the power cables. By bringing electricity to Leto, we have fundamentally changed the biology here. If we had never come, it is likely the change wouldn't have occurred, but now..." The ramifications were too large to comprehend. "We simply can't mine the Leto water for human consumption without further testing. We have to know that R particles are safe before we allow people to buy it."

"But these R particles," Zhong says coolly. "They make up less than a fraction of a percent."

"Yes," Charleston said.

"A statistically insignificant amount, isn't that right, Dr. Mack?"

Charleston nodded, and Birdy bristled at being intentionally left out of the conversation. Charleston noticed, too. "Yes. It is within official safety limits, but I have to agree with *Dr. Arnolds* that—"

"Your concerns have been noted," Zhong said. "PanGen has exclusive rights to Leto's water in one of the longest-distance mines that have ever been attempted. If the water can pass the Commission, we move forward with the operation."

Zhong had dismissed her then, but she wouldn't let him do it again. When she got home with the proof, she would not be silent. And Zhong and the PanGen dynasty would fall.

Like her mother said: sometimes, doing the right thing required doing the wrong thing.

She pulled on her pack.

"To doing the right wrong things," she whispered. "I hope it's not too late."

X

THE PRE-LAUNCH ROOM bustled with people monitoring various systems. People were everywhere, some in grey-green jumpsuits, some in white lab coats, and some wearing only the long-sleeved skin-suit top and clinging bottoms that Ezrie had on. From the holodisplays, she could see vital information on the team, including herself. From a few of them, she saw other names. Cassie Byrion. Jenny Candala. All flat lines. Sam followed her gaze.

"We think the Lock is blocking communication," Sam said weakly. "We hope, at least."

"Yeah. That's comforting," Ezrie said dryly. Her head was still pounding from the place they'd put the brain implant she swore she would never have again. Every thought from every human within a hundred miles danced through her brain. And the skinpants beneath the outlanding suit were threatening to strangle her asshole.

She picked the tight material out for the thousandth time.

"You get used to it," Sam said with a laugh. "It helps with water conservation. We recycle as much as we can, including our own."

Ezrie grimaced. *WELL, AT LEAST I'LL KNOW WHOSE WATER I'M RECLAIMING*, she thought. *IF I HAVE TO DRINK PISS, IT MIGHT AS WELL BE MY OWN.*

LEE: SURPRISINGLY GOOD ATTITUDE, BLACKER BETTY. YOU'LL BE LUCKY IF DRINKING PISS IS THE WORST THING THAT HAPPENS ON LETO.

She cursed herself as Lee shoved a large red pack into Ezrie's arms. She hadn't masked her thoughts for over ten years. She had to remember how to do it. Deeper thoughts, the ones that were more memory or impulse, didn't register as well. The ones that sounded like her own voice in her head that seemed to come through *louder* somehow.

Ezrie unzipped the pack. None of her things were there. No screen, no picture, and no laster.

"Hey! This isn't my stuff. Where's my shit, man?"

"You'll get your pack back when we get home, Blacker Betty," Lee snorted. "For now, all you need are a few supplies to survive the next day."

Ezrie gritted her teeth, shoving the stuff back into the pack. A few packages, food paste tubes, a portable fire pack, and Xtenz rope. She'd used one once. In the Davis house, they were all about family adventures. Ezrie had nearly crapped herself rappelling down the face of Red Rock canyon attached to the Xtenz's retractable metal line.

She reflexively put a hand to her ear. The earring was still there. She wondered if she should remove it, for safe keeping. But there wasn't a safer place to have it then right in the open, was there? Hidden in plain sight. As long as she didn't turn it on, it would stay that way.

"Do I need a helmet or anything?" Ezrie muttered to Sam after Lee left, double-checking that the earring was locked in place and not going anywhere. She hefted the pack on her back. It felt like a bag of bricks. "Can we breathe the air?"

"The air's breathable," a voice behind her said. Ezrie turned to see the skinny black woman that she'd met earlier. The talker. "There are no active airborne pathogens, at least nothing that's any worse than Earth," the woman laughed nervously. "But the outlanding suit has a standard hood, communication system, and environment controls to keep you warm or cool, filter air, anything you could ever want. A cornucopia of comforts—"

"Birdy is our resident Leto expert," Sam said. "If you have any questions about the biology, she is our brilliant mad scientist."

Birdy smiled at that. Ezrie thought "Birdy" wasn't the name she would have given her. "Horsey" was closer to the truth.

patted a water-filled bladder on Ezrie's back, then reached into the neck of Ezrie's suit. "May I?" She pulled out a thin straw hiding in a pocket where the hood connected to the neck. "Go ahead. It's clean." She blanched. "For now, at least. It's your water, remember, so you'll want to clean it out daily. There's nothing quite as unsavory as old reclaimed water."

Ezrie took a sip, her ragged throat reveling at the taste of the water. *The first pass is always the best,* Ezrie thought sardonically. *It won't taste so great the next time around.*

A large window hung on one side of the pre-launch room. Through it, Ezrie could see the huge porter that she'd traveled through a few hours ago and the control room that Lee had shot her in. How long ago had it been? Hours? Days? It felt like an eternity.

Lee handed out more large red packs to different people in various stages of dress. Ezrie recognized James, the doctor, but the rest were strangers.

"That's Rand," Sam pointed. "The Artemis Team leader." She paused. "And my husband."

Ezrie's trace identified him as Rand Everton, Mission Captain. It listed credentials for him: a Staff Sergeant General in the Southern War and the captain of PanGen mining expeditions to Proxima Centauri and Gliese. His sharp, hooked nose cut angles with his tanned cheekbones, making him look like a sculpture in bronze. A good-looking man, even with bags beneath his eyes and that world-weary stare. But he had a hardness about him that Ezrie had only ever known from tyrants. Rand whistled, and the room quieted.

"We have a short jaunt today. The goal will be to get on the planet, search the base, and get off again. The less time we're there, the safer we all will be."

Rand stared Ezrie down with ice blue eyes, his body ramrod straight. "Our newest team member, Ezrie Collings, will lead us out and back. This is a quick trip, let me reiterate." His words were crisp and sharp. "No one should be getting comfortable on Leto. I'll have you back here in time for lunch."

Ezrie's heart fell. She had hours to find Marcus, not days. She had to have a plan.

Before she could even begin formulating, Rand made a beeline for her.

Shit.

She instantly regretted thinking it, but somehow caught the word, pulling back at the last instant and allowing the thought to dissipate in her mind. It felt like almost, but not quite, remembering the name of a song. She willed herself not to finish her thought. The cursor in her mind next to her name remained empty. That, she supposed, was another silver lining on the shittiest day ever. She was getting better at having an implant in her brain.

"Ezrie Collings," Rand stated. "I'm Captain Everton. Most of the team calls me Rand. I'm leading this mission."

He seemed to look her over, even as his gaze never moved from her own.

"It's important that you understand how this team works," he said, his jaw flexing. "We don't need dead weight, do you understand?"

"Yes." Ezrie glowered, but still felt small under his scrutiny. She had a flash of living with the Serviers. Andy Servier, the father, had looked on her more than once with this same mixture of disgust and cold disappointment. Mostly after she'd used his login credentials to help steal a very nice Tesla Cordata from a local car dealership showroom.

"And I want to make it clear that you will be escorted at all times by someone from the security team. You are a guest on my team, is that clear? You will accompany us to the surface and then back. Then, you'll go back to where you come from. Do we understand each other?"

"I understand."

Like hell I'm going back, she thought with that same careless release. The words fluttered into the ether. Somewhere that wasn't tracked by Captain Anal, Boobs McShrinko, or Horsey Talksalot. They had no idea what she was capable of.

She caught a pair of eyes staring at her, belonging to a skinny redheaded guy. He looked away too fast for her trace to identify him.

"It's time," a voice said through overhead speakers. "We are go for launch."

A porter tech shuttled her into the porter bay. "All we need is your hand here on the porter, Ms. Collings. Once you've gone through, we'll be able to bring everyone else over."

She tried to steady her shaking hand as she placed it on the screen. Ezrie felt something like stage fright. What if she did it wrong? She had never ported even close to eight light years away. She'd never even had the guts to port to Io. The machine rumbled to life, the ions flickering yellow, the scanner beaming down, measuring her size, her energy. It created a perfect copy of her, down to the ion. Ezrie closed her eyes. She could imagine the shadow Ezrie, somewhere. A perfect replica whose ions built an invisible bridge that would call her into an unknown world.

The computer announced that the code had been received.

"The porter is open," the voice announced. She could hear whoops of excitement from the crew, even behind the soundproof glass. She glanced behind her and saw Birdy hugging Sam. Even Rand's military jaw softened with relief.

"Ms. Collings, go on through. The rest of the crew is prepped to follow."

Behind the scene, Ezrie knew that the Lock was taking her DNA, matching it, and using it to fill in key gaps in the porter programming. When she was through, it would ripple closed, eating all the data it could find, breaking down every electronic connection.

Did they know that? Were they aware that the end game of the Lock was a complete system failure?

It didn't matter. Not her problem. Marcus was on the other side, waiting. As long as she got to Leto, nothing else mattered.

Ezrie stepped through the door and into a concrete porter bay—the spitting image of the room she'd just left, but a study in grey instead of white. She nearly thought she had come out in same exact room except that it was completely empty and the air was sauna-hot and thick as paint. She gasped it in, the humidity making her feel like a fish out of water.

She looked around the bay. The H1 porter was outdated, and the porter itself was covered in strands of strange blue growths. She touched one, and it glowed with bioluminescent light. For a multi-trillion-dollar organization, it seemed they had put a lot less thought into their porter specifications and cleanup than they should have.

Orange light seemed to come from everywhere at once, and her head spun crazily. The porter bay featured a thin window, maybe a foot tall, that encircled the building, allowing Ezrie to catch a glimpse of the sky. She saw a purple-burgundy tree limb, soft and feathery. A tentacled creature shot through the air like a dart, leaving behind a red cloud of dust. *Was that an octopus?* She thought. Despite her singular focus, she felt a thrill of the unknown in her bones. She wanted out there. To see it for herself.

Ezrie tentatively walked to the exit. It wouldn't be hard to run. She put her hand on the exit scanner as the ion field hummed to life behind her.

Lee ported through, taking one side step before pulling up the laster and siting Ezrie between the eyes.

"I'm gonna need you to step away from that door."

Ezrie sniffed. "Are you always this friendly?"

"You and I are going to get along fine as soon as we understand each other." Lee sat down on a small bench that lined the octagonal building, her leg crossed wide, her elbow on her knee, the laster trained on Ezrie's head.

"Blackers like you are used to looking out for numero uno, aren't you? No use for anybody else's shit. I get that, I really do." Lee kicked the dust from her boot on the steel floor. It made a hollow boom. "But down here, we work together or we don't work at all. I'm sure that's new to you—"

Ezrie gripped the straps of her pack tighter, thinking of the hours she had worked with her father. Even Marcus had assisted, at times. She had been a part of that. "You don't know me."

"I'm telling you, Ezrie," she shook her head, her voice a bell of warning, "I do. And I know how you end up."

"So what if I look out for myself? No one else is doing it."

"Down here, we look out for each other." Lee's pulled a cigarette out of her boot, tapped it on the metal bench. "On Earth maybe you can go it alone. Lots do. But here?" She pulled the trigger of the laster, lighting the cigarette in the flame of the burst. Ezrie jumped back instinctively. Lee laughed roughly. "You can't survive on your own."

Ezrie turned away, feeling humiliated and small. *You watch. I'll be alive long after you're dead.*

Ezrie was pleased to find that her trace had gone dark, the ticker tape of constant information silent in her head, even with Lee within spitting distance. A closer look around the room told her that the walls were covered in grey sheets of mitrium. A good way to ensure that ports couldn't be impacted by outside stimulus. The dampening was so thick on this one that Ezrie felt a little jealous. She needed this for the trailer. Even a ICET troller or high-res scan wouldn't be able to penetrate it.

The others ported through every few minutes. She tried to remember them as they stepped through: Sam, Birdy, James, et. al. The mitrium in the walls made her trace blessedly quiet. Now to see if she could still use her brain without it.

There were three she hadn't noticed before.

One was a square-jawed man with a blonde buzz cut and sharp nose who didn't bother to introduce himself. When he stepped out, he scanned the room, pausing only momentarily on her face, then gave her an odd commiserative smile before going to join Birdy, Sam, and Aris, who had already ported through. It made Ezrie wonder if she knew him and had just forgotten.

The second was the redhead who had stared at her in the launch room. He was skinny, freckled, and had the reddest hair she'd ever seen—even redder than the android, Aris. She caught him stealing a glance at her, and he blushed deeply, giving her an awkward wave before jogging over.

"Hey," he said. "It's nice to meet you. I'm Finn, but they call me Purple. I'm the software guy, here." His voice didn't seem to match him. Even though he was easily a foot taller than her (and probably weighed the same as her soaking wet) his voice was big and booming and as Irish as potatoes.

"Ezrie," she said, trying not to laugh. "I'm Ezrie Collings."

"I know," he said. "I'm a big fan, a huge, huge fan. I've seen all your interviews. Your da, he's like, he's such a big deal."

She inwardly groaned. Great. A Nets fan. She knew his type: Alt-History guys who sometimes sent her weird conspiracy theories or unsolicited dirty pictures. Their reverence for Richard Collings verged on worship, and she sometimes wondered if they didn't love him more than she did.

"Thanks. Um. It's good to meet you."

"Yeah, it's too bad we're only going to be here for a few hours," he said. "I'd love to pick your brain—"

Oh no. Ezrie touched the wad of gauze pack at the back of her head. The trace was sore and annoying, but it was a good excuse to leave the conversation. "My trace," she said, gesturing to the gauze. "I don't think that's a great idea. Maybe I'll go check in with the doctor-guy—"

"James," he offered. "For sure, for sure." His face went a bright shade of red.

She turned away, finding the grizzled face of James and moving his direction. You'd think that halfway across the universe you'd be able to lose the creepers.

The last person to port through was a Viking of a man with an intense smile and emerald eyes. He was maybe the most attractive person she'd ever met in real life. He introduced himself as Alex Deifik, Security Lead. Then, he got violently ill, barely missing Ezrie as he vomited everything he'd ever eaten since second grade onto the floor. "Bad port," he said, wiping his forehead and smiling rakishly. "Do you have a mint?"

"Okay," Rand said, ignoring Alex. "We need to split up. Kenner and Alex will search the perimeter. Birdy and Sam will check the lab and engineering. Purple stays here with Aris and reconfigures the porter for launch home. The rest of us are checking out the base. James, you're with me. Lee, you have Ezrie."

"My pleasure." Lee flicked her laster on, giving Ezrie a once over.

"Masks on." Rand flipped the mask over his face. "And stay alive."

Ezrie put on her mask and heard the sound of the suction near her ear. From her trace she couldn't see any of the others' feeds—the mitrium walls doing their job—but she could see biometrics from her own suit. Her heart rate (121 bpm). The oxygen level (eighty-four percent and rising). Rand placed his hand beside the exit door and the bay door slid to each side, revealing a world in technicolor.

The sky hung huge and orange overhead—an orange that was vibrantly alive, as if every breath of air might be making her younger, smarter. In it were two suns that her trace identified as Pyrios and Aeos. She could almost look at them with her bare eyes. One fit inside the other like matching wedding bands.

Behind her lay an ocean, huge and red, that became deeper and blacker the further towards the horizon she looked. The seashore lapped against a midnight beach covered in black-purple sand, the water sluggish and lazy. Pink-tipped waves rolled softly, so unlike the ocean that Ezrie had visited when she had been small. The waves of the Pacific were wild and angry, *and acidic,* her mother had been clear to tell her. *Don't touch the water.*

Here the water was listless and bored. It kissed the shoreline softly, the black pebbled sand leading to a high berm covered in grey grass. Parti-colored trees grew dense and squat at the edge of the cliff, with those same purple-burgundy tendrils she'd seen through the thin windows of the porter.

From overhead, flying creatures warbled calls at them, their bodies dark black, or green, or sometimes translucent in the orange sky. An eyeless creature with wings like wax paper nearly flew into her head, then zoomed past with a throaty cackle, it's body envy-green. Other creatures swarmed in the trees nearby, snapping at passing insects, whipping out tentacled appendages with a crack as they snagged their dinner. They peered at her with fish-egg eyes, blinking orbs that swirled untethered, like pickled eggs in a jar.

Ezrie felt her breath catch in her throat. She felt like Dororthy stepping into Oz.

LASTERS TO DISABLE, Rand sent.

Ezrie's hand went to her waistband on instinct, but of course her laster wasn't there.

NOT YOU, EZRIE, Rand sent. YOU HAVE TO EARN A WEAPON.

Ezrie tried to be angry, but the missing laster didn't matter in the sparkling light of Leto's evening. She stooped to grab a handful of the black rocks, rolling them in her fingers. They were perfectly round and smooth like thousands of tiny marbles in her hand. She shoved them in her outlanding pants, not even really knowing why. Maybe to remind herself that this was real. All of this existed, and she was here.

A small, private conversation box opened on her overlay. Ezrie wondered exactly how private the conversation was.

We can sightsee later, Lee sent to Ezrie. We need to move now.

Ezrie followed the group towards the base with Lee close behind her. The building was a cancer on the hallucinatory beauty of the Leto. Against the backdrop of the colored sky creatures and multicolored tree fronds, it hunkered spider-like with glass and metal arms that seemed latently violent compared to the flow of the jungle. There were several small buildings nearby, each of them like dead satellites, their lights gone, their metal forms sulking in the humidity.

What happened here? Rand sent. Ezrie refocused on the reality in front of her.

The main doors had been pried open, and one of them hung at a postmodern angle. The short decontamination chamber between the outer and inner door was flooded with yellow light. From within, there was a low, almost whispered hum.

What is that? Ezrie sent to the team without even meaning to.

The emergency generator, Lee sent. She was turning from side to side, scanning the shoreline and woods, looking for someone. They turned off the main power.

Rand: I don't like any of this. Everyone needs to make their feeds live.

Birdy: Going live

Kenner: Live

Purple: Live now

Feeds filled the periphery of Ezrie's vision one by one. Images of Alex and Kenner moving towards the woods. The twin video feeds of Birdy and Sam jogging towards another small, squat building in the distance. She blinked into her own main navigation, focusing her attention on the yellow box with the word "LIVE" in superscript. It began blinking red.

I'm live, she thought.

Rand: The secondary doors are torn up, too. There were huge divots in the metal panels that lay haphazardly where a door should have been.

James: What could have done that?

Lee squinted in the poor light and touched the damaged panels.

An animal, maybe, if it was big enough. Lee squinted, her brows knit.

Rand nodded. Well the airlock is broken, he sent. We'll need to keep masks on until we've scanned the whole thing.

Ezrie walked into the building's belly and past the side hallways like great, hollow arms. The generators flicked off and on, spasmodically drenching her in sodium light. From the lights overhead, blue tendrils swirled, glowing incandescently. She reached up to touch one and it crumbled to grey dust.

Lee and Ezrie, take the professional hallway, Rand sent. James and I will take the bunks and medical.

Ezrie felt a sense of unease as Rand and James disappeared into the darkened belly of the base.

This way, Lee sent, nodding to a hallway on their left.

The motion lights attempted to announce them as they arrived, flickering once before dying. It left them in half-darkness, lit only by the orange light coming through a shattered window that looked into the forest beyond.

The west hallway window is broken, Lee sent. Looks like they had some trouble.

Ezrie saw Lee from two angles: one in real life and one in her mind. It was disorienting, to see her in two places at once. The other feeds made it even worse. She could see Kenner and Alex traipsing through the jungle underbrush. Rand recorded a room full of empty cots. In medical, James' feed showed an empty body bag that had been torn to shreds. From Sam's and Birdy's feeds, the lab was destroyed, samples upheaved and shattered glass all over the floor.

Ezrie's gaze landed on a perfect handprint in blood. A shudder went down her spine.

Blood, Lee sent. She held Ezrie back from going closer.

Whose blood? Ezrie sent.

Lee shook her head. She stooped down, her gaze following some invisible trail. Ezrie looked down and saw that there were footprints. Also small, but not much smaller than Ezrie's own footprints.

THIS IS WHERE SHE SLIPPED, Lee said. SHE WAS RUNNING.

SHE? Ezrie sent. SHE WHO?

Lee ignored the question, instead stepping over the footprints and down the hallway. Ezrie coaxed herself on despite the feeling that her muscles were suddenly made of glass.

Most of the doors in this hallway were closed, their security panels glowing red. Lee didn't even try them. Only one door was open, and it hung crazily by a hinge. Ezrie's trace lit up, highlighting that this was Dr. Jeffrey Sanger's office, the Leto Apollo Team Psychologist.

Ezrie had seen enough psychiatrists office to know that something in here had gone very badly. The soft chairs were torn, with synthetic stuffing all over the floor. The desk and table were covered in more black smears of blood. The wide screen that made up the shortest wall of the room was dark, fractured into a thousand shards of glass. The twisted husk of a metal chair lay beside it. In the center of the room was a glitching projector, errors running in a steady stream, fueled by the faint energy of the generator. Ezrie couldn't make out the code because it was rolling so fast, but it was clear there was a fatal circular error somewhere in the playback program.

From someone's feed there was a low whine.

WHAT IS THAT? Rand sent.

IT'S THE PORTER, Purple sent. WE'RE TRYING TO DISABLE THE LOCK, BUT IT'S NOT WORKING. EZRIE IS THE ONLY ONE WHO HAS ADMIN CONTROLS.

Lee stopped in her tracks, her gaze snapping to Ezrie. "What are you trying to pull, Betty?" she growled.

But Ezrie couldn't think of anything but what she was seeing.

Words on the ceiling, nearly fifteen feet up. Thousands of words scrawled in black and red like a child making crayon drawings. They ran in veins across the ceiling, then dripped down the far walls in nonsensical phrases that made Ezrie shudder.

NOT

WE ARE ONE AND NOT ONE

WE ARE ONE

WE SPEAK

RAND: LEE, COME IN.

SAM: BIRDY AND I HEADING BACK. MAYBE I SHOULD TALK TO EZRIE...

NO NEED, Lee sent. ON OUR WAY.

Ezrie reached up to touch the writing, but Lee stopped her with the laster on her arm. LET'S GO.

HEY GUYS? Purple sent. I THINK WE MIGHT BE IN SOME TROUBLE.

From his live feed, Ezrie could see Aris hovered over the control panel, her android fingers a blur on the controls. The whine from the porter was getting higher, shriller.

RAND: LEE, MOVE EZRIE NOW

PURPLE: I NEED EZRIE TO SHUT IT DOWN NOW WHILE THERE'S STILL TIME TO OVERRIDE. From his video feed, the porter processes were squealing like a bad fan belt on an old Ford. The Lock had eaten the safety program that managed the ionic field generators then.

"You heard the kid," Lee snapped, "get your ass moving!"

Ezrie gritted her teeth. She had come this far. She was this close. She wasn't going back now. Maybe not ever.

"No."

Ezrie planted her feet, bracing for whatever came next.

"You're going back to fix that porter, or you're going to regret it." Lee seethed, her eyes blazing as she raised the laster to Ezrie's chest. "Now move your blacker ass before I melt it."

LEE: EZRIE IS REFUSING TO COOPERATE. I MAY HAVE TO TAKE HER BY FORCE.

SAM: HOLD ON! DON'T DO ANYTHING. I'M ALMOST THERE.

From Purple's feed, there was the sound of a crescendo, increasing like the line on a parabola.

Ezrie's heart was racing. The sound of a porter overloading was one she had heard countless times. This time, it brought her back to the earliest sound, the sound of her father laughing and shouting. *It works, Z, it works!* He'd shouted it, wrapping her up in a spinning hug as she clutched his flannel shirt in her fists. To him, it hadn't matter that it had exploded. To do something great, sometimes you had to let mediocre things burn.

"Goddamit, Ezrie, this is your last chance." Lee's voice was cold. She flicked the laster's power and it made a distinct hum as it went from low to medium setting. Or was it high? It didn't matter.

Ezrie curled her toes in the steel boots as if she were gripping the floor beneath.

"Do whatever you have to do. I'm not leaving Leto. Nobody is."

Ezrie heard the pop as the ion field of the porter disentangled.

"This is on you," Lee snarled. "Everything that happens next, it's all your fault."

The yellow sheen of the porter ions snapped to black. The running light at the top of the porter frame blinked red, then went dark.

WARNING. WARNING. WARNING.

Alerts flamed across Ezrie's trace. Screams and shouts of confusion from voices both on and off the feed.

Lee screamed, pulling the trigger even as spittle flew from her mouth.

There was a ripping sensation as Lee unloaded the laster—a tearing pain that felt like it would destroy her very cells. She dropped, paralyzed, burning, dying.

Even as Ezrie's body shook, her eyes on fire, she heard the sound of boots on metal. She saw Sam leap at Lee, knocking the laster out of her hands.

The last thing she saw was Sam turning to her, her mouth full of echoing words. Ezrie wondered what she was trying to say, but it didn't matter. There was darkness coming to swallow her, and somewhere in that darkness, she could hear the faintest sound of a whisper.

PART 2
GREY IS FOR MORALS

"You begin simply, by learning how to divert systems. It only takes a bad piece of code or a carefully placed comma to confuse the machine. Diverting systems is about reorganizing the brains of the machine to follow a set of commands that will take it down the rabbit hole while you sneak up behind it and steal what you need."

The BlackBook, Last Accessed 2072

|

Ocean Base, *Leto*

Day 2

LEE WAS FURIOUS. Rand, who sat across from her at his desk, wasn't happy either.

The porter board was fried, according to Purple, with no chance of having one ready before the window closed. Phlax had choked out the air filtration system and the heating system, not to mention the main external database where backups of the team trace files were stored. They were stranded here, and there was no doubt in anyone's mind that Ezrie was to blame.

Twenty-eight days trapped on Leto with no way home.

"She knows more than she's saying, Rand," Lee said, finally breaking the silence. She flexed and unflexed her fingers. It still stung where Sam had dropped her elbow on Lee's wrist. If she weren't a friend, and Rand's wife, her neck would be broken by now. "I swear that she was planning on stranding us here from the start."

"Maybe," Rand said, his throat hoarse from shouting at her. "But if you kill her, we can't know for sure, can we?"

Lee thought about all the things she wanted to say, but she knew better. Unlike Ezrie, the blacker hothead that had gotten them all into this mess. And then there was Rand. He was in this up to his neck. Lee didn't know how, but she knew that he was.

Still, they had time between them. A lot of time and a lot of history. She wasn't about to call him out unless she knew for sure what he'd been up to.

"Lee," he said after a moment of consideration. "I need you on my team. We've always had each other's backs out here, and I need that now more than ever. I think someone on the team is trying to shut down the mission."

Lee thought about this, then hawked a wad of phlegm onto the metal floor. She would have to keep playing along. It was what Cassie would have wanted.

"I said from the first minute I laid eyes on her—" Lee started.

"No." Rand ran his hands across his sandpapery jowls. "Not Ezrie. One of us. One of the Apollo team."

So it had come to this.

Lee felt a cool anger. How could he sit there and lie to her face? After she'd saved his life in California, the only other living member of the regiment he had led. They had been inseparable, Rand convincing her to leave ICET at the top of her game to come work Snake duty for PanGen. Rand had been her stand-in for a daddy for almost as long as her own father had refused to take her calls.

"Who do you think it is?"

He sighed. "Marcus, probably. That's the obvious answer." He scratched his stubbled. "But I don't know, Lee. But it looks pretty bad when you try to kill the only person who might have a lead."

"Are you saying you think—"

"You are relieved of your weapons."

The instinct to punch him was so strong, she had to grab her right fist till her knuckles were white. "Excuse me?"

"That's an official directive," Rand snapped. "Are we clear?"

Lee's face darkened. She flung the laster on the table. Then she pulled the field knife from her belt and stabbed it into the laminated veneer of the desktop.

"Does that make you feel better?" he said quietly.

"A little," she snarled.

"Good. Go get some food and take a quaalude, or something. And stay alert. We don't know who is out here or what they want, but they certainly don't seem very friendly."

"Yes, sir," Lee snapped.

She stormed out of the office, her head spinning. They all thought Marcus brought Ezrie here, but it was too obvious. Rand was the one who split the teams. If Ezrie had stayed at the porter... She felt a pang of grief through the anger. She should have listened to Cassie when she had a chance.

She paused, finding herself in the control room, her arms itching to fight. She pushed over a rack of computer innards, swearing and punching, kicking a chair until it spun around and toppled.

From down the infirmary hallway, she could see Purple, hovering around the infirmary room where they'd taken Ezrie. As Lee approached, he started up, still holding a panel of the wall like a knight with a shield. From within the panel, sticky blue strings laced and throbbed with light.

"You," she seethed. He went red and dropped his eyes. "Waiting for your girlfriend to wake up?"

"H-hey Lee," he said, lowering the panel slightly. "Trying to clean phlax out of—"

She knocked the panel from his hands, and it clanged on the steel of the floor. Purple stepped back, looking even younger than usual. "You think you know who she is because you seen her on the Nets or made her the porno star in your wet dreams? You don't, kid. She's bad news. All of this is bad news, and she's as much a part of it as—"

She stopped herself. No. She couldn't out Rand like that. Not in front of the kid. It was bad leadership. Good news went down, bad news went up.

"Get the hell away from her, Purple. She is a user, and you're gonna end up being a stepping stone."

He said nothing, but his face flushed even deeper red.

Lee stalked away towards the bunk, fuming.

"Oh, Lee," Birdy said as she passed in the hallway, "I was going to tell you that it looks like some of the samples from the lab are missing—"

"Dammit, Birdy!" Lee shouted, feeling her voice breaking. "There are *people* missing. Your samples are the least important thing on this planet!"

Birdy scuttled away, leaving Lee in the angry silence of the bunk.

Lee sat on the side of the bed and sobbed, crushing the tears from her eye sockets as if she could hurt them, too.

Where are you? What do I do now?

Lee stared at the locker that used to be Cassie's and felt a pang of loneliness and grief. She popped it open with a practiced jiggle. All of Cassie's things were right where she'd left them. A beat-up grey t-shirt that was soft as kitten fur. Lee looked over her shoulder, then, convinced she was alone, breathed it in. She wanted to think of Cassie, but also not. It was too hard.

Where are you?

She picked up the flat penny lying at the front of the locker shelf. It was long and coppery, with a picture of an atom on one side and the words "Newtonian Museum, 2042." Cassie's eyes, grey and shining, had lit up as she explained the trip she'd taken with her sophomore chemistry class to the California Academy of Sciences in San Francisco. How it had inspired her to do whatever it took to go into space.

What if—

No. Not Cassie. Cassie couldn't. Wouldn't.

She peeled off her clothing, dropping them into the bin where they would be chemically sterilized and dried, then stepped into the chemical shower. The air in the evening was still stifling, and the cool liquid felt good against her skin. Through the domed sky room, she could see that evening was falling on Leto.

Where are you? What do I do now?

When she came out, she felt better. Still angry, but not in the fiery, destructive way that had seized her earlier. She was back to the icy, controlled rage that was more comfortable. And it wasn't Ezrie alone that was the problem. Although, Ezrie would help Purple fix the porter, Lee decided. Maybe she'd take Ezrie out and leave her alone on in the jungle for a while. Maybe that would knock her down a peg or two.

No, this was about Rand. Rand and Cassie.

The facts were this:

The Lock had been set on Leto.

The Lock had been designed to bring Ezrie—and only Ezrie—to Leto.

The Lock could only have been set by a super admin. That meant Cassie or Rand. Or maybe someone who could have hacked the system. Someone like Purple or Ezrie.

Unless one of those people gave super admin access to someone else, she thought. *That would mean that there were two of them.*

The thought was terrifying. Not only would it mean that the people that Lee thought she knew so well were lying to her, but that the possibilities were endless. Rand could have given his credentials to anyone.

Cassie could have done the same.

No, that wasn't real. Cassie would never have done that. Could never. Rand had to have given out his credentials.

But how? The voice in her head was her brother's, Paul. Even though he was still a Deacon in the same church home that Lee's father had been preaching at since they were kids, he still spoke to her. She went to him, sometimes, when she felt abjectly lonely for family. Paul was kind, though persistent that her chosen lifestyle was always going to come between her and her father.

How? Paul's voice said again. *How could he have shared those credentials? They're held on the trace.*

There were ways into the trace. She'd never shared hers with any of the girls she'd been with, but people did it, she knew.

But what if it *had* been Cassie?

No, she would never do it. Cassie had been rough and demanding on the surface, but so gentle beneath. She and Lee had that in common. Maybe that's why it hurt so much that she was considering Cassie as a traitor.

But Cassie *had* hidden things from her. Like the fact that she'd been married. To a man. Like the fact that her husband was on the PanGen board. It would have been easy to share her access with her husband and have an outsider influencing the Leto mission.

LEE, Rand sent, I NEED YOU TO CHECK ALL THE MANIFESTS.

"Dammit," she muttered, drying her short, buzzed hair.

OF COURSE, she sent.

How could she keep pretending? The fact was that Cassie had told her before the overnight that this was going to happen.

Watch out for him, Cassie had said. *He's stealing time. I know it.*

It's this planet. It's this terrible place—

The timing error on the porter? It seems a little interesting that it's off by five minutes. Every time.

What are you saying? How can you put that on Rand?

He was supposed to have Purple fix it, wasn't he? Months ago. And every time, it still lags.

Glitches. Technology on Leto is unpredictable.

But then she'd whispered one more thing to Lee in the quiet of her apartment after they had finished making love.

I'm scared. I think he's going to kill me.

Lee had held her, wiping Cassie's tears with her rough hands.

Whatever Rand had done, Lee was going to find out. And she was going to make sure that she didn't leave Leto without whatever was left of her Cassie.

II

LEE STOMPED out of the office, swearing a blue streak. Rand shook his head. Lee was mean, impatient, and scary, but she was as lethal and loyal as a well-trained Doberman.

She had been in his Mississippi squadron during the war of 2066, what the Gen kids called "The Uncivil War." After she had sniped a gunner who was tailing Rand, they had been nearly inseparable. Not that it was romantic—although it had gotten close once after they both began working for PanGen. Lee was like the sister he had never had, and Rand was like the father that Lee had always wanted.

"Hey."

He looked up from the report he was writing to see his wife.

Sam came into the room, that look on her face like she didn't know if he would kiss her or hit her. It frustrated him, that she treated him as if he were a monster that she was trying to tame.

"So?" Rand prompted impatiently.

"Ezrie is good. Stable." She sat down, her hands on display. She had been biting her nails. But it was better than drinking, he supposed.

"Good."

They sat in silence for a moment, Rand feeling his skin crawl as the seconds ticked by. This was another game of Sam's. She would wait him out until he said something. It was a power play, he knew that from the little psychology that he'd learned from her over the decade they had been married. He cleared his throat, telling himself he wouldn't do it. Not this time.

"How is Lee doing?" Sam couldn't hide the disdain in her voice. He chided himself for ever telling her about the time at the Halla Plains Mine on Gliese. The generators had gone down on the northernmost tundra while they had been fixing the porter. Rand and Lee had been forced to keep warm the old-fashioned way—"the church camp way," she'd called it, spooning uncomfortably in a sleeping bag for almost eight hours. Despite his assurances that nothing had ever happened between them, Sam had always been suspicious and jealous of their friendship. It made working with both the women much more difficult.

"You heard her." He flicked the knife. "She and Ezrie seem to not get along so well."

"Ezrie is a dangerous addition to an already fractured team." Sam's eyes were fiery, her hair down. She was beautiful, if you didn't know anything else about her. Rand felt something stir in him. He pushed it away. No. Not now. Maybe not ever again.

"For the last time," he growled, "I didn't have a choice. Zhong threatened to replace me if I didn't bring her."

"Well, it would have been someone else trapped out here, wouldn't it?" Her voice quavered. "We don't have a way home, Rand. Tell me that Ezrie doesn't have anything to do with that."

He sighed. "I don't know, Sam. I really don't."

He considered telling her what Zhong had said. That there was someone on the mission who was trying to sabotage it. No. Like the safety of the port—or lack of safety—that information was need-to-know. Sam was the psychologist. She didn't need to know.

Rand felt a pang of guilt. He had let his own guard down once or twice. In the heat of passion, sometimes he had allowed a penetration of even the deepest parts of his mind.

"Purple and Alex have been working for hours to get communications going." Sam paced, anxious. Rand did his best to focus on the problem at hand. "There's nothing. The porter is completely disabled, we have no way to communicate with home." Her voice broke, tears muddling her words. "And I want a goddamn drink."

Rand went to her and held her. He knew she was manipulating him. Her last-ditch effort to make him care. But he did care, despite himself. His arms around her felt different now than when they were first married. All the baby treatments had made her thick in the waist and face, which was insult to injury since they had never gotten pregnant. In hindsight, it was probably the best thing for them. At least there were no children to be hurt.

"Hold on," he mumbled into her hair. She smelled sweet. Like peaches. "Take a breath. Remember. All you have to do is make it through today. That's all."

She turned to him and smiled. She wiped tears from her eyes. "Thank you. Thank you for reminding me." She put her hands around his waist and he kissed her, softly.

He tried not to think of those other lips. The softness of her hair. The small of her back beneath his hands.

"Where are you," Sam said, pulling back.

"What?"

"Sometimes you go away," Sam said, looking at him with red-ringed eyes. "I wish you would tell me where you were going."

"Nothing. Nowhere. Just tired."

Sam nodded, wiping her face. "Yes. Of course. It's a good excuse because it's always true."

"Now hold on—" She was trapping him. She had been setting him up for a fight. "You're being stupid—"

"No," Sam said stepping back, letting the embrace fall away. "I'm not stupid, Rand. You trust Lee. You respect Alex. Even Birdy gets your sympathy once in a while. I'm the only person who gets nothing but a stone wall. I'm so—" her nose flared, her eyes catching his accusingly. "I'm so tired of being married to a stranger."

"You shouldn't be," he said quietly. "You deserve better than that."

She laughed bitterly.

"And it's not worth your time to be my friend, is it?" She put her hands to her mouth, tearing at one of the beautiful nails self-consciously, nibbling like a rabbit at a carrot. "I'm too much for you. I'm only good for making you feel tired."

"Sam—"

"No," Sam said stiffly, pulling her finger from her mouth as it if had burned her. "I won't bother you anymore. Maybe I'll kill someone with a laster. At least then you would be paying attention."

She stalked out of the office, and he could hear her sobbing echo in the hallway.

Something in his guts twisted. No, he didn't want to be Sam's friend. He had wanted to be her everything. But then.... He thought about all the months of trying and failing at making a baby, all the emotional backlash, the anger pointed to him. The frustration, the competition that had always been between them. The anger he had felt when she had gone behind his back and taken the job at PanGen. But he couldn't say it, could he? Not out loud. Because he had known she had done it to keep an eye on him. On him and Lee.

Too bad she'd been looking in the wrong place the whole time.

III

Santa Monica, CA, *Earth*

October, 2061

THE RAIN FELL HOURS AGO, but the sky is still dangerous. They cancelled school because of it, the rain that will eat through cotton and burn the skin beneath. But Ezrie loves the smell of the rain. The alien taste of the acid air in her lungs. She takes a deep breath in. It is new toys and Christmas after the presents are opened. Her father's cologne mingled with acrid sweat, like when he lets her work on the machine.

He is working on it now, without her, in the garage (the workshop, he complains to her often, you never call things what they are, Ezrie) even the holiday of rain unable to tear him away from his work.

From the teleportation device, he tells her.

To her father, it is the teleportation device, said with a mixture of loathing and love and boredom and possessiveness that her nine-year-old brain cannot suss apart.

To Ezrie, it is always the machine.

Tonight, she is not fiddling with the programming glitch in sandbox twelve or watching her father solder a new diamond core wire to the control housing (at her suggestion). Instead she stares up at the sky, the prickle of plastic from the astroturf against her Llama Pajama shirt. She can see the stars tonight, which are the real miracle. All because there was rain.

There is a waft of scent and fabric, and her mother is beside her.

Ezrie's mother's name is Molly, but not on this last night, the night before she leaves for good. Molly is the name that she tells people who ask her if she is Latina or Polynesian. The same kind who ask if Ezrie can speak Japanese or if she is proud of her Chinese heritage.

Now, as the sky begins to clear and the stars sharpen, her mother is radiant—is more than Molly. She is Miyu, the name that she is embarrassed to tell people.

Miyu. Miyu. Beautiful evening. Beautiful night.

Molly is the woman who pays the bills and makes sure that Richard has a sandwich in the workshop when he has been in there all day. Miyu is the one that once climbed the fence of a rich lady's house and went skinny-dipping while Ezrie stood watch.

"What are you wishing for, Z?" Miyu asks.

"I wish that we could stay here forever."

Ezrie looks at her mother, who is staring straight at the sky. The light is dimming, as the grey clouds begin even now to roll in. The small device that is attached to her mother's head blinks slowly. It is new, and Miyu has always loved novelty. She disappears into it now, for a moment, then refocuses on Ezrie. Ezrie hates it, even now, the communication device blinking in time with her mother, reading her mind, storing her secret thoughts.

Her mother is staring so hard into the sky. There is no mistake, there are tears on her face.

"What's wrong, Mama?"

Miyu sits up, her eyes flashing. Ezrie knows this look. It is the look that she gets after she and Daddy fight. It is the look she has before she drives the car away for sometimes days. Ezrie smells sourness on her mother's breath.

"I won't always be here," Miyu says, holding her arm so tight it begins to hurt. "But you will be okay. You are strong, not like me. You keep being strong, okay?"

Ezrie nods, and her mother's tears spill in the starlight. She brushes a stray hair from Ezrie's forehead. "The only thing faster than light is love. No matter where you are, we always travel together. Can you remember that? Tell it to me."

"The only thing faster than light is love," Ezrie mumbles. She is so sleepy and feels as if she is on the brink of a great cliff and falling. But there is nothing and no one there to catch her.

"Yes," Miyu says. "Love..." her voice trails off. Her mother's words are sluggish, the way they get when she's had too much wine. She lays back, at peace.

Ezrie closes her eyes and rests her head against her mother's shoulder, holding her hand. Not knowing her father will find the pill bottle empty. Not knowing the paramedics will soon be on their way. Not knowing that everything will change. A breath before Ezrie becomes a black hole from which no light can ever escape.

IV

Ocean Base, *Leto*

Day 2

EVERYTHING HURT. She had time to ponder this at length, now that she had made temporary residence in the infirmary—a cold, glass-walled room that felt exactly like the prison it was. Despite almost dying, she felt okay but for the excruciating muscle spasms that sometimes racked her. Little aftershocks from the electric earthquake Lee had unleashed.

Now, resting on a hospital bed in the paper smock that she still hadn't bothered to change out of, one of these aftershocks seized her calf, giving her the world's most agonizing charlie horse.

"Why didn't I die?" she groaned through gritted teeth, grasping at the calf as if she could force the contraction to stop. Lee really had done a number on her.

"Ezrie." Aris' eyes contracted, pulling her into focus. "You are lucky to be stable and conscious. You were wounded by an electronic emission device at near-lethal levels," Aris said. "The odds of your survival were forty-seven percent."

"Really?" The contraction abated, and Ezrie let out a breath of relief. "I would have put money on sixty-thirty against."

Aris cocked her head, her red ponytail bobbing. "A gambling reference." She smiled. "Very good. At least you have your humor back."

"I wouldn't say that exactly."

Ezrie's hand went absently to the earring. Aris was her jailor, and a good one. She was fast, made of titanium, and could tear Ezrie's arms off if she wanted to. But Ezrie had seen what the pin could do to an android brain. All it would take was one little pinprick and she would be jello.

But then what, Ezrie? she asked herself. *You don't have maps. You don't have anything.*

She would have to be patient. But until then, she needed to start gathering information.

Ezrie pulled on the outlanding pants that had been set beside her bed, newly sanitized. Every movement was pins and needles. But she was here. They couldn't cart her back to Texas if they wanted to. It was the one good thing that had come from all of it. Despite what they thought, it wasn't the end of the world. Almost any porter could be fixed.

Birdy fluttered into the room, her hair wild and her eyes shining. She was one of the few who came by to see how she was. Even though she could not shut up about anything, Ezrie felt her ridiculous optimism was slightly contagious. She hated it, but not as much as she should have.

"Oh my goodness," Birdy chittered. "You have pants on! This is going to be an excellent day, I think. How did you sleep? Do you feel any better? How are the muscle cramps?"

The barrage was overwhelming.

"I'm okay," she managed. "A little sore."

Birdy nodded, her eyes wide and sympathetic. "Absolutely. You know what you need? Food. And some sightseeing." Birdy smiled even wider. "Please let me show you around. So far, I don't think you've been shown the hospitality that you deserve. How would you feel about coming with me on a small trek? I can show you some of the more fascinating parts of Leto. You might even learn something!"

"How does Rand feel about that?" Ezrie didn't even want to bring up

Lee, who had been by several times to make threatening faces at her from behind the glass.

"I've already approved it with him," she said. "He didn't like it very much, of course, but we're all in this together, aren't we? Might as well make the best of a bad situation."

Despite Birdy's ridiculous school-teacher enthusiasm, Ezrie had to admit she wanted to go. Without a map or a weapon, it was no good trying to strike out on her own to find Marcus. Learning more about the planet could be very helpful, if she ever found a way to get out from under Aris' eye. And although she would never admit it to Birdy, she was curious about what secrets Leto was keeping.

Ezrie glanced over at Aris, whose unlined face was placid.

"I'm assuming we'll have a chaperone," Ezrie muttered.

Birdy laughed. "Well, on Rand's order it's either Aris or Lee. If I were you, I would choose the one without a laster."

Birdy led the way through the base while Ezrie straggled behind. She had to force her legs to walk as if they didn't feel like they were burning, but the aftershocks seemed to have stopped. The combination of the Leto water and Tylenol was surprisingly effective, and Ezrie felt the tingling in her fingers and nose begin to dissipate even before they left the medical wing of the base.

Still, she took as much time as she could trying to get the lay of the base.

Ezrie's trace filled her brain with passing information as she scanned her surroundings. The infirmary was protected by an ion door which led down a hallway that met up with the main control room. There were four different hallways that extended off this main room—a woman's hall and a mens hallway on the opposite side. There was also the medical wing (Ezrie knew that one well enough) and a professional hallway with offices. She'd been down that one, too. She shuddered at the thought of the scrawled words and the bloody handprint.

In the center of the complex was a large room with a high-domed, translucent ceiling. Through it, Ezrie's trace identified Pyrios and Aeos, Leto's orange suns. A huge rotating 3D model of the planet dominated the room showing bright green dots clustered at the place that Ezrie's trace identified as Ocean Base. A map of Leto. She felt a thrill of hope, but it was short-lived. Her trace only recognized avatars, not locations or directions, and none of the avatars belonged to Marcus. Dammit.

On the far side of the main control room was a dining area—cabinets and shelves lined the walls, and two long tables flanked either side. Alex sat at one of these, and caught Ezrie's glance as he hovered over a bowl of something. He smiled at her broadly. Purple, eating a snack bar, looked tiny beside him.

"Look who it is," Alex said, his Russian accent subtle, but pleasantly exotic. "Sleeping beauty."

Purple shuffled aside on the bench at the table and offered her a grey packet of something that smelled like cumin. "Here," he said, "You're likely hungry enough to eat a cow between two bread baskets."

She forced the smile from her face. Purple looked like a walking Irish caricature. *You like red hair, freckles, and potatoes? This is your guy.*

Ezrie sniffed at the hot grey packet. The packet read TACO DINNER, but the smell made her highly doubt it. Still, she took it and sat anyway. *Can't have a coup without an army*, she thought. "Thanks."

Purple beamed.

As Ezrie choked down the meaty gruel, Birdy peppered her with questions. Alex chimed in with several innuendos, and Ezrie couldn't help but feel like she was the new kid at school. So not everyone hated her, just the people in charge. The kid, Purple, couldn't even look at her. He nibbled halfheartedly at a power bar and nodded at everything Alex said.

"Hey there," said a voice behind her. "Let the woman breathe a little."

Ezrie turned to see the sharp-faced man. Her trace lit up with information. Kenner Strafe, Security Second and Survival Lead. He walked in, looking like a bronc rider she had met once. Kenner had that kind of wide swagger that came from hard work.

"My name is Kenner," he said, giving her a wide smile "I don't believe we've met."

"Ezrie Collings," she said. She liked the long drawl of his words. The south somewhere. Georgia, maybe.

"Ezrie Collings," he said, his name rolling her tongue thoughtfully. "So you're the reason we are on this little vacation." Kenner drawled his words and delivered them with an easy smile that never reached his eyes. He had the rugged good looks of someone who spent most of his time outside. But something about him exuded disdain beneath the laid-back exterior. "I've heard a lot about you."

I bet you have, Ezrie thought. Then, defensively, "From who?"

"Purple can't seem to talk about nothing else." Kenner said, his laugh loose, but mirthless. Purple's face went a molten red. "He says you're the closest thing to the porter inventor we have on the team. Except for Marcus—"

"What I meant," Purple spluttered, "was that you're savage, right? I mean, brilliant. Your dad. That's what I meant." His face went beet red, and he stared at the ground as if hoping earth would open up and swallow him.

Ezrie wanted to be offended, but it was so clear he was mortified. "Thanks," she said. "You're right. He *was* brilliant."

Birdy laughed nervously.

"I heard that Birdy's taking you out for a little trip," Kenner said. "I'd be honored to escort you ladies."

"We'll have Aris," Birdy said abruptly. She smiled then, apologetically. "You don't need to trouble yourself with us."

Anxiety rimmed Birdy's voice, but Ezrie couldn't see why. Kenner didn't seem to be stressed out about anything. His speech was as languid as his gait. But he was no slouch. He'd had some kind of military training at some point. He smiled, and Ezrie could see nothing concerning. Birdy, however, was compulsively tapping the table with her knee, not even knowing it.

"Suit yourself." Kenner said. "But you'll probably want this." He dropped the red pack to the floor beside Ezrie. "You dropped it when Lee shot you."

Ezrie grabbed the pack. "Thanks."

"Leto's a dangerous place, even more than Alabama." *So close,* Ezrie thought. *But I've never been to Alabama, so how would I know.* "I'd hate to think of anyone stranded out there with no supplies." Kenner winked at her. "Don't worry. You got at least one person on your team."

"That's very thoughtful," Birdy said, the strain evident. "I'm sure that we'll be perfectly safe. We're heading to the waterfall area. Aris and I will take good care of Ezrie."

"I could go with you, too," Purple mumbled. "I mean, if you need another, uh, driver or something."

"Yes," Alex said, dripping sarcasm. "Maybe we can *all* go. I'll pack a picnic. We can bring some ice cream. You and Ezrie can go swimming in the lake?"

Purple's face turned every color of red. Ezrie nearly laughed out loud.

Alex laughed. "Come on, kid." He grabbed Purple's arm. "Let's go fix the transmission lines so that we can go home. We'll go swimming later."

Ezrie caught a strange, sweating look on Alex's face. He burped and grimaced. "Shouldn't have eaten the taco meal," he lamented, his accent thickening.

As soon as they were gone, Kenner cleared his throat. Birdy dropped her gaze to the small salad before her. Ezrie realized Birdy had barely said a word since Kenner came in. Her fork lay where she'd left it, its mouthful of rehydrated salad forgotten. No wonder she was so skinny.

"Anyway," Kenner said. "Let me know if you change your mind, ladies."

"We can take care of ourselves, thank you," Birdy said, her words crisp and short.

"I'm counting on that." He gave a wide smile. "Stay safe, team."

Kenner slid through the ion door without a backward glance, and Ezrie felt as though she had missed some part of the conversation. Like he'd said more than what she'd heard.

I'm on your team.

Birdy visibly shuddered.

"I don't know what it is about him," she muttered, "but he gives me the most terrible feeling."

"He's a security guy, right?" Ezrie prodded.

"Yes..." Birdy paused. "But he's also friends with one of the CEOs of the biggest Leto investor, Living Waters."

"The water company." Ezrie knew them. They sold high-end water, the kind Ezrie only drank when she worked for very bad people. But hadn't she heard something about the company being connected to a church?

"Yes," Birdy affirmed. "They were tax exempt for a long time, but ended up turning too much profit, so the Reverend dissolved the church into the business. Kenner grew up in one of their boy's homes. He's fanatical." She drifted for a moment, and Ezrie wondered what kinds of secrets Birdy knew.

"But what am I saying?" Birdy snapped back to reality, a thin smile on her face. "It's nerves, isn't it? It's been such a hard few days." She grabbed her red pack and hefted it up. "Let's go explore, shall we?"

"Yes," said a cold voice. "Let's."

Ezrie turned to see Lee flipping her outlanding hood over her head. Ezrie's stomach dropped. Her stomach spasmed, as if merely looking at Lee could cause some kind of electrical seizure.

"I'm taking Ezrie to the waterfall to show her some of the species—"

"Sweeps," Lee retorted. "At least that way you can be doing something productive instead of making daisy chains."

The way that Lee looked at her made Ezrie feel like a bug on a petri dish. She clutched the backpack to her chest, as if holding it might offer some kind of protection. It felt heavier, somehow, and she wondered if that was something to do with the atmosphere or humidity or the fact that she had almost had all her cells explode a day ago.

"Looks like it's girls night out, then," Birdy giggled nervously. "What fun."

Fun was not what Ezrie was thinking. It was more likely that Lee had already planned some weird demise for her in the jungle. Death by octobird. Leaving her in a giant ant pile covered in taco meal. And, looking at Birdy's skinny frame and nervous eyes, Ezrie felt confident that no one would be stopping Lee from following through this time.

V

THE STATE of Sanger's office filled James with overwhelming sadness. It was hard to imagine that a man that he'd learned to tie a fishing lure from over too many cans of Pabst Blue Ribbon was gone. More than that—that someone or something could have changed his usually sharp mind into this fevered nightmare.

When Ezrie and Lee had shared the room on the live feed, James had been surprised, but mostly preoccupied with his own problems. Not only had he been forced to watch as Ezrie refused to assist with the porter and see her near murder in real time, but he had also been documenting the insanity of the medical wing.

So many of the Apollo team had died, and there were body bags to prove it. But they were empty, one of the bags torn apart. Two with claw marks on the inside of the bags.

"What does that mean, 'from the inside'?" Rand had asked him, privately. There was a level of incredulity that indicated James was mistaken. If one of his girls had spoken to him with the same tone, they would have earned themselves a whopping. James had worked too hard for too long to be treated like that from a grown man. Especially by a white man who had half the education than he did.

"It means that someone was put in while they were still alive, though I don't know who would have done that or why."

There were far more questions than answers, all around. James had found an Xtenz rope in one of the bags, covered in blood—the retractable steel cable was a standard issue in Leto packs, meant for emergency rescues or moving heavy objects. Then there were the boot prints in blood, most likely a woman's, in the professional hallway.

But now that they were going be on Leto for weeks instead of hours, there was at least time to try to make sense of it.

He cursed himself for what felt like the millionth time since the day before. He should have listened to his wife. He shouldn't have come. *It's only a few hours,* is what he had told her. *I'll be back in time for supper.*

But there were now twenty-seven days between him and Meryl's meat loaf.

Jeffrey Sanger's office was a mess, to say the least. The words scribbled on the walls didn't seem to have cohesion, all except the phrase "WE SPEAK" scribbled in some black substance. The flickering scroll of errors from the projector included symbols he had never seen before: curlicues and sharp-toothed letters that made no sense.

He engaged his v-feed recorder, narrating as he went.

"Written messages on the walls," James intoned, "and paper records. Someone smashed the wall screen with a chair. Broken glass, more blood."

Doc, Alex sent. I don't feel great. I think I'm gonna need to lie down for a while once we're done at the transmitter.

James checked Alex's vital signs. Some inflammation around his stomach. A slight fever, but nothing too concerning.

Sounds good, James sent. You're probably worn down. Get some rest.

It wasn't too concerning. The port had been bad. James had felt like throwing up himself, and he had a stomach like a rock. He made a note on his trace to visit Alex afterwards.

He opened the desk drawers, finding nothing but miscellaneous office supplies and scraps of paper. Some of these had symbols on them, like the ones from the projector feed. He recorded them, opening the other drawers. The smallest drawer, however, was locked. He frowned. What would Sanger have to lock away?

James blinked off his feed and sighed. His knees hurt. Meryl would be angry knowing how much he'd been pacing over the last day. *They're not meant to last forever*, she would say. Maybe something about how he was wearing out his knees almost as much as he was wearing her patience.

James rifled through the items in Sanger's office, careful to keep what little order he could. As good a friend as Jeff had been, he was messy and old-fashioned. Nobody, especially not psychiatrists, kept paper records anymore. It was expensive and outdated. Still, Jeff had stuck to his guns. It had come in handy, though, especially when the tablets that were left on Leto between launches stopped working correctly. He'd been allowed his eccentricism.

Many of the papers that littered the desk and floor looked like the walls. Others were filled with scrawling ropy letters, every inch of the front and back covered in words that made no sense. One of the documents stood out, one of the few that were written in the sloppy, yet legibly sane handwriting that must come standard with doctoral degrees. James picked it up and read:

"After speaking with several crew members, including Captain Byrion, Hector, and Norman (Chuck), it's clear that the dreams all deal with similar themes—loss and the inability to communicate.

"I myself have had a similar dream in which I am watching a v-feed and there are voices all around me. I try to silence them, but I realize I'm alone in a large, black forest. Still, the voices continue.

The worst part of this dream is that it does not scare me, but frustrates me. It's clear that the voices want to tell me something important, but they are unable to communicate fully. The first time I had this dream was a few days after we arrived, which seems to be a similar timeline with the others. I am going to do full evaluation interviews with the entire crew to see if the phenomenon is consistent."

He felt a sliver of fear. It reminded him of Meryl's nightmare. She'd been so scared, she'd called the girls. Brenda, as logical and even-tempered as himself, had talked her down from full hysterical. But Lonnie, with her musical theater degree and hand-sewn purses, had gone wild-eyed and passionate. *You can't be thinking about going. You know Mom was right about that car accident.*

Yes, Meryl had been right about that. His knee reminded him every day.

Even though Meryl's nightmare was recorded on his trace (as she had requested; you don't stay married for twenty-two years without knowing which battles to pick), James didn't need to replay it for himself. He didn't think he would ever forget.

You were in a room full of light. You were swallowed in trees and you were growing. I don't want to talk about it. But I don't want you to go. Tell them you can't. Please, James. Tell them you can't go.

James rifled through the rest of the papers, looking for others like it. He found only half of a ripped piece of paper that had fallen to the floor. He picked it up, and sorted the sheets until he found the accompanying mate.

"The crew has taken the death of Norman Walheim the hardest. Though they respected Lexi and Heitar, Norman (Chuckwagon, or Chuck, for short), was the most difficult to lose. Dr. Tukuafu has been looking for anything that would be a contributing factor to this possible infection, but she is leaning more and more on me for answers.

I've done as many searches as I can on potential mass hallucinations and suicidal/homicidal behavior, but I have not found anything that remotely connects with what we're seeing. I can't help but feel that the issue is a physical one, not an emotional one. I wonder sometimes if she's trying to discredit me to the others. I've always felt that she secretly wants me to fail here.

I've been locking my office with the psychiatrist code to ensure that she's not coming in during the night to look at my notes. She looks at me sometimes like I'm the enemy."

James picked up the last, near the top of the stack. It was different. It featured an uneven scrawl filled with broken sentences and words. He could understand, but barely.

WE see the dead now. After it's dark, sometimes they iaiiiillljljjjj I know who is watching me but its memememememee. I am here and I am not here and I know they are talking to me and I hear them when I'm awake. I am awake. Idon'tknow iidon 't slkklsj I'm so tired and my brain won't stop talkingtalki TALK SPEAK WESOEAK WPEAK. We speak.

The last two words were the ones that chilled James to the core. The scribbled, scrambled words focused into those seven letters: We speak. They were clear, cogent, and in handwriting that was definitively not Jeffrey Sanger's own.

He felt a prickle at the back of his neck. A feeling that someone was watching. Was there a crackle in the bushes?

The window, broken open long ago, let in nothing but orange afternoon light. A small spidery creature crawled along the window sill. It ignored him with a thousand black eyes, it's purple body hairy and looking for something to eat.

He gathered up the documents, carefully recording them on his trace, then stacking them on the desk.

By the time the floor was picked up, he was sweating heavily in his suit. He took a sip of water every now and then, aware, as always, that he needed to be sure to clean out the cache before it got too *dreck*, as Purple would say.

He took a final look around and found a small key on the floor beneath the bottommost pile of papers. There was a moment of sheer discovery. He nearly laughed, fitting the key into the drawer.

James carefully pulled the drawer open, but had a moment where his brain couldn't recognize what it was seeing. Then, he had a fleeting hope that it was some kind of practical joke. But the shine of the teeth—especially the silver-mercury filling on the back molar—and the blood on the desiccated and receding gums made him realize it was not.

It was a human jaw.

VI

BEING OUTSIDE on Leto was a sensory overload. Ezrie had nearly forgotten how breathtaking it was since most of the last two days she had been unconscious or trapped in a metal box. The suns painted the sky a supernatural orange. A mist rose up from the sloggy red waves of the ocean, creeping up the black sand and flooding the forest with haze.

They crunched across the gravel towards a long, squat building made of concrete and glass. Lee pressed her hand to a scanner, and the front of the building lifted up to show a row of shining, identical motorcycles.

They were gorgeous black bikes—long and round, as if edges had been removed completely. As the three women walked into the hangar, the bikes responded, powering up. Crystalline windshields lit up in red, green, and yellow, showing maps, temperature, and terrain information. Lee grabbed one, and it instantly connected to her trace, gears and wires personalizing the seat position and height. As she brought it into the light, Ezrie realized that the bikes weren't really black, but covered from stem to stern in solar scales that flickered an iridescent green and purple in the light.

"Wow," Ezrie exhaled. "That's a pretty bike."

"Don't get too excited, Betty," Lee snapped. "They are DNA coded. Only people with admin access can give authority."

She assessed the hangar. Ezrie saw her counting the empty bays. All but four bikes were missing. Ezrie wondered who had them, and she knew Lee must be doing the same. Lee didn't give her thoughts away, however.

"You're riding with me, Betty." Lee tucked her hands into the shielded handle recesses and addressed Birdy. "I'm turning communications on. Try to keep up."

Ezrie took her spot on the back of the bike, grateful for the handles attached to the massive saddlebag. Not only was the saddlebag big enough to fit a small child into, it meant she didn't have to hug Lee in order to survive.

Of course, it also put Lee's trace within killing range of her little device. Not very practical, wearing the outlanding gloves and a helmet, but it made her feel better. Like she wasn't completely powerless.

Yeah, you just try getting sassy with me, LeeAnn, Ezrie thought. *I'll melt your goddamn brain off.*

But she wouldn't. Ezrie sighed. She could kill cactuses and ferns, but she only had one human she ever wanted to kill. One was more than enough.

With a wave of Lee's gloved hand, they were rolling, and Ezrie's heart whipped nearly out of her chest as the engine engaged, rumbling and roaring through the misty morning fog.

Even though Ezrie didn't understand exactly what Lee had meant about "coms," she soon learned that the outlanding suit had the ability to communicate directly. And even though Lee didn't say a word to her (despite her threat that she would), Birdy wasted no time taking advantage of her captive audience.

But even the long-winded explanations of Leto bladder-fish or the mating rituals of poppisits couldn't diminish the magic of riding through the Leto forest. As the thick treads of the electric motorcycles barrelled through the underbrush, they disrupted iridescent yellow and pink flurries of creatures which floated up lazily, looking like a flock of fairy sheep.

"Zephyrs," Birdy chittered. "They're pervasive on this side of the planet. But they only come out at night."

The multicolored octobirds (slints) sat in the multicolored trees (rimands), cooing in harmonic intervals and waving their tentacled legs. They blended in seamlessly to their surroundings, and Ezrie might not have seen them at all but for their occasional startled bursts of color. One got so close to the moving motorcycle that Ezrie could have grabbed its red-and-yellow frond-like tentacle, but it squirted red dust on her instead and slipped up into the trees.

As they moved deeper into the jungle, the light diminished. Ezrie caught glimpses of luminous figures in the distant underbrush. A set of purple eyes—more than two—flickered, then disappeared.

"What was that?" she said. "Something with purple eyes."

"Lycants," Birdy hesitated. "It's possible it's a lycant. We were tracking them for a while. Ear tags to see their range." Her voice was stiff.

"What happened?"

"There was an accident."

Birdy was surprisingly quiet after that.

They paused at a small shack to the northeast of the base. Even though the ride had been amazing, Ezrie's ass needed a break. Also, she needed to pee.

She stretched as Lee circled the shack. Birdy chattered at her, showing her a large stand of flowers in bright orange and blue. "Like pitcher plants," Birdy said. "But they draw in their prey with vibrations. If you put your ear close, you can hear."

Ezrie leaned in and heard a low sound. It sounded like voices, a chorus of low, close notes making an infinite chord. She leaned in closer, sure that she could pick out a harmonic there, notes shifting back and forth, turning the chord major, then minor, then major.

"Not too close," Birdy giggled, pulling her back. "You're exactly the kind of dinner they would love."

"So strange." Ezrie shook her head. "They sound like voices."

Birdy got a faraway look in her eyes. "Yes. There's something to that, I think. You know, on earth, before the droughts, there used to be massive stands of birch trees."

Ezrie had seen birches before, at the Street of Trees in North Dakota the one time Molly had decided the family should take a road trip and "pretend we're really alive." The trees had been thin things with black and white bark. Their leaves had shimmered in the wind, and Ezrie had wanted to take a leaf so badly. But Molly had been in charge that day, not

Miyu, and so reason and responsibility reigned. Instead, her father had bought her a small gold leaf necklace. She'd lost that too when her father died, like she'd lost everything else except for a trash bag of clothes.

"Birch trees," Ezrie murmured. The sound of the flowers mesmerized her. Light, dark. Happy, sad. A rhythmic melody of loving and losing.

"What they found was that birch trees talked to each other. They would tell each other about diseases or parasites, and the trees would build up specific resins to protect themselves."

Her eyes were shining, and Ezrie was reminded again of her mother. Miyu had looked like that sometimes. But Birdy didn't look as if she might switch on a wrongly-placed word.

"I sometimes think that Leto is the same. I've observed that influences in one part of the forest sometimes impact elsewhere. There's a possibility that all of the trees and flowers are sharing information with each other all the time."

"Birdy," Lee called, "Come over here and see this. You too, Betty."

"I have to pee," Ezrie called back.

Lee's head popped out from the building's doorway. "Don't be prissy. That's what the suit's for."

"All water is good water," Birdy said as if it were a catechism.

"You guys do you," Ezrie said flatly, "I'd rather die."

"Suit yourself, Betty," Lee smirked. "But don't try to steal a bike or do something smart. You don't want to make me mad."

Ezrie shuddered inwardly. After the last few days, she was ready to stop being hit with high voltages of electricity.

"She's kind of an acquired taste," Birdy said, when Lee disappeared into the shack. "Protective and clannish, yes. But she's not really bad. You'll see. I think she actually is starting to like you."

"I don't think I would survive it if she liked me any more."

Birdy gave her a surprise hug. Ezrie stiffened, her eyes wide.

"Well, *I'm* glad you're here with us," Birdy said. "It's nice to have someone to talk with." Her eyes softened. "Not everyone listens."

As Birdy walked towards Lee, Ezrie considered it. Birdy was so positive and nice. Why in the world would she be glad *Ezrie* was here? Ezrie was the antithesis of everything Birdy was about.

Well, I'm not here for long, she thought, stiffening. *They'll be better off when I'm out of their hair. Purple's smart. He can get them home.*

Ezrie pushed through the ferns enough so that she wouldn't be caught with her pants down in the open, but kept the domed top of the shack in her sights. Even though the jungle masked most of the suns' light, it was uncomfortably hot. By the time she'd finished peeing, then wiping pee off her hands, then wondering why the grass she'd used to wipe it was slithering, she could feel sweat trickling down her spine.

The bushes rustled behind her, and Ezrie's stomach tightened to a knot. She wished she had a weapon.

Probably a squirrel or something, she thought. *Some weird bird.*

The air was too quiet, though. No noises, no animals. No insects buzzing.

She paused for another moment, willing herself to see whatever had disturbed the undergrowth. It had sounded big.

"Ezrie! Where are you?"

She tried to shake the feeling off, but moved quickly out of the underbrush. Lee stood in the doorway of the sweeps shack, with Birdy looking at something closely inside. Ezrie could see Lee getting a kick out of Ezrie being terrified of some Leto spiny crab-spider or some shit. Better to keep it to herself.

When she got to the others, however, Lee was sharp-eyed, steel-jawed, looking at something that wasn't there.

"What's wrong?" Ezrie asked.

Lee shook her head. "Looks like someone's been dipping out the cookie jar."

Ezrie stepped into the cool interior of the shack.

"The printer is missing." Birdy fingered the bare wires where Ezrie assumed a 3D printer should have been. Ezrie felt grit beneath her feet. She rubbed it with her boot, and it made a sandpaper sound.

"Printing medium," Lee said. "Again."

"Again?" Ezrie asked.

Birdy stood, brushing her hands on her pants. "Some of the manifests have been wrong in the past. A miscalculation, maybe."

Lee grunted. "Maybe."

They stepped back into the warmth of the jungle, Lee closing and locking the door behind her with a handprint.

"Let's roll," she said, pulling her hood back over her head, the mask over her face. "We still have a lot of land to cover before these pieces of shit die on us for good." She kicked the engine manifold, and grey dust puffed out of the ventilator shield.

WHAT DOES SHE MEAN BY THAT? Ezrie sent, trying her hand at a private chat.

"It means that phlax likes to ruin bikes, Betty," Lee snapped through the suit com. "It feeds on the electricity."

"Phlax is a growth that is unique to Leto," Birdy offered, her voice tinny through the com of her suit. "I've done a lot of research on it. It is beautiful, but pernicious. It grows on anything that is supplied by an electric current."

Ezrie reluctantly mounted behind Lee. The woods were choked in silence. Light slid down through the tops of the trees and drowned in the darkness of the jungle below.

Lee kicked the engine to life. It coughed and sputtered. Birdy roared out ahead, pointing the way with a gloved hand.

As they pulled away, Ezrie took one last look over her shoulder and saw a flash of something skittering away into the bushes. Ezrie felt her stomach clench again.

Say something. Tell Lee to turn around.

But the further Lee drove into the forest, the easier it was to not say anything at all.

A squirrel, is what she told herself. *Spooked by some Leto squirrel.*

It made sense, too. If it had been real, Lee would have seen it, wouldn't she? She would have had to see it.

Because despite what Ezrie tried to tell herself, her gut whispered that it was much, much bigger than a squirrel.

VII

Ocean Base, *Leto*

Day 3

ALEX DIDN'T FEEL RIGHT.

It wasn't a matter of being sick—sick he knew. Every winter growing up had brought homemade turnip soup, steaming garlic poultices, and mounds of blankets for him and his three sisters. Kirillov was known for the monastery—the greatest stronghold in northern Russia—and being as cold as a witch's tit. Alex couldn't remember a winter growing up where he hadn't gotten a fever. *Too much playing outside*, his mother would tell him, secretly proud that he was the fastest, strongest, and smartest in his class.

He hadn't been sick once since joining PanGen, and he'd used the health benefit to see that his last remaining sister hadn't either. Tati had died in the war; Nataly, the oldest, of cancer. Only Gasha was left now. She lived only a few blocks from where they'd grown up, across from the monastery on Lake Siverskoye. Gasha would half-heartedly tease him for his fine penthouse in Moscow Central. "What good is your fancy apartment if you're never home to sleep in it?" She told him once. She reminded him more of their mother every day and made the same turnip soup when her two little boys caught the chills. Of course, now they had the Republic medicines to keep them safe.

Medicine belonged to the victors.

He felt the tremors inside of him, some deep vibration, and pushed them aside, pretending more strength than he had.

"This morning you need a kick in the ass and a map of the world," Purple said, taking the rungs up the transmitter tower two at a time. "Your slower than a week in jail.

"That's how the ladies like it," Alex huffed behind him.

"They don't count if you have to pay them," Purple retorted.

Alex grimaced. "Funny."

Some of the tentacled birds that Birdy called slints rustled in the tall, particolored trees as they passed. From this vantage point, Alex could see almost to where the jungle became the browns. From far to the north, he could nearly hear the waterfall splashing.

Alex struggled over the grated landing at the top, trying not to pay attention to the rubbery feeling in his legs, as if they might give out at any point.

"This place got tozed," Purple commented from ahead of him.

As Alex tried to catch his breath, he saw what Purple meant. Phlax covered the transmitter tower in a cocoon of glowing blue filament. It had spread its web between the main antenna and the domed roof of the tower.

When they finally cut their way into the transmitter control room, Alex was surprised at the darkness inside.

"Apollo must have cleaned it out when they got here," Purple said. "Very faze of them."

"Very faze," Alex nodded.

Absence permeated the room. No light from the control console. No sound of an emergency generator. The trace relay was dark.

"No power." Alex picked up a frayed edge of a power cord as thick as his arm. A clean cut. On the floor were fragments of the central control board, with the control console smashed in. "How is the trace still working?"

"Mountain has a trace relay that simulcasts," Purple said. "For this exact reason, actually."

"In case someone smashed the hell out of the transmitter? Funny. I don't remember that in the safety orientation."

Purple laughed. "No. Just in case one of them goes down. Redundancy is the name of the game, especially where phlax is involved."

WE FOUND THE PROBLEM WITH TRANSMITTER, Alex sent, sharing the live feed of the cut cable and damaged porter on the team channel. SOMEONE DID THIS ON PURPOSE. IT WILL TAKE SOME TIME TO PRINT NEW PARTS, BUT WE SHOULD BE ABLE TO GET IT WORKING AGAIN.

I CAN PRINT SOME, Kenner sent. SEND ME THE LIST.

OKAY, Rand sent after a minute. ALEX, GET THE TRANSMITTER ONLINE. PURPLE NEEDS TO WIPE AND REINSTALL THE PORTER. IF WE CAN GET THEM BOTH WORKING, THAT'S ONE MORE WAY WE CAN GET HOME.

They took stock of the damage, making notes as to what could be fixed and what needed to be replaced. They had time to do the work—three weeks and some—now that the port window had closed. But who would want to make the transmitter inoperable, and why?

As they headed back down the ladder, Alex felt his bowels twist. He let Purple go first, only making it about halfway before he had to pause, a slight moan escaping his lips.

"Hey, man. Are you okay?" Purple looked up at him, his brows creased. He looked so much like a little kid from this angle that Alex wondered for the millionth time how someone so young could be on such a huge project.

"Fine," Alex said. "I think my stomach is predicting the future."

Purple looked up at him quizzically.

"We both know I'm having Taco Meal for dinner, too. It's my favorite form of self-torture."

Purple snorted a laugh, shook his head, and slid down the last few steps.

Alex came down much slower, feeling the pressure inside of him increase. Like bad gas, or like the feeling after you'd been punched in the kidneys. He felt something pull as he jumped the final rung. He would need to see James when he got back.

"Hey, Alex." Purple said, pulling on his hood. "what do you think about Ezrie?"

"A little old for you."

"Yeah, but she's lash, right? I mean, cherry—for someone who's a little older."

He clapped Purple on the shoulder. "To you, everyone is older."

His smile felt forced, the tremor from inside of him so small, yet so distinct.

It's a cold, Alex thought, pushing the alternative from his mind. *A little Leto cold can't keep me down.* As Purple chattered about Ezrie and the porter, Alex did his best to nod in all the right places. He tried not to think of the images he'd seen from the safety manuals—examples of what happened to a man when a port went bad.

Just a cold.

He shivered, despite the heat, and wished more than anything that a bowl of his mother's soup was waiting for him.

VIII

KENNER STILL HADN'T DECIDED who to kill first. He was reluctant to start the dirty business, but he knew better than to shirk his responsibilities now. The Reverend was counting on him to accomplish it all, and he had no idea what kind of help he was going to get to finish the job.

Kenner was alone in the engineering station, which was little more than a storage shed with a high-class security system. Tall shelves flanked each wall, filled with polyalmarine bags of print base and heavy barrels full of metal ball bearings. Some of the base was specified: cotton, polyester, and neoprene amalgam for clothing; carbon and titanium beads for machinery and tools; a rubber and oil solution for plastics. Explosives, heavy metals. Everything you'd need to build an entire base from scratch.

As he pawed through the bags of materials, he considered his options.

Lee was a good choice. She was probably the smartest of anyone on Leto, besides himself. And she was strong. Kenner pulled a bag of fertilizer from behind a barrel of steel ball bearings. Then, on second thought, he took a few handfuls of those as well. Eliminating Lee early was a good strategy.

But the killing bothered him. It always had.

Kenner activated the small, boxy MEG printer, and the robotic arm descended to greet him. It circumnavigated the room on its ceiling track, the metal ball bearings on its housing grinding. It glowed with that same blue that got into everything after a while. He pulled out and attached the feed tube from the machine to the kiln and printer.

"How can I assist?" the simple, robotic AI crooned.

"Gotta fix that transmitter, MEG. So, we need four Series Three connectors with Class K shell material, four rugged-use cables with thermoplastic chlorinated polyethylene jackets, one submodifier hex central bracket with screws and interface brackets," he paused and smiled to himself. "And a partridge in a pear tree."

"Unknown item," the MEG said as it sprouted small metal suction rods.

"No sense of humor," Kenner chuckled. "Cancel partridge in a pear tree."

The mobile MEG descended to the buckets of components and began its alchemy. It buzzed from material bay to material bay, inserting its small proboscis into fitted openings on the bags and barrels. Kenner could hear contents traveling down the tube that leashed the small robot to the kiln table like a dog on a chain. There was a snap and a hum, and an engine from within the print table began to thrum, vibrating the floor.

Halfway through the MEG's printing cycle, he blinked into the trace control, finding and activating a small, hidden file that he'd used God knew how many times.

"Printing error," the MEG intoned. "Duplicating print."

When he was finished, he had doubled his order—eight cables, eight connectors, and two brackets—but the print log only showed the original request for four. He put the duplicate parts in his red backpack, careful to wrap a sheet of mitrium over them so that Aris wouldn't get suspicious. He set up the next round of parts and decided to make himself useful while he waited.

Kenner grabbed a container of engine oil reserved for running the generator.

As he worked, he considered the others. Rand, James, Sam. He had gotten used to them. Even as he finished the explosive, he felt sad that he had to make it in the first place.

The only person he didn't consider was Birdy.

He reviewed their progress—the girls had gone out towards the sweeps shack, but had stopped at the nearby waterfall. It made sense. If there was anyone who could sweet talk Lee into pausing, it would be Birdy.

It made him feel uneasy, though. Lycants loved water. It had been at the waterfall where Brindle had been attacked.

Despite Birdy's protestations, no women should be unescorted in a dangerous area. Lee might be alright, but she was a wild one. Kenner couldn't trust Birdy's safety to her.

He tightened the strap on his backpack and began running towards the waterfall, only a half mile jog or so. Birdy wouldn't be happy that he'd come when she told him not to, but it was for her own good. Why was it that women didn't just appreciate being protected once in a while?

Kenner moved quickly along the shoreline, enjoying the feel of running. He ran through the underbrush as if he'd grown up here, as if he were back on his Alabama mountainside instead of through flowers and trees that all wanted to eat him.

He paused in a small glade, the trees revealing a field of tall, purple loosestreaf, their tiny petals opening and closing on passing specks of dust. The image was beautiful, although he didn't normally stop to wonder at stuff like that. That was Birdy's influence, he thought. Still, the vibrant purple against the orange sky and the psychedelic greens of the trees was overpowering.

As he scanned the skyline, always keeping in his sights the small beacons of Ezrie, Birdy, and Lee, he caught a strange flicker of something on his trace.

Footprints. Tracks.

His body went on high alert, and he crouched down out of habit, pulling the laster from his belt and flicking it to deadly force in a practiced motion.

Kenner stayed still for minute before creeping forward.

On the overlay, he could see that the tracks were weeks old. They measured 22.5 centimeters in length. Small, probably belonging to a woman.

The tracks took him up over a rise where the flowers became sparser and the ground drier. Stubby red shafts of grass poked up through the sand. As he scanned the ground, his trace lit up, identifying an object in the dirt.

At the same time, his trace picked up chatter from Birdy and Lee that they were on the move again, heading away from the waterfall towards the westernmost sweeps shack. Too far even for him to run.

Kenner scooped his hand into the sand, rubbed the object clean, the wheels clicking into place. Of course. It was dead, thank God.

He ran down the hill and through the jungle to the edge of the thick Leto ocean. He threw the smashed trace into the water—the device that had been so painstakingly removed to protect its owner. He shook his head, wondering how anyone could have been so sloppy as to not fully destroy it in the first place.

As he returned back, he decided that he would focus on the bomb first. When it was the right place and time, he would know it. And after that, he would be strong enough to finish the job. Then he would finally have the peace that God's word had promised him. All of them.

IX

SAM SAT IN THE INFIRMARY, navigating through the records, waiting for Ezrie. The records were spotty, with sections of video or trace notes that were unreadable, completely consumed by the phlax infestation. She suspected it the first night. The database had been near the broken window of the professional hall, and by morning, it had been covered in the fluffy yellow sky creatures called Zephyrs. Like little puffs of smoke, the night-dwelling zephyrs loved phlax.

But the increased zephyrs could only mean the thing that Sam dreaded most—the phlax infestation was worse than they'd ever seen it. Purple had helped clean up some of it, but there were whole days that were missing. Terrible days that Sam wasn't sure she was ready to see.

James had shown her Heitar's jaw privately, and she had nearly walked into the medical wing and grabbed a bottle of rubbing alcohol. She had not, but the urge was still there. Better to black out than see reality.

"It's been pulled from the skull," James had said. He looked at the ground, not touching the thing. It was too fresh to know if the person had been dead or alive when it had been taken. According to dental records and DNA, it had belonged to Manuel Heitar, the security lead for Artemis.

It was disturbing to see it so unattached. The silver fillings of Manny's back molar glinted in the phlox's bioluminescent glow.

Sam had to find out what had happened. But there were so many clues, so many records...How could she know where to start?

Aris arrived, with Ezrie in tow.

"Wonderful!" Sam exclaimed, though, to be honest, everything about her smile was false. She felt anxious, unhinged, and on the verge of a relapse. Ezrie was antisocial, oppositionally defiant, and narcissistic. It seemed like a bad combination. But she didn't have a choice. Mandatory sessions were protocol for all new hires, and working together would hopefully break down some of the walls between them.

Sam set Ezrie up beside a holoprojector and three consoles with recorders. Sam figured Ezrie would enjoy looking through the picture window into the infirmary room, the only view that the little room had to offer. From the overlay in her head, she could read the exact amount of time she had been unconscious for, the caloric value of the watery bile she had drunk for breakfast.

Aris' false eyes recorded every move.

"Could you not?" Ezrie snapped. "Your robot eyes are creeping me out."

"My current directive is to protect you—"

"Yeah, but maybe you could do it over there. I promise you can still kick my ass if I get out of line."

Aris seemed to consider this recommendation, and took a step backwards.

"Better," Ezrie glowered.

"I acknowledge your discomfort." Aris said with a cheery smile.

"Don't mind her," Sam soothed. "It's only a precaution. I'm glad we get to work together today. And I really need your help. The trace is set to back up team members' traces—"

"So everything on our traces is recorded," Ezrie said flatly. "Does PanGen always act like a Fascist dictatorship, or is it for my benefit?"

Sam nodded. "I know, but that's what it takes to be on this kind of sensitive project. PanGen records everything—personal notes, medical histories...but the storage container is covered with phlax." Sam tapped the grey metal box.

"The stuff that eats energy."

"Exactly! Except now the phlax is eating files." Sam smiled wider, and

Ezrie raised an eyebrow. "So, since you don't have access to saving any files on your trace, it's completely harmless for you to help me. And Purple says you're a genius, so I figure we should give it a try."

"Are all the backup files for the entire project on this one hard drive?"

Sam sighed. "Yes, it's very frustrating. But we have to reformat the porter operating system regularly, due to the phlax. This mass storage comes in very handy."

Sam sent Ezrie's trace a small folder. She knew the contents already: an impossibly long list of medical records from the Apollo crew. The files seemed infinite, with each entry having multiple documents attached. "There's a lot we need to recover." She nodded to Ezrie.

Ezrie opened the file on her trace with some effort. "Shit. Why won't it do what I want it to do?"

"You sound really frustrated. What do you think you can do about it?" Damn. Counselor talk, especially when she was trying to be one, was the wrong tactic. Ezrie rolled her eyes.

"I'll figure it out."

Ezrie seemed to be trying again, her brows knit and her hands gripping the table. Suddenly she relaxed, and almost smiled. "Whew. Okay. It's open."

Sam felt a smile—a real smile on her lips this time. "Great! I knew you could do hard things. Excellent."

But Ezrie was barely paying attention. She seemed to be looking the file. "What is it?" Sam asked.

Ezrie paused, as if picking her words. "The code on these files is wrong," she said. "I've been blacking for my whole life. I've worked in every language ever written—Slix, Rocketforce, even a little Tour8. I've never seen anything like this."

Sam screwed her forehead up in consternation. "What do you think it means?"

Ezrie shook her head. "Someone out here really knows how to mangle code." She squinted, then shook her head. "Not just mangled. Some of these symbols I've never even seen before."

"Can you clean them?" Sam asked.

Ezrie sighed.

"You could finally use your trace for good," Sam reasoned. "And maybe you'll learn something. Get to know us a little bit."

Ezrie sniffed. "Not likely." She scratched violently at the healing trace wound at the base of her skull.

"Don't do that," Sam said, trying to make her voice as non-threatening and friendly as possible. "Or I'll have to put one of those cones over your head."

Ezrie scratched harder, then sighed.

"Sure." She managed a strangled-looking smile. "I can remove the waste code and see what we come up with."

<hr>

They worked through the files slowly, Ezrie practicing her trace skills as awkwardly as a baby giraffe taking its first steps. They went through personnel files, medical records—anything and everything that could possibly be salvaged from the damaged drive.

Sam was surprised to see that Ezrie seemed to be enjoying herself. After an hour of opening files, sifting through the junk, and then sending it to Sam's trace for review, Ezrie still hadn't complained once. It was slow, but Sam didn't mind the pace. She was proud of herself, too, doing double duty. Managing the files and learning more about Ezrie. She asked lots of questions that Ezrie gave terrible answers to.

How long have you been blacking? A long time.

What is your favorite color? Invisible.

Who is your biggest influence? Satan.

Sam sighed internally after every attempt, simply seeing it as another level of challenge. After all, Ezrie could only stonewall for so long.

"You know what I wish we had? Ice cream," Sam said, trying something else. "When I was a little girl in New England, we had this shop that sold peppermint ice cream all year long. Did they have that in...where did you grow up?"

"California," Ezrie said, abstractly. Sam smiled. Win.

Ezrie paused, glancing at Sam and sighed. "I grew up in Santa Monica."

A handful of new files were dropped onto Sam's trace. She ignored them, turning her full attention to Ezrie. A breakthrough.

"Very exciting. Is that where you got your first trace?"

"No. My dad hated them. I got it...later. After..." Ezrie stopped, stalled.

"After your mother passed?" Sam had already read Ezrie's files. She suspected Ezrie knew, as well. Sam knew all about the foster homes, about the truancy, cheating. The allegations of abuse that had gone unnoticed. The incident at the college. And, of course, when she finally ran away for good.

Ezrie said nothing.

"I'm sure this has been hard for you, having to learn to deal with the trace again after having been without it so long."

Ezrie didn't answer again. A file flicked to the holodisplay projector. "What about this one?"

Sam glanced at the record, ignoring the misdirection. "No. We don't need those. Those are Birdy's field notes. Almost as exhaustive as listening to her talk about them." She smiled at her own joke, but Ezrie didn't seem to be paying attention. "What was she like? Your mother."

"Listen," Ezrie stopped, her eyes snapped to Sam's. "I really don't want to talk about that."

"Why do you think that is?" Sam turned fully to Ezrie.

Ezrie slammed her fist against the table, causing Sam to jump.

"You want to hear about my mother? Fine. My mother killed herself when I was nine, is that what you want to hear? She zoomed out and took a bunch of pills and my dad never talked about it, not once, until he was —" Her voice broke, and Sam knew that it was more helpful for her not to say anything.

"I'm done." Ezrie clipped, and Sam could see her visibly shutting down, pushing all the repressed anger and sorrow into the background where it would continue to manifest in unhealthy habits and choices. "You can work the rest of this garbage out on your own. I quit. Aris, take me back to my cell."

Aris turned to Sam.

"It's fine."

Aris escorted a fuming Ezrie out of the lab, and Sam shook her head.

Ezrie didn't want to talk about her mother's suicide or her father's death. She didn't want to talk about the time she threatened to kill Marcus in the very college where her father had worked side-by-side with him. She didn't want to talk about anything real. That was fine. They had time.

———

Sam worked through the whole stack of new, cleaned files. One that caught her attention was from Cassie Byrion, the Captain of the Apollo crew, and the one person who had tried to pin some of the Leto Mission's failings on Rand. It featuring complaints and arguments with Marcus Olet. To tell the truth, she didn't really like either of them. And Marcus was nearly as narcissistic as Ezrie. Funny that they had that in common.

As she read Cassie's files, key phases leapt out at Sam as she scrolled through the log files.

Undermining authority.

Failure to communicate.

Excessive loss.

An unusual turn of phrase, especially at this point of the mining mission. Excessive loss was usually recorded after mines started operating. Desalinators exploded, pipelines damaged by inclement weather. Usually you didn't see it until after pipelines were put into place. And the environmental survey that Living Waters had demanded meant that not a single drop had been mined yet.

Sam blinked into the v-file.

———

Cassie is in the admin office, with Marcus across the desk. He looks impeccable, as always, although red-faced.

"In the spirit of transparency, something you might be unfamiliar with, this is being recorded," Cassie begins, her voice pointed and sarcastic.

"I don't have anything to hide," Marcus explodes. "Record whatever you want."

Cassie hands him a report from one of the MEG units—a printing bot.

"Tell me what's wrong with this picture, Marcus," Cassie says. Her tone is cool but determined, like a school teacher who you don't want to disappoint.

"I don't know, Cassie," Marcus said. "Sometimes parts get done wrong."

"This isn't just a few parts," she snaps. "Three motherboards? Four main support legs? You're supposed to be the porter king. What the hell are we losing all this money on, Marcus?"

"The MEG is glitchy, like everything else on Leto." He sits back, his jaw set. "If you can't afford to do the job right, then you shouldn't be doing the job."

"Don't lecture me!" Cassie's heart rate is elevated, and Sam can see her blood pressure rising. "Ever since you came out here, you've been a pain in my ass. I know that you've been stealing printer compound. Whatever you're doing, I'm going to find out. This will be your last off-world mission, Marcus, God as my witness—"

Sam closed this. She'd heard this rumor before. She blinked the file away. Cassie had been so sure that someone was stealing, but to what end?

She perused a few more. On a whim, she opened up the folder for her husband. She felt a twinge of guilt. She was his wife, after all. But that made it more okay, didn't it? What did they have to hide from one another after nearly ten years? But he'd never shared his trace feed with her, even after the counselor suggested it might improve their sex life. He'd said something about how a man's thoughts should be the one place his wife never looks. Sam had respected that. But here she was, snooping.

She blinked into a random v-feed.

Jenny Candala stands in the press corner of the Society of Transnational Scientific Research, holding her gold statuete in one hand and a glass of

---

That's enough, Sam's sister's voice sounded in her head. *No good ever comes from snooping.*

Of course, she was right. But Sam remembered the STSR gala. Rand had been so nervous that night, worried that he didn't belong there. So, he had held her hand all night long. As for herself, she'd been completely prepared to impress, especially Jenny Candala whom she only knew from the Leto project and had celebrity status in more than one circle.

Jenny had sparkled like a diamond. Sam had felt jealous then, infuriated that she felt so small in a room full of her colleagues. She blanched, closing the file. If she watched her husband's feed much longer, she would see herself get roaring drunk later that night. But that had been before she was sober. She had the chips to prove it.

Sam blinked into the last upload from Jenny's trace. It was a rough-shot video, the camera angles skewed and jangling. Sam instinctively wanted to shut it off, but knew she couldn't.

She screams once, an agonizing, pained sound

The record ended, and Sam's heart was still racing. She had envied Jenny. She had been brilliant and beautiful. But no one deserved to end like that.

She wiped her face, blinking into the files of Nancy Tukuafu, the medic for the Apollo crew. Maybe there was more information on Jenny's death. As she did, the physical avatars of each of the missing Apollo team presented themselves, complete with their monitored heart rates—which were all flatlined.

"No," she whispered. "This can't be right."

She blinked into another file.

Jeffrey Walheim—friends call him Chuck—is in the men's bunk, staring at the wall. When Tukuafu says his name, he jumps, whirling around, stumbling, his back to the wall. He is holding something in his hand. His eyes are haggard and red.

"I came to see if you got any more sleep last night. Dr. Sanger said that you've been having bad dreams."

Chuck's eyes go wide. "You're not real." He is breathing heavy, and his temperature is dropping and spiking erratically. The warning in Tukuafu's trace says that his core temperature has come down to ninety-six degrees.

Jeffrey Sanger, Psychology Lead, is now beside Tukuafu. "Everything is fine, Jeff," Sanger says, moving slowly towards Chuck. "This is real. We're seeing some unusual temperature changes. Why don't you come with us."

Chuck presses his back against the wall, looking like a child avoiding a whipping. He is holding tightly to something in his hand, but it's impossible to make out. "Caroline...the men are here again."

HEITAR, Tukuafu sends, WE'RE GOING TO NEED BACKUP SECU-RITY. BRING MITCHELLS. CHUCK IS TALKING TO HIS DEAD DAUGHTER, AGAIN.

WHAT'S AROUND HIS NECK? Sanger sends. SOME KIND OF WIRE?

It's there—a thin rope of some kind that ties Chuck like a leash to the beam nearly ten feet overhead. Behind him is a chair.

Chuck lashes out again, swingy his meaty arm wildly, his bulk and speed unstoppable, the wire around his neck pulling taut. Sanger yelps and skitters out of Chuck's path at the last minute. Tukuafu moves towards Chuck slowly.

"Listen, Chuck. This isn't you—"

"I don't know what that means anymore," he sobs, his body going slack. He backs up into a chair and awkwardly climbs it.

There are others in the room now, and the large security lead, Manual Heitar, motions two others to flank the doctors, making a small semi-circle around Chuck.

"There you are," Chuck says with a dreamy smile. "I brought you a birthday present, honey." It is unclear who he is addressing. Adrenaline spikes in Tukuafu's own avatar. Lines of trace flood as everyone in the room realize what is in Chuck's hand at the same time.

Chuck retracts the Xtenz rope faster than they can stop him, flipping the lock so that it won't stop when he drops it. The handheld device, designed to lift two hundred pounds of dead weight, pulls him up, the thin wire lifting him up on the chair, his toes dancing like a ballerina on point before the weight of his body and the speed of the rope cut cleanly through his neck.

The head is still falling when the recording ends.

Sam choked back a sob. Chuck had told her in sessions about his daughter. She had drowned in the bathtub while he was zooming and Chuck had never forgiven himself for it. Still, he had never exhibited suicidal ideation, not once in the three years she had known him.

Marcus had to be the key to all of it. And he was alive, somewhere. He had sent Ezrie here, hadn't he?

But there was no record of his trace at all. As if he had disappeared.

Sam trembled as she blurred past all the other records to the last one, dated only two weeks before. Dear God. Fourteen days ago, someone else had *still* been alive. Cassie Byrion, the Apollo Team Leader.

It is the hallway between the medical wing and the main control area. Cassie whispers a rushed Our Father over and over again as she huddles against the wall.

"There's no one left but me and Marcus," Cassie's voice is thin. Her footsteps echo down the long hall towards the secure medical wing. Body bags line the walls beside her, shredded and empty.

Sam pauses the feed and slows the frame rate to read the names.
Jeffrey Sanger. Cause of death: Suicide by electrocution.
Norman "Chuck" Walheim. Cause of death: Suicide by decapitation.
Charleston Mack. Cause of death: Suicide by drowning.
Dead. Dead. Dead. Dead. They were all dead.

Cassie opens the door.

"Nancy died this morning. Walked into the ocean, like Charleston. I tried to stop her, but..." she pauses. There is the soft sound of footsteps, as if from far off. Cassie does not seem to notice. "Marcus's locked himself in the science lab. He swears that Jenny is still alive. That he saw her running around in the woods. But I've seen them come back, too. They don't stay dead."

The playback hesitates before the large viewing window looking into the infirmary. There is nothing inside. "Where are you? Where did you all go? The ghosts are getting closer, and I'm too tired to fight them. I don't want to be alone."

There is a jittering of the image, a scream, the recording falling to the floor then whipping back up. A huge, looming figure.

Chuck's body rises, his neck bleeding black.

Cassie is scrambling up, running. Through the corridors, through the control room, the recording bucks and heaves with every pounding step, from behind, the gutteral sound follows.

Cassie darts down another hallway, the recording stares through a hallway window into the orange Leto sky.

A scream, the sound of bone on glass. Arms reaching out, smashing. Cassie strikes again, breaking her bones as the window stars, strikes again to shatter it, then uses her head to—

From down the hall, there was a crash. For a moment, Sam wasn't sure if it was real or something from Cassie Byrion's memory.

There was a moan. Sam's skin went prickly. She feared that Ezrie was loose, that she'd somehow sorely misjudged the woman.

HELP, Alex sent, HELP SOMTHIGS WRONG

"Alex?" Sam raced out of the corridor and through the secure doors. Alex stood in the control room, his face slack and covered in blood that was pouring from his eyes. He was weaving as if he'd been drinking.

"Alex, oh my God." She grabbed him just as his legs gave out.

"Feeling so sick," he slurred.

MEDICAL ASSISTANCE, Sam sent, JAMES, I NEED HELP

Alex collapsed to the ground.

$$X$$

"ALEX HAS PORTER FLU," James cut the silence, and looked at Rand directly. He looked tired, "But I guess you all know that."

The mood was grim. Birdy's eyes were red, and Purple was so pale his freckles looked like paint spots on white canvas. Ezrie felt sick to her stomach. She never wished what was happening to Alex on anyone. Seeing it once had been enough.

She was suddenly thirteen again, feeling the flesh of her father's forearm as it shifted away from his bone like overcooked chicken. They never should have come. She should have never let them follow her here.

"What happened?" Sam whispered. Her hair was pulled up into a messy chignon, and her face looked tired. She caught Ezrie's gaze and turned away. "Our safety protocols are supposed to make that impossible."

"The safety protocols were overridden," Aris said. "It was the only way to get the team on the surface."

"What are you talking about?" Sam whirled on Aris. "Why in the hell would anyone remove the safety on the porter?" Sam turned to Rand, her eyes blazing. "Did you know about this?"

Rand held his gaze steady. "Yes."

Sam's cheeks were burning, her lips quavering. "How dare you keep that from us. That's our *lives*, Rand. You have put us all at risk. Everyone who has ported through is in danger."

Rand did not look away.

"It's happening so fast," Birdy said, her voice shaking. "Usually porter sickness takes weeks or months."

Ezrie closed her eyes. She did not want to be here. When she opened them again, the room felt as if it were swirling around her.

ARE YOU OKAY? Purple sent.

FINE.

"It depends on the severity of the code break," Ezrie said softly. "Alex was the last to port through, so the cascading Lock would have damaged his code the most. It's possible that we're all sick, but it would be less." She took a deep breath.

"Unfortunately, that is not the only issue we're facing right now." Rand said. His voice was low, but his face was still as firm-set as ever.

Sam reluctantly sat, clearly pissed. She had every right to be.

"From what Sam and James have shared, it's clear the Apollo team suffered from some kind of hysteria or mass hallucination. It started with nightmares, then paranoia, then suicide."

Rand blinked, and the holographic globe of Leto was replaced with a v-feed. Even though Ezrie didn't know any of the people on the projector, it was clear that they had undergone a transformation. When Cassie Byrion came on screen, Lee made a strangled noise in the back of her throat.

When it was over, there was a moment of hollow silence. "They all died here," Sam said, breaking the spell. "All except a handful that are unaccounted for, including Cassie and Marcus."

The room was silent. Kenner spoke first, his voice soft and swinging. "So, Rand. What do you suggest we do now?"

"Well," Rand said, dryly, "Since we haven't seen Marcus on the trace, he doesn't want to be found. Backtracking the signal only brings us to Ocean, nothing more. So we need to do more investigating to see if he left any bread crumbs." He shot a look at Ezrie, like she knew more than she was saying. *I wish*, she thought. *If I did, I wouldn't be here.*

"But if Marcus sent a message, it's not on the porter logs here," Purple interjected. "That means he must have used the porter at Mountain."

"Then we could use it to go home," Birdy said hopefully.

"What's Mountain?" Ezrie felt all the eyes on her. Rand gave her a withering look.

"PanGen installed a second porter on the west side of Leto in case of an emergency," Purple offered. "It makes sense that any survivors would be there."

Ezrie nodded her thanks. Purple smiled, but it was small and sad.

"As far as we know, the porter at Mountain had some phlax damage before the Apollo crew left." Rand said.

"Was that the timing issue?" Purple asked, "I fixed that."

"You did. This was different. They said the porter was reading an error."

"It seems Marcus got it working," Lee clipped. "Enough to send his girl-friend a love letter."

Ezrie ground her teeth. Lee was trying to get under her skin, and it was working.

"With all due respect, maybe we should stay here." Purple's big, Irish voice echoed through the control room. He looked around, all eyes on him, and licked his lips nervously. "I mean, we can print new parts for the trans-mitter we have. And now that we have Ezrie," he shot a furtive look in Ezrie's direction, "we should be able to get a new OS for the porter in no time."

Rand surveyed the room, letting his steely gaze rest on Ezrie for a moment before moving on. "My team, including Birdy, James, and Kenner, will go to Mountain and assess the situation, look for Marcus or any other survivors there might be."

Lee and Ezrie exploded at the same time.

"I'm going *after* that sonofabitch–"

"You can't expect me to—"

"No," Rand snapped. "You both stay here."

"You can't leave me with her!" Ezrie's brain was reeling. She had to get away from this base. She had to find a way to get on the team going to find Marcus. "She's a psycho. She almost killed me!"

Lee was up in an instant, grabbing Ezrie by the collar. She seethed, her jaw flexing, the snake on her arm tensing, "You want to find out how psycho I am? Keep talking."

Ezrie clenched her fists, her pulse racing. "You all know its true. The only reason you're *on* this planet is because of me—"

"I swear to God, Betty. One more word—"

"Enough!" Rand barked, his voice cutting through the tension."We don't have the time or energy for infighting. He stared down Ezrie and Lee. "Ezrie stays here with an escort *at all times*, under Lee's direction. *I* will find Marcus, after we know we have a safe way home. Got it?"

Lee let her go with a shove, and Ezrie sat begrudingly.

"Mountain Base is almost two hundred miles away," Birdy blurted, snagged on a detail of the discussion that was a million miles from reality. "The terrain is very dangerous. There are animals—"

"That's why you're going with us," Rand said. "No one knows Leto like you. We may need help navigating, especially where the maps are thin, out towards the mountains."

Birdy blanched, withering in her seat.

"We'll all get some sleep and start fresh tomorrow," Rand clipped.

"Rand," James said, "Alex is dying. Someone should be here to monitor him. Make sure that he has appropriate end of life care."

"Alex isn't going to live." Rand sighed, dropping his chin to his chest. He looked defeated. "I take that on myself. If Marcus is out there, we still have a chance to save him, or at least find out what the hell he's been doing here. I need you to be there when we find him. Sam is medically trained. She'll be monitoring Alex here and making sure he's comfortable."

"Of course," James said. "Sam is very capable."

Rand nodded and Sam smiled, though Ezrie didn't think the shrink looked very confident. "We need to find out what exactly might have triggered this whole mess. I need to have something to take back to Zhong and the board when we get out of here."

If we get out of here, Ezrie thought. From the looks on their faces, a few of them were thinking the same thing.

"As far as command goes," Rand continued, "I'll lead the rescue team with Kenner as second officer." Rand flicked the image closed. The room sat in silence. "Lee, you'll lead the home team with Sam as your go-to. Questions?"

The room was silent, but it seemed to Ezrie that everyone but Kenner was equally unhappy.

"My team leaves at 0400 tomorrow. Set your trace accordingly. Until then, you're dismissed."

The group broke up and dispersed to the living quarters, side conversations like discontented echoes. Ezrie sat, unwilling to move.

Rand turned to Ezrie, jaw sharp and militant. Lee leaned against the door, snake tattoo flexing, eyes slit. They faced her down like a pack of wolves over a dead carcass.

"Something you want to get off your chest?" Rand asked. His eyes glittered in the sallow lights.

"This is bullshit," Ezie said, slumping into her chair. "Marcus asked for me. There's no point in locking me up like a prisoner here when I could help you get that the other porter working."

Rand's eyes narrowed. "Purple is right. We don't know if the porter at Mountain can be fixed. We know for a *fact* that this one does. Or did." He glared at her, and she could almost hear his internal words. *Until Ezrie came through.* "You can prove yourself by helping Purple get this porter functional. That seems a fair punishment."

"Please," Ezrie hated the wheedling sound in her voice, but she had no other options but begging. "I have to find Marcus. He asked for my help, and I think you know you need me to find him."

"I'm sure they can manage without you," Lee said.

Rand's eyes flicked between the women for a moment. "Ezrie is here, whether she deserve it or not. That's a fact we can't ignore—"

"But I don't have to trust her. Or like her." Lee's eyes were burning holes in her.

"If it helps," Ezrie said, "I don't like you either."

Rand stepped closer, inches from her face. She felt naked under his glare.

"Watch yourself, Ezrie. Leto has made lunch meat out of better people than you'll ever be. If you want to get out of this alive, you'd be wise to listen to Lee. If anyone is going to save your ass, it will be her."

He had pulled up to his full height, towering over her by almost a head. She could smell the military on him, and it stunk.

"Yes, sir," she said, a thin smile at the corners of her mouth.

"Aris," Rand said. The android stepped forward, a scuttling beetle in the shadow of the control room. "Please escort Ezrie to her bunk."

"Of course, Captain."

Ezrie stormed out of the commissary before Aris could stop her, nearly running Purple over.

"Hey," he said. "Sorry. I was, uh, fixing up this panel..." He awkwardly attached an access panel to the door housing. "Phlax, am I right? Gets into everything. Loves electricity. Hey, so I saw this interview you did once on GrindUp—"

She pushed past him with Aris on her heels, walking faster until she was jogging.

"You must stop," Aris called. "My orders are to escort you to the women's bunk—"

There had to be other exits. She took a quick right down one of the long spider hallways and saw a yellow ion field door.

Ezrie began running, hands in front of her. Knowing that it was a door and a door meant a way to escape.

She slammed into the ion door as if it were a brick wall. Pain bloomed in her hand, and a bright red light went off in the trace across her vision.

DAMAGE. METACARPAL FRACTURE. MINOR.

Aris strode behind her, catching up without breaking a sweat.

"Shit," she cried, cradling her hand. "Goddamn it, let me out!" She screamed, impotently at the door, the world. She slammed into the ion field and it kicked her back, dropping her to the cool floor of the hallway.

"Ezrie," Aris' buttery voice sounded in her ear, "your genetic code is disallowed from going through the ion field doors without an escort. Please do not attempt to go through. I will be forced to disable you for your own protection."

She screamed in frustration, her tears making the metal floor wet and slippery. She could feel the others judging her, the white icon of the trace was watching. But they didn't matter. What mattered was that she was as far away from Marcus right then as she had ever been. The planet of Leto was a black hole. There was no way to even begin looking for Marcus. No maps. No doors. No escape.

Marcus was out there somewhere, waiting for her. He would probably die before she ever got to kill him.

"You have damaged your metacarpal," Aris said. "I'm programmed for minor medical service—"

"Shut the hell up and leave me alone!"

She lay there for a while, letting the frustration leak out of her until she was exhausted. When she finally sat up, wiping snot and tears from her face, she knew she needed a plan. She cradled her arm in her hand, allowing Aris to walk her slowly back to the women's sleeping area.

Ezrie crumpled onto the bed, defeated and tired. The pack that Kenner had brought her was in the way, and she pushed it off the bed. It made a hollow clunk as it hit the floor.

Weird.

She swung her legs over the cot and unzipped the pack, fingering through the jumbled mess. She decided to take everything out and do a careful inventory. Never knew when she would have a chance to blow this popsicle stand.

A change of underclothes, skin pants and tank top; a simple first aid kit; a water bottle with a filter; enough food paste tubes to choke a mule; a portable fire pack including a lighter and twenty fuel disks; a package the size of a book made of some waterproof material. A tent, maybe? Two or three portable chemical shower cannisters, bright blue. Then she felt something hard. She pulled the object out gently and opened the mitrium flap.

There was a knife in her bag.

Kenner. She smiled, secreting it away quickly so as not to arouse Aris' suspicious. She had to admit that it was nice to know there was at least one person on her side.

She showered, then changed. She was still tired, but now she was focused. She attempted to send Kenner a private message, but his feed was blocked. Sleeping maybe. And he'd be gone again in the morning.

"Ezrie, your arm is still hurt," Aris said. "Do you need help?"

"Yes," she murmured, realizing it fully for the first time. She needed someone in flesh and blood willing to help her. Someone who had access to the map files and admin files she would need to get moving.

Only one name even flickered as a possibility. As Aris began to bind her fractured wrist, she said it over and over again in her mind. It was her new mantra. She tucked it away, knowing that it was the only solution.

If Purple wouldn't help her, no one would.

PART 3

WHITE IS FOR FIRE

"Sometimes you think you know the solution, but that is only because you think you know the problem. A good blacker knows that the problem is often not what it seems on the surface, so the solution is only covering up the truth, not illuminating it."

The BlackBook, Last Accessed 2072

|

Ocean Base, *Leto*

Day 4

BIRDY PUT on her outlanding gear over her tank and skinpants in the dark, her spirits mixed. Although the circumstances weren't ideal, she loved Leto. And, perennial optimist that she was, she had never driven across it. She had only ever ported from Ocean to Mountain, leaving the physical trial of a trip to the more physically inclined members of their party. She told herself it would be good science. Unpleasant and uncomfortable, but that was field work, wasn't it?

And there would be duplicates of the experiments at Mountain. As long as that lab hadn't been destroyed, too.

The lab at Mountain had been demolished along with all the work she had done to connect the R-particles with the phlax. Someone had been using it as a place to live, complete with a chamber pot made from a bucket. It was littered with blood and broken glass, and someone had destroyed her samples with extreme prejudice.

With the losses were the R-particle experiments—all the proof that she needed to expose PanGen's willingness to play Russian Roulette with peoples' lives. There was nothing to do but record it all on her trace and cry.

She had tried to explain to Rand the gravity of the loss, but he didn't understand. He never understood.

"I'm am trying to get us home, Birdy," he had said, exasperated. "The experiments are not my priority—"

"They are the *only* priority." Birdy had been beside herself. "Without them—" she stopped herself before she said too much. "We need them as evidence to the Water Safety Commission. That the water is safe. Otherwise the Leto water might not pass."

"The water is not the issue, Birdy." Rand's face had been red and for the first time ever, she had sensed fear in him. "Zhong said its already passed the Commission with flying colors. *We have to get everyone home.* The water is the least of my concerns."

Something in his voice sounded desperate, and she didn't like that. Even more, she didn't like the idea that the water had already passed the Commission. That meant the mine would be running within a few months, as soon as the infrastructure was in place. The Leto water could never get back to Earth. Birdy would make sure of that.

It was unfortunate, but she didn't agree with Rand. She didn't feel their loss as keenly as he did. Charleston had been her colleague, so she was sad for his loss, but all the other deaths seemed so removed. Surreal. She had never been very good at caring deeply about people. Plants required no shows of affection or false pretenses. They were just so much more dependable.

But she could not get the image of Alex out of her mind. His body swollen, his skin waxy and seeping fluid. He had already begun to go into sepsis, which mean that the cell walls of his organs had begun deconstructing. Alex was going to die. That meant that from a purely scientific standpoint, the odds of death had increased for herself, as well.

She didn't want to die, she decided. Even more importantly, she couldn't. Someone had to return from Leto with proof.

Birdy could only pray that the proof was at the Ocean Base—for all of their sakes.

For what seemed like hours, the motorcycles jangled into the Wilds, the blur of black shadows whispering venomously from somewhere beyond the headlights. As Rand zoomed over sand, then grass, then into the black of the northern jungle, Birdy bounced and grappled with his rigid body, using every ounce of her skinny frame to simply *not fall off.* It was especially difficult to do when the engine would randomly cough and buck.

They moved through the jungle slower than Rand had expected, with several stops to pull gnarled bushes from out of the wheel housings and to clean phlax off the control panels. When they stopped for the evening, Birdy gratefully dismounted, stretching her aching spine out and trundling up a small rise. As she looked down on the shallow valley, the lights of the rising suns blooming in the southeast, she forgot about her bruised tailbone and aching back. Below her, the dark of early morning was illuminated with floating yellow and pink lights of a cloud of zephyrs gracefully drifting on an unseen breeze.

The creatures swam through the warm air like a flock of stars, glowing steadily and gently above the treeline. They always reminded her of dandelions she had picked as a child. Even in Chicago, they had the tenacity to grow at the edges of the concrete. She would blow and they would drift up and up, taking her wishes with them.

What do I wish tonight? Her heart ached for Cy. For his brown arm against her browner arm. His chest softly moving against her naked back.

I wish that you were not so far away.

Her heart ached as the ball of tendrilled white blew towards its brothers. She wondered if it felt loneliness. She missed the simple rocking of Cy's body next to hers on the back porch swing—the heart-clamoring, rested exhaustion that comes from making love deeply. A completion that was both sweet and sad all at once.

A rogue zephyr escaped from the cluster and danced about Birdy's face for a moment before lazily moving to join the others. She held her breath, as if she might blow it out like candle. The cloud of them moved over land, then slowly began descending into the tree line below.

"*Asteraceae zephuros.*" Kenner said in his slow drawl. "Isn't that what you called them?"

"Yes," Birdy said quickly. "Some interstellar cousin of the moth, I think."

"Greek," Kenner noted. "The god of the wind."

"Yes."

There were a thousand words that Birdy might have said in any other circumstance or to anyone else. That Zephyr was the father of Eros. It was the western wind—the one that was kindest and most gentle. In Egyptian mythology, Hutchai, the serpent-god, drove the west wind, and in Slavic tradition it was Dogoda, the goddess of love.

But with Kenner, she was much more careful.

Sometimes she would catch him staring at her. Not out of annoyance or confusion, the way most responded to her torrents of encyclopedic diatribe. But with a contained heat that made her stomach cold.

"I'm going to head down the ridge for a moment," she said. "Maybe I'll gather some samples. They're only active at night, and I have wondered about their migration paths. Will you stay up here and keep watch? I'll take my laster."

"You sure you don't need backup?"

Birdy tried to make her smile warm enough. It was easier now that Pyrios had peeked over the ridge.

She turned the laster on and held it up. "I'll should be safe with this, don't you think? Thank you all the same."

Birdy stepped carefully over morolith mushrooms with their wavy white tops and through the eldenwood trees and rimands. The bark was shimmery with the oil that they secreted to attract the small Persimmon bugs that were their prey. The bugs writhed in the oil, their bellies blinking white death lights—an SOS call that only attracted larger and more substantial food for the trees.

On Leto everything was always eating everything else.

She followed the trail of the zephyrs into the darker part of the forest. She looked back over her shoulder. Birdy glimpsed Kenner at the top of the ridge. He waved.

Why was it that he bothered her so much? Sometimes he said things.

Sometimes he would talk about God as if He belonged to Kenner and no one else. It was a possessive kind of love that left no room for anyone else to believe in Him.

But the worst was when he looked at her the same way.

She pressed through the bushes and saw a glowing structure.

The zephrs had lighted on a small hump that grew straight up in the air. It was about two and a half feet tall—kind of a rough pillar that came to Birdy's thigh. A tiny monolith in the darkness of the forest, built by the beautiful and flowing designs of phlax that Birdy had become accustomed to seeing everywhere on the base. But this was the middle of nowhere and still the monolith glowed with it.

She scratched the surface, and there was a moment of pressure. Her touch gave it an extra energy. She laughed despite herself, letting go and seeing it dim. Pressing it and seeing it light up. It was like turning on a switch.

Phlax was a funny thing. Like a salt crystal in structure, but able to bond and replicate incredibly quickly, usually around some kind of power source. But where was the power source for this?

"Interesting," she murmured.

COME ON BACK, BIRDY, Rand sent. WE'RE GOOD TO GO.

Birdy pulled out a vial from her jumpsuit vest and carefully scraped some of the shavings from the small square pillar. As she did, she glimpsed a second monolith about half the size only two meters away. This one reacted the same to her touch, but was less formed. It looked like an unfinished version of the first.

She made a note of the location and added it to her personal Leto journal. It was more journal than field guide, but a great place to begin research. She made a note to stop on the way back through and check on the growth. There seemed to be an uptick at the base. She wondered if it was the same as out here, so far away.

Birdy came back to the ridge.

"Did you find what you were looking for?" Kenner's voice was too quiet. Too intimate.

"Yes. Thank you. It was a very enlightening excursion. Most beneficial."

Birdy started walking to where James and Rand were revving the engines. Behind her, Kenner followed, his footsteps not making a sound. She had a sudden, rash knowledge that if he wanted to harm her, she would never know it until it was too late.

It was a paranoid delusion. It was.

Was it?

Yes it was.

But she couldn't stop thinking about it, even as they began to put miles and miles behind them. Even as the sun rose on the new world of Leto, Birdy knew that no amount of sunshine could warm the chill that he carried wherever he went.

All you have to do is get to the base. The experiments will be there. They have to be there.

She wanted to believe it, and held tighter to James as he drove up the winding mountain ridge towards the base. But something inside her whispered that there was something bigger going on and Kenner was a part of it.

II

Ocean Base, *Leto*

PURPLE'S ALARM went off at 6 a.m., but he was already awake with an anxious head. Feeling wrecked out and trying to figure whether he was feeling the beginnings of a complete genetic deterioration or not.

Did his head hurt? A little. But that could be from stress. His stomach was in bits, but that could be stress, too. He dithered back and forth: dying or not dying? He didn't want to think about the alternative, so he told himself he was fit.

But it was definitely a possibility.

He flicked the small, battery-powered tube on the shelf beside his bed. The poster of Marina Giles dotted into existence, shining in ultra retina perfection from the paper-bright laser feed through the slit in the top of the white tube.

Marina winked at him.

Rand had told him to disable the security defaults to wedge the lock open. Everything in him had protested, but he'd do anything to avoid Rand eating the head off him. The thing that fried him most was that he hadn't told anyone else. They's thought they were safe because he hadn't said anything to warn them different. Rand wasn't the only one to blame.

"What you wager?" he said to the poster. "I'm a right bollox, in'it?"

"You're so faze," Marina moaned. "I want you to take me home and turn. me. oooonnnnnnnn."

On any other day, this probably would have given him the want. But today it made him feel lonely and sad.

He blinked into his personal Trace files. The v-feeds he kept on file were from as far back as when he was eight. He blinked through feeds of Cami and Nola, taking a moment to revel in the smells and sounds and tastes of home. This was a football game, and Cami and Nola were passing the ball between them, Cami's feet lightning quick and Nola coming in to assist, then driving the ball in for a goal. This was one of his favorites. He could still taste grape freeze on his tongue, hear himself cheering with his sisters and mum: "Wreck 'em out, Nola!" They'd been thirteen and twelve, and their friends had been impossibly pretty. Still were, for the most part.

Purple blinked past feeds of Jennica's debate tourneys. Rach and Daph, the twins, giving each other pierced ears in the bathroom when Mum was out of town at a conference. Purple had sent her the feed to prove it hadn't been his fault and he had still gotten Nets limited for a week.

His oldest sis, Clare, was different. He paused on his favorite feed of her and felt his heart squeeze. They had gone driving before he'd left home to attend Cambridge. He'd only been sixteen, and it had been nothing but reports and interviews for months leading up to that semester. The Irish Post had done a feature story on him, and, even though it ran on the second-to-last page, everyone in Kinsale kept dropping in, wanting to know how he'd gotten so smart. What will you do at University? What's an AI-driven security system? Even Mum and the rest of the girls had become so nice it was spooky.

Clare had been the only one who didn't care. He paused for a moment, then whispered, "Ah, dreck it," and blinked into the feed.

They are at Clare's thinking place, at the end of the small dirt road off L5840 where it becomes Quay Coast Road. Around the bend is Rosmalley, with its farms and yew trees. But from here, their house in Westport feels far away, even though it's a short drive. Clare often brings him here to sit and look out over the Atlantic on days fit for drying, which aren't many. Today, it is not one of those days. It's not pissing down, but the air is damp and cool, September curling around Ireland like a welcome blanket of grey.

Clare pushes back her hair, squinting into the nothingness as she reads and marks his first year composition assignment—due the first day of class.

"How can you be so shite at writing when you can run laps around me at everything else?" she asks.

"I dunno," he says. "I guess I got all the brains that really count."

She laughs. "Yap it. Romance makes almost as much money as computering, if you're in the know."

Clare whispers a new thesis for his second main hypothesis segment. She is a writer foremost—romance and love, not the horror stuff that Purple is often drawn to—but she'll edit his work if he asks the right way. And since Purple has promised to watch her twin boys for a week as payment, she's not groused so much about having to review his thesis for the millionth time.

"Done," she says. "And don't bring it to me again unless its finished for good."

She flicks at something in the composition, then sighs. The file appears on Purple's main Trace home. He feels the weight of his life lighten. He can face Cambridge, as long as Clare is there.

A single moment where he was just another kid with his big sister. And even though he was the one in the papers, she was still the smartest, strongest person in the world to him.

Get up, kids, Lee sent on the main channel. Purple, you and Ezrie are going to fix the porter today. Aris will be your escort. Meet up at the control room in fifteen minutes.

Purple felt his heart jump. But also, he hated himself for it. How could he be thinking of life when his friend—almost his brother—was dying?

Instead of going to the main control room he took a side trip the infirmary. Sam was helping Alex eat some kind of soup. Chicken noodle with little chunks of chicken.

"I found it in the kitchen," Sam said. Her eyes were red, and Purple wondered if she had been up with him all night. "It was real food, not this dehydrated stuff. It was the best I could come up with, under the circumstances."

Alex's face sagged. The corners of his eyes were full of dried blood instead of sleep. But he didn't look like he was in pain. Still, Purple didn't want to look at him. When he did, he could only think of Clare, her white hand still while the machines breathed on her behalf

"Oy, lad," Purple said, careful to keep the emotion out of his voice. "Must be tough."

"Still sucking air," Alex said in a thick voice.

"So, you're still sucking? Same as always," Purple said, the joke feeling thin. Alex smiled, but it was dreamy and detached, slowed by whatever drugs Sam had given him.

Sam lifted the spoon and Alex declined. He lay back and closed his eyes. Sam wiped at bloody tears with a wet nap. Purple wanted to wake up from whatever nightmare this was. By the time she'd finished washing around his eyes and mouth, Alex was firmly asleep.

"He's not in pain, which is good. But he probably won't be with us when we port home." Sam wiped a hand across her red eyes. Purple sat on the chair beside the bed. "How are you holding up?"

"I'm...I'm okay," Purple managed, standing. "I should go."

Sam stopped him. "You know, you have a right to feel sad and angry." Her face hardened momentarily. Then she seemed to reconsider. "You should talk to him. He doesn't have a lot of time left."

"I've gotta skip," Purple muttered. "I'm working the porter with Ezrie."

Sam gave him a sad smile. "The porter and Ezrie will be there when you're done. I promise you." She stood. "I'm going to go finish up the medical records audit. Just shut the door when you're finished."

Purple sat beside Alex, listening to the regular beeps of his heart. He had sat the same way beside Clare every day for nearly six months. He had been hoping that she would recover. He had prayed, even. But there was nothing inside Clare but emptiness. Nothing inside the prayers but despair.

He had fought with Mum about it the night before he left for the port. She always wanted him to check in, but especially before he went on work. It was the least he could do, seeing as he hardly spoke to any of them at all anymore. It was just too painful without Clare.

"She's barely alive," he'd asked, his voice too loud. "Is this the kind of life she wanted?"

"It's what *we* want," his mother had said. "The doctor's say her brain activity is good. She'll be getting more communicative any day now—"

"You've been saying that for a year, Mum," he snapped. "It's millions of pounds, now, is it? How long can you pretend there's hope for her? You've got to wise it—"

"Don't. You. Dare!" she shouted. "It's mine and your father's money, and I'll do with it what I will. If he were here, God rest his soul, he'd do the same." She'd sighed, and she looked to be crying over the video feed. "There's new science being tried all the time—"

But the science was never right. And all Clare had now was time. Years of waiting for a miracle that was never going to come.

Purple looked over at Alex, the large man's face slack.

"I'm sorry, lad. For all of it."

Purple slipped out of the room, giving one last backward glance at the sleeping Alex. He couldn't help but wonder how much time the big man had left. He felt nauseous and headachy, himself. How long did any of them have left?

<hr>

Purple led the way through the base, his hands sweaty on the storage container for the hard drive. He needed to think of something to say that didn't sound stupid. Behind him, Ezrie trudged, with Aris bringing up the rear. They were on the gravel pathway that connected the base to the porter bay. The air was orange with afternoon heat, squid creatures rising up and down on the distant red waves. The squawks of alien birds were a distant background noise.

He wanted to say something to Ezrie that would mean something. That would prove to her that he was as faze as he thought she was. But he also felt like cat crap in a toaster.

"I saw your T-Nation interview, back in '67," Purple said. "You murdered it. Really. All that stuff about the The Black Door—"

"That was a long time ago," she said darkly. "I was just a kid."

"Well, people keep up with it. You know it got retted, right? There's some lads been searching for the Black Door configuration for years. Call 'emselves Freedom Travelers—"

"That's so dangerous and stupid," she snapped. "Porting on unauthorized signals is banned for a reason. You want to end up like your friend back there?"

Purple's stomach twisted.

"The Black Door isn't real." Ezrie's eyes were hard and her words were points. "I made it up so that people would remember my dad. Clearly it worked on you." She said it with such derision, Purple felt like melting into the ground.

"Right. Fine then."

So, so stupid. Purple knew better than to believe all the Alt-History feeds and Underground bullshit. He wished he would stop making an ass of himself in front of her. But that wasn't likely, was it?

From ahead of them, there was a crackle in the underbrush. Adrenaline washed over him, making his skin crawl and vision sharpen.

"I sense movement," Aris said.

They stayed still, listening for a few moments. The only sound was the call of the ocean birds and the thick water lapping the sand.

"A bird, likely," Purple said.

"Or a squirrel," Ezrie said, her eyes scanning the darkness behind the porter. "That's a pretty normal thing out here, I bet. Right?

She looked legitimately spooked, and it made his skin feel clammy. "Go check it out, Aris."

"My first priority is maintaining Ezrie's security. I am unable to explore further."

"Great," Ezrie said, her eyes still laser-focused on the underbrush. She turned a exasperated look on Aris. "Aris, can you put in your official record that you're the worst?"

"I have made a note."

Purple smiled, and the edge came off the moment. But Jesus, he was jumpy.

Can't imagine why, he thought. *Between possibly dying of porter flu and Alex....* He swallowed, trying to shut out the intrusive image of Alex's bloody tears. There was a lot to be jumpy about.

They hustled to the porter bay with Purple lugging the unwieldy container as faze as he could and trying not to think about it all. His trace went silent as he walked through the door, which always made him uncomfortable. To the rest of them, he was a blank avatar. And it forced him to listen to his own thoughts, which was a scary proposition, even on a good day.

"So, we're recording the error log, if anything is left from the Lock going tits-up, and then cleaning out the OS files before we upload them again." Purple said, filling up the space of the porter bay before his brain could start showing him horrible things. He popped the gorilla glass enclosure off the control panel. The panel gave off a delicious, plastic-y, freshly-baked parts smell.

"I can help with that," Ezrie said, her eyes brightening. "That's what I was doing for Sam before." It wasn't a smile, but it was the closest thing he'd seen her to happy so far. It made him feel amazing. *The* Ezrie Collings was here, with him, and he was not making her want to die. Faze as shit, that was, despite all the other terribleness that was going on.

Ezrie dropped to a knee and pried open the access shield for the power supply. She touched the filmy blue web. "Is this that stuff? Phlax?"

He laughed. Birdy was so predictable. She probably told Ezrie the exact weight of each molecule. "I'm guessing Birdy talked your ear off about it. It gets into everything. Total dreck."

"Dreck, huh? That's a new one. Clearly I don't hang around enough Gen kids."

"It's okay," he said. "I barely count, anyway. I'm almost twenty-five." Lie. But, she seemed to buy it. It chuffed him to know that he could get away with being a bit older.

They worked for a while, Ezrie cleaning files and sending them to Purple.

"It's been a while since I built a porter OS from the ground up," she said, breaking the silence. "Is this your main job here?"

He nodded, blinking the files into the untouched OS one by one.

"Mostly. The phlax gets into everything, even the porters. We have to reset almost every time we come, so it's not a far walk for me. It's the same with androids."

"Yeah," Ezrie said, standing and stretching. "I saw that you're an android guy. So, you maintain them, or program them, or what?"

"The whole ball of string," Purple smiled.

Purple told her the whole story, about how he had started nearly two years before, working for Jenny Candala, the hard engineer for Apollo. She was pretty—though that wasn't a detail Purple mentioned—and had literally written the book on the Aris models, being one of the key developers at Telluride Labs before PanGen siphoned Jenny off to help with water mining operations.

"Talking to Jenny feels like talking to a tiger who is trying to decide which part of you to eat first," he said. Ezrie half-laughed, and he gave himself an internal fiver.

"Phlax makes the Arises malfunction. So Jenny gave one to me to fix and I ended up optimizing her and adding in a custom language program —smoother language functions and the like."

On her word, Zhong had almost immediately put all the models in his and Jenny's hands. And, although it had been Cassie Byrion, the leader of the Apollo team, that had first mentioned the malfunctions of other android models—a Rold that wouldn't print as directed, a Gemini 6 that refused commands—it had been he and Jenny Candala diagnosing and fixing them.

By the time he was done talking, Ezrie had sent him the last file he needed.

"Faze," he said. "We should be ready to port in a few hours. I'm sure they'll be happy to see us," he smiled, then remembered. "Oh, bust. I guess it's not doing, is't? We can't port home, anyway." He gave what he hoped was a seductive smile. "So, what are you doing for the next bit?"

She raised an eyebrow. He instantly hated himself.

"Ha," he said, flatly. "Just joking."

"Funny."

The way she said it while flipping her hair from her eyes was rather cute. The earring glinted in the light of the oculus.

"That's very bouge," he said. "Looks like a program of a sort."

Her eyes went wide and she put her hand to her ear. She was genuinely surprised and it made him laugh.

"No worries," he said. "I've seen a lot of bodyware before. Everyone has a custom program nowadays. Nice to be able to access something that no one else can get to, especially with PanGen up our skills."

"Um, yeah," she blustered. "It's a...personal file. I'd rather if no one knew about it, you know."

"I've got your number, cold."

"Thanks," she gave him an uncomfortable smile. They stood awkwardly for a moment.

"Well, in any case, I have to turn on Aris," he said, breaking the tension. "Lee's probably already gotten the memo that she went into diagnostic mode. If she's anywhere nearby, that is."

"Yeah," she said. "I get it. Keep the team safe."

Aris came back online, and Purple finished the install. Ezrie watched everything he did. It made him feel important, somehow. That someone who was as experienced with the porters—someone who was literally a part of the porter lore—was impressed with what he was doing.

Lee met them halfway back. Her eyes were lighting fires everywhere she looked.

"I got a notice that Aris went into diagnostic mode," Lee seethed. "What the hell was that all about—"

"I was checking her for phlax," Purple said, feeling his face go hot. Dammit. Every. Single. Time. *Any redder and it would be Purple,* Alex had said once. *Once.* And that's all it had taken.

Lee paused, jaw hard. She swore under her breath. "Aris, get Ezrie back to the bunk."

"Of course," Aris said. "Come this way, Ezrie."

Ezrie bristled, but said nothing to her. Instead she turned to Purple.

"Thanks for letting me tag along. I learned a lot." She flashed a quick smile, and he got the impression it was more for Lee's benefit than his.

Ezrie walked away, Aris within arm's reach. After she was gone, Lee yelled at him for nearly a half hour, but none of the words stuck. He was too busy reviewing Ezrie's last smile over and over again on his v-feed.

III

Mountain Base, *Leto*

THE MOUNTAIN BASE nestled at the foot of Mount Prata. Prata meant "silver" in Portuguese, and Birdy thought it was perfect because of the metallic prang trees (*acer pragora*) that grew along its ridge. Birdy had never seen them up close, only on Charleston video stream. He was technically the biology lead for the mission, but he and Birdy had planned to co-write several papers on what they'd found. That wouldn't happen now, of course. Seeing the mountains that they had named together reminded Birdy of his good-natured, if preoccupied, smile. She felt a slight pang of sadness that made her feel more human than she'd felt in a long time.

The trees sparkled along the distant mountain ridge, reflecting the wash of reddish light as the second sun—Aeos—rose over the Chaldean Range to meet its mate in the southeast.

Rand pulled his laster from his pocket.

KEEP THESE ON, Rand sent. JAMES AND BIRDY, HEAD OVER TO THE PORTER AND TAKE A LOOK AT IT. I'M GOING TO CHECK OUT THE TRANSMITTER. KENNER, DO A SWEEP OF THE BASE TO SEE IF THERE ARE ANY SURVIVORS. ONCE YOU'RE DONE MEET AT MOUNTAIN CONTROL. KEEP ALL COMMUNICATION TRACE ONLY.

Sure thing, Boss, Kenner sent. He nodded, taking the bike from Rand. He moved like liquid in everything he did, mounting and flicking the bike forward in a nearly synchronous movement. If he decided to turn on her, she'd never even hear it.

Birdy turned her own weapon on. The lake at the foot of the mountain shone glassy and red. The light of suns glinted across the silvered trees, emblazoning the valley in orange sparkles. A smattering of bladderfish —*hydroxen piscelenis*—rose from the water as if by magic, floating in shimmer of the morning light. A passing tern dove for one, and the fist-sized creatures dropped into the water, making gentle ripples on the surface with the sound of a pail of golf balls being dumped into a lake.

On her trace, Kenner opened up a private channel. He was now fifty yards away, the bike tiny against the backdrop of massive evergreen trees with white, fern-structured branches. As he disappeared into the forest, the light shimmering off the tree branches seemed to give him a kind of halo in the early light.

Be safe out there, Birdy. You're one of my favorites.

Of course, my friend. You as well.

It felt forced because it was. His intensity made her uncomfortable. The way he spoke to her, like he had some kind invisible ownership, made her want to crawl out of her skin.

Birdy climbed up behind James, sealing her outlanding helmet. As they drove off towards the porter bay, leaving Rand to walk the short distance to the transmitter tower, a memory bubbled up from her past. Rupert Gelecki. He'd had two pet snakes, a Brazilian Rainbow boa and a Gopher. After school sometimes, to avoid the kids who would call her names, she'd go to his house and watch him feed skittish mice to the great, sleepy snakes. She would watch the mice run circles around the cage, mesmerized, while they eventually tired and forgot that the snake was even there. Then, death.

She listened to the thrum of the engine, felt the bumps as the bike rolled over sticks and navigated through the piney forest at the outskirt of Mountain. She sat, chest pounding, not even knowing why she was afraid.

The porter bay was as much a disaster as her lab had been. The secure housing for the control panel had been shattered, with elephant glass scattered all over the floor.

James whistled slowly. "That's a problem."

Birdy could only nod, her heart sinking into her stomach.

The panel itself had been pried open, and several cut wires were exposed. They were clean, sharp cuts, as i whoever had been "working" on the machine had left in a hurry. Although the power light was on, it blinked yellow—not enough energy. More concerning: where the main power controls had been severed, thick, fingerlike tendrils of Phlax had grown together, forming a makeshift connection. Even in the dusty morning light, they glowed a soft bioluminescent blue.

James cut at one of the thick growths with his field knife. The power light flickered as a few of the strands broke, turning a pale grey and crumbling to dust.

"Amazing," Birdy murmured more to herself than to James. "It's like they've healed the connection."

"Too bad they had to," James said, picking up a piece of the elephant glass. "Someone didn't want this porter to work, either." The glass cover had been smashed, the likely weapon a piece of rebar that lay discarded on the bay floor.

"OW!"

Birdy turned to see blood oozing from his arm, his other hand already applying pressure.

"Oh, are you okay?"

"Fine," James said. "A piece of loose glass. Don't worry about me. I know a good doctor."

She smiled thinly as he pulled dressings from his pack and began to wrap the cut.

Birdy stepped out of the porter for a moment and caught the signal of Rand nearing the transmitter with Kenner close behind.

Someone cut all the wires here, too, she sent. But for some reason, the porter looks like its working.

Get as much information as you can. Take all the video

you need, Rand sent. Hopefully it will help us figure out what's going on.

Birdy stepped back in to see Jame tapping on the emergency diagnostics screen.

"What is that?" Birdy breathed.

What spewed onto the small screen was a mass of images, numbers, and symbols. Strange geometries. Above, the porter oculus blinked yellow once, twice, then a steady green.

"I've never seen an error like that," James said, his bushy eyebrows knitted. "What do you think it means?"

"I don't know."

The ion field throbbed to life—the normally bright yellow translucent field now a bright and glittering blue. It grated against Birdy's already frayed nerves like a bell going off in her head. And somewhere from within the field, there was the rush of water. The sound of static on a bad telephone connection. A sound of voices.

Birdy could almost make them out. Without thinking, she began to walk in.

IV

THE TRANSMITTER LAY to the east of the base, and the way it looked against the red water of the lake it reminded Rand of a painting his mother had done once of a windmill at the edge of the ocean. She had been a good painter. Not amazing, but she'd had an eye for color before the macular degeneration blinded her. He felt a sudden sense of loss. A nostalgia that flashed bright and then was gone.

On the feed, he could see all the members of the crew, but that did nothing for his nerves. Something felt final and he couldn't help but think of sitting back to back with Lee, bullets flying overhead. He had a feeling. The clarity he sometimes felt that life and death are separated by the thinnest of lines.

A heavy set of thoughts, but he couldn't escape them. He had shit the bed on this mission and people were going to die. Everyone knew it, himself most of all.

He climbed up the ladder to the top and pried the door open. As usual, the phlax had grown strong here, attracted to the thick cables of the transmitter. As he stepped inside, the intricate patterns of blue astounded him. Circles and swoops. Geometric shapes trapped in three dimensions. And all of it glowing gently in the darkness of the tower.

Rand sat down and looked at the port history of the transmitter. The porter doors didn't work without a power to send someone's signal into space. It meant you had to have two parts to jump to Earth or Leto or anywhere. With the door closed, he would have expected the transmitter to be disabled. But no. Someone had needed to send something back to Earth. Not a person, but information. You didn't need a porter for that. Simply a very good signal.

He checked the dates. Someone had been up here as recently as a few days ago. Maybe the same person who severed the lines that ran the transmitter, and they had done it mere hours before he had brought the team on this godforsaken mission.

They sent a message. Not to Texas. That message came from somewhere else on the planet. No. Another message was sent. This time to Alabama.

"No," Rand whispered, his heart sinking into his feet. "Nonono..."

He blinked into the administrative panel, looking for a log of credentials. It was sloggy and backwards, showing the oldest logs first. He blinked past Marcus' name, Jenny, Cassie...

Who sent that message? Who sent it?

His eyes lit on the sender, even as he heard Kenner's feet on the landing.

```
Location: Alabama
   Message: Ezrie is on her way. Plan B is in
motion. Make sure she gets here on time.
   Admin Approval: Rand Everton
```

He heard the footsteps too late. Such quiet, sneaking steps.

Kenner unloaded the laster into Rand. He felt his body drop, every cell shaking and burning.

Why, Kenner, why?

Kenner knelt beside him, careful not to touch his wracked body.

"I'm sorry it had to end like this, boss. But someone had to be the first, and you're the one in charge."

You bastard! Rand screamed behind paralyzed lips. *You traitor! I will drag you down to hell with me...*

Kenner dropped the bag beside his head. Inside, there was a mass of wires and a small digital timer. Rand heard Kenner's footsteps trundling down the ladder.

Rand reached for the bag, but his arms wouldn't move. With all his mental faculties, he flicked his feed to LIVE. Hopefully they would see, hopefully they would know it was Kenner...

Sam.

Rand had time to think her name. The universe slowed and he saw their life: all the mistakes he had made; what he wished he had done differently. He had never wanted to leave her alone. But he had done it, over and over.

The light came, then. Voices whispered that she would not be alone. He would be with her. They would all be together soon.

V

JAMES GRABBED HER HAND, pulling her back from the alien ion field with a snap.

"Birdy, don't!"

From all around, she felt a cracking boom that split the air. The shock wave slammed Birdy's sternum, knocking the air from her lungs and dropping her to her knees. The drop seemed to break whatever magic the porter had woven over her. James stumbled to the doorway and she scrambled after him, staring at the black smoke that billowed from the transmitter tower.

"Oh my God," Birdy gasped.

Metal screamed and she felt a blast of heat and flame. The antenna of the transmitter wavered for a moment, then one of the tower legs, white with heat, crumpled, dropping the entire tower to the ground with a thunderous crash.

"Stay here," James said, grabbing the medical kit. "Don't go through the porter!"

"James!" she called, but her voice was drowned as the remaining tower legs crashed down. Flames ripped through the forest, turning the sky dark and making her cough. James disappeared into the fire.

Her trace blinked once, then showed a warning:

CANNOT CONNECT TO TRACE NETWORK

She felt tears at her eyes, and she put a hand to her forehead.

"No, no, no. This is not happening."

From behind her, the ion field of the porter flickered blue. The light above blinking green.

Come

Birdy dashed away from the porter, terrified that she had almost walked through, terrified of what lay in front of her. There was nothing in her mind—no maps, no trace markers, just a blank trace overlay with a blinking error: CANNOT CONNECT TO TRACE NETWORK.

Ahead of her, through the trees, she glimpsed James. He ran towards the burning hulk of the transmitter, then quickly change directions. Birdy pushed her muscles as hard as they could go. She nearly got lost in the smoke of the tower, but then saw the red of James' pack lying on the ground in a small clearing. As Birdy neared, she could see James kneeling beside the burned body of Rand, his head mostly gone. One of his eyes hung loosely from the socket.

She stalled, her legs stopping too slowly. *I don't want to see this, I can't do this.* Her eyes wanted to shut the horror out, but she forced them open, willing her legs to move forward. *Rand is in trouble. I have to help.*

But as she rounded a bush, Kenner came out from the smoke on the side nearest the burning transmitter, holding a laster in his hand. He didn't see her, it seemed. James didn't either. And by the time Birdy realized what he was doing, her scream of warning was too late.

Kenner pulled the trigger, and James' body dropped to the forest floor, the medical kit spilling on the ground.

"No!" Birdy's scream resounded in the forest.

Kenner's eyes snapped up to meet her own, his face pale and grim.

She wheeled around again, pumping her legs as fast as they could go in the opposite direction.

have to get through the porter, have to tell them—

Birdy's lungs burned, her breathing loud and pained. There was no time to think. She wove through the forest as best she could, praying for God to help her.

The door to the porter bay loomed closer, the ground giving way to the gravel of the base. No matter the color of the porter field, she would have to take her chances. She ran inside the porter, arms outstretched for the ion field that still seemed to be drawing her near—

The laster blast dropped her, her momentum flinging her almost into the field, but not quite. She felt an earthquake of pain, but couldn't scream. Her throat, her arms, her jaw were locked in a living rigor mortis, her body flailing without her permission, her eyes frozen open.

Kenner picked up a piece of bent rebar on the floor and smashed the scanner and the transmission motherboard beneath. He beat them mercilessly, enraged, red-faced and slathering. For a moment, Kenner became alien, his face sharpened with intent. A creature she feared.

Please stop, please don't

Kenner turned on her, the rebar still in hand. The porter flickered, the ion field snapped dark.

The world slowed for a moment, and she had an acute pang of loss that she would die here, without Cy.

Then Kenner tossed the weapon aside.

"Are you okay?" Kenner said, his voice tender. Her brain reeled at his tone—the warmth of his concern. She wanted to pull away, to spit and scream. But her muscles could only flex and unflex impossibly fast. He brushed a curl from her face, his fingers leaving a track of burning fire across her cheek. "I'm sorry. But I had to."

maybe James is okay, maybe Rand is alive, maybe this is a nightmare, maybe

Kenner was so close now, his face hovering above hers. Then she was in his arms, still shaking, being carried like an epileptic bride over a threshold. He put her down, setting her back against the porter frame, trussing her arms behind her back with a lynchtie. She could feel the chips of glass and metal pressing through her outlanding slacks and into her buttocks and thighs.

He pulled out a small vial and a hypodermic. "This is not goodbye," Kenner said, his eyes soft. "It's until we meet again."

She felt the needle bite into the fleshy part of her thigh, and in her mind she cried out.

"Why..." she choked at last. "Why?"

"Because this world is too good for them," he said softly. Kenner was close, his eyes gazing into hers. She knew what would come next. The predatory muscles would flex, the reptilian head down and low, as if in sleep. She had the fevered knowledge that Kenner was going to eat her, bite her with fangs that he'd hidden for all these years. "Because the people of God need a paradise. And it wouldn't be paradise without you."

He kissed her, pushing her back with force like a waterfall. She could feel his tongue sliding inside her mouth, that snakelike slither that made her want to scream.

He murmured against her hair. "I have been wanting to do that for a long time."

From the back of her head, she felt a sharp pressure. The world went black.

VI

Ocean Base, *Leto*

Day 4

EZRIE HAD SLEPT BADLY. She had dreamed of her father all night long, although it wasn't quite him. Somehow, he was made of water, a red, aqueous figure that slithered up the side of the cliff she was standing on. He grabbed for her foot, and began to pull her down into a sea of lights—

If only she could get out of here.

Aris sat in the corner of the bunk, beside the little sink and mirror, guarding her like a dog. The android sat so still, her red hair and ponytail making Ezrie wonder if Purple had chosen her exterior himself. She looked like she could be his sister.

Of course, she didn't ask. Ezrie had no interest in talking with her, and had politely told the android to stop communication until further notice. The exact words were, "Shut the hell up or I'll kill myself." The android had gone silent.

The chatter from her trace had also gone silent after Birdy announced they were almost to the other base. Ezrie figured Lee had pulled her off the main team chat. They were probably there now, learning all the magical

166

secrets they needed before traipsing off to track down Marcus which was HER JOB. Instead, she was trapped in a glorified shower room with a broken wrist and a robot nanny.

Ezrie kicked a chair, and it spun haphazardly for a moment before falling. Aris eyed her carefully.

"Aris, what am I doing here?" she yelled, feeling her chest tight, her throat hard.

"You are being confined for your safety." Aris smiled approvingly.

Ezrie sunk to the cot. She was an empty, hollow shell. A relic of a past that no one, *not even she* cared about.

A small private window opened up in her mind.

MARCUS: I NEED YOUR HELP. COME AND FIND ME.

On her trace, there was an alert in red caps.

ADMIN PERMISSIONS GRANTED.

Suddenly, her head filled up with information. Maps.

Leto bloomed before her eyes, locations with names, distances. Ezrie's heart hammered, her vision went sharp. She could see Marcus' location pin clearly embedded in the map of the planet.

EZRIE: MARCUS, YOU PIECE OF SHIT! WHAT'S GOING ON?

But there was nothing else. Merely a blinking cursor on a private chat inside her head.

What could I possibly be able to do for him? She realized she was pacing.

"I'm detecting elevated heart rate," Aris said. "Do you require medical assistance?"

Ezrie was hit with another barrage of files. He was uploading weapons access. Porter access. Aris' controls. She had the entire world in her hands.

It was time to act.

Ezrie blinked into the Aris file and disabled her. The android went slack, rendered lifeless with a single blink of Ezrie's eye.

"I'd say it wasn't personal, but it is," Ezrie said as she stepped past the android to the door as another alert flashed across her trace. At least she hadn't killed her. Ezrie rubbed her earring, like it was a magic lamp. She talked a lot of game, but she'd seen the program in action. Even an android didn't deserve that kind of death.

Then, the trace in her mind gave a warning.

CANNOT CONNECT TO TRACE NETWORK

Ezrie paused. She was off the network.

She blinked quickly to affirm that the maps were still there. Even though she wasn't on the trace, the files had been downloaded. Marcus' location was clear, the map to his location pin still showed perfectly across her trace overlay.

She grabbed her pack and flicked through her new files.

"Schematics," she whispered. "There's got to be a way out of this place."

She found the file and put it onto her overlay. That was a skill she'd learned from Sam, at the same time she'd been earmarking files for herself. She'd pretended to work slowly. But that's because she'd been making copies and hiding them in a subfolder in the only other thing she had access to—or hoped that Purple could give her access to—the porter operating system files.

Purple had been helpful, after all.

As Ezrie snuck past the control room, she saw Lee and Purple. Something was going on, playing out on the massive globe at the center of the room.

"Rand!" Lee shouted. "Birdy!" She turned on Purple. "What the hell is going on over there?"

"I don't know," Purple spluttered. "Everything was fine. The chatter on the feed was totally normal and then it just went dark—"

"Rand," Sam was shouting into the void. "Rand, come in. Can you hear me?"

"Double-check the transmitter," Lee barked. "We need to see if it's a tech glitch on our end."

Ezrie slipped out the exit at the end of the women's hallway, careful to move quickly, but as quietly as possible. Once she was outside, she was keenly aware of the crunching sound every step of her boots made on the on the gravel.

Come on, Ezrie. Got to move faster. Got to get to the bikes.

She nearly bypassed the porter. Why go back for it when Marcus had already given her all the maps she needed? *Because you can't trust the hand that feeds you, ever,* she thought.

The porter bay's door opened easily for her, her newfound admin permissions putting everything in her power. Ezrie popped open the control console and manually navigated to the core running files. She was relieved to find that her little stash of documents was still there, embedded in the new, clean OS. While Purple had been yammering on and on about androids, she had been transferring her folder from Sam's phlax-infected storage. Birdy's personal Leto maps complete with annotations. All of Marcus' personal logs.

She blinked into the folder and began downloading.

"Stop."

She turned slowly.

Purple's weapon was shaking, but trained on her chest. He gulped hard, his hand fingering the trigger. He was angry, the blood at his cheeks like circles against his pale skin. "I'm such a knob. I completely believed your whole bag."

"I'm here to find Marcus."

"None of it!" he spat. "You gonna blow us up, too?"

"I don't know anything about that," she said. "All I know is that Marcus is here, and he probably knows a shit-ton more about what's going on that you or me." She took a step towards him. "You can come with me. We can do it together. I promise we'll come back and fix the porter."

On her trace, the download completed.

"You can't leave," he said, "And if you don't stop on your own, I'm going make you."

Purple pulled the trigger, but Ezrie rushed him at the same time, knocking the weapon from his hand and sending the blast into the ceiling. He grabbed her by the wrist before she could run, twisting it up behind her back.

Ezrie yelped, the bone of the bad wrist flaring with acid pain. She turned into him as hard as she could, jabbing her free elbow into his neck.

Purple's grip faltered, and she punched him with her good arm. He stumbled back, and she dove for the weapon, turned, and shot.

Purple dropped to the ground, shuddering from head to toe.

She glanced at the laster, but couldn't see the setting in the dark. Knowing Purple, it couldn't be more than stun. That meant he'd be fine in a few hours. But she didn't have time to worry about it, now. It was too late anyway. She'd already shot him.

Ezrie stepped around him, sticking the laster into the waistband of her outlanding gear and closing the door behind her. At least that way no one would see him before they needed to.

She ran across the campus towards the motorcycle hangar, thinking about what Lee had said. If the bikes were DNA-coded, how would she be able to get one to move?

She took a gulp as she pressed her hand to the control panel. To her amazement, the bike lit up.

Welcome, Ezrie, the bike integration flickered on her trace overlay.

She slipped her hands into the handlebar recess and felt the bike smooth and shift to her size. The engine roared into life, a deep rumbling beneath her.

"If you're gonna travel Leto, do it in style," she muttered.

"Stop right there, you little blacker bitch!"

From over her shoulder, Ezrie could see Lee racing towards her now, her arms pumping, her face red and murderous. Lee shot the laster into the air between them, seemingly ready to kill Ezrie at a distance, if necessary.

Ezrie twisted the accelerator, and the bike wove and slid below her in the sandy soil. She cursed the bike and the ground, but then the bike leapt forward, thrusting her into the jungle too fast for Lee's laster blast to connect with.

"Don't you dare run from me!" Lee shouted. "I'll kill you!"

Ezrie caught a glimpse over her shoulder of Lee's wild-eyed glare as she mounted the other bike. The snake on Lee's arm writhed as she twisted her bike into motion. Ezrie barely missed a massive tree branch, almost losing control of the bike in the process.

Focus, Ezrie, she thought. *No time to look back now.*

Even then, she could barely keep the bike from smashing into the colored tree trunks that seemed to appear out of nowhere.

Ezrie could feel Lee behind her, gaining. She was stronger, more attuned to Leto than she ever could be. Ezrie didn't have time to be scared. She only had time to survive.

VII

LEE LEVELED her foot to the floor, speeding through the deepening dark like a devil. The motorcycle made deep gouges in the tall, brown grass, but none of that mattered. Ezrie couldn't outrun her forever. Besides, she was untrained and on a foreign planet. When Lee caught up with her, there would be hell to pay.

On her trace, Lee zoomed in on Ezrie. The woman had guts, but no brains. Marcus had given her maps, a bike, everything. And it was Kenner's bag that showed in the last few seconds of Rand's feed. She swallowed hard, blinking back tears. Rand had been innocent. Cassie had been wrong.

But now, they were both dead. Lee would make sure that Kenner and Ezrie paid for what they'd done.

Lee gunned the bike faster. She could hear the other motor up ahead. They were almost to the sweeps shack. Lee made a vow that Ezrie would never make it.

She gave the bike as much energy as it could take, and it leapt forward at the same time as a pale figure ran across her pathway.

What the—

Lee swore, pulling the bike hard to the left. The motorcycle slipped out from beneath her body, wheels churning the air as it smashed into a tree.

She tumbled, head over heels, through the brush, her head nearly missing the trunk of one of the multicolored trees. She felt herself flying, crumpling, then coming to rest at the foot of a large pink pitcher plant.

Ahead, the green iridescence of Ezrie's bike lit up on Lee's trace, retreating into the darkness and out of range.

She got up, running, staggering after Ezrie despite the pain in her arm and leg.

"You can't run forever! We'll find you!"

Lee stalled out, the pain catching up to her like a freight train, then swore again. She looked behind her, to where the figure had been standing. Lee could only see grass and ferns and the light of the afternoon slipping through the trees.

It couldn't have been her. It couldn't.

But it *had* been.

She picked the bike up, grunting with the effort, ignoring the searing pain from her right shoulder. The bone wasn't in the socket correctly, and she could feel it click and give way.

There was another shift in the underbrush. Something was stalking her. She thought of the blind purple eyes of the lycants, Brindle's arm hanging in ribbons. They didn't attack, usually, but sometimes...

No. If there was something out there, it was human. Lee wasn't crazy. She'd seen a woman in the darkness.

"Cassie?" Lee said hoarsely. "Are you there?"

It wasn't impossible. They hadn't found Cassie's body, maybe she was out here still, hurt, and afraid to come closer.

"It's me, honey," Lee said. "Come on out."

Lee pulled the laster from her belt and scanned the area briefly with her trace, flipping through settings. Infrared. Ion waves. The sweeps shack stood exactly how they had left it a few nights before. The only thing that showed were some small skittering creatures and the flighty bodies of a few zephyrs.

The woods were silent. No echo. No birds.

Had she imagined it? She couldn't say for sure.

Lee mounted the bike, putting the weapon back. She needed to get back to the others. She paused, giving the shack one last look. Cassie was here, she knew it.

A sound in the bushes stopped her. A rustling. A not-quite-human sound.

"Who's there?"

She turned quickly, but not quick enough.

VIII

SAM PUT her pinky fingernail in her mouth and bit it as hard as she could. There was a satisfying tear in the nail, and a pain that suddenly made everything focus. She breathed, then carefully brought her hands to her sides, ripping the broken nail from her finger and smoothing the edge as best she could. Bad habits died hard.

The great globe map of Leto was empty except for a flashing error message: CANNOT CONNECT TO TRACE NETWORK, over and over again. All the icons that represented the Artemis team—her team, her friends—were gone. There was no telling who was alive and who was dead.

The base was quiet. And it was getting dark.

WHERE ARE YOU, she sent to Purple and Lee, already knowing the response.

CANNOT CONNECT TO TRACE NETWORK

"Shit," she muttered under her breath. Sam felt a wave of numbness trickle down her spine.

She wanted to leave Alex, to follow wherever Lee and Purple had gone. But she couldn't bear to stare at the empty globe. Couldn't bear to keep calling out to her husband who had gone silent. Couldn't leave her last and only patient. The last person who needed her.

Sam worked in the infirmary until late into the night, connecting Alex's trace locally to the lab monitor. As he slept, she monitored his progress. Systolic arrhythmia. Kidney failure. Lung incontinence.

Sam scanned her own database—the only database she had left—for saved files from nursing school. There had been an entire four-week segment in the last year of nursing school on porter flu, complete with a two-hour lecture on different ways to categorizing the death for billing purposes: genetic deterioration, teleportation malfunction, mass organ degeneration. There had to be something about best practices.

Alex moaned, his eyes fluttering for a moment. When he opened them, there was blood trickling from their corners again. His skin had gone flaccid, especially around his cheeks, and it gave the impression of a demon wearing a costume that looked like her friend.

She brushed hair back from her face. There was no time to mourn, no time to think.

Oh, but there will be plenty of time now, won't there? Said a cold voice in her head. *Because we're not going anywhere, Sam. No one is going anywhere.*

It sounded almost like Rand.

She knew better. Rand was dead. Just like the rest of them.

Just like you'll be, soon enough.

"No," she moaned. "I won't believe that."

She had seen Rand cry over the broken body of Junior, the yellow lab that had become their surrogate baby. She had seen him sweat over the exact wording of public debriefings, asking her for suggestions on words that sounded "smarter than he was." She had held his head to her chest, their bodies slick with sweat, and listened to him tell the dark secrets about what he wished and dreamed when no one was around.

And now he was gone. She hated herself for being angry with him. Their last words shouldn't have been in anger.

But his last word wasn't. Sam had felt it almost as much as she had read it, the last word that came across her trace before it blinked to black: SAM.

Now there was nothing but a dead space in her brain where his avatar should have been. Where they all should have been.

She went into the larger surgical room where Alex was not, and opened up the cupboards. His vitals still beeped on the display, highlighting his diminishing lung capacity. It wouldn't be more than a few hours and he would go into renal failure, then lung failure or heart failure. And then, it would only be her.

She flicked the IV bag. Empty. She should refill it.

What I should do is put him out of his misery, she thought. *Turn up the opioids and let him drift painlessly to sleep.*

Yes, she decided. *That's what I'll do. But first...*

After a few minutes of desperate scrambling, she found a bottle of plain old-fashioned rubbing alcohol. She sat on the floor, cross-legged, the way she had always done when she was in high school. She tried to imagine it was her mother's whiskey, the one she filled up with water to make the difference invisible. Sam swallowed the alcohol, cringing at the taste and anticipating the dark nothingness that it brought.

She gagged but forced herself to swallow it back down.

I don't believe it, I don't believe it, I don't believe it's real.

She blinked into her own trace record, her eyes tearing, her stomach tearing.

Rand would know what to do. He would come in and hold her hair back, like he had in the early days. He would murmur the mantra that she had created: This is the first day of the last drink.

She heard herself crying, screaming. The walls echoed the sound of her voice back to her.

"Rand," she said, when she was able to speak. She blinked her trace open. "Show me Rand."

She was suddenly in Oceanside. The day shone bright, even beneath the protection of the sun hut. The invisible ion barrier made it look like they were out in the open, and had cost a pretty penny even compared to the money that they had spent on food, luxurious hotels, and vintage wine. There were other families and a few couples in their own little protected bubbles. The ocean was visible, though far too acidic for swimming. She'd read about an immigrant family earlier in the year that had ignored the ban. The whole family was hospitalized. The little boy had lost both of his legs below the knee.

But inside the sun hut, it was only Rand and her basking in the smell of sea salt and virgin margaritas. There were seagulls casting shadows on their food—Sam had made a cold pasta salad from scratch and Rand had pretended to be thoroughly impressed with her domesticity.

She knew she was really in the cold medical wing on an alien planet. Still, on her trace, Rand looked so real and close by. He was reading a book, barely paying attention. She could see the stubble on his face. But his eyes had that disconnected look to them, even when he looked at Sam. Especially. Like he was zooming, but not quite. As if he were in some invisible world far away.

"Tell me you love me," she says.

He touches her leg, his face melting into a smile. He had always been fond of her legs. He called them "come-on legs."

"Of course I do," he says, reaching over and kissing her.

Sam dims the sun hut so that no one can see them. But he does not open up his trace to her, not even now.

The v-feed ended and Sam dropped her head in her hands.

Something about it was odd. What was it that she felt she was missing.

Tell me you love me.

Of course I do.

That's what it was. He didn't tell her he loved her. Not at all.

"No," she slurred, her lips tasting the metal of the floor as she did. "I'm not thinking that."

That's the denial again, Rand whispered in her head. *That's what a professional would say.*

"You shut up. You don't know anything."

The world was doubling up. She finished the bottle and vowed that she was done. Just because everything had gone shit-side-up didn't mean she could be unprofessional.

"I'm being very professional," she said to the beeping monitors, too loudly.

"Sorry," she whispered. "Now. Now, I'm being professional. Starting now."

Sam staggered out of the room and closed the facility door behind her. Her head was so light and fuzzy, like a feather blanket. Or a balloon wrapped in fur. This idea made her giggle, and when she drooled on her outlanding shirt, she broke into a crazy mixture of laughter and sobbing that made her feel fulfilled and hollow all at the same time.

She couldn't help but remember the snippet from Rand's trace that she had seen. The small, embarrassed smile from Jenny.

No. Not now. Rand is dead, goddammit. I'm undergoing trauma and imagining things. Time to be professional, not jump to conclusions.

"I'm...being...PROFESSIONAL!" she shouted down the metal hallway. "This is me BEING PROFESSIONAL!"

From down the hall, she heard bootsteps.

"Unidentified—" Aris' voice snapped off, mid-sentence.

There was the sound of metal being smashed, a motor running down. Sam tried to pull herself up from her place on the floor, but she slipped, and fell. The door to the surgical room opened, there were muddy boots. Women's boots. Small.

"Lee?" The words tumbled, and the room was spinning. "Did you find Ezrie?"

She saw inhuman eyes. An impossibly perfect hand. Then nothing.

IX

EZRIE RODE DEMONICALLY, as if the past were chasing her. On the trace, Leto rose before her in the groves and trees of the jungle. Names of animals flittering across her brain as Birdy's field notes integrated with the map that Marcus had sent her.

Tontors.

Ulilax.

Kimbas.

These creatures were strange, and were made stranger by the infrared of the trace's night-vision. She blinked it on, catching a flurry of activity everywhere she rode.

By night, Ezrie had moved out of the jungle into a green grassland area. There were rolling hills here, and river ran through the middle of it. She decided to follow the river up, since Marcus' map suggested it. Birdy's field notes also mentioned that the river—the Chalice River—wound through the mountains all the way to the north side of Leto's great landmass, and that it was "the largest and most impressive river" that Birdy had ever seen.

The evening was hot and muggy beside the river. She unloaded from the motorcycle, stiff and hungry and still. Lee could still behind her, but Ezrie thought she'd lost her, the sound of the other bike vanishing hours before.

She filled the water bottle from the stream and put the water filter head on top. The water was red like grape juice. Ezrie was dubious. She ate three food tubes instead, and spent the next hour bungling about, attempting to turn the the book-sized package into a tent.

By the time she was finished, it was well past dark, and there were hooting noises coming from the clusters of long-haired trees that grew alongside the water. She fiddled with the button on the side of the tent and an ion field projected over the tent like a bowl over a mouse.

There was no bedroll or blankets, but Ezrie didn't mind. The air was warm and the ion field kept out the bugs. She would have to look up Birdy's notes on how to avoid being eaten alive by them. Already she had two huge welts where something had tried to suck her blood while she was setting the tent up.

Ezrie gazed up through the ion shimmer that protected the tent and tried to count the stars. So many. Thousands and thousands. Far above, a distant blue orb hung in the sky. Leto's only moon—Delos, is what the notes said. Ezrie snacked on a peach cobbler dessert tube in the quiet of the Leto night and felt something like peace. Purpose.

She blinked into Marcus' files. Notes on the porter issues. Medical records. Personal logs.

It was funny to be so close to him after all this time and still not know anything about him. All she knew was what she remembered. What was on the news. There were few records of his personal life, and she was curious.

March 7th, 2078

Frustrated with the lack of respect from members of the team. Cassie clearly doesn't understand what I'm here to do. The porter setup is my jurisdiction, and I really need a full support staff to make sure that it's going the right way. I'm tired of her degrading me in front of the other crew

members. Really fed up. Talking with Zhong
later about potentially going to Toron
instead. This has been a nightmare.

She snorted. Egotistical, entitled, and complaining. That sounded about right.

Ezrie closed the files, convicted by her plan. Whether or not Marcus needed help, she had come here for one reason and one reason alone.

She got up and grabbed the knife from the pack. Kenner had known she would need it. She ran her thumb over the blade carefully. It reminded her of that other knife so long ago. The one she brought from the DePalma's and had hid while she walked down the bustling hallways of Elsevior University.

If I had been older. If I had been stronger.

Ezrie nestled the knife beneath her, both hands on the handle. She felt like a child—weary from a hard day and holding to her best toy. She raised her hand to the earring and rubbed it. There was some comfort in the knowledge that, this time, the game was for keeps.

$$X$$

Elsevior College Campus, Santa Monica, California, *Earth*

February, 2066

MARCUS SITS in the leather chair that should have been her father's. He is young, his hair dirty blonde and his eyes brown as coffee. Through the door, she can see the security guard waiting outside the door. Ezrie is four-teen and she knows that the De Palma's won't take her back. Not after this. She feels the knife in her pocket, not really knowing why it's there, but also knowing exactly why it's there.

"What do you want to say to me, Ezrie?"

"You said that you would make things right."

Marcus nods. "And how do I do that?"

"Tell everyone the truth. That's all I ever wanted."

He sighs. He looks tired.

"You and I both know that if your father's name is on this invention, Ezrie, no one will buy it. Not the way he died. It will be a liability even before we can get it to where it will help people the most."

"But..." She can't think of words fast enough, big enough. Her skin feels exposed, raw. Like when she first got to the group home. The resident leader tried to make her stop taking chemical showers, but she snuck in anyway to wash phantom blood from her skin. She could never wash it away, the rasping, wet sound of her name on his lips.

"I wish it was different, but you're old enough to at least understand that, aren't you? I can give the machine credibility. I can get it to the people who will immortalize your dad's life and work. Do you understand? And really, it doesn't matter who gets the credit as long as the right thing gets done. Does that make sense? You'll know the truth. I'll know the truth. And when the time is right, I'll tell everyone."

She does not have the words. There is sorrow in her throat, clogging them up, pushing them back into her brain where they would fester and infect and become a rage that would eat her piece by piece.

"You're a liar," Ezrie whispers.

"What?"

"You said you would help, and you didn't. You came and I told you—"

Promise, Ezrie. Promise that you'll get rid of it.

"—I broke promises for you," she says. "This isn't what my dad wanted."

"Your dad was sick. Richard Collings was brilliant, but at the end, he wasn't in his right mind. Neither were you."

She gripped the knife so tightly, she nearly cut her own hand from the pressure.

"I promised to get rid of it," she says, pulling the knife out. "I promised."

She lunges across the desk, but she is so small, so unprepared. He grabs her wrists and holds them tight.

"You don't want to do this, Ezrie," he says. "You can't bring him back by killing me."

He's right. She doesn't want to kill him. But she wants something, and she doesn't know what it is or how to say it.

Then the guard is pulling her off of him. He puts her in handcuffs, and blinks a message.

"No," Marcus says. "Take her home."

"But Professor," the guard says, "that's not how we manage—"

"Ezrie didn't do any harm. Find out where she needs to be and get her there."

They scan her trace and call Lisbeth De Palma. She flies in from Newark, asking questions that Ezrie doesn't answer: How did you get here? Where did you get the money? What in God's name were you thinking?

It is not long after that the De Palma's give up on her. And not long after that, she arrives on Matt and Bethany Peterson's doorstep. And soon she realizes that if someone is to save her, it will be herself.

PART 4
GREEN IS FOR GROWING

"Blacking, like any performance art, is about diversion. Like a magician, you learn to keep your audience's eye on the cards in your hand, not the one behind your back."

The BlackBook, Last Accessed 2072

I

Mountain Base, *Leto*

Day 5

BIRDY AWOKE COUGHING AND SPLUTTERING. Feathers. There were feathers in her throat. No. It had been a dream. Cy's birds had flown into her mouth. She had been screaming, but making no sound.

She tried to scramble to her feet, but her wrists were still tied behind her and she wrenched them uncomfortably in her shoulder sockets. She had a crick in her neck. Where was she?

She coughed, blinked awake, and then remembered heavily. She was in the porter bay.

"Let me out! Let me out, please!"

The half-completed porter bay was silent but for the ringing from her empty screams. The porter bay door had been shut, the porter itself silent and lifeless as the hot, dead air trapped inside. The only sound was the buzzing of a tetchfly. On the floor rolled the empty glass bottle of whatever Kenner had drugged her with, the syringe nearby. The air was close and sweet—thick with decay.

He'd left her to die.

Birdy used her tongue to wriggled out the straw hiding in the neck of the outlanding suit. She took a sip, trying not to think of the water that the suit had collected from her body. Then, failing, heaved a watery vomit, the taste of her tongue suddenly repulsive.

Kenner had kissed her. He had killed James and Rand, and then he'd *kissed her*.

She struggled against the bindings. They were tight, but if she stretched her chest a little, they stretched with her. Her shoulder knocked against something, and it fell behind her. She strained over her shoulder to see a bottle of water rolling towards the curve of the porter bay wall.

The Living Waters label flashed around and around as the bottle rolled towards the body of James.

She screamed, tried to struggle away, but managed only to clock herself in the back of the head. She moaned.

Kenner had left James in here *with her*—such a misplaced and depraved offering. She could see the charred mark against his temple where the weapon had burned his flesh.

What if he comes back? What if he's waiting until I'm awake to open the door and finish the job, what if—

Stop it, the cool voice in her head retorted. *It's time to be smart.*

She took a deep breath, trying to push the fog and fear from her mind. *Okay, Meshelle. What would a smart girl do?*

It was something her mother would say. The kind of gem Ladora Arnold would pull out when Birdy as wilting over a math problem that was too hard. It was the voice Ladora Arnold had used right before the only time she'd ever hit Birdy.

"Don't you dare give up," Ladora had said, her wiry arms on her hips, out of breath. Birdy had been talking about the girls who said she shouldn't be a Berylhurst Prep. She had said the one word that she knew she shouldn't: *quit*.

Ladora Arnold had slapped her, her hands dry and ashy from washing dishes after her long day of working at the desal plant. Wherever there was water, her mother was working.

"You ain't no shadow, baby. You're smart. So don't let me ever hear you say that word again, clear?"

Birdy's cheek smarted from the memory. Her mother had been right. So she'd gone back to Berylhurst with a new goal: find friends and keep them. Birdy had been smart enough to know that she needed people. Numbers. There was safety in the herd.

Now, there was no herd. Except James. And she didn't feel like keeping company with him.

Birdy looked around, willing herself to focus. There were shards of metal all over the floor, but it looked like Kenner had picked up all the broken pieces of elephant glass and thrown them into a pile of scrap metal beside the door. Still, she wondered if there could be something, some small sliver of something that she could use to slice through the ties. The first aid kit had been abandoned, contents strewn on the floor. There would be a scalpel in there. That could cut through a lynchtie, easy.

She kicked her heel out and managed to catch a thin piece of metal beneath her boot. She dragged it closer until she could position the metal behind her back. After several attempts she had it in her fingers.

A small success, but it flooded Birdy with accomplishment.

"That's how we do it in the 'hood," she said, channeling Marley Jameson, a braid-wearing, big-assed girl that she'd palled around with until getting into Berylhurst.

Back and forth, she worked her makeshift blade over the Kevlar line. By the time the sun went down, she was drenched in sweat, her throat burning. She could feel the sting of salt in blistered patches on her wrists, and her hands ached from crimping around the tiny piece of metal. The rope had given up only a few fuzzy strands. She bowed her head and cried.

Night moved in without a sound. It made her skin crawl. Even the tetchfly that had been inadvertently sentenced along with her had fallen silent. Perhaps it had become a victim to the heat, or was simply following a Circadian-type impulse to rest when the greater of Leto's suns went down. Either way, she watched Aeos sink lower until it was swallowed by night, the silence from her trace deafening.

She hummed some old songs from the Nets to pass the time. Her raspy voice creeped her out, though, especially as James' body began to deteriorate and emit decay smells and gas. She had to focus on something else.

Birdy dug through her database. She wasn't a music-saving kind of girl —she wanted to keep her space open for field notes and downloading articles she found. But she had saved a few songs. The one she played now was "Lonely," by General Reep, and it became the soundtrack of her capture—a melodic, moving, and surprisingly hopeful balled that Cy had sung to her more than once. If they ever got married, she had hoped it would be the song that they danced to for the first time.

> *"There's never a night dark enough*
> *Where you can't shine.*
> *There's never a place high enough*
> *Where you can't rise.*
> *So when all the world falls down*
> *And there's no one to care*
> *Baby, when you're alone, I'll be there..."*

She replayed it over and over as she worked. It made her think of Cy, chasing her down the cobbled street with his umbrella, trying to cover her from the rain that she didn't know was coming. She often found that she was crying without knowing it.

Her shoulder blades ached, the post of the porter door jutting into her back, pulling her chest out uncomfortably.

"Baby, when you're alone, I'll be there..." she hummed, her voice raspy and dry. She had been sawing for what felt like hours, mostly to pass the time. It wasn't doing any good, she knew. Kenner would be coming back, but how soon? She needed to think of something better. But all she could think of was that she was hungry.

Dear God, she was hungry.

James' body gave another urping blat, filling her nostrils with methane and the sweet smell of overripe fruit. She could imagine the lycants now, somewhere nearby, the smell of decay as attractive to them as pollen to a bee.

Don't think about it. Try not to think

But she couldn't not think of their slippery wolf bodies and glittering purple eyes. How they would open their smiling mouths that nearly encircled their long faces showing teeth like metal barbs. She had been there when Tukuafu had wrapped Brindle's arm, the skin hanging in shreds like torn piñata paper...

She sobbed, a little moan coming from her throat unbidden. She could see it now, the lycants outside the door, unhinging their jaws like a reptiles to swallow her whole.

She closed her eyes tightly.

You're going to die here. You need to be aware of the high probability.

"Stop," she whispered. "I don't need that right now."

He said he'd be back. He promised.

But what did that mean? Her stomach hitched again, but she managed to keep the bile down. He might be back, but would what he was planning be worse that what she knew was out there in the wild?

Don't you give up, Ladora whispered in her ear. *Don't you dare let him win.*

Birdy dropped the little metal shard. There had to be a smarter way.

She stretched her neck up, feeling the tendons strain on the verge of crimping. She had studied the design of the porter in college—a prerequisite for anyone interested in offworlding. She'd found that the biology of a machine was almost as interesting as the biology of a creature. It ran on mechanical and chemical processes, and there were parts to be dissected, categorized, and examined on a microscopic level.

The two pillars which supported the porter doorway were made of a titanium-beryllium alloy. They rose up and connected in an arch where the receiver, the oculus, sat at the apex of the machine. On one side, the side she was tied to, luckily enough, a control box was situated. Birdy tried not to think of Kenner smashing through the elephant glass that protected the controls. She'd been lucky she hadn't been closer. A shard of elephant glass could through human skin fast as a field knife.

"Oh. My. Goodness," Birdy spluttered, wishing she could smack her own forehead. "As if the answer wasn't literally right above your head."

She ignored the stabbing pain in her back against the jagged pillar as she pulled herself to her feet. Her legs, mobilized after sitting for almost a day, screamed pins and needles. She moved slower, positioning the broken scanner box above her hand.

Birdy misjudged, bringing her arm against the destroyed box too soon. She hissed a breath in, feeling her skin slice open like soft cheese. The outlanding suit was built tough, but not that tough. There was a bloom of red along her forearm.

"I'm not going to die," Birdy said through gritted teeth. "I'm too smart to die."

She slid up slower this time, finally at a vantage point to see the scanner box fully. It had been smashed, the glass broken. But the elephant glass protective housing—held in place by a tension hinge—was sticking straight into the air, the shattered edges making it look like a sundial in the pale, blue moonlight.

Birdy could see no moon through the window.

She heard a gasping, raking sound from the ground behind her.

She pulled towards the sound thoughtlessly, feeling the sharp edge of the glass against her hand, cutting it open. She gasped in pain and surprise. On the ground behind her, James' body rocked from side to side. His gaping eyes and mouth revealed a thin, blue light glowing from somewhere inside. It reminded Birdy of Halloween, when they would put flashlights in their mouths and the red light would flow out wherever it could—the cheeks, the eyes, sometimes lighting up a nose.

It's not happening, none of this is real, death is the end of the life cycle, there is nothing real here, this is a hallucination brought on by stress and hunger, drugs—

Birdy sawed madly at the lynchties, straining to see her work. From behind her, James slowly, heavily, propped himself up on his elbows and knees, the light bleeding from every pore.

She screamed as she felt another of the strands give way. She pulled her hands apart, stretching the final cords taut as she sawed at them. The glass beneath her wiggled dangerously, the vigor of her motion threatening to rip it from the hinge.

The throbbing blue light was now bright enough to illuminate the entire porter bay. James launched himself up, staggering, to his feet. James' mouth, fixed in a perfect "o" of a silent scream, searched the bay, eyes shining like lighthouse beacon.

The light landed on Birdy for a fraction of a second before the last of the kevlar cord cut loose. She felt as though that stare was looking inside her, burning whatever sanity she had left. James stepped toward her, the light bearing down from his eyes, his mouth.

She dropped to the ground, scrambling backwards on bloodied hands, her chest tight with the screams she was suddenly too afraid to release.

James tracked her, but poorly. His awkward body staggered, as if drunk. He flailed towards her, grasping with meaty, swollen hands. She launched herself to the door lock, her hand pressed as hard against it as she could.

ACCESS DENIED

James lunged at her, his head lolling from side to side. She picked up a piece of rebar from the floor. When he stepped closer, she swung at him feebly. He knocked the bar from her hand, and she tumbled to the ground. He leered, groping at her, his face fiendishly blue with ethereal light.

She ducked away, scuttling along the walls, tripping over debris from the half-finished porter.

James was slow, his synapses impaired. She was fast. She was smart.

She was skinny.

Birdy looked up at the slim window that edged the dome of the porter bay, her brain calculating probabilities. Not good. Even if she could jump eleven feet up, she'd have to find a way to break through the glass...

She ducked as James came at her again, nearly doubled over as he grabbed for her. She spotted the rebar and lunged for it, scrambling up just in time to hit James in the back.

The blow was lucky, catching his unsteady legs off-center. He sprawled forward, moaning.

There was no way she could make it, unless...

Birdy clamored up the porter support beam, using the control panel as a foothold.

All you gotta do is jump. You can do this...

James got to his feet quicker than she'd anticipated. He was getting faster. He lunged.

She leapt to the small lip of concrete that ridged the porter bay, her legs flinging free while her hands scrambled for purchase. The rebar in her hand clanged, but the bent section caught on the edge of the window. She pulled herself up as James grabbed at her, nearly catching her foot.

Birdy shimmied away from the edge where his bloated fingers grabbed at her boots. She swung the rebar at him, hitting him in the face until he stumbled back.

"Get...offa...me!" she screamed, punctuating with the weapon.

James roared, stumbling back. She turned again, intent on breaking through the glass. She brought the rebar down in an awkward motion over and over, her own screams and cries far off and dim.

The glass cracked, starred. Behind her, James reached up, his fingers touching the fabric of her jumpsuit. She screamed, bashing at them, knocking herself in the leg in the process. She winced, then wriggled closer to the window, finding purchase on the ledge, giving herself as much room as possible before one last kick through the window.

The glass panel disintegrated into a framework of shatterproof cells. Then, Birdy kicked the whole thing out, letting in the first real breaths of air she'd had in what felt like days.

Birdy rolled through the window and dropped, not able to stop herself from flailing as she fell nearly twelve feet to the ground. She landed, feeling a twinge of pain in her ankle, but managed to scramble up. She ran, half-limping, as fast as she could to the science lab, locking the door behind her and sliding against the door as if her tiny body could block another attack. She didn't think, just held to the iron staff of rebar with pink knuckles, hardly aware of her own cries.

"I want to go home, I don't want to be here, please, I want to go home—"

After hours, unable to think, unable to be afraid any more, she curled around her makeshift weapon in the safety of the science lab. In her nightmares, James screamed at her soundlessly, his yawning mouth full of eyes.

II

South Chaldees Checkpoint, *Leto*

AS MORNING TURNED into sweltering afternoon, the mountain crawled into view. Kenner pushed the bike up the final incline, engine willing, but phlax-gummed. He flicked the oxygenator of the outlanding suit when he began to feel breathless.

All around him, Leto lay in pale pink blanket of snow, the deep red of the lake and the brilliant purples, greens, and whites of the trees far below him. The mountains were jagged, covered in hoary pink frost, the snow reminding him so much of the store-bought cupcakes the Home would bring in on birthdays. Far below, he could see a flock of sharp-nosed creatures flying through the tops of half-dead trees. Far to the north, he could imagine the white desert beyond the curve of the horizon. Beyond that, destiny.

He killed the engine, drinking in the silence.

But there are voices in the silence, aren't there?

He shuddered the feeling off. No. There were no voices.

Kenner blinked through the settings of his trace. He pulled up the options for connection. *Trace network offline,* the device whispered in his head.

"Damn right, it's offline," he said, gently pressing the pain spot at the back of his head. It had started a couple days before, but it throbbed incessantly now. He took three aspirin and waited for the pain at the back of his head to subside a little before he checked in.

He blinked the numbers that he'd memorized. Kenner had turned them into a cadence, like a Catholic's Hail Mary. An homage to the great work that he was destined to do.

seven four one dash arrow-up dot dot dash

seven four one dash arrow-up dot dot dash

Kenner blinked again, executing the search command. He sat on the ledge of rose-colored ice, strong and exhausted, as if from baling hay or going nine rounds with someone bigger than he. The quietness of the moment was sweet and sad at once.

But listen, Grandam whispered in his head. *If you're very quiet, can't you hear them—*

His trace hitched and buzzed as he trace connected to the other transmitter. Even with the exact knowledge of its location, the transmission whispered *TRANSMISSION: WEAK LINK...TRANSMISSION: WEAK LINK* in his head. It felt almost like a recrimination.

A sliver of guilt wedged in his brain. A sudden fear.

Weak link. As if Leto itself knew what he was doing. Or not doing.

Never.

There was that feeling again. As if everything around him was connected somehow. Watching somehow. Judging him in silent chorus.

He pulled out the letter, hands shaking. He was embarrassed by the creases. How many times had he read and re-read his sacred commission? It helped in the anxious moments. The ones where he felt sure that Leto was a trap he'd fallen into.

My Son, My Disciple,

You are so highly favored. Your dedication
and skill have always been one of my highest

joys. From the time you were small, I saw the spark in you to do great things. This is your chance.

We know that God does not suffer mercy to be robbed by justice. It is for this reason that he has put Living Waters, God's Good Flock, on the earth. The wicked must be held accountable for their acts, and when the blood of the innocent cry to God, he sends you and I to mete out his justice.

There is no malice in this duty. You have always been a reliable disciple. You are a swift angel of justice in a world where evil is justified by even those who believe them-selves righteous.

Now, this is the moment for your great work.

As Joshua called down the walls on the wicked Cannanites, as He struck down the Israelites for their murmuring, as he swal-lowed Korah, Dathan, and Abiram in the earth for their self-righteousness, you shall strike down the enemies of God's people now.

Your work is to take the life of so few. And in return, you will place God's people in a new paradise. You will save millions of souls from eternal death.

There is no single life that it worth the loss of God's holy work. No matter how much you are tempted, no matter how much your physical man revolts at the work, you must complete it so that the ultimate right-eousness is accomplished and God's people no longer must act as avengers for the unholi-ness of the world.

    With this new world, the blood will cease
    to shed, Kenner. And God's people will
    praise you as Aaron to my Moses.
        Doubt not. Fear not. The sword of God is
    in your hand.
        Your Father and Brother in God,

    Rev. Percy Andrews

Tears filled his vision. Yes. The Reverend was right. Seeing her face that last time, her revulsion, her fear. Birdy didn't love him as he loved her. He had always been fooling himself. She could only see her own selfish needs, never to what he had to offer.

She had no place among God's people.

He wiped his face and carefully folded the letter. He tucked it back into its envelope where the two cyanide pills sat like watchful eyes. The Revered had confidence in Kenner—he'd said it a hundred times. But every brilliant strategy had a backup plan or two. If anything went wrong, the Reverend had been wise enough to give Kenner a way out.

Kenner opened up the new transmission window.

COME IN, SECURE 1, Kenner sent.

SECURE 1: IT'S GOOD TO SEE YOU MADE IT. I WAS STARTING TO GET WORRIED.

SECURE 2: I'M HERE.

SECURE 1: SO, THEN. EVERYONE IS TAKEN CARE OF?

He paused. He could not lie, not now. But he had made his mind up, hadn't he? Everyone would be taken care of this time tomorrow. Birdy was safe with James, protected from animals and visually dead, if not truly dead, yet. By the time he returned, he promised himself, he would be stronger. More resolved.

SECURE 2: EVERYTHING AT MOUNTAIN IS CLEAN.

SECURE 1: OCEAN IS ALSO CLEAR.

WHAT ABOUT EZRIE? Kenner sent. Thinking about her part in all of this made him nervous. They had sacrificed so much to get her here. He was about to sacrifice everything. Ezrie was a risk, and one that he had never fully trusted.

And what if he was being double-crossed? What if there was death waiting for him at the end just as sure as it was waiting for Ezrie?

But that's what faith was. Trusting that someone had a bigger plan than he did.

I believe. Help my unbelief.

SECURE 1: DON'T WORRY ABOUT EZRIE. SHE'LL GET HERE. BUT I STILL NEED YOU TO BRING UP THE REAR IN CASE SHE STARTS TO SLOW DOWN.

OF COURSE, Kenner sent, I'M HAPPY TO SERVE.

He wanted to serve. But he wanted her, too.

I MAY NEED TO TAKE THE LONG WAY BACK, he sent. THE BIKE'S ENGINE IS STARTING TO GO.

Also not a lie. He would be taking the very long way back, all the way back to the porter bay where Birdy was waiting for him. If all went well, the engine would remain functional until then and he could swap the bike out for one at the secondary base.

SECURE 1: I SUGGEST YOU MOVE AS QUICKLY AS YOU CAN. THE WINDOW OPENS IN ELEVEN DAYS. WITH HELP, SHE SHOULD REACH THE MOUNTAINS IN A WEEK.

Kenner considered the strands of blue filling up the engine of the bike. It would be gathering in the other machines as well, reconfiguring and rerouting. And the bike wouldn't last forever.

But he had to ride back for Birdy. He could get a new bike at Mountain. He still had time to do it right.

He considered it.

I'LL BE THERE SOON, he sent.

There was silence on the other side.

Is there a chatter in the quiet? A voice like an angry woman heard from beneath water?

SECURE 1: MAKE SURE SHE GETS HERE, KENNER. IF EZRIE DOESN'T FIX THIS DOOR, NONE OF US ARE GOING HOME.

I'LL MAKE SURE, Kenner sent. I'M GOING OFFLINE UNTIL THEN.

He blinked the transmission off before he could get a response. He didn't want to hear alternatives or reasons why not. He had to finish it.

Even though the outlanding gear covered his skin from toes to fingertips, he could feel the wind gusting at the top of the mountain. An animal howled somewhere below. Others joined in, singing their wild song to the red sky.

It was a sign, he knew.

With a grunt, he kicked at the engine one time, watching the dust crumble from the motherboard, the battery housings, whatever the phlax could eat. He would go and find Ezrie. Of course he would. He was a disciple. He served the greater good.

But he would go back to Birdy first. He would keep his word.

He raced down the incline, pushing the engine to the limit. Birdy was waiting for him. Hungry. Broken. He felt a warmth spread through him despite the chill of the air as it rushed across his suit. A dizzy, sick desire for blood or pain or kindness.

Kenner knew that whatever watched him felt it too.

III

The Eastern Wilds, *Leto*

EZRIE FOUND that Leto had a rhythm. A dangerous beauty. As she rode, she soaked it in. The jungles fell away to a new kind of land—open brown swaths of dirt that reminding her of Texas, except without all the lip-cracking dryness. The tall stands of trees besides the ribbon of red river—the Eriset, said Birdy's notes—reminded her of old-timey Nets movies about Redwood forests that had once filled the world.

Despite the unparalleled beauty of the scenery, Ezrie found herself yawning. She had slept badly. She'd had a terrible dream that was too vivid. Her father had been there, his head half-missing and dripping yellow ichor. He had been trying to sing, but all that came out was flecks of phlegm. She tried to shrug the dream off, but it lingered. And the driving for so long made her feel nauseous and light-headed.

She pulled the bike to a stop, trying to wash the image away by focusing on the rushing sound of the river and the cacophonous hooting calls of birds in the high trees. She unzipped and undid all the straps from the outlanding suit, then peeled it off down to her ankles. Leaning against a tree, she peed. "Lady-style," her mother once put it, making sure she kept her ankles as piss-free as possible. She could see the bladder-fishes levitating above the little stream, and could hear the *plop-plop* sound as they dropped back into the water, maybe hunting for bugs or running from predators.

There was more than enough water here. No need to drink her own fluids if she didn't have to.

When she finished, she stripped off her boots and the rest of the suit, standing in her underwear and wishing she had something other than the skinpants. She walked gingerly back to the bike and grabbed the knife from her pack, going at the too-tight pants with relish.

"Take that, you ass-chokers," she muttered. "And tell your friends."

She set the knife down and looked at her handiwork. The shorts were ragged, but sufficient. At least now she would be able to breathe.

From over her shoulder, she heard rustling in the distance.

She whirled around, nearly falling, knife still in hand.

If there were animals out here, animals that could eat her, she didn't know if a knife would do her much good. She slipped it into the belt loop of her newly cut shorts and pulled the laster from the saddlebag of the motorcycle.

Ezrie pulled on her boots roughly, attempting to walk as quietly as she could towards where she'd heard the sound. It was an undergrowth area about 100 yards from where the bike stood. *What am I, Superman?* she thought. *How could I have heard anything from so far away.*

Because you didn't. You're imagining things.

Yeah. I'm tired. My brain is having a minute, that's all.

She kept walking, though, until the rocks beneath her feet became short, green grass. Light filtered down through the trees turning the little glen into a cathedral. Quiet. Too quiet.

Who's there, she wanted to call. But she was afraid someone might answer.

There was a wild flutter, a squawk and a rain of colorful spray. Ezrie pulled the trigger on impulse, adding the smell of burning laster to the malodorous liquid falling on her face and hands. A school of angry stints puffed away through the tree-tops.

Ezrie wiped red goo from her eyes, dropping the laser in defeat. "Gross."

She trudged back, past the bike and down to the river.

Ezrie stood there for a moment, wondering if it was even safe. The last time she'd had a bath in real water, she'd been fifteen years old. That had been one of the only good things about the Peterson house. She'd gotten in trouble more than once for using their allotment of water all by herself.

But there was no lack of water here.

She took off the shorts and tank top, carefully placed the boots on a flattish rock. Ezrie dipped her toes into the red water. Cold. She snatched her foot back. But the suns were already rising, and the warmth of them on her back made the cool water inviting.

Ezrie splashed in, nearly forgetting to take the earring out. She place it carefully in the front pocket of the outlanding suit before stepping out on the slippery rocks beneath. She was pleased to find that, further in, there was a sandy bank. She stood on it, in the red water up to her waist, and splashed the inky, stinky residue from her body. She splashed the alien water on her breasts, her armpits, and her face. "Screw it," she said, dropping her body beneath the waves like a baptism.

She gave a little underwater cry at the coldness of it, but she refused to come out. The sensation of being surrounded by water was exhilarating. Real water, not some cloggy chemical scrub. She waved her arms, feeling like a mermaid, spreading her legs so that the water could reach all the unreachable places and make her clean.

She had a sudden urge to breathe the water in, to let it be both inside her and outside. Something about how light it was—like air, like swimming in the sky—made her feel as though she could breathe it if she really tried.

So stupid.

She bobbed up, splashing out of the water, wiping red from her eyes and mouth and laughing.

Ezrie pulled herself onto the bank, slipping only once on the rocks, and sat for a long time. The suns rose and filled the sky with that impossibly orange light. They dried her body and warmed her. While it did, her mind felt truly clear for the first time in years. The spell was broken by an old song, and she sang along to lyrics she didn't know she knew.

"Baby, when you're alone..." she sang out-of-tune, "I'll be there..."

When she finished, she felt cleansed. Complete.

IV

Mountain Base, *Leto*

Day 6

NO ONE HAD YET ARRIVED to keep Birdy company, which (for the first time in her life) was a good thing, considering that two of her former teammates had tried to kill her in the last forty-eight hours.

She had found food in the lab (not entirely professional, but necessary when one was working all night long in the lab). And had made several meals out of peanut butter and jelly that had been left. It was okay without the bread, and she'd washed it down with some of the bottled water (Earth water, of course) they kept below the sink. It felt like the most delicious meal she'd ever had.

There were a number of problems with the events of the last few days, but Birdy was being as pragmatic as she could. Of course, James could not have been killed. Perhaps he had been comatose. Maybe Kenner had stunned him. But then, there was the issue of his physical deterioration. Rigor mortis. Methane gas release.

She didn't like it, but the facts were not adding up.

The first thing she'd done after eat and drink was to open the fridge where the living experiments had been kept. The generators for the base were still running, had not been turned off, it seemed. She was ecstatic to find that the R-particle tests were there, completely intact, with new field notes recorded in TELO—the Terrestrial Experiment Lab Operator. Charleston had been here then, at least for a while, before the porter had been destroyed and rebuilt by phlax.

She had closed the fridge again, grateful for at least one shred of good that had been accomplished.

The next thing she had done had surprised even her.

She had crept out of the lab, her outlanding suit "zipped and flipped" as they said (cut in two places though it was) to the porter bay. Yes, she was shaking like a tree in a hurricane. Yes, she held the rebar in her hand like a baseball bat. But she was going, dammit.

Because he can't be alive, she thought. *Or he is, and I made it all up.*

She had steeled herself, willing the scientist to come up from wherever she was hiding. It couldn't have happened. It had to be a hallucination. She had to face the hallucination and accept that she had imagined all of it. Or she had to know that it was all real. Sam had said hallucinations were what drove the other team mad. Birdy couldn't afford to go mad. Not when Kenner would be back to find her.

The direction of the lab to the porter meant that she saw the window first. It was open where she'd kicked it, the glassy panel smashed but cohesive. A sliver of glass and polyvinyl material hung haphazardly from the corner of the frame far over her head.

No. She had not hallucinated.

Crouching, she walked slowly to the front of the porter, her arms tensed to fight, her breath quickening.

The door had been torn from its hinges, the control panel destroyed. But it was empty inside. The only sign of what had been James were footprints in the sand, disappearing into the forest, uneven and red.

Inside, she stepped in gingerly, her eyes on the door at all times, half-sure that Kenner would appear to trap her again in this chamber of torture. When he didn't, she stooped down to where James' body had lay (before it reanimated, but that's not a thing to think about now), and captured a sample of the blackish, bloody fluid that he'd laid in.

"Live analysis of R-particle Test Bank Four," Birdy said, satisfied to see the "LIVE" icon blinking in her trace, even if the round trace network icon was dim. No one was listening and the network was down, but she was live-streaming her work, dammit. It made her feel better.

The experiment had been from evaporated water. The R-particles had been left in the dish and she and Charleston had subjected the forty-some samples to different catalysts. Alcohol, UV rays, plasma. She pulled out her own micrometer and blinked it on. The samples buzzed on her trace overlay, showing the experiments in ultra-high resolutions at sixty-four thousand times the ability of the human eye to see.

Birdy passed over most of the bank, pulling out only the ones she needed: human plasma and electrophoto cells.

She started with the human plasma. Each of them had blood samples taken before coming, and Birdy had requested clones for safekeeping and experimentation. She had the team (so to speak), lined up in front of her now, filling a rack of beakers. In the temperature control unit (the body fridge, is what Charleston had lovingly called it), the samples, as well as the R-Particle experiments themselves, had been maintained at 97.6 degrees and subjected to oxygenation—a simulated body for the particles.

Birdy looked at the R-Particle slides. There had been no changes to any of the blood samples of the crew. A perfect control.

She gave a sigh of relief. Maybe Zhong had been right. Maybe the R-Particles had no effect. They were too small. Easily sloughed by the body.

But you know better, don't you, her mother's voice said. It brought to her mind the nightmare she'd had the night before. A dream in which Ladora spoke wordlessly from behind a curtain of vines that reached out and choked Birdy till she gasped awake.

She pushed the dream aside. Can't let the hallucinations take hold.

The R-Particles worked on electricity. They were galvanized by it. That much she knew.

Birdy was careful with this last sample. It was the real sample. The one that would put Zhong and PanGen out of business.

The sample had been water, at one point. But with the addition of electrolysis, a constant stream of electrical impulse over months, now, the sample was something new.

She felt overwhelmed with emotion as she looked at it now. "Beautiful," she whispered.

As she'd suspected, it was phlax. Whorls and circles of crystalline blue. Building and organizing. Structured. Her trace captured it's perfect, pristine glow, measuring the angles and geometry before saving it in the biomechanical drive that was the foundation of her research.

"Findings," Birdy said out loud, "The water of Leto carries the R-Particle which is inert except when exposed to consistent electric impulses. We can conclude..."

Birdy swallowed hard. She touched the device at the back of her skull almost subconsciously. The ramifications were unthinkable.

"We can conclude that any Letan water-based organism, or organisms that consume Leto water, that come into contact with consistent electrical impulse is a potential host for phlax."

But that's not all, is it? her mother's voice said, softly. *There's much, much more.*

She pulled out the new samples with shaking hands from where they were tucked away in the small breast pocket of her outlanding suit. The phlax from the monoliths in the forest. The black biological substance that had once been James' blood.

She prepped the phlax first, taking the sample from the site in the forest and comparing it with her own experiment.

"TELO," she addressed the AI of the lab. "Please compare the cellular profiles of slide three and four. Hypothesize growth behavior, assuming this was a one micron sample thirty days ago."

"Completed," TELO said.

There was a soft pinging noise. On her trace, a twelve-sided cell structure appeared, four connective ganglion nodes on one side.

"The growth rate is .04 milimeters per day at a constant energy output of .003 joules," TELO said.

"What is the difference between the current growth rate and the growth rate thirty days ago?"

"An increase of 1126%."

Why? Why was it growing faster?

She didn't have time to find out.

Birdy prepped the next two slides, taking a little of James' blood from the control group and creating another slide with the black ooze from the porter bay. It was only one data point. Not great science, but it was better than nothing.

I'm crazy. What am I looking for? What am I trying to prove?

"TELO," Birdy said. "Analyze and compare slides five and six."

Another ping. New information lit up her trace.

Time of Death: -24.3 hours

Blood type: error 330

Error. That made no sense.

"Compare with R-particles on file."

"No R-particles in sample," TELO announced.

None of it made sense.

But what if the particles weren't there because they were something else? Something different.

"Okay, TELO," Birdy said. "Remove hemoglobin from the compound," Birdy said. "Remove any traces of blood type O positive. Refine the compound within those directives. Call it X-particle. Run the scan again."

Time of Death: -24.3 hours

Blood type: O positive

X-Particle: 97%

On her trace, the image of the blood makeup was red. James sample had been rife with something. Something different than R-particles *or* phlax.

"Dammit," Birdy whispered. She stared at the blood sample on the slide, hating that she knew what the next experiment was. Hating that she knew what came next.

"TELO, expose slide six to constant electrical output starting at twenty joules. I'll be back in a couple of hours."

Birdy gathered the R-Particle petri dishes, packing them in a slim, cooled case. It was designed to carry thermally-dependent experiments for up to two weeks, or as long as the batteries functioned. Birdy couldn't think about the odds of them being infested now. She could no longer wait to get away from the base.

She did a quick sweep of the base, adding in what she could. Food tubes and MREs, a water purifier (although she packed as many bottles of real water as she could), a first aid kit which she used to glue the elephant glass cuts on her arms and hand closed. A sewing kit so she could sew up the outlanding suit on the go. It was still torn open from her collision with the gorilla glass.

There were no lasters on base that she could find, and she didn't have permissions to print any. She would have to do things the old-fashioned way. She got two kitchen knives and a laser scalpel. Then, as a final measure, she took the rebar. It would make a good weapon. It already had.

She pulled the pack on her back, feeling tiny compared to its bulk. She was not down to her last task, the last thing on her list.

Birdy came back to the lab, already knowing what she would find.

James' blood, the black, dead thing it had been, was sprouting visible strands. Blue, detailed wisps that glowed with ethereal light. And the blood itself was once again red.

Her eyes might tricker her. Her brain might try to fool her. But data never lied.

"TELO," Birdy whispered, clutching the straps of her pack. "There is one more thing." She leaned against the table, suddenly dizzy, eyes closed. "Scan the room for the unknown compound. The X-particle. Overlay it on my trace. Please. Thank you."

"Completed."

She opened her eyes, her gaze lighting on her hands. They were a fireball of color, her veins like rivers of red water.

She unloaded the pack, ripping off her shirt, and traced them with her fingertips. The rivers of the particle were in her skin, in the bones. It made her body into a map of blood.

Not blood, she shuddered. *Something* new.

That was the connection. The R-particles came from the water. The phlax came from the R-particles. But the phlax was creating something brand new inside of her. Inside of all of them.

V

The Eastern Wilds, *Leto*

THE POND NESTLED in a stand of weeping trees with pinkish berries and white leaves shaped like stars. It was only a few hundred feet wide, and narrow on one end, that side covered in bluebell-like flowers and orange-and-green bushes. The hum of the flies melded with the smallest trickle of a stream that fed the pond from the west.

As Ezrie pulled her clothes off and waded in, she felt spoiled. After years of not having water, she was hungry to feel it. This desire had slowed her down some, as she had nearly ever chance to wade in, not even bothering to put the earring back on.

She noted as her fingers skimmed the surface that this was the first water she'd see that wasn't red. It was crystal clear. Ezrie wished that Birdy was here to explain the science, but she wasn't.

Ezrie took a breath and dove in. It was a gorgeous feeling, the temperate water so much more comfortable than the river. Ezrie wondered if there was a spring nearby, and she relished the feeling of warmth against her legs and breasts.

She swam down, and the water seemed to part before her, as if welcoming her. From below her, the warmth intensified. There was a soft rush against her ears like a whisper. She imagined tiny fishes swimming into her ears, and covered them instinctively.

She came back up, gasping for air, her hands covering her ears. She should leave here. The night was drawing in. She treaded water for a moment, still spooked by the idea of fishy bodies crawling into her cracks. But an ethereal light from the bottom of the pool caught her attention. In the dimming evening, she could make out something glowing bright blue at the far end of the pond.

There is something down there. Someone.

It wasn't an idea. It was one hundred percent real. Someone was down there.

That doesn't make any sense. Of course there is no one down there.

But she was sure. *People* were down there.

Another whisper in her ears, like when you played telephone in school. Whispers where you couldn't quite hear what they were saying. She shivered, shuddered. But she couldn't stop herself. She took a deep breath and dove towards it.

The water seemed to flow her forward, down. She passed waving fronds of whitish-blue plants that stretched down into a bright blue abyss. She followed the light, her eyes stinging, her chest burning, reaching out—

hands hands below the water

Something jagged and angular sat at the bottom of the pool, full of light.

Ezrie swam closer, the sound of the rushing blood in her veins was a throbbing hush.

As Ezrie closed in on the structure, she saw that it was an intricate arch of the filmy stuff that Birdy had called phlax. Within it were two pillars, about six feet apart, looking unfinished. They were angular, but rough. Ezrie reached out her hand and touched it instinctively. The light increased, then dimmed as she let it go. She heard a sound in the water as she did, a feathered, foamy sound like the audience before the curtain goes up.

They needed her to come down.

Ezrie's oxygen-starved lungs felt heavy, full of bricks. She needed to get back up to the surface.

But why? Why leave when everyone you want is here?

Something wrapped around her ankle, soft and slithery.

She jerked, pulled away. A twist of the filament caught her wrist, swirled and drew her close.

Ezrie screamed below the water, the last of her air clouding her vision in bubbles. From below, a light. Voices in the light.

speeak

She wrenched her arm, nearly dislocating it from the socket. In the light, she could see a gauzy figure.

Ezrie pulled away, desperate for air, clawing against the slithering arms that held her fast.

Ezrie, the voice called. *Come to us.*

For a moment, she stopped struggling, her eyes keenly sharp. Her mother's hand reached up from the pit below, a yellow scarf tied around her wrist.

Mother. Molly. Miyu.

Ezrie, light-headed and drowning, took her mother's hand and felt herself being towed down towards the light that was expanding and contracting with each heartbeat.

She felt a violent, tearing sensation as another arm pulled in the opposite direction. Stronger, faster. Perfect.

Ezrie tried to pull away, to go towards where her mother waited, where she was wanted. But the other arm insisted, and Ezrie's nails against the flesh didn't even cull blood from the wounds.

Ezrie moved towards the surface, dragged behind a form she couldn't make out. She reached back towards the fading light, calling for her mother, her mouth full of water.

She broke the water's surface, coughing and retching, the form dragging her to land and dumping her unceremoniously. Ezrie attempted to crawl back in, but found arms around her chest holding her tight.

"Let me," she gasped, "Let me go. She wants me. She needs me!"

"Stop," the woman said, turning Ezrie to face her.

Ezrie tore her gaze from the water, the light dimming from beneath the waves as her own breathing became even. She knew this face. The ridiculously red hair.

"A-Aris," Ezrie sputtered. "What are you doing here?"

"Protecting you," Aris said. She held Ezrie's wrists as tight as handcuffs. Ezrie screamed and tried to pull away despite the pain.

"Please," Ezrie sobbed. "Please, let me go back."

"No," Aris said. "You are not allowed to harm yourself. Your safety is one of my prime directives." Aris smiled, her eyes strangely still. "I mean you no harm, Ezrie. I am programmed to watch over you, and so I am fulfilling my purpose."

Ezrie noted that her voice had taken on a jagged quality, more similar to the androids that Ezrie had come across in her own work. Herky-jerky voices that were always a fraction too slow between words. Someone had reprogrammed her. But why?

"Who sent you here?" Ezrie refocused on Aris. "Did Purple program you to find me? Did Lee send you? I'm not going back, I swear—"

"You are the only remaining human member of the Leto Artemis mission." The android looked at her with a curious, gentle calm. Her eyes still as stones. "I am here to ensure your survival."

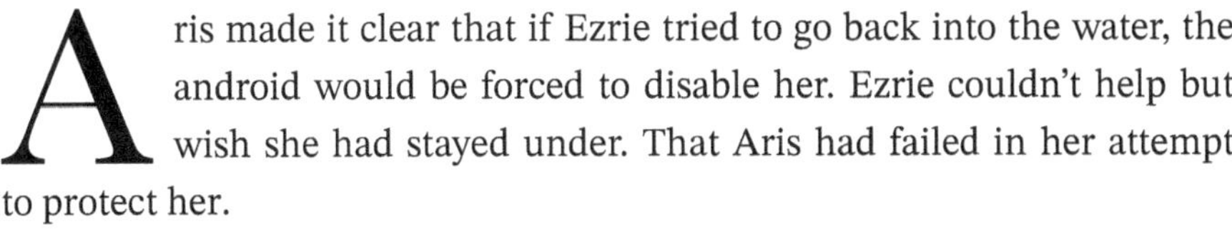

A ris made it clear that if Ezrie tried to go back into the water, the android would be forced to disable her. Ezrie couldn't help but wish she had stayed under. That Aris had failed in her attempt to protect her.

They sat now in the darkness, the glow from the fire pack warming her outwardly. But nothing could touch the cold, sickness she felt inside.

"What happened to the others?" Ezrie managed. "How did they die?"

"Sam and Lee were terminated. Alex suffered from genetic deterioration. Purple..." The android paused. "Cause of death: unknown."

But Ezrie knew. She had shot him and left him for dead. She had tricked herself into believing she hadn't, but Aris was the proof. Ezrie's stomach rose into her throat. The information was too much.

"Terminated—Who terminated them? How did you survive?"

"I am unable to answer those questions—"

Ezrie punched the ground. "I order you to tell me—"

"You do not have that authorization." Aris said, her face twisted into a face of concern. "Please accept my condolences—"

Ezrie's sprang up, grabbing the laster. Somehow this was her fault. She had left them there, and they had all died. And Purple. She had killed him herself. They had followed her here and now they were all dead. She stood, her hands shaking, the laster pointed at her own head. "Tell me what you know, or I'll kill myself right now."

There was not time to think. In a single breath the android had stolen the laster from her hand and had Ezrie on the ground, her hands behind her back.

"Ezrie Collings, I wish you no harm," Aris said. "I am unable to lie and I have your safety as one of my top priorities. You must trust me. I am all that is left."

VI

Mountain Base, *Leto*

Day 7

IT DIDN'T MAKE him angry that Birdy had escaped. He found that part of him had actually expected her to. Was even proud of her, a little. But he'd never admit it.

Kenner stood in the porter bay, wondering if he could have tied her tighter. Given her more of the sedative. It didn't matter, now, though. Whether by accident or by some subconscious desire to see her free, he had made mistakes. The only thing left of his plan was a damaged porter door, nearly ripped from its track, and a black stain where James' body had been.

So, the animals had come for James, after all, despite Kenner's best efforts to protect the man's body. It had been a mercy. Another mistake.

Maybe they'd killed Birdy, too. It gave him a sad, inevitable feeling of relief. It had been done for him, then. God had made up where he had lacked.

But then he noted the broken window and followed the footprints to the lab, then north into the woods. They were fresh. Maybe only hours old.

There was still time.

He had decided it then. He would follow her and track her. Then he would kill her. It was the only way to end it.

───────

He went west, following the telltale markers of her passing. The broken reeds near the lake. A boot print at the edge of the river. She was smart to lead him into the mountains. Soon, there would be no maps for him to follow, and once there weren't they would be on equal footing. Kenner knew how to survive, but Birdy knew Leto better than anyone. You could say they would both be on home turf.

He pressed his fingers to the headache that seemed to grow stronger every day. She was somewhere in the woods, and he thought he could sense her watching him.

Not her, them, his Grandam's voice croaked. *They are always watching.*

"Stop, Grandam. Stop," he said. "You're dead."

Kenner blinked on the scanner, the infrared still showing nothing. It seemed to ease the headache, even though it gave the experience of tracking Birdy a hollow, electric taste in his mouth. He wanted to track her like an animal. Hunter and prey. Skin and skin. The way that man was always designed to find his mate.

A trio of octopus-birds—slints, she called them—flitted overhead, fighting over a fish they'd snagged from the river. His trace highlighted the small bodies of rodents beyond the rise of the hill, darting down and up from their burrows.

The hairs on the back of his neck prickled. Something was watching him.

You don't pay attention, do you, boy? His grandam's voice in his head was deafening, even as he strained his ears to hear.

Except that this time, there *was* something watching him. He silently pulled his knife from his belt. In his left hand, he flicked the laster to lethal.

He heard a soft rustle from the woods before him, and all his senses went needle-sharp.

The thing that stepped out of the forest shadow was unlike any creature he'd ever seen, but he instantly recognized it from Birdy's report on Brindle.

Lycant.

It was reddish, foxlike, nearly five feet tall with purple eyes, that were blind. Hearing like a bat, she'd said. Blue phlax grew from its head as if crafted by a metal artisan—an intricate headdress sewing itself in and out of the flesh in snowflake-like patterns. The growth, hornlike, was luminous. It pulsed with light, illuminating the shadow of the deep forest beyond.

A hollow wail chambered from somewhere inside the beast, and it bared an impossibly wide set of teeth that almost brought the flesh from the sides of its jaw to touching behind its bulbous eyes.

Then it lunged.

Kenner braced himself to strike, willing the animal to come to him. Then, he heard another hollow wail. He aimed and shot at the one he could see. The animal tripped, then tumbled, rolling and stunned.

Kenner ran.

He flew through the deep woods, the sound of his own labored breathing swallowed up in the echoing howls of the things that followed him. The creatures were gaining, their otherworldly feelers sensing his fear and tracking it like a scent. He crashed headlong through snags of muck, his boot getting irrevocably stuck for one moment. With only a moment of hesitation, he pulled himself up by a low-hanging limb, foot naked, at the same time a lycant's iron jaws clamped down on thin air.

The second lycant climbed the tree like a cat, jumping and snarling onto Kenner almost before he could process it.

They fell together, the branches snapping like bones beneath them. Kenner plunged the blade into its glowing eye. The thing howled and reeled back, jaws snapping even as its mate closed in.

He shot the laster directly into the second beast. It paused only long enough for Kenner to scramble to his feet, then jumped at him, slashing and slavering, the blue eyes throbbing. Kenner waited until the very last second before he feinted, slicing the creature's neck with deadly force. He felt the bolt of electricity, still coursing through the thing's veins as it slammed into his chest, unfazed.

Using every ounce of strength he had, Kenner brought the serrated butt of the knife down on the headdress of glowing phlax.

The animal choked, slumped, and Kenner managed to roll out from beneath it as it fell lifeless to the forest floor. The other lycant reared back, the impossibly smiling fangs opened to reveal the double rows of blade-like teeth. It howled, angry, mournful, and retreated back into the thicket.

He stabbed the dying lycant in the heart, through the back. It made a dry, haunted sound, like October leaves. A croaking, sandpaper sound.

He stood for a while, the muscles in his legs shaking. His shirt was torn. He was bleeding from his shoulder and his knuckles on the knife hand. Kenner stood over the dead lycant, the blue of its eyes fading, the throbbing of the light ever slowing.

The blue light glowed strong through where he'd crushed the skull. He cut down into it, flaying the skin open at the skull, even as the animal whined.

"What have we here," Kenner mumbled.

Inside the skull he found a mass of blue tissue. It throbbed in some parts, in other parts it had taken on a dull dead grey hue. It faded slowly, from the edges in. The center of the mass glowed keenly for a moment, barely bright enough for Kenner to cut it out before it went dark.

He kicked the body over roughly, a gesture that somehow soothed the fear in his hammering heart. It was over now. He peered at the small nub of tissue that had been at the center of the growing mass.

Kenner wasn't a scientist, but he had shot animals on three different planets with devices exactly like this.

An animal tag. A tracker.

He wiped his blade and slid it back into his pocket, then scanned the grass for his laster. Nothing but pieces.

He cursed himself twice. Once for the laster and once for losing Birdy's trail. But at least he could fix that one.

Kenner was careful to place the tracker in the protected breast pocket of his outlanding suit. He would keep it safe. Birdy would want to see it. She would know what to do with it.

If she was alive.

He jogged back to find her trail, knife in hand and scanning for more of the creatures.

You saw what I did to your friend, didn't you? Kenner thought. *You best be finding somewhere else to be.*

Kenner moved faster now. "I am worthy," he whispered into the jungle dark. "I know you are worthy."

VII

Chaldean Mountains West, Leto

Day 8

IT TOOK NEARLY two days to make it out of map range and into the blank canvas of the uncharted Chaldeans. Birdy spurred herself on, stopping every so often to listen for a distant motor. She did not hear one. It made her wonder if Kenner was tracking her on foot. The thought made her blood run cold. He was stronger and faster. He knew how to kill silently. She had seen him do it.

Birdy made small, quick meals, adding a few of the juicy kingenberries whose bushes dotted the forest beside the Eriset River. They were red and tasted like apple-cranberry juice—a perfect supplement to her dwindling supplies.

The Eriset River was the obvious road—it cut through the entire land mass of Leto, at least the part they had surveyed—and Kenner would assume she was clinging to it. So, she decided to take a more difficult path, pulling deeper and higher up where she was more protected but could still see it slinking through the mountains. If he tracked her this far, Kenner would have the same short-range scanning capabilities that she had, and it meant that she needed to keep as far from him as she could.

She looked over her shoulder often. She slept in snatches, and when she woke, she was drenched in sweat from nightmares. Last night, Kenner had trapped her in a glass box where he peered at her with wide yellow eyes, hissing words that she could almost hear, his snake jaw opening, the forked tongue crawling down her throat until she suffocated.

Kenner said he would be back, and she had never known him to break a promise.

Birdy shuddered to think how many times she had been alone with him, tracking the animals that she had on her wish list to identify and add to her named specimen report. What had he been thinking on those quiet walks through these same woods? Had he been imagining kissing her like he had in the porter? Had he known he would kill the same people he ate with in the mess hall?

She knew he had. As much as it shamed her, Birdy knew Kenner better than anyone. Because, at his core, Kenner was a predator. Kenner might understand animals on a level that even she didn't understand, but she could identify a predator when she saw one. Kenner followed biological imperatives, and she understood them better than anyone. Eat, procreate, protect, find shelter.

She hiked up, ignoring the burning in her calves and the blistered sores that had broken and scabbed, climbing through thick stands of gasping flowers that breathed in her scent as much as she breathed theirs. She grunted as she walked, her arms sore from the walking stick. She had whittled it down with the laser scalpel so that it fit her hand pretty nicely, if she did say so herself. Still, she wasn't used to having to support her whole body weight with her arms. Birdy wiped the sweat from her eyes, not quite fast enough to save them from stinging, and looked out.

She stood, breathing heavily, at the top of a ridge looking down into a deep chasm. It followed the ridge for miles, and Birdy could see levels of forest, like great stone steps, that branched down between her and the darkness below.

There was a rush of movement, and she gasped as thousands of fire-red animals flew up out of the darkness, opening fibrous gliding wings in a rush of airborne frenzy. They cackled and hooted, a blanket of sound and color, sending trills of harmonies floating into the orange afternoon light. Despite the ache of her chest, she didn't reach into her pack for her inhaler. It felt like it would break the magic, somehow.

She recorded them as she walked, keeping an eye on the chasm's widening and slimming as it traced the spine of the range. Birdy noted the far-off trees nearest the cliff's edge. Some kind of subforest? Birdy noted it for further study.

There wouldn't be any further study, now, would there?

She paused, defeated. She wanted to go home. She wanted to see Cy and her mother. It would take at least a week to follow the Chaldeans southeast to the Barrens. From there, it would be another week at least to Ocean Base. At her current rate, she would probably make it just in time to miss the to port window.

"That's negative thinking, Meeshel," she told herself dryly. "More likely you'll get killed before that."

But she pushed deeper into the forest, determined, keeping the suns at her back and ensuring a northwestern route. Birdy trudged through the woods as gently as possible. She'd seen Kenner track down creatures that made no sound or scent, finding them merely on basis of wind direction and gut instinct. Every broken branch and bent frond would betray her.

Yes, he would find her.

It wasn't then a matter of not being found, but being ready when she was. But what did that even mean? She passed through a copse of tight trees, cringing as they scraped across her face. As awful as Kenner was, she could never kill him. It wasn't in her nature.

Birdy came to a virtually impenetrable wall of thin, reedy trees. She stood for a moment, panting.

"Darn it," she said.

She sat down unceremoniously and took a swig of red water. The filter light blinked a happy green. She knew better, but she had no choice. She could feel the particles inside of her, could hear them if she listened closely enough. Birdy considered the scalpel. Taking her own trace out might be the only way to—

There was a crackle in the bushes behind her.

There was a flutter of motion and Birdy shrieked. From the low, clawed bushes behind her, a silvery body, sleek and liquid, bounded jaggedly towards her and stopped short, snorting through a waving halo of golden tentacles.

Birdy's heart hammered in her chest, nearly too afraid to recognize the beauty of the thing. Her brain began to scan and categorize. She blinked notes onto her trace as it pawed the damp earth.

```
A beautiful quadruped, fur instead of hair,
tentacular appendages from the cranium, and
multiple eyes. Incredible golden and white
coloring—
```

It snorted again, breathing heavy out of the thick gold-tinged tentacles that formed its mouth. It stamped, nodding at her, then bounded away.

"Oh, no," she breathed out. "No. Don't run away."

It disappeared in the bramble of bushes that had seemed impenetrable a half hour before. She stalled at the hidden entrance, taking a moment to collect a tuft of golden fur that had caught on a branch, then followed the creature's trail.

She walked as quickly and quietly as she could through the woods, following the breaks in the branches. The woods were thick here, but she followed the sound of hooves crushing through the bracken. She sped up, letting the sound lead her.

The drop came too suddenly to even shock her.

Birdy screamed, flailing, her pack hitting her face and slipping from her shoulder as the ground crumbled from beneath her. She slid, then tumbled. She felt a crack and a bloom of white-hot pain in her knee as she launched, propelled by some solid mass into the rocky scree below.

oh dear God, please stop please stop stop stop oh no

She felt her stomach flip as her body flew into open space. She flailed her arms, reaching for help that wasn't there. She hit a huge rock, and her body flew again, this time tumbling.

As Birdy rolled, she scrabbled for purchase, for any way to make it stop, but there was nothing to hold onto but red dirt.

She rolled off another ledge, and she was falling again, this time branches smashing her mask, her body weightless.

Birdy hit the ground hard, her right foot taking almost all the impact. She felt the snap, the twisting pressure followed by a galaxy of pain, and then all the motion stopped. Above her, she caught a glimpse of the golden beast through the thick treetops, disappearing into the long purple grass that grew on the ridge, now nearly forty feet above her.

She moaned, a whimper of a sound that seemed trapped in the oppressive underbrush. Birdy tried to move, but everything was on fire. The pain in her knee was merely an *amuse-bouche* to the all-consuming hell that was her ankle. She tried to lift it, but the pain was so intense that the world began to go spotty.

Don't pass out, don't pass out, don't pass out...

The world came back into focus. Birdy looked around. Turning hurt almost as much as the break itself.

She found herself in a thick grove. The earth was springy and mossy. There was almost no light down here, just a dark green haze filled with shadowed trees. Overhead, she could see the faintest glimmer of orange sky and the slight ridge the beast had taken to wherever he called home. If she squinted, she could see the spine of the mountain where she had fallen from. But even that was more imagination than reality.

She was trapped.

Birdy made a screaming, choking cry as she struggled to sit up. She rose again and again, each time her chest constricting more, her breathing becoming faster and faster. She needed her inhaler. Worse than that, her leg was very broken. She thought of the emergency medical kit. The epimedic would have a rudimentary surgical setting. The bone could be set. She could use the laser scalpel to seal the wound.

She'd put the scalpel in her pocket. What if it had fallen out?

She patted herself down, a frenzied motion that caused searing proximity pain in her knee and ankle. But the scalpel was there, in her side pocket. She flicked it on, and a three-inch light blade brightened the darkness. At least one piece of good news.

Now to find her pack. Birdy looked around, grunting at the pain of moving the leg even a tiny bit. In every direction, there was nothing but trees.

No pack. The weight of that reality sat on her all at once.

No weapons.

No food.

No water.

No inhaler.

I'm going to die here, she thought. *After escaping and fighting and running, I'm going to die here.*

No, you're not, her mother said. *You're too smart to die.*

But there was no thinking to be done here. No solutions to be gathered.

Birdy sat alone in the dark of the deep woods, hyperventilating, and realizing that death was coming, one way or another.

VIII

EZRIE FOUND Aris had a lot information that neither Marcus nor Birdy had given her. She seemed to innately know where the dangers were, as evidenced by her suggestion to go around a nest of crested cores, a type of snakelike reptile that shot poison-tipped spikes from its tail. Aris ran beside Ezrie's bike at phenomenal speeds, despite Ezrie's attempts to lose her.

"We are making excellent time," Aris said, the next afternoon, no sign of flagging, "I am pleased with our progress." Somehow Aris had connected her vocalizations to Ezrie's outlanding hood, so Ezrie was stuck listening to Aris talk whether she liked it or not.

"Time," Ezrie said into her hood, slowing the bike. "What time?"

Aris didn't respond.

Having Aris around was exacerbating the terrible sense that something was going on. Things were combining in places she couldn't see. Like the water of the pond, there were things happening far below the surface of Leto, and they were happening because of her.

In the evening time, they would stop and make camp. The zephyrs would come, as if they were following the pair, lighting on Ezrie's skin if she had taken the outlanding suit off to sit beside the fire. They glowed as they sucked moisture from her skin—at least that's what she assumed they were doing. They turn from white to yellow and then red.

At night, she had dreams where she was trapped in a room full of sparks. Snakes drank her brain, dipping slivered tongues into the hole where her trace used to be.

And always, voices she couldn't understand.

She knew that she was hallucinating. The Apollo crew had suffered from paranoia, too. Then they'd started killing themselves.

She shuddered to think how close she'd come to that same fate. But she felt more than fear. It was a pang of loss. She had wanted to go to the bottom of that pool and be with whatever looked like her mother. Ezrie could still feel the burn of the hand on her arm, the yellow of the scarf so clear in the water.

The river gave way to a brown expanse of short, ugly trees. The mountain range, which sat solidly to Ezrie's right, rolled down into squat hills, with the main range one hundred miles further. The mountains were curving like a crescent moon, but the trail was straight— through what Birdy's field notes referred to as "The Browns."

The Chaldeans are a range that extends approximately 300 miles to the southeast of Mountain base, cut through by the Eriset River and its tributaries, and flanked by wide portions of scrub desert called "The Browns." Very little is known about this area and I'd like to explore it more fully in the future.

The shimmering sand reflected the orange suns as they danced across the sky, making Ezrie's legs burn despite the temperature controls and homemade shorts. She had ceded to Aris that she should put her outlanding suit back on, but refused to trade skinpants with the creature.

Still, she was so hot, she didn't notice the heat from the bike's engine until it was actively sparking out.

"Shit!" she yelped, dropping the bike and jumping clear as the engine emitted a spray of energy that looked like a child's toy laster. She felt the impact of a small boulder in her side and wrenched to protect her still-sore wrist.

The bike ignited in flames.

"There is a critical error with your vehicle," Aris said.

"Yeah. I noticed that."

Ezrie struggled to her feet, unzipping the outlanding hood and wiping sweat from her forehead. The browns were becoming increasingly yellow, and the sun made shimmers of heat in the near distance. She stretched her side slightly, then grimaced. Good thing that rock had stopped her fall.

Aris cleaned out the bike for what felt like hours, assuring Ezrie that she had in-depth knowledge of the bike. Still, when it was put back together again, the engine merely whined and then sparked out again.

"You said you could fix it," Ezrie said.

"I believe that there are connectivity issues with the main controls and the motorcycle," Aris said. "We need to have a new part that has not been affected by the phlax."

"Goddamit!" Ezrie shouted into the bleak, brown void.

They set up a camp, although it was early. There was no point going on with the suns so low against the horizon. Aris said that she could carry Ezrie further, but Ezrie declined. Something about that seemed infantile. She didn't like the idea of riding piggy-back on Aris, even if it did make sense.

Besides, she still didn't trust her.

"I am a machine," Aris said. "I can go faster and further by foot than you can."

"Yeah, I'm not in a hurry," Ezrie said.

Aris didn't say anything, but Ezrie wondered if there was a timeline she wasn't seeing.

Ezrie soothed herself by focusing on the small, yellow rodents that seemed to find their campfire so entrancing. Although their fur blended almost perfectly with the grass, their huge purple eyes were like beacons.

Ezrie wondered if they weren't what she'd seen on their sweeps run. How long ago had it been? She tried not to think of it.

Ezrie blinked into her saved copy of Birdy's notes, grateful for the second time that day that she'd stolen it.

```
Much    like    the    parasaurolophus,    the    Kimba
uses    their    bony    ridgeplate    to    sound    warn-
ings.    It    is    possible    they    make    music,    as
well,    since    their    attendance    to    pitch    is    so
keen.    I    tried    to    teach    one    to    sing    "Happy
Birthday,"    and    it    was    able    to    follow    the
first    three    notes.    I    hope    he    teaches    his
colleagues.    Can    you    imagine?    A    choir    of
Kimbas!
```

Birdy's notes were preternaturally chipper, and it both annoyed and soothed Ezrie. Even ridiculously cheerful was better than the emotionless blank slate of Aris' false smile.

Kimbas intermittently popped up from the ground to glare at the intruders or trumpet a warning from the bone ridges on their foreheads. They were adorable, in a hungry, hunted kind of way. They ran up and down the tree nearest the fire, carrying some kind of nuts in their huge jaws.

Ezrie held out a glob of nut paste. One of the Kimbas crept towards her slowly, its miniature snout wriggling at the foreign smell, its stubby tail wagging attentively.

Aris opened her mouth as if to protest. "Don't. say. anything," Ezrie hissed. Though not one for pets, especially not rodents, Ezrie had to admit that it *was* pretty cute.

The Kimba scrambled up and swiped it right out of her hand. It raced back to its burrow, its brothers and sisters cackling and blowing their trumpets, knocking their little horns together like kids fighting over kitchen scraps.

"They seem very intelligent," Aris said. "Error," she said. "Conjecture."

"More than can be said for some of us," Ezrie said, licking a smear of trail mix paste.

Aris looked at her quizzically. But her eyes, Ezrie noticed, were silent.

The biology lab table is cold beneath her back. The students are gone. In their place there are floating white orbs. The alight on her face and arms, drinking from her skin.

Mrs. Green, the biology teacher, is telling the orbs that they will dissect her. But Mrs. Green has no voice. She only mumbles, her throat sounds claggy and choking.

From the corner of her eye she can see her father lying next to her. He is the same, but his eyes have gone white. His skull is open, the pink of his brain raw and glistening in the floating lights.

Aris comes close, her eyes spinning. She reaches her android hand into her father's brain, grabbing a great handful like a child with a bowl of Jello. Like its nothing. It squeezes from between her fingers, dripping into great red pools of water.

We speak, *she says.*

Ezrie woke gasping. The smell of food was in the air.

It was a strange, incoherent dream. A hallucination, maybe, but it had been so visceral. So *real.*

She came out of the tent, blinking her eyes as the big sun slipped up over the horizon.

Aris smiled, her eyes still for once. "I have prepared a meal that is high in caloric value. Would you like some?"

Aris set what looked like a small roasted chicken before her—golden-brown skin crackling, with juices dripping down the sides. It smelled like Thanksgiving and Christmas and every birthday Ezrie had ever had.

Before she even really knew what she was doing, Ezrie had eaten it, licking her fingers clean.

It was only after she was finished that she picked out the little trumpet-shaped bone.

Ezrie decided that she would stick to food paste.

IX

Unknown, *Leto*

Day 9

THE HUNGER WAS bad and the thirst was worse, but the pain was the clear winner. Birdy spent a least a day in and out of consciousness, unable to even think because the ankle hurt so badly. She had been awoken by what felt like an earthquake.

Overhead, the wings of red bat-birds fluttered. They swarmed over the wide trees and Birdy made herself smaller on instinct, instantly regretting it, the pain billowing up from her ankle.

She was so hungry. So thirsty. The water in her suit was nearly gone, the reclamation cycle shorter and shorter.

She had to get back up the mountain. There was no way around it.

With a lot of effort and many tears, Birdy pushed herself up, hobbling slowly towards she'd taken her terrible fall. Twenty feet above her she could see a red dirt shelf. Green rabbity creatures popped their heads in and out of burrows, then scuttled down on long, retractable legs. Above that, some thirty feet, was the incline she'd fallen down. In the center, nestled by a large rock, she could see what remained of her pack. Broken, split, hanging from a jagged edge, the food tubes scattered like party favors.

She moaned. It made her leg hurt to even consider how far that was. How impossibly high.

"I can't," she whispered, her voice gravelly. "You can't expect me to. It's not fair."

So, maybe she would have to leave the pack. But she couldn't stay here. That meant doing something about her ankle.

Taking off the outlanding suit was almost as bad as the initial break, and Birdy heavily considered simply cutting the suit off after the second or third time she accidently moved her leg too fast and upset the mangled bones. She did get it off, however, and laid, sweating and shaking in her tank and skinpants for a while cursing God.

It made her feel better.

The leg was discolored, blood-congealed, and black on her anterior tibia. A compound fracture. The tip of one bone had torn through the skin. Looking at it made her feel like she was going to be sick again.

I'm gonna die, I'm gonna die, I'm gonna die.

What do you have? Ladora whispered in her ear. *Tell me something good.*

It was cool down here, and protected. She hadn't seen any huge bugs, which was a blessing. She had the laser scalpel still, miraculously. She had a couple of cups of water left (at best) in the outlanding suit. Enough for a few days, if she was very conservative.

No pack. No rope. No trace. No help—

"That is counterproductive," she said, feeling her mother's words on her lips. "Let's try to focus on solutions, Meeshel. What are the priorities?"

1. Water
2. Food
3. Leg
4. Kenner

The wind rustled in the trees, something moved in the darkness beyond.

"Stay away from me. Get away!"

She fumbled in the pocket of her outlanding suit, pulling the laser scalpel out and flicking it on. It's light was so small in the darkness. A small exclamation no bigger than her hand.

It would be easy to end it, something in her whispered. *It will be better than whatever Kenner has planned.*

No. She wouldn't think that.

Instead, she tried again.

1. Leg
2. Everything else

Right. That was more like it.

She took stock of the trees. It was a pity that her walking stick had been lost in the fall. And her rebar. Either one would have made a good splint. She sighed, reviewing her new options. There were a few jade trees and rimands, but they were both soft wood. Jade also had the habit of causing her to break out into hives any time she touched them. Neither would work for what she needed.

She spotted a greyheart tree and hope flashed bright. The Leto version of *chlorocardium rodiei* offered incredible strength and a lemony scent. The leaves, if you could call them that, were fronds—typical for about half the trees on Leto. They waved like ostrich feathers, clutching up small bugs and passing dust to feast on. They picked Birdy over, and she didn't hate the tickle of them on her naked arms.

Another thing to be grateful for, she thought. *To be out of the suit for a little while.*

She searched for a suitable branch, doing her best to not touch her bad leg and ending up sweating and panting in the process. Once she found a good one—a faded orange—she used the scalpel to strip it. Then, she pulled the tool belt from the outlanding suit and laid the branch beside her mangled leg. It was stiff, which was good, if not completely straight.

"It'll have to do, I suppose," she giggled hysterically. "All the Leto doctors are currently occupied with more pressing matters."

She slid the belt below her calf, lining it up with her tibia. She tried to stay clinical. She had splinted animal bones. So what if she'd never splinted her own leg before?

"Doesn't mean it's not possible," she told herself. "Gotta be tough."

When she pulled the leather belt tight, she heard the bones snap and grind. An ocean of pain flooded over her, drowning out everything.

She passed into darkness, haunted by people without faces who lived in her bones. She knew what they were saying. Something about home. About how she didn't have to be alive if she didn't want to be.

———

She woke and slept. Nightmares washed over her whether she was asleep or awake.

When she was sure she was awake again, she tenderly touched the splint. It was good, but not good enough. She cut up the white tank that was her only other clothing, strengthening the splint until she felt like her leg wasn't about to snap in two. It hurt like hell, but at least she could pressure on it. That meant walking, which was good. She didn't like the sound of the trees at night, here. She was sure there was something moving in them. Watching.

Birdy sweat and swore getting the outlanding suit back on. By the time she managed to fit the splint and stick into the outlanding suit leg, she felt like she'd finished a marathon. She rewarded herself with a small sip of the reclaimed water, wincing at the sour taste. The suit would be dry soon, she knew.

She needed her pack.

She pulled herself up with the cane she had made—another of the orange tree limbs, hobbling slowly until she caught sight again of the cliffs above.

Her heart sank. No, she was not going up there.

What was she going to do? The pack was up there, a beacon in the forest. It was her only lifeline.

And a sign, her mother's voice insisted. *If anyone sees it.*

Anyone. You mean Kenner.

Birdy felt her stomach curl. He would know she was down here. That meant only two options: get the pack back or run away.

But where? Where do I go?

She looked on all sides. The forest crept alongside the cliff for as far as she could see. But if she was very quiet, she could hear the far-off sound of static. Surely there were streams that fed into the . It was possible it flowed down here, or that there were tributaries that broke off and dropped down this side of the mountain.

What if it's in my head? What if I'm imagining it like I imagined them.

But the quadruped with the tentacled face. The beautiful golden beast with the liquid eyes. It had bounded down the hill like she had. It wouldn't have come if there wasn't food and water and shelter nearby.

Above her, she could see the purple grass of the short cliff that separated her from the sheer mountainside. What if imagining wasn't the worst thing she could do. She closed her eyes, picturing the creature as it had bounded away.

Focus, Ladora said in her ear. *What do you see.*

Birdy imagined a deer trail, a wearing of the purple grasses that snaked up and around the point of the mountain, leading to the river. This vision clarified, and she could see the pack, moving languidly towards the resting place. The leader called his does to him, a mournful sound that she could almost hear.

It felt like more than a fabrication of her mind. It felt connected to them, somehow. But regardless of whether or not she was hallucinating, if she followed that route, he *would* lead her somewhere, Birdy felt sure. Somewhere, her forest would connect with that main elevation. She could find a way up, backtrack, then find her pack.

If there's a way up, a cold voice said.

"There's a way," Birdy argued. "There's always a way."

X

Desert of Solace, Leto

ARIS WAS NOT HER MOTHER. Ezrie knew that logically. But after hours of walking through the desert, Ezrie's thoughts were slipping. Ezrie's legs felt like they would break, the sun baking her despite the protection of the outlanding suit. Ezrie wanted to pull it off and strip naked, run barefoot across the white sand, but Aris spoke and she heard her mother's voice.

"The suit protects you from heat and reclaims your water for future use," Aris said breezily. It had her mother's cadence. Ezrie stopped removing the suit, a feeling of déjà vu taking over. "Taking it off will only allow moisture to escape."

Molly. Miyu. The woman that could have been.

It's not real. I'm hallucinating.

In the tent that night, as Aris kept watch, Ezrie tenderly touched the memory like you might tongue a tooth that was loose. Her freckles, the way she would catch Ezrie up and dance her around the house when she was in one of her happy moods.

But the happy always came before the sad.

No, Ezrie thought. *I don't want to.*

But something in her brain refused to give.

See, it said. *See.* And it would show her the times Molly had screamed. The times when she had driven away in the blue car. The sound of the ambulance screaming the day they took her away. The urn.

<hr>

Ezrie had not slept well, despite the ion protection field. She'd had dreams. And when she woke, she was sure she could hear whispering from somewhere below the sand. Every so often, she heard her own name on the wind.

She brushed it off, or tried to. It was crazy.

What is crazy?

And was Aris plotting something? Sometimes as they walked, Ezrie wondered what was going on in the android's phlax-riddled cortex. Aris continued to identify errors in her own programming. Ezrie wondered how much the phlax had to do with that. When she stood watch at night, Ezrie could see the soft blue coming from somewhere in her skeletal cavity.

Stop it. You're going to drive yourself insane.

But it was getting harder and harder to fight the gut instinct to fight or run. And the voices *were* there. As they walked, she reached down and picked up a handful of sand, yellow as gold. She held it to her ear.

If you listen you can hear the ocean, her father's voice said.

Ezrie shook her head, banging her palm against the outlanding hood. There was an annoying, incessant whine that had begun the day before. It hummed the same note, and she was dropping the hood more and more often to get away from it. Even in that noise, she could sometimes hear a crackle. Like a transmission that was almost getting through.

She needed to focus. The deterioration of the Apollo team had taken only weeks. The thought made her chest constrict. How long would it be before she was infected with whatever they had?

"Aris," Ezrie said, "Do you have any records of what happened to the Apollo crew? Did you download the footage Sam found?"

Aris looked at her quizzically. Ezrie stopped walking.

"The files. From the other crew. Do you have access to personnel files?"

Aris smiled. "I detect an error in my programming. You will need to request that information at another time."

"A goddamn magic eight-ball would be more helpful," Ezrie muttered.

Ezrie opened up her own files with a pang of guilt. She had killed Purple for these files. *Oh, kid. I didn't mean to hurt you. I'm sorry.*

She blinked through them, reviewing what she'd saved. Of course there were Birdy's notes and Marcus' files—although she still didn't feel up to fully opening that can of worms. But she had other files, too. She'd set up to save any documents that had a high security level (mostly personal records and medical records), thinking she would figure out a way to hack them.

Fortunately, Marcus had saved her a ton of work.

Ezrie blinked through records for what felt like an hour before she found anything even remotely interesting. When she did, it was a coroner's report for Manuel Heitar, the security lead for Apollo, written by the doctor, Nancy Tukuafu. Ezrie skimmed it, then stopped on cause of death: Drowned.

There was a v-feed file attached marked "Sensitive." Ezrie blinked into it, the video feed playing over the live backdrop of the yellowed desert.

Heitar is standing in the men's bunk in front of a long mirror. He is muttering words to himself: "Stupid, stupid, shouldn't have, so stupid—"

There are only two cots open. There are no sounds. It's as if the base is abandoned.

"This is my last will and testimony," Heitar seems to settle himself enough to get the words out. His accent is light, but it's clear he's from South America somewhere. Ezrie's trace responds to the unspoken question, highlight Heitar as originating from Guadalajara, Mexico.

He brings the razor up to his face, running the blade along his jawbone on the flat side, his eyes half closed as if he were feeling the touch of a woman's hand.

"There are ghosts here," Heitar says. "First at night, and now when I'm awake. Sometimes I'll be standing there, doing my job, and then I'm gone. Like I'm somewhere else."

There is a hitch in his voice, a strangled sob.

"I saw my brother today. Again. It's getting so I'm afraid to close my eyes because I know he will be there, and I will say the same stupid things that I said the first time."

Heitar puts down the razor for a minute, grabbing a can of shaving cream. The smell is sharp and minty. Heitar rubs a glob of the stuff on his face, his eyes glazed over as he stares in the mirror.

There is a flicker. A flash of blue in Heitar's eyes.

"No," he moans. "No, get them out of me. Get them OUT OF ME—"

It is like watching a mime pretend to fight himself. Heitar pulls at his hair, screaming, while his other arm tries to wrench it away. He is slippery, the shaving cream all over his face, throat, dotting the mirror before him.

"I can't, I can'tIcan'tIcan't—"

His eyes are wide open, but they are blind. He fumbles for the razor, which knocks to the floor. From somethere beyond the feed, Ezrie hears the sounds of running. Someone calling Heitar's name.

His hands are working together now, hands in his mouth and on his face, pulling his mouth open as he screams. It is a deep, ugly sound, like a howl. His tongue flicks in and out, lolling and gasping as if to escape.

There is a cracking from somewhere in his neck and Heitar's scream deepens.

Something is breaking in Heitar, but his hands are too strong. They keep pulling and pulling, the scream drowned by blood coming from whatever has broken in his face.

And the hands keep pulling.

With a final burst of strength, Heitar breaks the jaw from his face, tearing it off awkwardly, skin still attaching the pieces to his face.

His hands drop limp, his body collapsing to the floor. Ezrie can feel nothing but the choking of Heitar's blood in her throat.

WE SPEAK, he sends.

Ezrie blinked out of the v-feed, her body shaking.

"What is wrong?" Aris said.

"Nothing," Ezrie bent over, flipped the hood back from her face, and vomited.

Aris came to her side and put her hand on Ezrie's back as she heaved again. Ezrie pulled away, her mouth still dripping.

"Don't touch me," Ezrie snapped. Then a wave of anger and fear poured over her. It was blinding, and she felt like Heitar—grabbing for something to destroy with, grasping for anything to hurt Aris and drive out the overwhelming knowledge that death was coming. "Don't touch me! For all I know, you killed them all. For all I know, that's how I die, too. Do you understand? DO YOU?"

She fell to the ground, sobbing. Everything hurt. Her stomach. Her head. Her heart. The yellowed desert of Leto swam before her eyes. In the distance, were there figures. The glint of glasses, the pink-and-yellow of a silk scarf?

Stay in reality, Ezrie, she told herself. *Can't lose it now.*

"I am here to protect you, Ezrie," Aris said softly. "I will never do you harm."

When Aris came close, wrapping Ezrie in her arms, Ezrie did not fight. In her mind, she imagined it was her mother's arms. And when Aris began carrying Ezrie across the sand, Ezrie found it strange that the android began to sing.

<hr>

After two days of traveling with Aris, Ezrie's outlanding suit shorted out, the whine replaced by dead silence. She stripped it off (against Aris' recommendations) and started trudging again, somewhat grateful to be out of the thing, her skin soaking up the sun. About ten minutes later, after she'd felt the first bite of sunburn, she had the suit back on, sweating and swearing until her voice had gone hoarse.

"I warned you of the danger," Aris said, her voice with that tinge of jerkiness that put Ezrie on edge. "I encourage you to wear mine."

And so, like sorority sisters, Ezrie and Aris had changed clothes.

Ezrie was surprised to find that Aris' outlanding suit fit her perfectly, and still had all the environmental controls running. As Aris had never turned it on, the phlax had not gummed up the circuits. Aris, in addition, seemed pleased that she could help Ezrie, although she mentioned several times that Ezrie needed to have her burns tended to.

Ezrie was becoming accustomed to the constant watchcare. It still made her nervous, like if she let down her guard too much, she would end up like Heitar and Cassie and the others. But there was an uneasy truce. Aris had carried her for miles. That meant something, somehow.

That evening, as the shadows fell, Ezrie invited Aris to sit with her. The android looked puzzled. "I have no need for sitting," Aris said, "but I appreciate your social gesture."

Ezrie felt rebuffed. She didn't even know why she had asked in the first place. To talk, maybe? For the first time since school, she felt like she had a friend.

XI

Chaldean Mountains West, Leto

SECURE 1: Come in, Kenner. Where are you?

Kenner dangled for a moment from the rope, his feet slipping on the treacherous rocky slope. Birdy had taken a dangerous fall. In his hands, he held the backpack, split open, with many of the food pastes opened. Small creatures had been nibbling at them, their droppings littering the side of the cliff where the pack had fallen. Birdy's tracks disappeared here, falling down into an abyss of gnarled roots and tree limbs.

Secure 1: COME IN

The pack was cold, the animals had come. If she had survived the fall, she would not have survived being on her own for four days. His heart sank. He had wanted to see her at least one more time.

The alert buzzed across his trace. He blinked his message, scanning the most likely direction of Birdy's fall. Scanning for a heat trace.

Secure 2: I'm here.

Secure 1: Where the hell have you been? We've lost Aris. Ezrie is offline. And Purple is alive.

How? Kenner looked up, as if he might see the kid standing there. He saw only the forest. How did he survive?

245

Secure 1: I don't know, but Aris is offline. We have no eyes on them.

Far below, the cliff face rolled down to a ledge, then dropped twenty feet or so to a small landing of forest no more than fifty feet wide. Beyond that was a chasm, maybe a half mile across.

She could have fallen off. It was not impossible. He set the idea aside. She had to have stopped somewhere along the forest ledge.

He had a sudden vision of her, lying dead, her entrails exposed, her fine features eaten by the wide, insane jaws of a lycant.

Secure 1: Why the hell are you on the other side of the planet? Is this a joke to you?

Tying up a loose end, Kenner sent, his deception now made bare. Birdy is alive.

secure 1: We're in a shitload of trouble if Ezrie isn't here, alone in three days. Got that? I don't get paid, the Reverend will excommunicate your ass, and neither of us will get off this planet. Do you understand?

"Don't worry," Kenner said, his trace matching his words on the channel. "I'm finishing Birdy off now. Purple is a non-issue."

Secure 1: Better fix this "non-issue" fast. You're running out of time.

Yessir, Kenner sent.

Secure 1: Don't give me that bullshit. Just take care of it.

The line went dead, and Kenner was again alone.

Something about it wasn't right. He tapped his finger against the bag. Birdy had been here. Birdy had fallen. But she had not died. He didn't know how he knew this, but he knew. The pressure at the back of his head intensified, the whispers creeping in on all sides.

She ran away from you.

She is hiding. She is going to them. They *will have her.* They *will love her.*

"No," he said. He shook his head.

They *will have her.*

"No!" He hit himself in the ear, driving the voices out. "Stop."

He shook his head. Hallucinations. Sam had said it. Some kind of infection.

Kenner could not let that stop him now.

He gathered her things in his pack and descended.

XII

Pleasant Grove, Utah, *Earth*

September 2067

MRS. PETERSON IS the last foster mother. She is sugary sweet, with a deep gift for manipulation. She convinces the case worker that Ezrie's trace needs constant monitoring, and so gains legal control to collect and review Ezrie's deeds, saving her thoughts and using them against Ezrie whenever it is most hurtful. And Bethany Peterson *loves information.* Of all the punishments Ezrie ever endures, seeing Marcus' picture—signed, like he's some kind of rock star—is the worst.

You have to learn to forgive, Mrs. Peterson says. Her eyes glitter from the fun of it all. *Then maybe you'll learn how to let people love you.*

The Petersons enroll her in a real school, having been kicked out of several online ones for unethical behavior ("She's too smart for her own good," the case worker tells potential fosters). There, Ezrie skirts the edges of the cliques with the shoplifters and the dealers, already skilled in finding people to use as doorways to what she wants. And this time, she wants out of it all.

One day, after the trace alerts them all to the end of lunch, she is approached by a girl who looks much older than eighteen.

"Bum a smoke?" the girl asks.

Ezrie lends her a cigarette and notes her eyeball tattooed with a tiny gold star.

"I have to go," Ezrie says. "Class is starting."

The girl nodded, "They keep you on a short leash." She pulls a tube of chapstick from her pocket, switching the cigarette out long enough to apply it on perfect pink lips. It smells like cherries.

Ezrie feels the pull of something she has not felt before. Not any of the times boys have kissed her, or the foster father who knows no know will believe her.

"Robyn," the girl says, holding out her hand, the cigarette dangling from the other. "I don't exist."

Ezrie laughs at that, self-consciously, and shakes her hand. The girl smiles. Ezrie can't stop herself from staring at the star, which glitters from Robyn's eye with every flick of the girl's long lashes.

"Staring isn't very ladylike," Robyn says. Her laugh is deep and throaty. It makes Ezrie's insides flutter.

"Sorry," Ezrie stutters. "I've never..."

"Seen someone with stars in their eyes?" She laughs again and crushes the cigarette beneath her boot. She bends over, and Ezrie is sure she is about to scoop up the ash. Instead, when she flicks her head back up, her eyeball is in her hand. The empty eye socket is hollow, the eyebrow aslant.

"Oh my god," Ezrie says, stepping back. She laughs despite herself, a mixture of shock and horror and unadulterated awe.

Robyn holds it out. "Go on. Let me get a look at you."

Ezrie takes it, examining it. It's glass, or something that looks like glass. From a metal burr at the back, there is a soft, blinking green.

"My mom's shitty ex-boyfriend," Robyn says. "Got piss-drunk and smashed some bottles. My eye didn't make it."

It is clear it is more than a prosthetic. The star is tattooed in some kind of ink that shimmers as Ezrie turns it over in her hand. And it's heavy. Robyn plucks it from her hand, pops it into her mouth like a jawbreaker, then slips it back into place.

"I got it from a guy who does things for people. If you have money, that is." She looks Ezrie up and down. "You don't look like his type."

"Maybe not," Ezrie says. "But I know how porters work. I can hack any porter."

Robyn screws up her face, thinking.

"Okay." She says. "I'll let him know."

From around the corner, she can hear the footsteps of the security guards. It means detention, which will end with something painful that Mrs. Peterson will devise. A trip down memory lane, perhaps. Her own worst memories played on a loop as a bedtime story.

Ezrie turns to go, her chest already tense from the horror she'll endure later.

"And, yes," Robyn says with a wicked grin. "I will be your girlfriend."

After that, Ezrie spends as much time with Robyn as she could.

Robyn is a good friend. A soft, kind friend.

Her first sale is to the guy who *did things for people*. It was a program—the first program—The Black Door.

"Invisible port, huh?" The man's name was Ajay, and he had a wide nose and deep acne scars. "How does it work?"

She doesn't tell him that part. Instead, Ezrie rerouts the porter transmission back, connecting into the original transmission field that was still there, hiding in plain sight. A transmission field that no one knows about but herself. And Marcus. The transmission field that killed her father. The one hand-edited by a thirteen-year-old Ezrie.

Ajay is impressed. "I'll buy it," he say. "I want the core code."

"There is no code," she lies. "You know it or you don't. Like an easter egg in a Nets game. I know it, you don't."

Ajay smiles and gives Robyn a glance. She seems pleased with Ezrie's answer. "Smart girl," he says. "Okay. So, package it up and I'll sell it for you."

"Thanks, but no thanks."

Ajay's steps closer, menacing. "You want to do business with my people, you work through me, you got that? You don't follow that rule, you try to steal my clients? I'll break your leg."

Ezrie considers the alternatives. Stay at the Peterson's and become whatever Bethany Peterson wanted her to be. Get a job scraping code for an hourly wage. Get married and pump out kids and some day eat a bottle of pills.

"Fine," Ezrie says. "I'll build the program for your clients. But in return, you take out my trace."

He smiles like a wolf. "That's a done deal, Idgie."

"Ezrie," Robyn says. "You better remember it. Someday you're gonna be working for her." Ezrie feels like she's glowing.

She does enough work for Ajay to save for a place. And it is only a few months later that they schedule the trace surgery. Ajay backpedals on the days leading up to it, making Ezrie promise that she'll stick around and keep building Black Doors. She tells him what he wants to hear, but Robyn knows the truth.

Robyn drives Ezrie to the appointment in a blue car Ezrie buys in cash. It is mostly empty but a few of Ezrie's belongings—the screen left over from her father's own lab, her mother's yellow scarf, and the too-expensive tourist picture of them all. Robyn has tucked one last surprise in the back seat, snapped into the seatbelt like a toddler: A little green fern in a yellow pot.

"You have to have something to take care of." Robyn is doing her best not to cry, but it's no good. Robyn is the one who told Ezrie she would have to disappear. She is the one who gives Ezrie a handful of contacts out east. Robyn is the one who convinces her it is the only way to find Marcus. And now Robyn is falling apart.

Ezrie wipes her friend's cheek and tries to think of something to say. Instead, Ezrie touches her chin, lifting Robyn's mascara-stained face to her own and kisses her softly.

Robyn kisses her back—passionate, delicious kisses that makes Ezrie's head spin and her heart ache. Real kisses that bloom in her chest like twin stars and taste like Marlboros and cherry chapstick.

When she wakes from the surgery, Ezrie is alone. She drives away in the little blue Toyota, nothing but time to think as she travels towards Texas. In the rearview mirror, she glanced at the little plant over and over, as if it might speak. But Ezrie is a shadow, and her only companion is silence.

XIII

Unknown, *Leto*

Date Unknown

SHE SLEPT, she woke, she walked. She walked, she slept, she woke.

Time was nothing to Birdy, only the pain and the hunger and the voices that mumbled beneath the earth.

The pain whispered in the aftermath of her nightmares. They had become as constant as the hobble-step of her stride. The dreams that had started almost the minute she'd come to Leto were becoming strange, frantic nightmares. People that she knew morphing, fading. The mouth of her Cy gone, then sewn shut with thick, black yarn. The kind her aunt had used to knit the blankets she sent for Christmas every year.

Except, last night in the dream, his fingers were field-knives like the one Kenner always had. Cy drew them across his face, and she screamed out. Not for him to stop, but in relief. When she cut the yarn, strings fell out of his mouth like entrails. Yards and yards, flowing, blue threads that reached out for her, filling her eyes and nose and mouth, stuffing her head with yarn.

Birdy stretched her bad leg as roughly as she could, clinging to the very visceral feel of the pain there. It was quieter now. The pain was not much more than a dull ache, but it was real. The dreams were not.

Voices that sounded almost like her mother's and almost like Kenner and almost like her own. But none of that was right. It was *them*. The more she walked, the more she knew that was true. *They* were so many. Like if every grain of sand on a beach was humming, making the whole beach vibrate with the almost-noise of what they were saying.

"Keep it together, Meeshel," she said, shaking the thoughts out like dust from a pillow. It was better when she was talking, even though she knew that it scared away anything she might eat. It was better than the dark silence of the wood; the voices of her mind.

The water was there, still far off, but close enough to hear properly. That was the static she was hearing. The water. She needed to find a way to get there.

Birdy pushed herself up, her body on pins and needles from sitting so long in one place. After a moment, she was able to shake them out, glad that, at least, her leg could feel.

She put some weight on it. It hurt, but it was usable.

"There you go," she coaxed herself. "Look at you, learning to walk."

Birdy's eyes had become accustomed to the shadowy world of the forest. Her trace helped in that regard. Everywhere she looked there were signs of movement—pod squirrels gathering snails, turrets diving for the squirrels with their slimy claws. Still, as much as she had wished, there were few things she could eat. She came to a stand of luminous berries, white as stars and thick as raindrops. She hesitated though, even in her hunger. No animals had touched these. She sobbed as she walked by, hating herself for not having the courage to at least try.

Cy and her mother were always on the stage of her mind. Sometimes Kenner. In her imagination, they would remind her of things she had forgotten. The time she crushed her fingers in the car door and had to get her hands stitched. The boy in second grade who had stolen her padlet and she had told everyone that he was a booger-eater.

These stories were things she had forgotten, but now remembered.

And, as she walked, the memories of them became clearer, like the sound of water somewhere ahead.

Her suit's environmental controls stopped working on the third day of walking. It was not very noticeable since the forest was cool and her body was sweating, but there was a distinct crack and fizz of the main energy compartment shorting out.

Darned phlax. Goshdang Leto.

Birdy found that she had lost much of the spark she had started out with. She could not recall the shiny woman who had been so excited to explore the hidden treasures of Leto. She dragged herself, step after step, hour after hour, day after day, towards the north, following the trail of the golden beasts that had brought her here.

She had begun thinking of them as friends. She caught glimpses of them sometimes, far off in the undergrowth. Their skin like gold, their masks like feathered tentacles, wrapping around the colored moss. They always were further on, further up. One evening, she saw the tops of them as they ran in a pack, a river of gold pouring over the cliff above the subforest floor.

Birdy fantasized about steak and potatoes. She heaped up cornbread and oranges in her mind. She imagined lavish meals and muttered their ingredients to herself as she walked, every day feeling her stomach knot itself, her body eating away at her muscles for the strength to continue.

And always, there was the feeling of being watched. The voices in the shadows. They hid in the sound of water that grew with each day. *They* were there, too. *They* were everywhere.

On her trace, a note flashed, circling a far-off stand of greenery.

"Oh Lord," she whispered, picking up speed. "Oh Lord, I hope I'm not hallucinating."

She nearly ran, dragging the bad leg behind, breathing heavy.

Don't pass out, don't pass out—

She grabbed handfuls of the kingenberries, swallowing them whole, rejoicing in the flavor of anything that wasn't her own water. The berries exploded in her mouth, sweet and tart and crunchy, and her tongue felt as though it would burst.

Birdy ate until she felt sick, then ate more, too tired, too grateful, to fight the rising tide of sound from inside her own head.

Home. They told her she was home.

And she believed them.

XIV

EZRIE COULD FEEL the heat through the suit, making her feel very much like she was being fried in her own juices. It had been yellow sand for miles, now. So when she saw the stand of tall trees in the distance—impossibly green against the brown wasteland—she was sure she was hallucinating again.

Ezrie blinked, feeling a snicker of fear. Were *they* hiding in there? Were *they* waiting?

Who was they?

She didn't know, but she regarded *them* more and more. She could feel *them* just below the surface of the water and in the sand. *They* were above her head, in the air...

"You can see that, right?" Ezrie asked.

"I see a number of trees," Aris responded. She was not functioning properly herself, increasing in self-diagnosed errors. The singing had been a disconcerting anomaly, but not the last. "Scans indicate that there is a water source approximately 1.1 miles beyond the tree line."

Stepping into the patch of grass felt surreal. It was soft, but purple, and not really grass. Ezrie stepped down and ran a gloved hand along the surface. The fronds were like tiny tentacles. They seemed to gently pull at her fingertips.

"What is this?"

"Unknown," the Aris said. The android wore the heavy motorcycle saddlebag over her head, looking like the world's most hardcore newspaper delivery girl. "This area is not currently surveyed, but included on the original map."

"Whose map?"

"I'm unable to say," Aris responded.

"Of course." Whoever had programmed her did not want to share that information. But it was clearly noted on Ezrie's trace as well. It had no name, but it showed to be about a mile long and half a mile wide. And there was water. Ezrie didn't think that anyone had ever given her better news.

As she walked over the purple fronds, they clung to the outside of her outlanding pants like tiny fingers. There was a shimmer which came from somewhere ahead of them, and silvery dapples of light made lazy circles as the ocean of purple undulated beneath their feet. It was mesmerizing, like a kaleidoscope that Ezrie's father had once bought her at a corner store. The light caught the fronds and highlighted nearly-invisible colors: tips of light blue, the purple stalk, and a base of silvery white.

Ezrie was so busy staring at the living carpet beneath her, she ran straight into Aris, who had stopped. Ahead, there was a grove of tall silver-barked trees standing like columns upholding a thick canopy of red, veined leaves. The bark threw silvery specks of light like a chandelier glass, covering the purple carpet with sparks. Small, busy bugs crawled up and down in thin, glistening trails.

Ezrie felt as though she was walking through a forest of Christmas lights. The trees fairly hummed with energy. Aris stated the statistics as she gathered them, giving Ezrie the eerie feeling that she was both there and watching from far off.

"Approximately twelve feet in diameter, covered in layer of silver hairs. Fifty-three percent of the sample size is surrounded by smaller saplings, four to seven centimeters thick—"

"Almost as if they're bracing the main tree up," Ezrie interjected.

"Conjecture, but noted," Aris said crisply.

"They look like birches, kind of," Ezrie said. "I saw some once." She had loved how they looked like they were dancing. She had loved that she was with her father on an outing. It felt so grown up.

"This is kind of weird," Ezrie said, stooping at the closest one. At the base of each tree, whether or not it had the small protective grouping of saplings, there was a well of deep red liquid, almost like a viscous moat. Despite the growing darkness in the sky overhead, the radiance of the trees made it seem like broad daylight. The pool was still as glass, and was virtually impossible to see unless you were very close.

"Unknown." Aris said. "Structure most resembles Great Redwoods from the western banks of old America."

"Beautiful," Ezrie said, rubbing her gloved hand along the hairlike fibers. There was a sharp prick through the webbing of the suit. She pulled her hand back sharply. "Ouch."

She shook her hand a couple times and backed away. It wasn't so much pain, but it was a shock. She flexed her hand. It felt tingly and warm.

"Biometrics indicate a flesh puncture—" Aris began.

"No shit, Aris. I'm fine. It's just a little poke."

Ezrie went to pull the glove from her hand and the world went spinny.

"My hand..." she said. The words came out slow and thick. She felt as if the world was being pulled through molasses. The Aris was suddenly at the end of a long tunnel. She tried to reach out and take her hand, but the darkness was pulling at her.

There was a shifting in the ground beneath them.

Ezrie stumbled backwards as a tree as thick as her leg, dappled and white, rose from the thick mat of black bracken like a tentacle. The branch sought her out, wrapping her and twisting around—

Ezrie tried to scream and run, but her legs felt slow and her body felt like it was made of cement. She fell on top of another thick trunk as it rose from the ground. Her legs were so heavy.

There was a slurping sound as a fan of tree trunks rose up, forming a shape like a slithering, upside-down umbrella. Except the tines were made of snakelike vines. They wrapped around the core silvery tree trunk like a medusa standing on her head. They tore chunks of the soft, purple carpet as they rose through the air searching.

Ezrie screamed as she felt herself lifted, caught by the writhing stalks.

She tried to struggle, but a numbness had seeped into her arms.

She pushed, trying to remove herself from the grasp of the trees as they pulled her ever closer. Her foot slipped, and the toe of her boot slid into the red liquid. There was a hissing and bubbling. She yanked back, her whole leg feeling like dead wood, and fumbled to grasp something, anything that would keep her from the liquid. The top of her boot was bare metal.

Aris came forward, grasping the roots, tearing them from the tree as she could. Larger roots rose up, gripping the android's legs.

"Take my hand," Aris said calmly.

Ezrie tried, but the tree grasped her, tiny limbs like bean plants climbing up her body and wrapping her up tight.

There was a sound as from far away. A thumping, then a shouting.

From behind Aris, Ezrie saw another Aris.

The one turned from her, deflecting a killing blow from the other, tossing her back. The other Aris scrambled up, her face placid, her arms swinging. The two androids grappled with each other, their simultaneous mechanisms moving as if synced, their programming equal, their strength perfectly matched.

"Ezrie!"

She saw the shock of red hair, the skinny arms pumping fast.

"Purple," she slurred, "you were dead, she said you were dead—"

A finger of flame burned from the laster as he cut though the thickest of branches holding her leg.

"Hold on," he panted. Limbs snaked around his wrist. He cut through, yanking his arms away from new, curling tendrils.

She heaved her leg up against the trunk of the tree, feeling as though she were manhandling a dead log, wedging herself between the arms attempting to hold and crush her against the spiked core of the tree. Ezrie looked down at the pool of red directly below her and saw bones.

Shit, Ezrie thought sluggishly. *It's gonna eat me.*

"Purple," she slurred. The limbs pulled her tighter, and she felt her breath puff away.

This is not how I die, this is not how I die—

But then, Ezrie couldn't see much of anything but an encroaching blanket of black, the voices beckoning her into the darkness.

XV

PURPLE DROPPED TO HIS KNEES, rummaging through the underbrush, nearly being snicked by webbed roots that seemed hungry for him. He pulled out the cannister of chemical shower and popped the top, dumping the contents in the pool of bubbling fume.

Please make this work, please make this work—

There was a gawdawful cracking sound coming from where Ezrie was now pinned against the trunk. She was pressed, unconscious, against the bosom of the tree like a babby to its mother's teat. The tree was crushing her.

There was a horrible shriek from behind him. He whirled around, to see Aris. She had sustained damage: her left arm dangled from a clutch of cables, but she did not seem to notice. Instead, she trained her blue eyes on Purple, then leapt towards him like a panther, her fist drawn back to smash his skull.

He pulled the laster's trigger, unloading it into the android's face, pitching her backward.

New tree limbs sprung up, catching his boot, and twirling around Aris' leg. The Aris pulled free easily, lunging for him, a monstrous metallic skull and bare eyeballs peeking from beneath the melted biosheathing.

"P-priority one," Aris said, her voice box jittery, "Eliminate Artemis Crew."

She launched at him again, slapping the weapon from his hand before he could even press the trigger again.

He stumbled back, no weapon, and desperate to run.

Aris was yanked up short. The cables of her broken arm were entangled. Aris tried to pull free, but new shoots sprouted from the underbrush, winding her back to the main tree like a fish on a line.

From the base of the tree, there was a sputtering bubble of fluid. Another large bubble formed, then popped. Purple winced as it splashed droplets on his face. He took his chance, grabbing the laster and burning through branches that glommed onto at his arms and legs. He dropped below a mess of web, narrowly avoiding a root as thick as his arm, like to choke him out.

The Aris struggled against the branches, bashing the tree with hell on her mind. But the tree was pliable, responsive. Every blow activated another layer of webbing, each dragging her faster and closer.

There was a squeezing, crunching sound of metal, and the Aris disappeared into the layers of writhing roots until the tree closed into a cocoon of silence.

Purple looked back to where Ezrie had been. She was gone.

The root webs of the tree were wilted and flaccid, the deep red a muckish brown. The spilled contents of his pack were strewn around the forest floor, with the hastily torn packet of chemical shower floating in the mire.

"Purple."

The voice was Aris'. *His Aris.*

She held Ezrie in her arms. The android's face was severely damaged, and it was clear that the other Aris had tried to smash through her skull. The way she had before.

But this time, Purple had been ready.

By the time Purple had finished washing every part of the The Browns from his skin, Leto's blue moon was glimmering overhead, and the shimmer of the trees was a burnished glow behind them.

Purple sloshed back to shore, soaking and shaking. The pain of his wounds had fanned down, but the sores were still there. He wrapped them in bandages, and then did Ezrie's as well, grateful that he'd been smart enough to at least bring the medical kit. And he'd been there to help her, even though that had not been his plan.

His plan had just been to follow her. But when he realized that he wasn't the only one, he'd fallen back, observing until the right moment.

He hadn't had much of a plan beyond that.

But now, he was here, and Ezrie was breathing. He didn't know if it was good or bad. She was a thief. A gowly liar. And possibly a killer. If he was smart, he would rack her up so she couldn't escape.

Ezrie shivered in her sleep, mumbling. Purple pulled out the silver heat blanket from his pack—luck have it, he had two. He waved off the zephyrs that had collected on her shoulders and back, and draped it over her. Despite who she might have been on Earth, or even what her plan was on Leto, there was no way she was killing anyone today.

No, he wasn't going to tie her up.

He looked over at Aris, a little disconcerted by her damaged face. For the thousandth time, he was so glad he'd moved her main controls to her chest cavity.

"What the shite am I to do now?" he whispered.

"What the shite am I to do now?" Aris parroted. Purple shook his head. If his ma heard what he were teaching this poor robot, she'd string him up.

"Familiarity of speech makes a stronger collegial bond," Aris said in response to his stare. "Is this correct?"

"It's just cracked to hear you talking like a person. I'm not used to it."

Purple set up the tent and heated an MRE, then cleaned out the outlanding suit. He carefully refilled the suit's water cache, adding new water from the lake after he'd filtered it.

As much as he didn't want to, he went back to the trees. He sent Aris to grab the other android's broken body, and she easily maneuvered around the searching tree roots, pulling them apart almost unconsciously. He salvaged what little hadn't been crushed by the impact of the trees. Fortunately, the other Aris' head had sustained minimal damage. The suit, however was trashed.

It was on a wild hair that he went through the pockets of the thing, half remembering some adage about dead men's pockets. He was shocked to feel the tiniest poke beneath his fingernail and pull out a tiny obsidian object.

Ezrie's program.

"What are you doing in there, lad?" he asked the thing. He found a small vial in the medical kit he'd brought and placed the earring inside. It went into his breast pocket for now. He'd give it to her, sure. Just as soon as he knew what she was up to.

As he worked on fixing Aris' face, he talked through the steps. Aris listened quietly. Zephyrs gathered round, as well, alighting on his arms and back, their little bodies glowing. He felt almost important.

"...and so," Purple mumbled as he worked, shooing the little creatures absently, "we need Ezrie to stay alive. At least I think we do if we want to get home."

He blinked into her ops file and ran the facial expression engine. She began making a series of faces. Surprised. Amused. Enraged. None of them fit with the words that came out of her mouth.

"What is home?" Empathy. Frustration. Surprise.

"It's where you're from, I guess." The program finished. Aris face went back to that blank, almost seeking look that she'd had since her reboot. The scratches on her new cheekbone suited her, he thought. They kind of made her look like a badass.

"Is Ocean Base home?" Aris face lit up in recognition, the electric synapses firing as the concepts made new pathways in the biochemical brain.

He smiled. "Likely, to you." To him, home was Mum and Rach and Daph. Part of his home was the graveyard where Milton O'Neill lay. And a big piece of home was linked to machines in a hospital room far, far away. "Home is where your people are. Family."

"Family is a relative bond, through blood or marriage."

"Yeah, but you can have other kinds of family, too." Sam's maternal questioning. Alex's jokes and disastrous confidence. A lump formed in his throat. "Family is..." He paused, trying to find the right words. "Family is the people who you care about and they care about you. People you want to protect. Spend time with."

"You spend time with me."

Purple felt the smile on his face again. She was so quick, so intent on learning the things that he had to teach. In the light of the electric torch, she looked so human. "Yes. That's true."

"Am I your family?"

He looked at her, considered the biomechanical processes that hummed behind the diode eyes. *Tell me something real,* Sam had asked him.

Is this real? He had to wonder.

"Yeah," Purple said. "I guess right now you are."

"I will protect you," Aris said. She said it simply, but there was such an emphatic, concerned crease along her perfect forehead. "I will be your family."

"Right now, you just be Aris, deal?"

"Then I will be Aris." Her face shimmered with a new thought. "After I am Aris, perhaps I will be family?"

He smiled again. "Maybe someday you can be both."

Ezrie groaned and stretched, spooking the blanket of zephyrs that had been rest on her as she slept. Somewhere, something rustled in the bushes. Brindle's face flashed in his mind. The Lycant marks deep enough that you could see the white of his bones.

Ezrie's eyes fluttered. She mumbled something that Purple couldn't make out.

"Purple," she said.

"Hey," he said, raising his hand in a half-wave. Despite everything, he suddenly felt as if he were seeing a celebrity at his high school prom and he'd forgotten to wear pants.

"You—" she croaked. "You were dead. Aris...Aris said—"

"Stay still," Purple said. "You're okay. We got you out in time."

"We...speak..." she muttered. In the light of the trees, she was ghostly pale. Purple glanced at Aris who stared blankly at them both. Whatever was going on was above his pay grade. But it didn't matter. He was the only one on the job.

PART 5

BLUE IS FOR BECOMING

"Transitions are the hardest part of any project. A new blacker, a new program, the place where digital organisms meet biological ones. In the limin, we recognize the soft places of our own experience and learn how to either tame them or expand them."

The BlackBook, Last Accessed 2072

|

Green Springs, *Leto*

Day 10

EZRIE'S MOUTH tasted like carpet. There was pain like tiny fires all over her skin, the feeling of muscles awakening after falling asleep. There was a snatch of a dream in the back of her head. Something about being in the desert, looking for water. She brought a leaden hand to her temple, and everything swayed in slow motion. From beneath her, she felt herself sinking, and she scrambled to her feet.

Someone was watching her. She could feel the whispers in her head, sliding below the surface of her consciousness. *They* were getting closer.

She shuddered.

"Careful," Purple said. "You're lucky that thing didn't snuff you out."

He was naked from the waist up, and his skin was slick with water. The blue Leto moon, Delos was what Birdy had called it, was reflected in its inky surface. Surrounding them on all sides were tall, weeping trees. The grass was soft, and it pulled at her, as if it were kissing her feet. She was not in her outlanding suit, either, just her skinpants and tank. She sat up, the

269

heat blanket falling from her shoulders, the zephyrs puffing away like smoke. Her body grumbled at the quick motion, her head throbbing.

"Where's Aris?" she said, pressing her hand to her forehead. "What happened?"

"Hello," Aris said, a slight lilt to her voice as well. Damned if the kid hadn't turned her Irish, too. "My name is Aris. It is a pleasure to meet you."

Her voice had smoothed out again, and there was a blank look about her. The rest of what had happened dawned on Ezrie. Everything hurt, but it seemed to act as a sharpener for her senses. And she did feel better. More cogent. "Purple." She almost hugged him. "Aris said you were dead."

"I disagree," Aris said with a smile. "I am not capable of deception."

"I think you mean 'thank you,'" Purple said. Ezrie looked at him blankly. "You know. Cause I saved your life. You're welcome."

Ezrie's face went hot. She exploded at Aris. "You told me—"

"*She* didn't tell you anything," Purple interrupted. "She's been with *me* for six days. The Aris that was with you is the one who said I was dead. Probably because she thought I was."

"What are you talking about?"

"The Aris with you wasn't the Aris that came with us. Somebody sent her. Likely it's the same person who wanted you here."

Purple sat near the electric torch fire that crackled between the tents. Ezrie noted that he had put hers up as well.

Ezrie shook her head.

"I don't believe that. There were two of them? Why?"

Purple grabbed the white tank undershirt and pulled it on. He had lost that puppy dog look, merely glancing at her like she were slightly unpleasant. Whatever star blindness he'd had when she'd arrived was long gone. There was a hardness in his face that had replaced it.

"I don't know," Purple said, flatly. "But I know that the one who was with you killed Sam and Lee."

"What? That's impossible." She had been Ezrie's friend. As Kenner had put, she had been on Ezrie's team. She had protected her. She had watched over her. "She never hurt me. Why would she kill anyone else?"

Purple was hunched over, and the thin white tank shuddered. Ezrie looked away. She didn't want to see him cry. When he looked back up, his eyes were red.

"She's a machine," Purple said quietly. "With the right programming, she'll do whatever you tell her to. Marcus wanted us dead and you alive. It's simple as that." He paused to slip the outlanding suit on.

She shook her head. The same reasoning bubbling up from her that she'd been nursing on for days. "I can't believe it. He isn't a killer. I mean, I hate him, but—"

"I agree," Purple said. "He's not a killer. That's why he sent Aris to do it for him. And the only reason I'm still alive is because you shot me."

Ezrie felt the information catch in her brain. Of all the things she had done, shooting Purple was the one that hadn't been a complete screw-up. She laughed. "Aris wouldn't have been able to see you since you were in the porter bay—"

"Thank God for mitrium. Exactly," he said. "I guess that's how I figured that you hadn't cacked 'em. If you had wanted all of us dead, you would have killed me, too." He gave her a sad smile. "And there's no real reason for you to want me alive. Except for this."

He held up a small vial, and Ezrie's stomach dropped.

"That's mine," she said. "Give it back."

"Hold your tits," he said, tucking it in the pocket of his outlanding suit. "I'll pay it back when we get there. Just in case you want to do me any more favors."

Ezrie was livid. He had no idea what he was messing with. Fifteen years of working towards this and now it was going to be sideswiped by some idiot Gen kid?

"You have no idea what that is! That's the whole reason I'm here." Ezrie wondered if she could steal it from him. She might have to. Except that Aris was his bodyguard now. Shit.

She rubbed her empty earlobe out of habit. Why had she forgotten about it when she traded suits with Aris? What was wrong with her brain? "Why don' you just leave it with me, okay? It has nothing to do with you."

"But it's all to do with Marcus, oy?" Purple said. "And that has everything to do with me. All of us, like."

"Listen," she bargained, "I'll go after Marcus, with the program. You go back to the base and send a message. Then, I'll meet you there, with him. And we'll be able to all go home together."

"We can't," he said. "Kenner razed the Mountain transmitter. The Ocean transmitter, too. No transmitter, no porting off Leto. Not even a message."

"Kenner? That doesn't make sense." She shook her head. No. Kenner was a nice guy, one of the few people who actually didn't hate her. He had made sure—

"I could give a bob if you believe it," Purple snapped. "That's truth, for you. Kenner was doubling up parts that he used to make a bomb, the logs showed it. That's what took down the tower."

Ezrie's head felt like is was being crushed. Not having a door wasn't really a problem. She could fix that. Not having a transmitter was a different story.

"You could fix it, right?" she said, looking up. "You could get the transmitter working—"

"Not alone. You were the key to get here. I wager you're the key home, too."

The quiet of the glade was filled only with the sound of a pair of echoing birds from somewhere nearby. Ezrie felt her heart sink. No one had been on her side all along. Not Kenner. Not Aris.

Ezrie felt something inside of her shift. It wanted to be anger. It wanted to rage against Purple's words. It wanted to explode and say that none of it was her fault, that she had no idea what was going on any more than anyone else. There was something else there, though. It wasn't anger. It was guilt. It was regret.

They had all died. They had all died because Marcus had only wanted her. The Lock was meant for her only to pass through. The rest of them were never supposed to come.

They had paid the price for her unwillingness to let the past go.

But it's not my fault. I didn't know—

It doesn't matter, her father's voice said in her ear. *You were willing to put them all at risk, and they died for your cause. Is it worthy?*

"I—" she started, the words to defend herself thick and sloggy in her brain. "I'm sorry. I'm so sorry." She crumpled, the weight of what she had done, what she had caused too heavy to bear. "I didn't know. I didn't know they would die. I'm sorry. I'm sorry—"

She fell to the ground, racked with sobs. They had been snuffed out on her behalf. Birdy and her brilliant, self-effacing notes. Sam with her nosy, good-natured questions. Kenner and his kindness—

"Kenner," she said, her throat full of tears. "Kenner said he was on my team. Am I on the bad team?" She felt the weight of that, saw it in Purple's eyes as he turned away. "Am I the bad guy?"

She buried her face in her hands. All this time, and she had assumed she was the hero.

Ezrie flinched at the soft touch against her shoulders. Aris clutched her in a gentle, awkward embrace.

"Aya," Purple said softly. "But you don't have to be."

Before they left the oasis, Purple insisted Ezrie look at the contents of the files he had wrangled from the Anti Aris' control center.

"Put it back here," he said, brushing her hair from her neck. His hand was surprisingly gentle, and the feel of his hands on her skin made her breath catch.

She pulled back, flustered, and he blushed deeply. "Sorry. Um, you have to get it close to your trace. It should connect by proximity."

She put the drive beside her trace, and chided herself inwardly. *Don't get all weird, Ezrie,* she thought. *Things are weird enough as it is.*

Ezrie blinked open the dead android's files and saw what he'd wanted her to see. It was all there. All those files that had come to her like a magic bullet. It had been Aris who sent those files using Rand's permissions. It had been Aris' secondary goal to lead Ezrie back to Marcus, alone. It had been Aris primary goal to kill anyone else or anything else.

Still, something about it rang false.

The video files of the crew deaths were violent. Even Lee, whom Aris had kept from following Ezrie. Ezrie watched, horrified, as the android waited until Lee's back was turned, looking for survivors, before tackling her, breaking her laster arm, and bashing in her skull.

TRACE NEUTRALIZED, the record stated. FULLY CONTAINED.

Unrestrained. Heartless. It was more than murder. It was a demolition.

"Marcus will be peeping us to come up direct by the river," Purple said. "We could come round the back way, through the Flats and give him the skip."

"Well, well, well," Ezrie said, impressed. "Look who grew up overnight."

He blushed, looked at the ground. "Maybe."

"It's a good idea," she said, her hand on his shoulder. He looked up at her, and she quickly removed it. She suddenly felt very warm. "It, um. It means we'll have to go through the desert, though. We need to carry as much water with us as we can. Right."

Ezrie left feeling awkward. Like she was fifteen again.

She filled the bottles, cleaned and filled the outlanding suits, and took inventory. At the same time, she was trying not remember Purple's hand brushing her hair from her face. How he'd looked in the moonlight, his chest bare, his hand on her waist.

"Oh my god, stop," she muttered. "He's a kid."

Twenty-five is pretty grown, she considered. Sure, it was probably a lie, but it had to be close, didn't it?

Purple did a final check on Aris' new parts. Aris' new brain was in her chest—a little trick that had kept her alive when the Anti-Aris had tried to kill her—and she was opened up now, her new little saline heart right between her silicone breasts. Purple stared at them quizzically, scraping out her insides with a small metal brush.

Ezrie considered saying something. Something about how it only made sense that a man would put a woman's brains in her boobs, but didn't.

"Hey!" Ezrie shouted. "You were holding out on me."

She held up the MREs that he had tucked at the bottom of the pack.

"Keep your mitts off them," he said. "They're for special."

She grimaced. "What's a more special occasion than me not dying?"

"Learn how to be nice," he smirked. "That'll be special enough."

Ezrie shoved them back to the bottom.

"Oh Purple," she sighed. "You better get used to food paste."

T he hills beneath the bike's wheels became mountains, the grass growing sparser and the river becoming a stream. Aris ran before them, wearing the Anti-Aris' saddlebag and scanning for easy paths that the bike could travel through.

Ezrie was angry that Purple was keeping her program hostage, but she didn't really blame him. She *had* shot him and left him for dead. Keeping her program was insurance. But she'd have to get it back sooner or later.

Purple set up a direct communication channel through the suits so that that they could talk while they rode, but Ezrie still didn't feel much like sharing. Besides, the outlanding had begun to hiss like a balloon with a puncture, and she was sure that it wouldn't last long.

But although she felt no need to talk, Purple didn't share the sentiment. So, she let him talk to fill the silence. And she *was* curious. It had been terrible to think that he was dead, and she wanted to know how he'd survived. Whatever had happened, he seemed different somehow. So when he started talking, she listened.

II

Ocean Base, *Leto*

Day 4

PURPLE STUMBLES TOWARDS THE BASE, his legs still watery from the laster hit. The late afternoon sunlight burns the sky red, the twin suns a fiery single ring as they near the horizon. The woods are quiet, broken only by the awkward call of a bird as it glides through the air overhead, its talons tucked against its mass of red feathers which trail like a kite.

As he passes through the airlock into the base, he sees boot prints on the floor, red as cherries.

He spies Aris' hand on the ground and jogs over to where she lies broken. Her head is crushed, leaving nothing but broken wires and a still-oozing saline sac where the main cortex controls should have been. He hears a moan from further in. From the infirmary.

"Alex? Sam? Lee? Where you at, mates?"

His own voice is thin and reedy against the steel walls. He waves the infirmary door open, his skin crawling, his laster in hand. If it's a trap, he's not prepared to fight. He fears that somewhere further in, Ezrie is waiting for him.

He sees the brown of Sam's hair and stifles a cry. That is all of her that he could recognize.

Sam's face is an absence, her skull a bowl of human soup where broken pieces of brain and bone float in red and ocher fluid. The bones of her spine are visible above the neck of her outlanding suit.

He touches her hair and calls her name, as if saying it might make this nightmare disappear. He hears another moan, and is not sure if it is from him or her or someone else.

"Who goes?"

He glances up at the monitors on the walls. Alex is still alive.

He goes across the hall, the pain of his legs now secondary to the panic in his chest.

"Alex," he calls, "Alex, mate. How goes it?"

His friend is turned away, his body curled up on the bed in a ball. The smell was overpowering. Vomit and feces and the deep, sick-sweet smell of rotting. He tries to stop the vomit from coming up, blocking with his hands, but he can't.

No. No it can't be. Not Alex.

Alex gives another moan, and Purple wipes his face shakily on the sleeve of his outlanding jacket.

"I'm here, lad. I'm here now."

Alex breathes, and it is a mucousy, watery sound.

"Helph," he mumbles, "hurts..."

Purple comes around to face his friend and is nearly sick again.

Alex's hair is gone in huge patches, and where the patches are gone, so is the scalp. The skull bones pulse with each breath, losing shape and integrity before settling precariously back into place.

Alex tries to reach out for Purple, but straps hold him to the hospital bed, cutting through his bleeding flesh like a gutknife through a fish.

"Sh—shh," Purple whispers, grabbing the mans' hands. His foot slips in the pool of his own vomit, but he manages to hold his friend back. Purple's fingers leave bruises on the man's flesh, dents where the blood pools beneath the skin.

"Oy, mate," Purple smiles. He is crying, but he doesn't even bother to wipe the snot coming from his nose. "Lad. It's me. It's Purple."

Alex struggles to speak, small chunks of pale-colored material falling out of his mouth with each word. Purple shushes him, feeling his stomach seize. He retches again and wiped his face on his sleeve.

Alex looks up, his blue eyes still untouched by whatever horrors have eaten the rest of him. He stares at Purple, then at the laster still in his hand. Purple, pale and freckled, half-holds him, giving him enough air to hack out a stream of sloppy words.

"You'll be okay," Purple says. "We'll have you back to rights soon enough."

The bag of drugs is empty. Purple rummages through the supplies, looking for something that can help. Anything.

"Puhleese," Alex slops the words, his hands grasping slowly for the laster. "Puhleese..."

Purple pauses, understanding now.

Alex makes a series of low grunts that could have been words had his tongue not lolled grey and dead in his mouth. The skin around his eyes is loose and gaping, as if it has been sewn on poorly and the seam is starting to tear.

Purple flicks the bag of pain medication, fumbling, crying as realizes what he has to do.

He puts the gun to Alex's head, closing his eyes as he presses the trigger. There is screaming, but the sound is swallowed by the crackle and buzz of his laster. He only realizes when she stops that the screams are coming from himself.

He buries Sam and Alex on the hill overlooking the base, digging the hole as deep as he can despite the pain that lingers in his muscles and head. He knows the graves are skim. Protocol is to save the bodies in storage until the port home, but he has simply flagged out and doesn't care.

There is almost nothing left of either of them, neither Alex nor Sam. Whoever has killed Sam has mangled her, left almost nothing to identify her by. No face, no brain, no trace. Just a broken body he wishes was someone else. Alex is a shell. Alex's face has gone gashy, the bones of his skull losing rigidity and the cells crumbling like sand. He is a monstrous shadow of the man that Purple had known.

Purple downloads what he can from Alex's trace and lays him beside Sam at the top of the hill. He piles up colored stones on the mounds for his friends—a rainbow of purples, reds, and blues.

He feels a sickness of anger well up in him. A guilt. If he'd have told Rand to kick it up his hole, or been savage enough to tell Alex how dangerous it was to come—

But he hadn't.

He holds the laster, turning the power up, putting it to his own head. He doesn't deserve to live while they are dead. He turns the power up, listening to the electrons moving. They sound like an invitation.

Come home, his mother and sisters say. *Come back to us.*

Aya. It could be that easy.

He sits beside the small graves he had made, the urge to pull the trigger so attractive. A release. A going home. That's what it will feel like.

But there are things to clean up first.

P urple makes his way back to the engineering shed. He stares at the pieces of the tozed android for a long time, unsure of the next steps. Aris' is nothing but broken wires and a still-oozing saline sac from the neck up. He laid her on the printing table, his head bowed.

Why would anyone cack Aris? She never did a harm.

Finally, the tears wells up. Tears for himself for not being faze enough. For Alex and Sam. For Aris. For himself. He is scared and alone, and knows that he needs to find Ezrie. Wherever she is, she is the key to it all.

Purple picks Aris' head up carefully (as if she can feel anything, now), and considers what it will take to rebuild. It'll take time, but it's possible.

There is no way to save Sam or Alex. There is no way to bring back Rand or the others. But he can save Aris. That has to be enough.

III

Ocean Base, *Leto*

Day 5

PURPLE'S ADDITION to the Leto team had been a complete surprise, considering he was green as grass. His mother invited all of his sisters over, and it was one of the last times that Clare was as he loved her most—loud and annoying and full of life. She slugged him and asked how many tests he'd cheated on, fully knowing that Finn O'Neill had never had to cheat a day in his life. It was full craic, it was.

Despite his mother's fawning and his sister's gushing compliments, he suspected most people from Mayo County thought him taking the piss. Doober Byrne said to his face what he knew everyone was thinking: "Who the eff goes to Cambridge for engineering at sixteen? I'd say you got a goat of a girl in the way, but your willy's never seen the inside of a broken barn."

But those who *did* believe the stories in the papers had their own earful to spit. And it didn't get better when he finished his five-year program in just over two years.

"Master's Degree? Master of what?" His auntie Fedelma had said with a sniff, taking a huge helping of broccoli. It was Easter and everyone had already had too much to drink. "If he's such a master, he should've done better'n water mining like a galoot. PanGen be damned."

"PanGen is one of the big ones, so no one here is complaining," his mother had said. Tigla O'Neill was a strong-minded woman, but never brash or loud. Her sister was another story.

"Well, it's true," Fedelma said smugly, reaching for the biscuit bowl.

"It's true you're fat, but we have the good manners to say it behind your back," his mother had retorted, pulling the biscuits from her hand. Fedelma couldn't have looked more surprised if a mouse had crawled up her knickers.

She was right, though. PanGen *was* one of the big ones, but not one with faze. The job wouldn't win him a Nets channel or score him a fine wife. Purple suspected that he was only hired because having a Generation kid filled some diversity checklist that the Board is keen on.

But, when it comes to androids, Purple can sometimes see why they'd want him. Even Jenny had seen his knack for it. He understands androids like Birdy understands living things. And Aris is much less complicated than any woman he's ever known.

———

Purple is possessed in work, losing track of the days like a dog running blind. He gathers parts from what is still usable in the engineering shed, then prints the rest.

As Purple rebuilds her, he keeps the door pushed open, his eye on the forest and the base beyond. The laster is always at his side and always set to kill.

He can't stop rolling everything over in his head. As he works, he pieces the parts together in his mind just like he fits new connectors for Aris' corpus collosum.

It's all a bad sum that doesn't add. Aris is a case in point. Whoever had harmed Aris hadn't wanted her disable, they'd wanted her demolished. *El splatto.* He puts the image of Sam out of his head, the empty hole where her face had been. *El splatto.*

So Ezrie kills Sam and Aris, but no Alex. Then she runs away? It didn't make sense. He picked up the spine and connected it to the new skull, a satisfying snick as the connectors coupled. If Ezrie killed Sam, she would have definitely have killed Alex. Although Richard Collings is a footnote in most origin stories of the Olet Porter, he is there. And in the Blacker circles Purple runs in, it is fact that Richard Collings was the first casualty of his own technology and Ezrie watched him die. It would be cold of her to let Alex go the same way.

Plus, Ezrie it all pointed to Ezrie having an accomplice. Clearly Kenner is working with her, because someone gave her the access codes for the bikes—all of which are now missing. And, from what he knows, every person with security access besides Kenner, Ezrie, and Marcus, is dead.

So, he needs to find a way to go where they are, because being here feels like living in a morgue.

When he is tired, he walks down to the ocean. The zephyrs dance over the water—dipping down and kissing the surface, then shifting up in a circular tide. He has the irresistible desire to walk in and take a deep breath. There is something down there. Someone that knows him and is waiting for him.

Purple counts the days by the amount of progress he makes on Aris. On day seven, she wakes, the newly printed cerebral cortex housed safely in a refurbished saline sac. The only problem now is to rebuild her operating system.

Without the trace, all he can offer her are the backup Aris program files from the infected hard drive. It is tozed with phlax—error messages warning that containment failure is imminent. He prizes it open anyway, removing as much of the phlax as he can before downloading her new running files.

Purple transfers the Aris files directly to the android. The process seems to last a donkey's years, with Aris' eyes shifting and dilating rhythmically as she absorbs information. He is sure that, even after all he's done to salvage her hardware, she will encounter a fatal error from the server and cack it right in front of his eyes.

But Aris surprises him by blinking slowly and sitting up.

The next morning he takes her for a walk to test her new wiring, all the way out to the motorcycle bay. He has to stop himself from punching the bay door. All the bikes are gone. He will have to build some kind of harness for the android. He tries not to think about how stupid it will be to ride Aris' back to find the others.

As Purple considers this image, Aris steps badly down a sandy slope and he instinctively puts out an arm. Her face, which is still in need of an emotional upgrade, shows bored resignation as she falls stiffly.

"I am falling," she intones before crashing face first into the ground. It strikes Purple as exactly like one of those goats that fall over when they are scared, and he bursts into laughter.

"Why are you laughing?" She asks.

"Sorry, I was trying to help and it didn't work very well."

"Perhaps you should not try to be helpful again," Aris says pragmatically.

Purple smiles. "You're not wrong."

He takes her back to the engineering shed, disables her and solders a handful of new connections. As he works, he is sure he can hear Aris talking to him, even though her eyes are dark and logically it should have been impossible. Once, he is sure she calls his name—his real name.

Finn.

That night he has dreams where he cannot hear. His mind is full of alien shapes that leave traces of meaning on his eyelids.

———

P urple awakes in the middle of the night out of sorts, having fallen asleep on the cold metal of the printing table. From outside, he hears the snap of a branch.

Cold fear catches in his throat. His muscles feel like rubber as he forces himself up from the table. He grabs his laster and slips out hesitantly.

The pale blue of the moon shines overhead, lighting everything in ominous shadows. Through the large-leafed Rimands that tower over the sand, he spies movement at the top of the hill.

Ezrie. Come to cack him off, too.

But the sound is loud, bulky.

Not Ezrie, Marcus. Or maybe both. Yes. That's what it was.

He turns the laster up to its highest setting with a shaking hand.

Purple keeps low to the ground, fighting the urge to run. If Marcus really is out here still, waiting for a change to finish him off, Purple needs as much surprise as he can muster. He moves to the trees, studying the underbrush where he saw the flicker of movement.

Purple pauses, heart pounding, his breathing shallow and silent. The forest is still, but there are no sounds of birds or animals. A faint soft wind from the southeast caresses the ferns and hushes through the leafy canopy.

It moves again, and this time there is no mistaking. It is a human figure.

From his vantage point, he can see its form but not its body. It is camouflaged. The only thing that Purple can really identify is the size. Over six feet tall, and twice and wide around as himself. The creature gives a spluttering bark.

Purple shifts to get a better look and a branch breaks beneath his feet. Purple stumbles back, dropping the laster as he falls.

The thing snaps its head around. It's Alex.

Alex's face is nearly unrecognizable and covered in blood and dirt. There is an unearthly glow coming from the broken bones of his legs and skull, and Purple can see the phlax twisting in sinuous tendrils up through the dessicated flesh of Alex's crushed face. He clutches a small bird in his hands, though they are less like hands than bony claws. He tightens his grip on his prey and gives a low, screaming cry, a sound that is both lonely and legion at the same time.

"Alex," Purple's voice quaked. He rose, his mind wheeling. "Wait—"

Alex's screams turns to a hiss, and he darts away, through the moon-soaked trees.

Out of his mind, Purple chases him, unable to cob any thought but the one that compels him forward: Alex is alive. *Alex is alive.*

Purple stumbles, fell, then picks himself up and surges forward. Ferns slap him in the face as he rushes past them, the greenery growing ever thicker as they move up the coastline together. Once, Alex turns back to him, pausing and hissing, his mouth open and blue light streaming from inside him like fire. Alex chomps the bird between his broken jaws and plunges headlong into the darkness of the forest, this time on all fours and moving at a speed that defies the brokenness of his body. He does not shamble or veer. Alex is a predator, seeking some prey that is beyond Purple's sight, bounding on bones that glow with moonlight.

Purple falls to the ground. His side aches from the chase. His heart mocks him for his stupidity. Sam had said it herself: this was only—could only be—a vivid hallucination. Some broken part of his brain tries to conjure up a way to undo the horrible thing he has done.

He feels the eyes of the forest on him, then, and he knows it is true. He is sleeping. He is losing his mind. Purple wipes droplets of tears or sweat from his face, knowing that they are all the same, really, as every other drop of water on Leto. He starts the heavy, long walk back towards the base.

By the time he makes it back, the red light of Pyrios has begun to illuminate the jungle in brilliant orange. He sits in the sand, watching Aeos follow it. The light of the suns sparkles over the red sea, and the zephyrs flit through the air, making the world ethereal in the dawn. Despite being flagged out and brain-weary, the sun cleanses even this damned world. Purple feels something that has been tight in his chest loosen. He lets it unwind, trying not to think of the monster he has created in his mind.

Finn, they call. *It's time.*

He strips off his clothes and walks towards the ocean. Aris couldn't save him. He had no way to go where Ezrie was. He was done with fighting them. Because even now, he can hear them calling and wants to come.

Come home, Clare says. *I'm safe here. I'm well.*

Come home, his little sisters says. From beneath the sluggish, bloody waves, he could almost see them giggling: *We want you to stay.*

"Let me say goodbye first," he whispers. "Then I'll right it."

He picks a handful of pink flowers that yawn in the red light. Purple goes to the graves and lays the flowers down.

But something is wrong here.

The mounds of rocks have been scattered, the ground where he has buried Sam and Alex has been troubled. Instead of the rising mound of purple sand, there is a depression. Something has been here and has been digging.

"No," he says. His voice strange and high-pitched, even to his own ears. "No. It's not that. It can't be that."

But no matter how many times he says it, he cannot deny the footprints that trail from the grave into the forest.

Alex had gone without him, somewhere.

Purple turns back, his eyes searching the red water. They were all waiting for him there. And he hoped they would wait a little longer. For now, he had to find where Alex and Ezrie and Marcus had gone.

The next morning, he takes Aris on his first wide sweep since the dark day he woke in the porter. When they come to the eastern shack, Purple spies the downed bike and nearly splits himself.

"Unreal!" he shouts, hugging the downed bike as if it were his best mate. There is no sign of the driver.

Aris cocks her head quizzically.

"It's a hug," he says, pulling away. "You give it to someone when you're happy. Or sad. It's kind of an all-purpose gesture."

"Are you happy or sad?"

"Both, I guess."

She nods, something in her eyes seeming to light up.

Aris carries the bike back to the engineering shed, and Purple and Aris work on it all that night. Purple carefully removes and replaces components while Aris cuts away thick swaths of phlax that fall in dusty piles all around the workroom floor.

On the eighth day, they leave. Purple pushes the bike tentatively through the brush, a vague hope that Ezrie's DNA fragments will be enough of a scent for Aris to track her.

The android pauses as they visit the sweeps shack one last time. Ezrie or Lee have been here, otherwise the bike wouldn't have been left behind. But he's cobbed that Lee had been chasing Ezrie before something or someone stopped her.

"Do you see any matches, Aris?"

Aris scans again. He was a tool to think that he could bring her back to life using mismatched parts and gowly code. He was a kid who had a great brain and always needed someone in front to follow. He closes his eyes, sure that she will say they were dead flat. No signal to follow.

"I have found a match," Aris says.

Purple lets out a breath, then smiles.

"Run the front, Aris."

Then they are off, with Aris running ahead, her body quick as lightning through the dappled green of the forest, looking the world like his setter on the scent of a rabbit.

IV

Chaldean Mountain Range East, *Leto*

Day 10

PURPLE TOLD her about putting Aris back together again. About how he had rebuilt her from pieces and parts, rebooting her OS from the contaminated storage containment. As he did, the mountains fell back, veering to the east as they maintained a northerly route. When he had finished, they had all but disappeared, nothing but hard-packed white salt beneath the tires.

When he talked about Alex, Ezrie almost forgot to breathe.

"Alex was alive? After you killed him?" She couldn't quell the incredulity in her own voice. She could hardly believe him. Her own thoughts had been so bizarre and untrustworthy. Something out of a monster movie. "Is it possible you dreamed it?"

"I can't say," Purple said, his body rigid. His voice was flat and tinny in the outlanding hood's speaker. "But I wager it's why there's none of 'em buried. Apollo, I mean," Purple said. "They don't stay."

"Where do you think he was going?" Ezrie said. The com box spluttered and hissed. When Purple didn't answer, she wasn't sure he'd heard her at all.

The niggling voices at the back of her brain shuddered as if in laughter. *Where were any of them going? Where were they all going?*

She didn't ask any more questions and Purple didn't tell any more stories.

Marcus dominated her thoughts. Ezrie was remembering the past, so clearly. The smell of his leather jacket. The way that he would sometimes laugh with her father at the dinner table when they played cribbage. About the reason she had come. A snippet of the BlackBook bubbled up from her memory, a quote that she had underlined when she had been trying to do things the right way. It had struck home to her in a way that was visceral—a truth that had been guiding her for her whole life.

When you understand your enemy, there is the risk that you will love him.

She had spent a decade learning everything she could about Marcus. She knew his favorite color was red, that he preferred Jaguars over Royces. She knew he liked blondes and drank Long Island Ice Tea when he was drinking alone. She had known all this and never loved him. And because of it, she had never found him.

To black your enemy, you have to understand him. You have to run the risk of loving him.

Tentatively, she blinked into Marcus' trace records she had stolen from the containment unit.

Much of it was bland. Insurance forms. Reports on porter usage. Supply orders.

She paused at Marcus' personal log folder, then blinked in.

The entries were short and perfunctory. It must have been a requirement of the team—probably from Sam or someone like her—to barf these internal feelings down on the trace. Looking through these files felt like peeking in on him as he was showering.

To black your enemy, you have to understand him.

Okay. Okay. I can do this.

––––

May 19th, 2078

The work for the second porter is going okay. Jenny Candala is supposed to be my number two on this. She is very nice, but not as capable as she could be. She's broken nearly every part she's printed. We're using up huge amounts of printing compound, and I can hardly order them fast enough to keep up. As far as I'm concerned she should probably stick with androids and assisting Nancy. Kind of flirty, too. Not that it bothers me. But I get the impression that she's up for anything.

––––

July 3rd, 2078

I'm feeling a little disjointed. I'm thinking a lot about Elsevior and Richard. Ezrie is saying things about how I didn't invent it. It's really frustrating, because I have never said that Richard wasn't a huge part of the creative process.

I feel stuck. I remember Ezrie when she was a kid. Smart and nice. She's out there saying all kinds of stuff that is half-true,

and I can't even speak to it because of all
the NDAs and gag clauses in this industry.

Ezrie paused, reading the entry over again.

"Hey, Purple." She hesitated. "Did Marcus ever talk about me?"

There was a long pause, the vibration of the motor the only sound.

"Yeah," he said. "Once or twice."

"What did he say?"

Purple seemed to consider his words.

"He said you were whip-smart. He said he knew you when you were a kid. He really mostly talked about your da. Told us about all the groundwork he did for the porters. He really respected him, I think."

Something about the way he said it made her feel guilty.

Had she been wrong all this time? Had she—

No. She shut down Marcus' files. She couldn't have been wrong. She remembered the way it had been. Sitting across from him at his office. Calling him up when her father had died. He had taken advantage of her and stolen her father's legacy.

But she felt the first tremor in her bedrock of hate. And the closer they moved towards his location, the more she seemed to feel him watching her.

They stopped early because of the rain. It wasn't dangerous like at home, but it was red and sticky, and Ezrie could feel how soaked the outlanding suit was over her sweaty skinpants and tank. The zephyrs, their recent nighttime companions, abandoned them. By the time they had made camp, however, it had started to clear. Still, they didn't appear, leaving the sky empty but for a rash of stars.

"I'm making a fire," Ezrie declared. "I've got to get all these clothes off."

"All of them?" Purple asked, his eyes wide.

She rolled her eyes. "Just keep your eyes and hands to yourself, and I won't have to destroy you."

Ezrie stripped off her wet things, shivering in the crisp evening air. The desert was cold at night. Purple was looking down, presumably counting the rocks between his feet.

She set up the Xtenz line, attaching one end to her tent and the other to Purple's across the fire. It was good enough, she thought as she hung her things over the fire pack. It was small, but hot enough to make your skin feel burned if you sat closer than two feet away. And if she was lucky, it would provide enough heat that her suit wouldn't be drenched by next morning.

Ezrie slipped back into the tent and pulled the silvery heat blanket around her. A clutch of trees surrounded the little glen that they'd made camp in. They were softly luminescent, giving the sky a green tint. Ezrie was almost cozy.

"Okay, you can open your eyes," she said. "Goodnight, Purple."

"Finn," he said.

She paused. "Finn?"

"Yeah. That's my name back home."

She smiled up at the stars over the tent. Finn was a good name. It fit him. "Goodnight, then, Finn." It was a little too intimate, and she found herself fighting in her own head. Do I really want to start this? Now? "On second thought, I'll probably just call you Purple," she yelled.

He sighed audibly. "Yeah. I thought you might."

———

That night, Ezrie had her first dream of Marcus. In it, he was sitting in her father's shed, the tools packed up, holding the entangler for the porter in his mouth. When he tried to speak, the scanner burned her skin to the bone, her eyes going blind from the bright, blue light. Above him, stars were falling.

Find me, he whispered soundlessly. *Help me.*

V

Chaldean Mountains West, *Leto*

Day 11

BIRDY KNEW KENNER WAS COMING. She knew that whoever *they* were, they were getting stronger. And something was happening inside of her.

She shuddered. The berries had been the start, but she'd had no choice but to eat them. She popped them in her mouth as she walked, ever stronger, ever faster, the sharp pain ebbing to a dull ache. And no matter how fast she walked, her lungs didn't burn.

The earth called her name. The air she breathed breathed her back.

Birdy, come, they said.

No. I won't. You're not real.

What is real?

"Stop," she said, her voice shaking. "Stop."

The moons were half-visible through the subforest now. She could see enough to walk. And she *could* walk. That was the miracle. But she knew better than that. She must have imagined the bone that had been protruding from her skin. Because the bone had set. It hurt still, but it had healed itself in just a few days.

293

It was impossible.

With God all things are possible, Ladora told her. *You must keep going. To the place.*

Birdy knew the place. She saw it in her mind sometimes along with the visions of the past. Visions that were more real than any trace v-feed. Replays of the past, but she was *there.*

Birdy sits at the kitchen table, the old sewing machine in front of her, her mother paying bills. She wants to make the dress herself. It's for the dance, and her mother can't afford a fancy dress. But they have material from an old prom dress.

Birdy is sewing the seam, her hand on the material too close. She is tired from studying, and she is running out of time. So she presses on the pedal too hard and the metal tool rips the material forward, taking Birdy's finger along with it.

She sees the needle puncture her finger, sewing one stitch before she can stop. She screams and her mother, flies over, dropping receipts and bills on the floor.

"It's okay, baby," she says, her voice calm. "Take a breath. It's okay."

She pushed herself forward, the past fading. There was a coppery taste in her mouth, and she realizes she was sucking on her finger, which still stung from the sewing needle. It was bleeding.

Birdy trudged up the steeply sloping hill that connected the sub-floor with the edge of the mountain. As she came over the rise, a golden hue shimmered into view.

Tears began to well up in her eyes.

They lay there, their great solemn faces regarding her with gentle curiosity. Several smaller creatures loped away, hiding among the larger of the beasts. Their long faces licking pale lips. The King, the great beast that had brought her here, stared at her, his great headdress moving slowly, thoughtfully. He seemed to glow, the deep gold of their his luminescent. He turned his face, and she followed his gaze to the gentle rise that connected the deep subfloor with something like a deer trail.

Birdy dropped to her knees.

"Thank you," she said quietly. "Thank you so much."

The King nodded, or maybe she imagined it. His eyes gleamed yellow in the dark.

Faster, he said. *He's coming.*

Even though she had removed the splint days ago, the hill taxed her healing bones to the limit. She struggled up the incline, sweat pouring down her neck. It chilled quickly in the damp pre-dawn darkness, sending shivers down the back of her outlanding suit. From all sides, she could feel *them*, hear their voices vibrating in her head.

Faster, they said.

She grunted as she heaved herself up, her hands grappling to find supports as she climbed. It crossed her mind that she had lost her crutch somewhere. She didn't really need it, anyway. Still, it would have been nice to have it on this last climb.

One of the creatures stared as she passed—a female, Birdy mused, nursing her young. Birdy considered how comforting it was to find mothers, even here. That Leto herself was a kind of mother. And her children were multitudes.

Birdy came to the top of the hill and collapsed, her mouth to the same pale dirt that had stolen her pack nearly a week before. But that pack was far behind. And she didn't need it anyway.

When she could stand to roll over, she could see the full light of the moon overhead. There was a breeze up here, warm and insistent. There was a howl and a snarl from somewhere nearby.

Coming, coming...

She came up to her knee, then to her good foot. She realized that she, since hers had been left behind, probably when she'd almost fallen back into the dark. It didn't matter now, anyway.

He was coming, and it would come down to death. His or hers. Or both.

Death? they asked.

But she could not answer their question. Not now. Birdy began to hobble faster. Her bad leg felt stronger with every step, the pain duller.

Not far now.

There was water up ahead,

something up ahead more than water

She could hear it now, every step vibrated the knowledge to her. She had to go forward. She had to get there, where it was safe. She pushed past boulders, ducked below nearly invisible trees as if she'd lived there all her life.

VI

KENNER JOGGED THROUGH THE UNDERBRUSH, Birdy's signature a clear map. She had stopped at the berries. The broken branches were the tell. He could feel her hunger as he touched them. A gratefulness.

He ate his fill, and things became clearer.

He jogged silently through the woods, his mind feeling at once clear and also malleable. He remembered things he'd forgotten—things before Leto and Birdy. Sometimes he took the cyanide pills out of his pack.

Grandam told him he didn't have the stomach for it.

He could smell the baby powder that she put on her skin. Then the forest was gone. It was nighttime, and they were in the farmhouse. The oil lamp was burning, and the old mahogany clock was ticking down the seconds. Tock. Tock.

He shivered. It was a dream. Of course.

"Boy," Grandam says. Her voice is froggy, like she hasn't had her bread and milk yet. It calms her stomach before bed. "Do you have something to confess?"

She pulls the picture from behind her back. The picture of the girl that he's picked up from the street outside the corner store, her breasts exposed, her eyes slitted with pleasure. It has been folded and refolded so carefully, then safely tucked beneath a board in the cellar closet where he thought Grandam wouldn't go. At the sight of it, his bowels twist.

"You're dead," he said. "This isn't real. You died."

"What is the penalty for the sin of the flesh?" she demands. "Tell me the scripture."

"The unrighteous shall not inherit the kingdom of God." Tears threatened his vision.

Grandam nods, her face stone. "Put out your hands," she says, a wad of phlegm cracking the words, fracturing them like old china.

Kenner puts his hands out, but they are so small. He is trapped in a boy's body. The pressure in his bowels is fierce, and his stomach is sick with fear.

He is going to shit himself. He has done this, but only once. The time that Grandam had whipped him so hard he wished he would die.

What is die.

"Please, don't," he whispered, the realization coming on him. *This is that time.* This was that time *again.* "Not this. Please, not this," he whispered.

When she began to strike him, he could taste the blood in his mouth, could feel the splintered floor beneath his cheek when he fell to the ground. He shat himself, and she struck harder.

"Be not deceived," she said, breathlessly, "neither fornicators, nor idolaters, nor adulterers, nor effeminate, nor abusers of themselves with mankind–"

He wished for death, both the boy and the man. Grandam did not hear, her words rising to a dizzy climax of pain.

"–nor thieves, nor covetous, nor drunkards, nor revilers, nor extortioners, shall inherit the kingdom of God."

From somewhere in his head, *they* watched and learned.

H e was back in his own body again.

It had been a dream. But not like the others. He could feel the strike of the lashes on his back, could taste the blood in his mouth.

What is dream

Then again, it had been too real for that.

From somewhere not too distant, there was the sound of a hollow wail.

They were real. He patted the pocket on his suit where he had pulled the tracker. The lycants had been real. Birdy's pack, that had been real. Everything else was a mirage.

He jogged faster as the trees spread out to a grassy field. The mountain rose up before him in a rocky slope, the subforest and the stone creating a small pocket of protection from the wind.

He reached the crook of the mountain and touched the place where the grass had been laid over. Some kind of beast, large. He could nearly feel them speaking here. He bounded up the mountain, Birdy so close he could almost taste her.

VII

Sand Flats, *Leto*

THEY FELL INTO A FITFUL SILENCE. The land was too flat and white, the sky empty overhead. And then there was the constant feeling of being watched. As if even the scuttering animals knew her name. As if they'd been waiting for her.

Her brain conjured up visions in the whiteness—a yellow scarf flying on the breeze; her father's body walking in a shimmer of heated haze. The rhythmic stomping of Aris punctuated her own irregular heartbeat. The android circled the bike, running forward and back in hypnotic circles. She was so fast, the slight smile always on her lips. If Ezrie didn't know better, she'd think that Aris was enjoying the journey.

According to Ezrie's map, they were getting closer to where Birdy had outlined a safe northern passage. The Chaldean Mountain Range was a huge moon-shaped arc that cut through the land mass that made up the largest segment of contiguous Leto. The signal from

Marcus was pinned on the other side. It was good to be moving, but not great that they were still so far away.

Still, although they were going out of their way at least by two days, it was good to feel like, for once, she was thinking ahead of him.

They travelled as far as they could during the day, pausing regularly to clean Aris and the bike. Ezrie didn't love relying on Purple to drive, but the bike only responded to him, the benefit of custom-building a motorcycle from scratch.

Still, Ezrie had her own insurance—she was the only one who could see Marcus' ping. Although it was annoying, the impasse meant that neither could make it where they were going without the other.

There was a hum in her suit, one that she knew well. Inside of it, she could hear *them.*

Come

She knew it wasn't real. Nothing dead comes back. Nothing gold can stay.

The snatch of the old poem bubbled up from her memory. Her father reading a book of poetry, flipping the pages and pointing out the words as Ezrie snuggled against him. For a moment, it was such a real memory, that Ezrie could smell his cologne. She could hear her mother doing dishes in the kitchen, singing badly to some song on the radio.

Nothing gold can stay.

The suit would give out soon, Ezrie knew, and the reclaimed water was starting to take on an acid taste from not being cleaned out for days. She hoped they would get through the desert before it went out completely.

The stars over their camp that night were a nice change from the blank whiteness of the sand. In the air, the zephyrs had made their return, though seemed less interested in Ezrie and Purple than Aris. The little creatures swarmed the android, making her look a little like a large stuffed bear.

"Should I dismantle them?" Aris asked in her naive country lilt.

"No," Ezrie said, thinking of the adorable kimba that the Anti-Aris had killed and cooked. "Let them be. They're not hurting anyone. I don't think."

Purple was quiet now, having talked for hours as they drove. She wondered what he was thinking. About Alex, maybe. She recognized that pale, dark sorrow in his face. She had worn it once.

When Purple handed her the beef stew tube, she thanked him.

"A bit of common decency?" He gave her a puzzled half-smile. "That's unexpected."

"Don't get too used to it," she retorted.

The food warmed her up a bit. Somehow, even the cold paste seemed better in the safety of the fire pack's flame. Despite all that had happened, she felt something of peace in the moment. She glanced at Purple, who looked away quickly.

"What are those?" Aris asked. Her head was thrown up, her mouth slightly open. The zephyrs fluttered white and yellow, in and out.

"Stars," Purple said. "They're like the suns here, but tons far away."

Aris nodded, "They are pleasing, aren't they?" She looked at Purple for approval. "They are very faze," she said reverently.

He chuckled. "True that. I guess I don't look up as much as I used to."

Ezrie wondered at the difference between this Aris and the other two. Being raised by Purple had made an impact. Where Zhong's Aris had been calculating and businesslike, Purple's Aris was empathetic. Where Marcus's Aris had been utilitarian, this Aris tended towards emotion. It was funny. Seeing all of them was like seeing the insides of their trainers, the way that dogs sometimes reflected the personalities of the people who owned them. A good dog would fetch. A bad dog would bite.

A good Aris wondered at the stars.

They ate their food quietly, and Ezrie couldn't help but notice how different Purple looked in this light. She could see the strong jaw, the usually hidden chisel of his arms and shoulders. He was young sure, maybe not even twenty-five. But there was no doubt he was a man. He had steel in him. It appealed to her in a way that was inexplicable, this mixture of innocence and hidden strength.

"I never said thank you."

Purple looked up, stirred from whatever thoughts he nursed.

"I mean," she stumbled. "For the life-saving thing."

"Life-saving thing," Aris repeated. "Thank you very much."

Purple gave a sad smile. "Yeah. I don't think I ever could have, before. I've always been...I don't know. Things change when—" he paused, stumbled. "Things change."

"Yes," she said, thinking of her own shuddering reality shift. The realization that maybe she didn't really know Marcus at all.

Purple looked at her, and she sensed something wilder in him than she'd ever considered. There was a flash of something like desperation, something like hunger. There was a rise in degrees, a bright electricity that hummed between them. It shifted, a palpable magnetism that started a slow burn at the tips of her fingers and danced across her skin. Her heart became a throb, a rhythm that opened some closed cage that she had forgotten she owned.

She looked up at him and their eyes met. His burned into her—an ancient open invitation.

"If you could have anything before you die, what would you pick?" he asked. His voice was low, and it was more a command than a question. It vibrated something in her core, and she felt suddenly exposed. "Name anything."

"We're not going to die," Ezrie said, trying desperately to avoid his gaze. Her head was reeling. She wasn't in the habit of lying, but she felt the lie so clearly on her lips.

"Fine," he said. "But still. What do you want most?"

She looked at him, again trying to avoid that heat. It had been a long time since anyone had looked at her so softly. So friendly.

"Um, a cigarette," she said. The words were awkward. Misplaced and random. She hadn't had a cigarette since she had known Robyn. There was that vibration again. A string of something desperate, but now it was coming from her.

She paused, then looked at him. "What do you want?"

He looked at her again, then at his feet.

"I don't know," he sighed. "I wish my sister was—" he stopped himself. "My sister and I were best mates. Really close. She was in an accident about a year and a half ago. She's been in hospital ever since."

He looked down, and Ezrie sensed that juxtaposition again: a man made of steel with a center like glass.

"I'm really sorry," Ezrie said. "Is she going to get better?"

Purple shook his head. "She's been on breathing machines for a long time. My mum and dad can't let her go. I don't want to, either." He paused, throwing a rock into the fire. "I sometimes wish that I could go back in time, you know? Fix the things that went wrong. I would have stopped her from driving."

How many times had she wished she could be that little girl in Marcus' office? How many times had she wished she'd destroyed the porter when she had the chance? How many times had she wished that her father had never invented it?

"Yeah," she said. "That's what I want, too. Go back in time. That's better than a cigarette," she said. Then gave a wry smile. "But not by much."

Aris stood, her face suddenly concerned.

"Ezrie, your face is malfunctioning." Aris' voice was sharp, her senses alert. "You may be in danger."

Ezrie laughed. "No. It's not a malfunction. It's a smile."

Purple laughed, and it was a nice sound. After a moment, Aris joined in, her cadence matching his, her head thrown back in a caricature of a laugh. Ezrie blurted out a laugh despite herself.

"Another malfunction," Aris whispered, instantly sober. She turned to Purple. "Should I disable her?"

"She's fine," Purple said. He smiled apologetically. "Aris is still learning a lot about people. She's only had me to teach her about socialization."

"Oh great," Ezrie chuckled. "Exactly what Leto needs. Another nerd."

"Be careful," Purple said with a twinkle. "The Nerd Party on Leto is very compelling, especially if you're hungry or a mathematical genius. We have pi."

Ezrie groaned, then really laughed because Purple looked equally ashamed and proud of himself. Then Aris joined in, throwing her head back and cackling with the most robotic version of laughter imaginable, making Ezrie roar until tears streamed down her face.

VIII

Chaldean Mountains West, *Leto*

Day 12

AS THEY CROSSED into the shadow of the western Chaldees, the white of the flats turned a grainy pink. Ezrie tracked her progress on the map that Marcus had given her as well as the ones on Birdys' field notes. The whine from her outlanding suit had become an incessant buzz in her ear.

Life burgeoned in the shade of the mountains. White snakes that bisected when they rode by, slithering in opposite directions away from the bike. Sky creatures of brilliant red, their wings like bats. Orange lizard creatures with segmented bodies flitted in and out of hand-sized holes in the pink dust.

Birdy's blank map did not bring up any information for the creatures. It seemed they had gone beyond the area where Birdy had explored. And, as unlikely as it was, Ezrie missed Birdy's voice in her head. She missed knowing what was alive and whether or not Birdy wanted to turn it into a pet.

As the bike passed, the lizards reared up on knobby knees, screaming. Riding past them was like listening to a murder in progress.

Ezrie recorded the lizards on her trace, then added her own commentary to Birdy' field notes.

The Marcusis are mean-looking bastards who like to scream at things they don't understand. You can tell them by their orange skin and the screaming.

Not as scientific as Birdy's, but she felt as though she were doing justice by the woman's memory. It was the least Ezrie owed her.

Overhead, the bat-like air creatures circled, their translucent wings like red parachute silk. They cawed occasionally, circling lower or landing to stare at them. They were curious. Patient. Ezrie wondered if they knew something she didn't.

There was a trickle of fear in her blood. *They* were watching. *They* were closing in.

The sound of the suit whining in her ears was the sound of voices. Hundreds of them. Thousands of them.

We. Speak. We. Speak.

Stop, Ezrie thought. *Please stop.*

"We have to stop," Ezrie said, the suit was dead, the line gone with the electrical output. Her grip on him was iron as she zipped and flipped the hood, yelling into his ear. "Purple, stop!"

He pumped the brake. As soon as it had stopped, Ezrie jumped from the bike, feeling the anxiety rising up from the ground and into her feet. Something lay beneath them. They were in danger.

"What's going on?" Purple pulled the mask from his face. Aris jogged back from where she had been scouting out the mountain. The Chaldean Range South towered over them now, blocking out the largest of Leto's suns like a blight.

They had stopped so close to the mountains that Ezrie could see the rough trail that Birdy had outlined as the best northern pass. Here, the constant head had melted the sand into a sheet of red glass. Every so often, there were large shattered holes surrounded by splintered spears of glass. Whatever made them left an opening large enough for a car to drive into.

"My environmental controls broke on my suit," she gasped, tearing the mask from her face, shaking white dust from her hair. "I don't know how to fix it."

Ezrie, they whispered. *Listen...*

Stop it.

She pressed her hands to her head.

"Hey," Purple said, looking around for the source of her freak out. "What's going on? You're bugging me out."

Aris was staring at her as if she had grown an extra arm. Ezrie had the wild urge to jump at her and cut the shifting eyes right out of the android's head.

From somewhere over her shoulder, she heard a whisper.

Ezrie.

"What?" Purple looked around.

"Nothing," she said. It was flat, red glass as far as the eye could see, but for the mountains at least a mile away. "I thought I heard something."

Ezrie.

From the corner of her eye, she saw a flicker of movement.

"What was that?"

Purple shook his head, his face sharp. "I don't know."

DANGER

Ezrie felt the words, the voices indescribably small but overwhelming. A rumbling beneath her feet.

"We have to go," Purple snapped, as if reading her mind. "Now."

He grabbed her arm and dragged her onto the bike. Purple kicked the engine, which coughed and sputtered.

Ezrie saw another flash of some movement in the dirt. A shift in the throng of voices screaming in her mind.

DANGER

The bike leaped into motion, Ezrie clinging to Purple's back as it did. She flipped over the hood and held on to him as tight as she could as Purple gunned the engine, roaring against the growing tremors beneath them.

The rumbling turned into a full-blown tremor. Then, in a crescendo sound, the ground in front of them exploded.

Ezrie screamed.

A beast erupted from the glass, scattering shards like shrapnel, a single, thick horn slicing through the earth like a scimitar. Ezrie covered her head with her arm, the glass bouncing off the outlanding suit. The creature pulled itself up by great four spidery legs, nearly fifteen feet tall. It's eyes were golden and black, saliva or mucous dripping from two holes on its face that were both a nose and mouth. Its body was hairless, with huge blankets of skin that hung from its armpits, its neck, and below a vestigial tail. In the moment, she had a flash that it looked like it was wearing a robe of grey cloth.

The beast sighted them, lowering its huge curved horn and bellowing a demonic scream.

Purple yanked the bike aside, narrowly missing the thing as it swung its huge horn to smash them, its eyes as glassy as the ground. Behind them another creature burst up like a mutant groundhog. It flung shards of glass to every side and barreled directly for them.

Purple nearly slid out as the second beast swung and missed. They pivoted so fast, that Ezrie's boots scraped the dirt and she could fee the sheet weight of the animal splitting the air over her head. Purple urged the bike faster, weaving around holes even as more of the creatures surfaced, crawling from the ground like spidery giraffes, howling and swinging their horns.

Ezrie held to Purple tight, and the bike sputtered. The engine began to smoke, and Ezrie couldn't help but the other bike, the one that had gone up in flames.

"Ohshitohshitshitshit—"

One of the beasts caught up to them, the huge head sweeping the bike. It slid and skittered on the glassy ground, and Ezrie felt the impact reverberate up her spine, the wind knocked from her chest. She tumbled, rolling and pitching, without even time to feel the impact.

Save Ezrie. The thought was so pointed, it seemed like it might have come from the trace. But the trace was dead. The com was dead. Yet Purple's voice echoed in her mind.

There was no time to think, to feel. She scrambled to her feet and began to run towards the looming mountains. Half a glance behind her showed the bike being swallowed up into a hole as another monster rose from the plain.

She screamed, pitching forward faster than her legs could run.

Ezrie tripped, falling to the shaking ground, the sound of a half-dozen creatures galloping towards her, hairless elephantine skin flapping as they stampeded closer.

Then, Aris was there, yanking her from the dirt, then bursting into preternatural speed. Aris' legs were moving too fast to see, and Ezrie's eyes bleared from the pressure of the air.

Over Aris' shoulder, Ezrie could see the animals howling and gaining, their claws rending the glass with every pounce. But Aris met them measure for measure, weaving through the shattering landscape like a ballerina, feet sure on the glassy surface.

Where was Purple?

The mountain jutted up from the ground in front of them. Aris leapt up the rocks, her feet smashing them as she landed, jarring Ezrie with every bound up the mountain side. From the vantage point of the ledge, she could barely make out a speck of red hair being chased by at least five of the horned beasts.

"Purple," she screamed. "We have to go back!"

"My directive is to protect you," Aris said, setting Ezrie down on the ledge.

There was a howl from below, and Purple ducked, narrowly avoiding the thick, pointed jaws bursting up from the ground. The creature lunged at him. Purple reeled back, the momentum sending him head over heels to the unforgiving surface. He rolled, found his feet and launched towards the mountains again.

"Run, Purple!" Ezrie screamed. She couldn't go down the mountain, not the way Aris had come. But she had the Xtenz rope.

It pounced, the powerful horn skewered the ground where he'd been moments before. The tremor dropped Purple to his knees, a new creature rushing to finish the job.

Purple scrambled up as the animal struggled to remove the horn, now buried skull deep in the red earth. The others were all coming, now.

"Purple!" Ezrie called. "Aris, hold on to me!"

Ezrie threw the rope down from the cliff above as the android grasped her around the waist and settled back on its heels. Purple ran towards them, trying to find a way up. From behind him, the creature gave a frustrated bleating wail as it struggled to pull its tusk from the ground. The others stampeded towards it, and Ezrie felt fear choking her. "Jump, Purple! C'mon—"

Purple ran, sweating pouring down his face, the animals behind him. He grabbed the rope and Ezrie flicked the Xtenz rope to retract. She felt the motor inside straining then stopping at least to feet from the ridge. Purple hung on, mere feet above the monsters straining to crush him in their jaws.

"Hold on," Ezrie shouted. "Aris, pull the rope, okay?"

Aris drew him up with inhuman strength, forcing Ezrie to let go.

Below them, the animals turned their rage onto their brother whose tusk was firmly rooted in the ground. They gnashed their teeth, belching screams before impaling and devouring it.

The beast with the trapped horn screamed. Then went silent as blood spattered the glass plain and the feeding frenzy began.

Purple's arm reached up and Ezrie grasped it, pulling him awkwardly over the shelf of the mountain's obsidian face. She fell back, Purple rolling on top of her, his face buried in her chest.

He raised his head, covered in pink dirt, sweat dripping lines down his face, his breathing was jagged. "Sorry."

She smiled, stunned. Then, hugged him.

I could have lost him. We could have died.

Aris put her arms around both of them and lifted them to their feet.

"Hugs," she said. "An all-purpose gesture."

They stood like that for a long time, holding each other till the suns went dark. Below them, the beasts eventually retreated back into their holes, clicking along the glass with their spidery legs, gorged and slow. It was surreal, the silence of the flats swallowing the memory of the creatures almost entirely. The only evidence was the open, bloody carcass like an island in the ocean of glass.

IX

Chaldean Mountains West, *Leto*

CLARE TURNS *off the autopilot to take the curves around the lake fast and furious. Purple holds on to the handle above the passenger seat, feeling his stomach churn with every turn.*

He wants to tell her to slow down, but he doesn't.

He sees the plank on the road, but thinks nothing of it. He does not know that there is a nail sticking out of one end. Clare accelerates into the next curve.

The truck's back wheels spin as the front left tire explodes.

Everything turns around, the truck tumbling end over end down the ravine towards the ocean. There should be screaming, the crunch of bone, Clare's body going slack.

But not in this version.

This time, he looks over to see Clare, her mouth stuffed with bandages, her throat wrapped tight, her eyes black as holes.

We speak, *Clare says, her voice a thousand souls.* Come home—

He awoke, gasping the words: *We Speak.*

The tent was dark. And he could feel *them* all around. *They. They* were here. Everywhere.

Purple stepped out of the tent and through the ion field. He looked down over the landscape of black glass. From overhead, the blue moon of Leto shimmered down, reflected.

Clare. He had been dreaming of the accident.

Purple looked over the edge of the mountain.

He was so tired. He didn't want to be afraid any more. He didn't want to remember any more.

Purple, they whispered. *Come*

Would the drop kill him? He didn't know. It would be bad, but not as bad as whatever *they* wanted him for. He teased his foot out over the ledge, a shimmer of scree dropping to the rocks below. He had turned Aris off to protect her circuits. The spare parts he had used were growing phlax faster and faster. She would start glitching soon. He didn't want to think of it.

And she couldn't stop him.

"Hey."

He turned to see Ezrie. She was small in the dark without the outlanding suit.

"What are you doing?"

"Bad dreams," he said. "All night, every night."

"Me too," she said.

There was a long silence.

"*They're* coming," he said, the words sounding tinny. It sounded crazy, even to him. "They're growing." He looked at her, expecting her to laugh and to call him a stupid kid. She didn't. Just hugged her arms to her chest and looked out into the glassy dark.

The rise of their voices was steady, like a far off crowd that was heard through a window. Purple didn't know where he began and where *they* ended. *They* called his name. Finn. That was his real name. No one called him that here. Just *them.*

Far out over the glass, a flash of light shimmered as if hovering a few inches above the frozen sea. Soon, others had joined it. They floated, seemingly aimlessly. Darting down, then lifting back up high overhead on an invisible updraft. They sparked, like Certs when you chewed it under blankets.

"It's beautiful," Ezrie said. "What are they?"

"Zephyrs. Birdy named them. They come out at night. They like people. At least, they liked to hang around the base. They love the transmitter. Loved, I guess. Past tense."

The lights, white, yellow, and now red, flickered and glimmered out across the endless sea of glass.

"You told Aris to save me."

He suddenly felt gaffish. It had been stupid, old-fashioned chivalry. The kind of thing that his sisters ate up when they played pretend princesses and he had to be the king. He suddenly wanted to tell Ezrie everything about them. He wanted to say nothing at all and sweep her into his arms, to have her body melt beneath his. He wanted to hold her and kiss her and push her off a cliff.

"I'm starting to forget what Clare looked like," Purple said, his voice sounding to himself like from far away. "In my nightmares, I can't cob her face. It's all wrong."

"Forgetting doesn't seem too bad. I wish I could." She stared at the stars, her arms over her chest. The moon made her face blue, illuminating her perfect, heart-shaped face.

"Forgetting's not your problem," Purple said. "Forgiving is."

She bristled at this, and he immediately regretted it.

"I'm sorry. I don't know what I'm saying—"

"It's fine. You don't know." She drops her head, and he wonders what she's not telling him. He has a flash of a memory, this time it is not his. She was in the garage (*the workshop, Ezrie*), holding onto Marcus as the dry leather of his jacket swallowed her tears.

The memory was so real, but it was gone as fast as it had come.

"I don't know," he said softly. "But I can imagine it takes someone very strong to have lived your life. It must be hard to always be that way. There has to be somewhere it's safe to fall apart."

The zephyrs blinked in and out of existence, giving the solid ground an additional depth, as if there were another, deeper sky below the glass. It reminded Purple of the old movies about snow. Except it seemed to be softly falling light, drifting down in hazy shades of gold and amber.

She stared out over the glass, and he felt a hollow loneliness. He would die here, alone. Away from anyone who loved him. Clare would never speak again. His mother and sisters would mourn him as he had watched them mourn her. He would fade away. Would that be so bad? "Maybe it's better that way," he said.

"What?"

"Maybe it's better not to care. If you don't care about anyone, you can't get hurt, right?"

She turned to him, her eyes glistening in the darkness. "It doesn't work that way. Because no matter what you tell yourself, you *do* care. And it hurts whether you pretend or not."

Her eyes met his, Ezrie's gaze ethereal in the light of the falling zephyrs. She was so close now, he could feel the heat of her body in the frigid mountain air. The tank top was taut against her breasts, and he wanted so much to touch her that his head felt like it was spinning. *They* were persistent, clamoring.

They wanted to be with her just as much as he did.

Ezrie looked up at him and Purple pulled her close—his hands on her face, her waist. He kissed her, wrapping his arms around her, relishing her softness again his hard, and letting all the sadness and want drown him. Letting all his pain drown in her.

They made love beneath the stars. Ezrie opened up, her body taking him in and surrounding him with heat and visions of stars. Mathematical equations. A door of blackness where no light could be seen.

He could feel her rising, her body so full of need, and when they both spent, he kissed her tears. They tasted like cherry chapstick.

X

Chaldean Mountains, North, *Leto*

Day 12

SHE DREAMED OF THE PORTER, but not one made of metal and glass. It was formed by her father and mother, but their bodies writhed with tentacled plants, their arms stretched overhead, the oculus blinking down like the white-blind eye of god.

Marcus sat below them in some kind of chair, like a dentist. He lay in a blue cocoon of light upon a web of blue strands that made symbols. She could not read them, but the meaning was one of worship and love. A desperate sacrificial sign.

Marcus opened his mouth as if to scream, but phlax exploded from his mouth like webs, covering her face and choking her until she woke.

She came out of the tent to find Purple beside Aris, the android's chest open, her eyes blinking.

"What's wrong?" Ezrie said.

"As if you don't know," Purple snapped.

"What the hell are you talking about?" she retorted. "I was with you all night!" She felt stupid bringing it up. Something about it was embarrassing. It made her vulnerable. She had let him split her open and hold every dark pieces up to the light. She didn't know if she wanted to be seen like that. Not here, when so many other eyes were watching.

"Someone has been editing her circuits and software," he hissed. Something about the wildness of his eyes was unfocused, the eyes of a drug addict or a man possessed. "Every time I clean her out, someone is going back in and messing her up. And you're the only one here."

"You think I'm messing with Aris? You're crazy."

Purple clenched his hands and kicked the android. The android flinched, her eyes blinking.

"I apologize," she said, her voice reedy. "I am malfunctioning. It is my fault. I am a bad family."

Purple stormed down the mountain, mumbling threats to himself.

See, a voice whispered. *Where is he going? What is he planning?*

Ezrie picked up Aris' control fob and attached it to her trace. She looked at the log.

It was a maze of alien shapes and symbols. The same language she'd seen at the porter and in the infected database. *They* were trying to communicate, but what were they saying?

From inside Aris, the phlax grew plentiful. It had developed strong fibers in her chest cavity, creating a saline cocoon around the control board and the battery it attached to.

How is she even working? Ezrie wondered. *She should be dead by now.*

When Purple came back, he was calmer.

"Sorry. I'm a little...edgy lately."

"No shit."

"We're going to have to shut her down," Purple said quietly. "She won't be reliable much longer. It's not you. It's the phlax. I know that—" he looked down. "I get scared sometimes."

"Of me?"

"Of everything," he said. "But especially you."

They had only been moving for a few hours when the sky went dark. Burgundy clouds roiled in the sky, the air stiff with electricity. The channel of the river basin acted like a wind tunnel, and she was nearly knocked off her feet several times.

"We need to get away from these trees," Purple shouted, coming back to help her. She took his hand, nearly falling over from the violent gusts howling through the canyon. "Aris is showing a cave across the river."

The clouds were angry now, brilliantly lit with fingers of lightning that reached down into the mountains. The bellowing crack of thunder instinctively made her cover her ears. Red drops began to splat against the visor of her outlanding hood.

"How far?" Ezrie shouted. She could barely hear herself over the snap-boom of the storm.

His response was lost in another deafening crack. Ezrie flinched.

Aris motioned them to follow, and then jogged as quickly as they could out of the open and into the reedy trees. A thick red mist was coming up from the ground as the cold rain drenched the soil. The Aris slowed as the bracken became thicker, moving towards some unseen target. Ezrie followed, the outlanding suit hood sleeting the water barely enough for her to see Purple's trail. They came to the bank of a filthy red river. It wasn't very wide, maybe ten meters. But the river was gorged and raging, full of broken debris and rising rapidly.

"Across here," Purple shouted into the wind pointing ahead. The sleeting rain made it virtually impossible to see anything. "Across the river."

"Are you crazy?" Ezrie shrieked, "We can't cross—"

"We don't have a choice," Purple shouted. "The cave is the safest place right now."

There was another crackle and lightning exploded a tree not twenty yards away. Ezrie jumped, finding herself leaning against Purple. She felt his smile before it happened, a flicker of thought: *I guess she can't be badass all the time.*

"You just watch," she shouted.

Ezrie stepped into the churning water, gasping as the cold red waves grasped at her legs.

Aris reached out and grabbed Ezrie's hand, even as the water swept her feet out from beneath her. She yelped, flailing and Aris grabbed her other arm, pulling her from the water before she had a chance to sink.

"I will assist you." Aris stepped into the river steadily, her heavy feet as solid as oak trees."Take my hand."

"I'll hold on, okay?"

Ezrie threaded her hands through the opening of the saddlebag that hung around the androids neck. It was thick and heavy. Perfect for keeping her relatively safe.

The thunder rumbled overhead as the android towed her carefully to the other side. The water made it all the way up to her waist, the outlanding suit providing some protection, but not much now that it was completely dead. She shivered as Aris deposited her on the other side. Through the trees, she could see the dark opening of the cave.

Aris began to cross back, the water swirling around her waist.

"Go!" Purple pointed to the cavern opening almost invisible through a stand of squat trees. "You'll be safe in there. I have to go now."

There was a kind of resignation to his cadence. She had the sudden and sure knowledge that Purple was about to do something incredibly stupid.

"No! Purple—"

Before Aris could reach reached the other side, and Purple slipped beneath the waves.

Ezrie screamed.

There was a crackle and bang from the sky. Ezrie flinched as a burst of fractured light broke through the clouds overhead and touched down within feet, the sound like a bomb. Ezrie cowered, then looked up.

"Go get Purple," she screamed. "We have to get him!"

Aris dove into the rapids, red ponytail sinking beneath the rapids. She surfaced once, then was lost in the churning waves. Beyond her, Purple's body sank below the water.

He's going too fast, it's so fast—

She ran down the muddy bank, dodging tree trunks and huge blue ferns. The water sluiced down her mask, making it almost impossible to see anything. He was almost fifty yards away now, too far to run, too fast to catch up with—

Ezrie had the sudden urge to jump in the water. She would be safe there. Above her the sky split again, pouring out another deluge of rain.

It's crazy. I can't swim in this, not in this suit—

Come, they said. *Come and see.*

Sobbing, she tore off the hood and depressed the lock. The suit cracked open, and she flung it off.

Please, don't let him die, don't let him die—

What is die?

She splashed into the cold mountain water, immediately pushed downstream at a rate she could have never run. Though frothy, the water was smooth and bouyant. It sharpened her senses. It made her feel strong.

From beneath the waves, there was something reaching for her. Was there a hand? The flicker of a yellow scarf? The flash of her father's glasses.

Come and see.

But Purple needed her.

Ezrie swam hard, the water seeming to rise up at her will, pressing her forward. Purple was nowhere. There was nothing to chase, no one to follow.

Purple grappled, then gripped a stone, then slid over a small fall to the churn beneath. He is so happy. At peace. And Clare is coming for him. She will take him to where they *live. The Nexus. The thing* they *have built—*

Ezrie focused in on the thoughts, willing him to life. *Don't die, don't die, goddamn it, if you die I will kill you—*

She strained her muscles, pressing the water behind her. She caught hold of the stone that Purple had grabbed, and felt the pull of the water drag her under.

The water was soft and quiet below. The world became larger, and she saw Purple as if he were a long way off. He lay trapped against the rock, floating languidly.

There was so much peace here. So much rest.

Submersed, the rush of the water was a memory. Below the water, there was warmth and light. She needed to breathe it all in. Let them be as much a part of her as she was a part of them. There were arms on her legs, blue-white eyes coming for her like lights on a subway, blinding and drawing her down. She swam deeper, feeling the pull of them, taking her down, taking her away.

Away. From Purple.

She shook her head, fighting the urge to breathe in the water with her whole being.

Ezrie closed her eyes against the visions, for a moment losing which direction was up. Then, she breathed out what little air she had left, following the bubbles to the surface.

She came out and the world was cacophony and confusion. Ezrie swam against the current, then grabbed hold of a tree root, pulling herself back branch by branch to the large rock where she was sure Purple's body had been trapped.

Ezrie dove towards the rock, barely grasping it. She bobbed beneath, still holding fast with one hand, digging her fingernails into the red muck to claim her purchase. She spied him, his body limp, floating gently as the water called his name. *They're all here,* the light called. *Come...*

She caught Purple's outlanding suit, grabbed his belt, anchoring herself, then came up for air.

Ezrie dove one last time. She felt along his outlanding suit for the release and pressed it. The suit cracked open. She fastened the belt around his wrist as another slash of lightning ravaged the sky. His arms were limp, his body a rag doll in the crush of the rapids. She pulled him from the suit using her makeshift tether, wresting him, wrenching out of the unwieldy material with strength she didn't know she had.

There was a tension, his feet stuck, the suit waterlogged and drowning. Then, he pulled free. The pressure tore Ezrie's tenuous grip from the rock and she flailed as the river dragged them downstream.

Water flooded Ezrie's eyes and mouth, but she held fast to Purple, his body slack. She clutched at anything that might stop their progress. But her slimy fingers and overwrought arms couldn't seem to catch hold. Her head dipped below the water, and she felt her lungs burning. She was so tired.

But then her feet touched ground, and she pushed as hard as she could back towards the surface, slashing her arms through the water like she were fighting it.

She pulled him out, sobbing.

Ezrie breathed into Purple, filling him up with her shaking, terrified breaths.

One, two, three, four, five, breathe. One, two, three, four, five, breathe.

Purple spluttered, coughed, then puked onto the red mud of the riverbank, the red rainwater covering them both like a bloody shroud.

She kissed him. She slapped him. Then she cried, her body weak, holding him safely in the mud of the riverbank. It was long after the rain stopped before Ezrie realized that Aris was gone.

XI

Chaldean Mountains West, *Leto*

THE RAIN BEGAN some time before dawn. It poured down, heavy and red. The clouds were angry. In the distance, there was thunder and the intermittent flash of lightning.

Birdy could not care less about the lightning, but opened her mouth wide to the rain, the red drops bursting on her tongue like summer strawberries. It was sweet, this water. She stopped, resting herself long enough to catch what she could in her mouth.

She had pulled away from the lip of the mountain, not wanting to repeat her mistake. Although the sub-forest was far behind her, there were others—a hundred feet below, a thousand feet below. She didn't want to take the risk of slipping in the shale and not being able to climb out again.

But she had to move fast. He was coming.

The waterfall came into view, the churning water red with white caps where it crashed into a pool and then created a small rivulet that wound its way through the rocky crags and back into the deepest part of the forest.

Where she stood now, however, was marked only by tall, sparse evergreen trees.

She stripped off the outlanding suit and threw herself fully into it, mouth wide.

The water coursed into her mouth, over her skin, sanctifying every dry pore and muscle. She let it coat her organs, making everything new. She breathed it. She knew better. She coughed and pushed herself up and out of the water. Too much water after being so dehydrated could kill her, but she couldn't stop.

don't stop don't stop

It was the rasping hum of that directive in her skull that made her stop at last.

Carefully, she pulled herself back. She would need to be smarter. The sound would bring him.

Come home, they said, there is more to show you

For a moment, she simply stood, the light finally cresting the barren ridge of the mountain peak. It warmed her, but the voices that hummed below her feet and in her brain called to her.

Come and see.

She dove into the water, down deep. There was no pain here, no loneliness.

But what about Cy? a part of her said. The name brought up the image of a distorted face. She barely recognized it. Was it someone she knew?

What about Cy? Holding an umbrella? Lying in a hammock.

Cy was real.

Birdy limped out of the water. The suit was a dead skin, a husk like a snake molt. She left it behind.

Birdy climbed up the rocks, her hands strong, her body sure. She pulled herself to the top of the waterfall, a climb whose concept would have dizzied her back on Earth.

what is Earth?

When she reached the top, she found herself overlooking a wide expanse of brownish trees. It was a valley that led to another set of mountains with the larger Leto sun rising to the south of them.

Her brain churned slowly, her hands still shaking from the adrenaline.

She wasn't going to die. Not today.

Despite the headache and fog in her head, she knew those mountains. She was facing nearly due southeast. She had tracked the Lycants all along where the two ranges met in this valley. Hetradyne Valley.

She nearly laughed, despite everything. For a moment, standing in the sun, a belly full of water, and the sure knowledge that not all of her mind was lost, she knew where she was. And she knew that, although Kenner was coming, something was happening inside of her. She flexed her foot and ankle, feeling the stretch of new tissue, the ache of growth.

She was healing.

Come and see, they whispered, *come and see.*

"Yes," she murmured. "I'm coming."

There was a feeling replacing the fear. Something about going to where she needed to be. Never being alone again. There would be time for fighting

what is fight?

and killing

what is kill?

but now, there was only going to be where the others were.

So she ran.

PART 6
BLACK IS FOR DOOR

"Humans are a messy machine, prone to breakages and self-repair. This is why it they are so much more dangerous, and why a Blacker who truly knows how to manage the human machine is so much more valuable. He not only must know what will divert them, but how they will respond to the diversion."

Some will respond with violence, some with fear. Others will stall out, not knowing what to do. It only takes one to surprise you with intelligence and to break all your plans."

The BlackBook, Last Accessed 2072

I

Living Waters Happy Home, Mobile, Alabama, *Earth*

October 2048

HER NAME IS CALLIOPE. *Kenner carves it in the hickory stump at the very edge of the play yard at the Happy Home School for Boys. She is a nurse that visits the school once a week. She has brown hair that looks like honey in the sunshine. He invents illnesses to go and see her.*

He is wearing a brown and blue checked shirt that was given to him by the intake counselor, Brother Bill. It is scratchy, but he knows better than to complain. Complaining means bible study during lunch, or breakfast, or sometimes during all the meals. The desk butts up against a window that is a few inches lower, making a shelf that other boys sometimes stack treasures or stolen food.

The little room where he is sitting is cramped with the little bed and a few chairs. The plastic on the bed is beginning to fray, and he messes with it while he waits. There is a poster of monkeys covering their eyes, ears, and mouth. No evil, never, Reverend Andrews says. When he kicks his boots, there is a soft thud, and he stops, worried that he might leave scuffs. He left scuffs in the rec room once and had to clean floors for a week.

All the details are so real. Am I here again? How am I here?

Kenner can hear Calliope in the infirmary. "Make sure to put a thin layer on twice a day, alright? It's powerful stuff, so be careful."

She opens the door, and a whoosh of cool air come out along with a skinny, pock-marked boy that has been here only a few months. Kenner has not bothered to learn his name. He will wash out. He is weak.

"Kenner," Calliope says, "Again." She shakes her head, and her eyes betray her happiness to see him. He smiles back, but not too widely. He holds up the bleeding thumb which he has managed by punching the fire hydrant near his class's lunch line-up spot.

"That looks painful. Might be broken." He wonders if she knows he's done it on purpose. Calliope fusses over it, splinting it with the silver thumb guard. From the open window he can hear the sound of the younger boys playing on the slide and fighting over the rusted swings.

"There you are," she says warmly. "You be more careful."

He feels happy.

what is happy?

She goes to open the door, but then she pauses. "I won't be here after next week."

"Why?"

"I'm going to a city," she says. Her face is bright, but there is sadness in the eyes. "But there will be a new nurse. Sister Roberta is very kind. Reverend Andrews said it would be best. Hopefully you won't have so many accidents."

It slaps him in the face, leaving a pain that is so much more than the broken thumb. He wants to cry, to scream, but he knows that those things don't stop the pain, do they?

"Are you okay?" she says, after a moment of silence. "I'll be back to visit, I promise."

He has so much he wants to say. The pain in his chest is blooming, growing, setting his ears on fire. Stay, he wants to say. Take me with you, he wants to say. She shows him a picture of a man. Tall, shaved head. A military uniform. "He's a very nice man," she assures Kenner. "He will be a good husband and protect me."

Kenner has too much to say, but the silence chokes him. He leaves without saying goodbye.

He waits until the teachers are at dinner, and goes to her car. He slashes the tires over and over, telling her how much he hates her as he stabs them. He can smell the rubber, feel the grip of the knife in his hand. Feel the adrenaline and then the guilt as she runs out, screaming his name.

He rushes her, still slashing, screaming, the tears finally coming. There is blood and pain and love and the deep, deep knowledge that he can never be saved.

I'll kill you. I swear I'll kill you before I'll let him take you away.

They *understand.*

Kenner drank the water *they* had left for him, and it made him strong. It made his mind clear.

He brought the cyanide pills out and laid them beside the water.

It would be better to die than to relive any more. It would be better to die.

why die? why kill?

They were insistent. The questions nagged at him. Why was he here? Why was he working so desperately to prepare this place for the Reverend, the church? Why was he willing to give up the thing he loved

what is love?

for some higher, holier purpose?

Because someone deserved something beautiful and perfect, and it was never going to be him.

The pills were so pretty in the orange light of the big sun. The sun *they* called father.

He picked one up.

He could become a part of them. Then he would be beautiful and perfect too.

He could feel Birdy, she was close. He could feel her walking through the concrete jungle of Chicago. Smell bread in the oven as Ladora baked it, ashy arms and all. There was something beautiful in Birdy, and he wanted it more than he wanted perfection.

Kenner put the pills back into the suit and flicked over the hood. He didn't need to track her anymore. He knew where she was going. Then, he was moving so fast across the Leto hills that he imagined he was flying.

II

Eriset River, *Leto*

Day 13

THE STORM LEFT the sunset land misted and quiet. Ezrie gave up on the idea of dragging Purple back to the cave. He was too heavy and she was too tired. So, she set up the tents beside the river, covering him in both the heated blankets. She lay next to him as well, hoping her heat would help keep out the mountain chill.

She warmed the contents of the last MRE with the red water of the river. Her hands shook as she scooped it into the plastic casing where it mixed with the chemical warmer. The water made her skin crawl. It was more than just the color. It had spoken to her. Showed her visions of what she wanted more than anything else.

Ezrie came back to the tent, holding the MRE held gingerly in her hand so as not to burn her. She shook him gently. He stirred, then bolted, cringing from Ezrie as if she were holding a knife to his throat.

"We're dead!" he shouted, his eyes raving, "We're all dead—"

She backed away, holding the food.

"Purple," she said, her throat thick with emotion. "It's me. It's Ezrie."

Purple's glazed eyes flickered, then the stony flatness of his expression melted into a softness that she recognized. Her chest flooded with relief.

"Ezrie," he said.

She handed him the spaghetti packet and he ate it. His eyes were red, the whites taking on that hazy blue that made her skin crawl. But he no longer had the peaky blotches like fever on his cheeks. Purple gobbled the food, then, when he looked like he wanted more, she tore off a hunk of dry bread from her own food packet and gave it to him. He nodded his thanks.

"Special occasion," he mumbled.

"Aris is gone," she said. She had gone to look for her, but it was half-hearted. She couldn't leave Purple alone, and water was too fast, too deep. Wherever Aris was, she was probably so full of phlax errors that she had shut herself down.

But what really hurt is that her program was gone. She had been so focused on saving Purple that she hadn't remembered he'd be keeping it in the breast pocket of the outlanding suit. When she did remember that detail, the suit was as gone as Aris.

So much for revenge.

"She needs to be dismantled." Purple's face was blank, his mouth chewing like a wind-up automaton. "That's protocol, at least. We send the tozed androids to research."

"What kind of research?"

He shook his head, half-heartedly. Ezrie wondered if he was even hearing her. His mind was a web of unfocused thoughts. Thoughts of death. Of going back to the water. She wiped at her tears, cursing herself. Dammit. She needed him. She thought of their hushed moment at the top of the ridge and closed her eyes. Not like that. She needed him to be okay.

She got up, her legs feeling twitchy. She was on the verge on figuring it out. "There's only one reason Marcus would send me to the opposite side of the planet."

He looked up.

"You said that they were going to build a transmitter out here, but they didn't." Ezrie ran her hands through her hair. It was stiff and dry from the river water. "I think someone did."

"They didn't." He pressed his hands to his head. She felt bad for making him work so hard, but she needed whatever information he had. "They sent drones to check it out, but they never picked a location."

"Why?"

"I..." he was fading. "Rand said that one of the board investors threatened to pull out if we cracked into the third transmitter." Purple was struggling to focus, but his face was more lucid, more engaged. "Yeah. Living Waters said they wanted a working mine before moving out to the other side. But they were also the ones who put up a fight when they tried to get the pipes laid down here. They said they wanted an ecological survey done. That was Birdy's whole job."

Living Waters. That had been Kenner's job. "Why would Living Waters want to slow down the mission? Why—"

The answer hit her like lightning.

"Purple," she asked, her voice shaking. "How many Aris' models were decommissioned and sent to research?"

"Um," he threw back his head, his eyes squinched. "Four or five."

"And were any sent back? I mean," she ran her hand through her dirty hair. "Did any of the Aris' that you decommissioned ever get used again? Did you ever see any of them again?"

"Not that I know of," Purple said. "But I didn't have anything to do with that. They were used for research."

"Could one or two Arises build a transmitter?"

He paused, looking like he'd been hit with a bat, then turned away. She could see that what she was saying was sinking in.

"That's mental," he said. "It would take at least two MEG printers and a shit-ton of compound..." he paused.

"Like the stuff that was missing from the sweeps shack, right?" Ezrie's brain was on fire. "Kenner had security access didn't he? Couldn't he have doctored the records like he did for the bomb?"

He turned to her, for a moment, looking like the old Purple that she remembered.

"It's possible." He stood, seemingly confounded. "But if he needed a transmitter, why not use the ones that were already here?"

"Because," Ezrie said, the realization dawning as she spoke it, "Those transmitters didn't belong to him, they *belonged to PanGen*. Marcus, or

Kenner wanted one for themselves—or Living Waters did. One that no one on earth would know existed. Especially if no one was alive to talk about it. That's why they stalled the mine."

"But why would they want that? There were already people here—working transmitters, bases, research...It doesn't make sense to tank it all—"

"And take it for themselves?" She laughed bitterly. "The infrastructure is still here. The research—if that's what was really going on—is ready to pick up with whoever Living Waters gets to replace Birdy. But this time, they won't have to share. No governance. Nobody getting in their way." The idea was insane, but she knew it was right. "Living Waters would have its own planet, its own eternal source of water, and no one would ever know."

"But the porters," Purple blurted, "They're tracked. Every one is registered, the signals monitored by ICET—"

Ezrie sat hard. Her head felt fuzzy, and the world was spinning.

"What?" he said, "What's wrong?"

"That's why I'm here," she whispered.

"What are you talking about?"

From the back of her mind, a guilt shuddered up to her conscious. She had promised her father she would destroy the porter, but what had she done instead? She had used it. That weighed on her mind more than anything. Not only had she used it, but she had shared its secrets, selling even the best for whatever she could get away with.

And the Black Door was the best secret of all.

She stuttered, her voice feeling thin and reedy. "Marcus...Marcus would have known about the Black Door." She looked up at Purple's confused face. "It was the original configuration of the porter schematics, the one that me and my dad built."

Purple paused. "Wait, you said Black Door was a myth—"

"I lied." She tried not to say the words, but they spilled over, unwilling to stay locked away. "I fixed the code mistakes for the original entanglement field—The Black Door—after my dad died. When Marcus took it all over, he made changes so that he could say it had been him, but it was me all along. It's the reason I came here. I've been wanting to kill him my whole life."

"Marcus brought you out here to custom-code his porter, so that he could sell the access to Living Waters. They would be able to mine Leto without any detection."

"And keep all the profit, all the time."

She hung her head. That's what it had all been about. A secret way to get water on and off Leto with no one else to know. And only Marcus had known she could do it. She was the only one who ever could.

"What are we going to do?" He ran his hand across his chin, which boasted a red, powdery stubble.

"We need to go," Ezrie said, standing. "If there's a way off this planet, Marcus has it. We have less than two days before that transmission window closes."

"And play right into Marcus' plan?" he blurted. "He backed everyone. He killed—" he stumbled. "He killed them." He sagged suddenly, his face going slack. He doubled over, and sicked up a thin stream of bile. He wiped his hand across his mouth.

With that feeble motion, the right path was clear.

"We don't have a choice," she said. "You and I have to leave. If we don't, we'll end up like the Artemis crew."

"What if—" He stopped himself, his red, bleary eyes meeting hers. He looked so old then. So afraid.

What if it's too late, his voice whispered in her ear. What if they are already inside of us. What if they are already inside of me?

She held him close, holding his rigid body until is softened almost imperceptibly.

"It's not too late," she mumbled into his shoulder. "Hold on. We're almost there."

He pulled back, his blue eyes encircled by darkness.

She felt a gut instinct to crawl away, to run until Purple and Leto were a distant memory. Because, for a moment, she saw them inside—a body full of minds, a body full of mouths, whispering her name.

III

Chaldean Mountains, North, *Leto*

THERE WAS little need for sleep or food. Birdy felt nothing but the compulsion to keep going.

As she traveled, the world became feverish. She ran in and out of the past. There was no pain. In her mind, *they* whispered things to her. Ideas. Places she had never known about. The people from her life before melted into the background, even as she relived experiences she had forgotten.

Eating a peach stolen from a food stand on Madison and Pulaski.

Laughing with Marley Jameson. They'd smoked under the bleachers at West Garfield Junior High and told each other's fortunes.

Cutting open the dog that had been the second dissection in her freshman anatomy class. Holding the liver, measuring the intestines, scared and excited and revulsed at the same time.

All of these things happened in real time, as if she had been transported in time. She awoke still smelling formaldehyde, the nylon edging of the lab coat scratching at her wrists. Birdy knew all the names of her classmates, could count the minutes until she would meet Brendan and Dally for lunch in the Commons. Knew that the boy who took money at the cash register would give her thirteen cents in change after she bought her salad and yogurt.

Then she was gone, and the memories were gone with her.

These memories didn't matter. Only the feel of the ground, the burning light from inside her head, the whisper of *them*—Only *they* mattered. She was going to her home. It was ahead, not very far now. The knowledge of this eclipsed anything she might have lost along the way. It filled her with a kind of happiness that was consuming. Whatever lay ahead blotted out whatever had been or would be.

And she knew he was following. That somehow he was a part of her. Of *them*.

They were learning about loneliness and fear. Love. Loss.

She experienced some of these things in her dreams, as if she was Kenner. She could see herself, watched from the outside. She saw Grandam and knew the fear of that lash. Birdy awoke from this crying and shaking, but unable to remember any of it.

Other times, she ran through the mountains, across a great, glassy plain with monsters that slept below. They reminded her of tusked creatures from her own world (rhinoceros), but she could not remember what they were called when she tried to say the name out loud. Lycants had protected her. They were a part of *them*, too. When she began to climb the black rocks, larger, wilder animals with thick, muscular bodies slithered beside her.

Birdy climbed as if she knew every secret handhold and pocket of the mountain face. She looked back only once, and almost flung herself to the ground, knowing that she was lost and also that she was no longer Birdy. She was *them*, too. But the world became Brazil, and Cy was teaching his birds to say her name and feeding them mango. Birdy awoke feeling the juice on her fingers and at the top of a great ridge, the orange sun so near that she reached out to touch it.

Now she scrambled down into a valley. They whispered and whispered, the throbbing in her head no longer painful, but insistent.

Come. Come and see.

She could see the spike of the structure that the humans had built, a small group of buildings tucked behind the mountains. Birdy slowed, only because she knew that there was another now. Someone whose name escaped her, but that she had known in that other life. It didn't matter now. Now there was only *them. Us.*

She found herself winding through the rocks, past the human stronghold, towards a small hillock of red sandstone where she knew there would be an opening.

It was small and tight, but she was not afraid. *They* whispered tiny changes to her body, a flowing that emanated from her head and her leg, both of which could not feel pain. Minute shifts, stretching, that made going into the craggy hole feel like it was made of water.

The first few yards of the cave were lit by the bright young suns of Solace, but it was then cut off abruptly by the blackness of isolation.

But it wasn't.

All along the walls she saw a thin, unending web of pulsing blue veins. It pulsed inside the cave walls, like far off dying stars. It was terrifying and mesmerizing. She wanted to run to it, to hide from it.

The ocean of sound in her head grew, the voices increasing.

Come and see.

Within, she knew she would find peace. Finally, to be one with the great whole. The arms of the dead reached for her. The filaments beckoned from beyond the granite wall, and she followed their trail of light.

"Birdy!"

She whirled on him, her eyes flashing. Her teeth pulled back into a sneer.

The cave pulsed with their light. He knew that they were inside. He could hear her voices as he could hear her. Not on the device. He could her hear speak through them, as they spoke through her.

She was beautiful in her monstrousness. Her clothes had been shredded from running, but her body was strong.

Do it, Grandam said. *You came all this way, and now you don't have the guts.*

"Stop," he shouted. "Please." He pulled the small token of his affection from his pocket, holding it tenderly in his hand. The vial with the trace that he'd cut from the animal. "I brought you a present. Stay."

The voices from the Nexus understood this word. It was what *they* desired more than anything. For her to stay. For all of them. It spoke through him, feeding on his own fear, his own twisted need for Birdy.

Kill or be killed, he thought. He raised the laster.

But she was Birdy. She was Calliope. She was himself.

I know you, their voice spoke in his head. It was Birdy's mouth moving, but he could hear all of them, understanding, knowing his pain and his past.

Do it, Grandam said, *kill her or be killed, boy.*

Protect our people, the Reverend said. *With blood, if necessary.*

Please. His child's voice was so small against their loud. *I don't want to, I don't want to—*

Come home, she beckoned, their voices drowning him. *Come with me.* She held out her hand, so wasted and twisted.

She was his Birdy, but she was not.

But her hand was so soft.

I will not leave you, she whispered. *Be one of us.*

He took her hand, and she pulled him close.

Her mouth was on his, her hands on his face, and he was enveloped in them. It was Chicago, and Ladora, and the dandelions in the cracks. It was Cy and the birds and the girls at the prep school. They were taking him in, stealing him away.

There was a pain in his back, a searing burn, and he flung himself away from her, knocking the laser scalpel from her hand. She smiled, her eyes so blue, her mouth wide and soundless like a black hole.

They were taking her away. There would be no more Birdy.

What is Birdy, she said, her smile too wide, her eyes too blue.

He pulled the trigger, but not to kill.

Birdy dropped, screeching, her body rigid. But he knew better. He had seen the Lycants. She would not stay down for long. She was almost one of them now.

He flipped her to her stomach, the electricity of her body sending aftershocks up his own arm. Kenner pulled out the field knife.

Kill or be killed, Grandam said.

He saw the thoughts of many. Chuckwagon with his noose. Tukuafu and her needle of poison. Lee with her guns on the red dirt, a child's jacket covered in blood tucked in her ammunition belt.

Himself as a boy, holding his bloody blade.

Which one was he now, the boy or the man?

Kill or be killed. There is only this answer.

There was no other way. This was the solution that they had been taught.

"No," he said, dropping the knife. "There is another choice."

What did you want to be?

A savior.

He picked up the laser scalpel and began to work. The cave filled with the smell of flesh.

She screamed, thrashed, as he knelt on her back, cutting her. He remembered the lycant, the contour of the device in the flesh. He cut like he was there again, like there was no risk.

Birdy twisted, ripping the laster from his hand and crushing in her fist. She was bleeding from where the cut had been made, the device hanging from a last piece of flesh like a macabre piece of jewelry. Her eyes burned blue.

He had done it wrong, then.

"Kill or be killed," she spat. "*We see.*"

Kenner steeled himself and lunged, her neck in his hands, so close that he could have kissed her.

She brought the knife up, through the rib cage and into his heart.

Something in him broke. He felt them sigh, a sound of release and sadness that brought tears to his eyes.

Home, they said. *Come.*

Kenner's body shook, a spitting black blood as he went limp. She pushed him off with inhuman arms, unable to feel the sorrow that tinged whatever she had been before them. But it was swallowed in the bathing blue light behind the wall. Around the corner, through a crevice, they waited to take her, so beautiful and warm.

He shuddered one last time, coughing. Then, he went dark.

No, she thought. *Only dim. He would return as they all did.*

But something was wrong.

The voices were quieting. They were shrinking.

Wait, she thought.

No pain. No death.

Wait!

Her head was splitting. The voices shrinking, screaming.

They were dying.

No. *She* was dying.

The words, fractured and frantic, raced through her head. She struggled, but her head was wrong. The world was going black. She couldn't breathe. She couldn't breathe.

The voices in Birdy's head reached a fevered agony.

"Air," she croaked. "Air."

She pushed back, away from them, away from their screams into clear air of the mountain. Above, the two moons of Leto nearly kissed in the sky. In their light, Birdy saw that her hands were covered in blood.

The last she remembered was screaming.

IV

Chaldean Mountains, North, *Leto*

SHE IS *in the room with her father. His skin is papery, his eyes leaking blood. He pulls her close, and she can smell the death on him. It is coming for him. It is coming for them all.*

Promise, Z. Promise you'll destroy it.

I promise, dad.

She hugs him, feeling the sickly softness of his bones, knowing that she is leaving bruises on his destroyed skin. But she cannot remember what it is like to hug him any other way, and she is so tired.

When she pulls back, it is not her father, but Marcus who lies there.

He is covered in plastic. Overhead, there are lights dancing, like fairies. They are both malevolent and kind. Marcus has an umbilical cord attached to his head, and it wraps around his wrists and ankles, strapping him down.

Come he says, come and see. I'm so hungreeeeee

———

She snapped her eyes open and she was on the mountain, walking. She stumbled on the trail. Her face was wet and she was calling her father's name.

They had walked all through the previous day, barely stopping to eat, each step more precarious than the last. Purple moved fast, stopping every so often to wait for her to catch up. She didn't know if it was because his outlanding suit was gone or something more, but he moved faster all the time. She didn't know how he could do it, the cold making her hand and feet feel like blocks of ice inside the broken outlanding suit. But it didn't seem to affect him. He would just walk, jaw slack, zooming, or something like it, for hours. He was somewhere else, with or without the trace.

And then, there were her visions.

She was seeing the past sometimes. Not like the dreams. No. It was if the dreams were morphing into some new version of reality. She would be walking, climbing, and then she would be at the Peterson's, locked in the closet, hungry and in the dark. She would be in a hotel room, putting her clothes back on, feeling sick and ashamed that she didn't even know the stranger's name.

Ezrie shivered, clutching her outlanding suit close while blinking back whatever waking dream she'd been having. Marcus was ahead. She could feel it. And there were others, too. She could sense them on the periphery. Flashes of images. Chicago. Blood on his hands. Purple in a hospital room holding Clare's hand. Wishing she could speak.

we speak

Zephyrs scattered like feathers in the early morning light, small puffs of yellow in the early morning dark. They were like the fairies in her dream, dancing around her. It made her feel that, somehow, her reality was fusing with some other existence.

"Purple? Finn?"

She called his name, convinced that he, too, was a mirage. He turned to her, the preternatural glow of his eyes was so dim as to be a trick of the morning light. But he stared at her as if she were a stranger.

Ezrie pulled back, a blind fear of him constricting her chest. The was a shiver of certainty that he would push her off the cliff if she came closer. Her legs stalled and stopped.

He's going to kill you. He's one of them. This was his plan all along—

She shook the paranoia from her head.

No. No, that's not right.

"Where are we?" she said, trying to keep her voice from shaking.

"Mountains somewhere," he said. "It's a short leg, now. Twenty miles, maybe a little more."

"Very faze."

He smiled, his eyes distant. She wondered what dreams he was walking through. What dreams they had to walk through still.

Sometime in the afternoon, Ezrie gave up. It was the rock face. She climbed, her legs weak, her arms weary. But her heart stopped. Purple held on impossibly, pulling her up with newfound strength. He still looked like the same person she'd met nearly two weeks ago, but he was wiry and strong. It was more than that, though. Whatever was inside him was changing him.

It was changing her, too, but slower. She wondered how much longer it would be. By the time they got where they were going, she wondered if she would even be able to do what she came here to do. She touched the small pin at her ear. Would the phlax have ruined that as well?

She didn't know. And she didn't know if it mattered anymore.

Overhead, the suns danced newly across the sky. Where once it had been a child's figure eight or a Venn diagram of two things with very little in common, it was now combining, coalescing to become a circle within a circle. A world within a world. She looked at Purple, making his way effortlessly over the rocky jags as if he'd grown up here. She had through they were so different, but she'd been wrong. He had lost, too. He had hidden. He was trying to make things right in his own way.

The water cache beeped empty. It figured. No water bottles. No Aris with extra supplies. And all she could see was black and rock and rock and black. And the suns were going down again, drowning Leto in purple-brown.

It is evening. Her father has taken her for a milkshake to Tibby's. The sky is dark and warm, and she is happy that it is him and her.

"I want to see the Ocean," Ezrie says.

Her father laughs, licking his peanut butter brickle quickly to save the drip from splattering his pants. "I'll take you some day."

"Can't we go now?"

"It's too far away. It takes time."

"Is that where mama went?"

Richard Collings licks the cone thoughtfully.

"There are places that people go that we can't get to," he says.

"Where? Where did she go?"

He smiles sadly, and she takes his hand. The chocolate is rich on her lips, and she can see his eye glisten in the fluorescent lights of Tibby's drive-and-park.

"We can get there," she says. "With the door, right? The door will take us anywhere."

He hugs her. "Yes. You're probably right. That's why we have to keep working on it. Who knows where it can go."

Ezrie came to herself still tasting the chocolate. Despite the outlanding jacket's threadbare material and blasting mountain wind, the summer night of the vision warmed her.

"It's just over the hill," Purple called. He stood at the edge of the rise. For a moment, she thought he was her father standing there.

"No."

She sat, the vision threatening her.

"I quit. Here's where it ends."

He stared at her. "What do you mean, you quit? You can't quit."

She was crying again, sobbing. There was too much truth in the vision. Death was a places you couldn't follow. And the only thing worse than that truth was the idea that on Leto, you could. She would stay here, and her mother would come. Her father was here somehow. If Ezrie waited long enough, they would find her and take her to the place where she belonged.

She wiped snot from her face unceremoniously. "Leave me alone to die here, okay? I'm done."

"They're waiting," Purple said, shaking her shoulders.

I've done nothing but hurt and hate, and I'm tired, she wanted to say. *I came here because he wanted me here. I waited on Marcus like I waited for everything my whole life.*

She crumpled, curling up on the snow and stone. There was too much at stake here and the truth she'd been pressing down had turned into something diamond hard. It cut through all the bullshit she'd been telling herself for a lifetime.

Purple stood, immovable.

Maybe you never wanted to kill him, he said. *I don't think you ever really did.*

But he didn't say it. She just heard him, felt his words in her mind.

Purple knelt beside her, reaching into the little pocket of her outlanding suit. Before he even pulled out the vial, she knew what he'd done. She could see it so clearly, tucking the little vial into her suit while it hung to dry. His eyes throbbed that luminous blue in the shadows of the setting suns. "It's been there for nearly a week," he said softly. "You could've killed me and left any time you wanted, but you didn't."

Purple knelt beside her, and there was softness in his eyes.

"You're not going to quit," he said. "You're afraid. And so am I."

She looked up at him.

"Whatever is waiting for us down there, we have to do it together. No matter what, I'll be here. I'll always be here. I'd rather die doing something stupid with you than doing something smart alone."

She looked at him and felt her eyes go hot. Purple had been the only one on Leto who was really here for her. He had been here for her since the moment she arrived. Had she been there for him?

"Come on, then," she said. It felt like an apology, but it came out sounding like a promise.

V

North Base, *Leto*

Day 14

THEY DECIDED to go around the perimeter, keeping out of scanning distance, they hoped. There was no way of telling where Marcus would be exactly, since his pin wasn't live but a downloaded location, but they assumed that whoever was there was in the small clutch of buildings that stood below the transmitter tower.

The evening was quiet. The transmitter stood sentinel above the whole miniature base, and Ezrie noted that it was much shorter than the others had been, hovering over a squat version of the porter bay at Ocean. It was smart, really. Having it up so high in the mountains meant that it was already closer to the satellites than the other porters, and having the porter so close to the transmitter meant that there was less distance for the signal to travel. The entire thing was covered in phlax, making the two buildings look like some fused, half-melted dessert.

She was starving.

"I'd cob that's where we're headed." Purple was hazy, staring at the porter with an odd far-off look. She felt that his words were coming from somewhere that was quickly becoming foreign lands.

"No," she said emphatically. "That's where *we* get out."

From this vantage point, they could also see that there was a pipeline in place. Ezrie realized for the first time that she had not seen anything like it so far on Leto. While Zhong had been testing water and setting up buildings and research, Marcus and Living Waters had been printing pipe and laying it down.

The long, wide segments of pipe went all the way to a yellow, shimmering lake on the east of the small valley. She stopped, transfixed.

Zephyrs. Millions of them rolling along the waterline of this mountain pool. A few drifted up and towards them, and Ezrie suddenly realized why they hadn't seen the small creatures for so long. They were all here.

The small creatures floated lazily to the transmitter, where they joined others that were coalescing around the thick power lines that ran to the squat building that housed the energy supply and solar converters. It was an ethereal sight—their bodies glow-warm and golden-bright. Ezrie felt her heart lift a little.

"They're nearing to pump, if they haven't already," Purple said, his voice hoarse. "Someone's has been working overtime." He pointed to the building where the pipes ended. "That's the main filtration station. Those big blue water jugs are brand new. It would be a bloody miracle if they haven't already gotten their first shipment off."

To the east of the pumping station, she saw the porter bay, a twin of its predecessor at Ocean base. To the south, there were two other small buildings. Ezrie stalked down the hill, Purple slowing perceptibly behind her. It was so odd to be in the lead, and she could almost feel his reticence with every lagging step.

From her trace, she could see Marcus' avatar blinking slowly. He was in a squat grey building south of the porter bay.

She felt her heart squeeze. Ezrie touched the earring. She had come all this way. Like Purple had said. She couldn't stop now.

"We should split up," Ezrie said. "Anyone who is willing to kill you once is willing to kill you twice."

"Good idea," he said, rubbing his head. He blinked his eyes slowly, scanning the eastern slope of the base. "There's something over there. Something big. I can feel it."

Ezrie looked to where was, and sensed it, but only lightly. There was something over there. *They.* The whispers ticked up to a sound like a seashell to her ear.

"Purple? Hey, Purple." Ezrie grabbed the sandpaper stubble of his chin. "Finn," she said softly, catching and keeping his gaze. "Stay away from it, okay?"

"Yeah."

"I'll check out the porter. I'll be back here in an hour, okay? Just wait for me an hour. Can you do that?"

"Fine. Sure."

She didn't know what else to do. His eyes were glazed. He was hearing things she couldn't. It was like the pull of a current, and he knew who was in it—Clare. Ezrie turned to leave, but then spun back, kissing him hard. When she pulled away, his eyes were searching hers, as if she were someone he almost remembered.

"Please, Finn. Wait for me. Don't go without me."

Something in him flashed awake, and he smiled. "I'll wait."

Ezrie slunk down towards the porter, her laster in hand, grateful that at least Marcus hadn't strewn this base with gravel. Her feet padded softly in the thin mountain grass. The air of the evening smelled of ice. She shivered, her jaw clenched. Her stomach felt queasy.

As she crossed the campus of the makeshift base, *they* fluttered inside of her, jittery. There was a sense of pain and fear. But there was something there as well. A familiarity. She knew this place.

She needed to be smart, to catch Marcus by surprise. She opened the door as quietly as she could, met by a flood of glowing lights. Zephyrs flitted past her face, and she felt like they might choke her. As they passed, the terror that had seized her dissipated incrementally.

Ezrie stepped inside the room, startling at the crunch of dead, grey zephyr corpses beneath her feet.

Have to stay quiet. Have to stay quiet.

But nothing moved in this building, which was no more than a small science lab. Marcus' avatar remained quiet and still, and Ezrie realized he was probably sleeping. He sat motionless behind a sealed plastic quarantine tent. More zephyrs danced behind the plastic. And it smelled in here. She felt her gorge rise. It stank of rot. Of metal and flesh.

abomination, abberation, unclean, unholy

Behind the plastic, she could make out some kind of chair with two figures beside it. The translucent plastic made it all look like a puppet show. On the wall beside the quarantine tent was a large imaging screen showing a trace overlay. It was spotty, with areas where the image was out of focus—some of it in the same corrupted symbols as the data in the containment unit she'd stolen. In the corner, there were location avatars. Two of them. Her thoughts flickered to Purple, interrupted by only

DANGER

the thought of *them* calling, warning.

A few zephyrs suckled at the sockets of the great light overhead as others paled to white and fell like ash to the floor. But the rest drew her towards the plastic wall.

She drew it back to find the mangled, misshapen form of Marcus.

He stared at her with blind, milky-blue eyes. His arms and legs were shriveled, his body emaciated, a bag of some clear fluid hanging from a rafter overhead that ran down to the dripline in his arm. The zephyrs crawled in and out of his mouth. Into his nose and ears. They kissed his skin like some writhing patchwork quilt. Red, white, yellow. An Aris knelt beside him, as if bending low to hear a promise he was whispering. Between them was a mass of blue veiny phlax. A network of light that grew and cascaded down their shoulders like a shared head of hair.

desecration, abomination

Ezrie felt fear on an atomic level. She felt Marcus in her mind, along with the rest of them. An agony of pain, the place where they lived dirtied and muddled by the foreign mind of the Aris. He was reaching out to her, a pressure of need and regret.

There was a moan from him, a wordless sound like hunger.

He was hungry.

help us help

She felt the laster on her neck before she heard the voice.

"Ezrie Collings," a woman purred. "I'm so excited you made it. We have so much work to do."

VI

Crater Lake, Oregon, *Earth*

July 2077

JENNY WISHES she were at home. There, she has awards on the marble mantle above the zen waterfall in her living room. Robotics International. The Society for Advanced Intelligence. There, her lab is full of dismembered Aris cortexes and phlax that has been reanimated and cultivated. She is so close to learning how the phlax can be manipulated to hack a trace. It is the science she has risked everything for.

Now she sits in a crappy mall cafeteria, trying to ignore the stink of teenage hormones that is probably permeating her Burberry jacket. There is a huge holoscreen in the center of the food court that is highlighting the sales from each store. Forty percent off spring casual wear at Amazon. Buy one get one free at Orange Julius. A gaggle of Gen kids are zooming out over the newest Nets video, slack-jawed and staring into space. She hates the trace, but it is a necessity. It will be the thing that wins her the Nobel Prize, some day.

She picks at the salad in front of her, wondering whether it's worth it. Jenny has done things she never thought she'd do. Stolen. Hurt people.

She cringes at this thought, more ashamed than she has a right to be. Rand is so lonely, such an easy target. And she'd needed a way to make the changes she needed to make. She, of all people, had known that hacking a trace is impossible—uploading dangerous code was not. Fortunately, hacking people is her specialty, and Rand has so many exploits in his code.

Jenny wonders if he knows. If he had felt her stealing his passcodes and DNA signature files while they made love.

She shakes this lapse in empathy off. It hardly matters now. She is getting the hell out of dodge. If all goes well, she will officially retire from Leto as soon as Reverend Andrews gets out of Hot Topic, or wherever the hell he is.

Jenny bites into a tomato that explodes juice down her blouse.

"Good hell," she mutters, wiping with a napkin. "As if this day isn't bad enough."

Jenny dumps the salad and napkin into the trash, pushing her blonde hair out of her face. When she comes back to the table, there is a trace fob. She puts the little fob to her trace and she is on a secure transmission. Jenny accepts the Reverend's video chat request begrudgingly. Such an old-fashioned thing, doing business face-to-face. But she understood. She'd wanted to meet Ezrie face-to-face, after all. And look how that turned out.

"Cassie suspects," she says. "I know it. I want out. I don't want the money any more. Get someone else to make your paradise for you."

The Reverend laughs.

"Oh, sugar," he says. "It was never about the world. It was about the water." He pauses. Two tables down sits a very large man. Above her, beside a jewelry kiosk, stands a skinny man with a moustache. How many others had the Revered sent? "No, you're not getting out. God's work will move forward whether you help or not. Leto will be our own little cash cow. Water coming out—free, gorgeous, and untaxable. Money coming in."

"I don't want to be a part of this—"

"You made your choice." His voice is razor-sharp. "You're built it, you own it. And you're the one who's gonna ship that water out. Did you get that little program?"

Jenny pulled the little flag-like drive from her purse. The Black Door. Ezrie was nearly exactly what she had expected. Angry. Chip on her shoulder. And she'd worked on trade. The kill code, another Caskade, was Jenny's underground specialty. Everyone wanted someone's brain turned to ashes. Ezrie was no different.

"Cassie knows, goddamn it. She's going to the board—"

"Watch yourself, blasphemer. Don't use God's name in your foul mouth."

Jenny choked on her anger, the urge to smash the drive insistent. One of the Gen kids laughs uproariously, and the rest join as they share feeds. A woman with a tray passes near her, child in tow.

"This only works if no one knows," Jenny said, her voice too slow, her words too crisp. "What happens when they find out?"

"I want you to get rid of them and then shut the doors down."

"You can't really expect me to do this alone," she says. "My porter hack is only five minutes. It's enough for me to smuggle an android or some parts, not an entire crew—"

"It's up to you. Find a way to get them off safely, or I'll send in Kenner to get rid of them whatever way he sees fit."

"And what if I don't?" she says. "What if I quit now and never go back?"

But the Reverend just laughed. "I think you'll find that I can be persuasive."

There's a man sitting on a bench outside of Macy's. His hand hidden inside a Victoria's Secret bag. He catches her glance and gives her a nod, a smile never breaking his lips.

Jenny breaks out in a cold sweat.

"Besides, if you do this last thing, your job is finished. I can make sure that you get any offworld job you want after Leto. Any face, any history. We have all the best people working for you."

"This is the last thing," she says. "Then we're done."

She takes the fob off and crushes it beneath her boot. She leaves the drive on the table, where the Reverend's goons can inspect it. The next time she goes to Leto, it is in the pocket of her outlanding suit. She realizes that she has no recourse but to complete the job she set out to do. It's a good thing she doesn't have to do it alone.

Jenny thinks of the little earring sometimes. Yes, whenever she needs Ezrie, it should be no trouble at all to get her here.

VII

Nexus, *Leto*

Day 14

PURPLE RIMMED the outskirts of the base, steering away from the thing

we are here

that called him from the eastern mountains. The voices, so dim this morning, were now stronger than ever. *They* seemed closer, somehow, calling him by some secret name that only *they* knew.

Finn...Finn...

They whispered about love and family and loss and promises. He knew that where *they* were, there was belonging as he had never known it.

But that wasn't true.

He racked his brain, trying to recall the name of the one who had made him belong. But the memory was split now. The girl in the truck and the girl on the mountain ridge. They mixed and merged in his mind, and he didn't know the word for the thing he felt, but belonging was a part of it. Sorrow was the other.

The moons slivered up, even as the last of Leto's suns crashed down into the horizon. From this vantage point, he could see a circlet of the planet, the top cut off some great vast king's diadem. To the east, the mountains wound away. To the west, the white plains and lake of glass was flooded with the deep red of sunset. Overhead, purple night encroached, with stars as bright as floodlights. He could see it all from here

we see

and he knew that *they* had chosen this place for them. Somehow, this had always been and would always be the place that he found where he belonged.

home is where you are from

Yes. You understand.

Rach and Daph are in the lobby. His mother is thinner than he remembers her. She has not been this thin since Purple's father died, when he was barely two. He has seen her pictures.

In the room, there is the antiseptic smell of hospital. The sound of quiet feet. It is not like the Emergency Room he visited when he broke his arm falling out of the Scots Pine. This is a quiet wing. Even the air is hushed, as if it is waiting.

He does not know why he is recording, except that they have told him that Clare may not speak again. Somehow, he has to capture her wit, her vivacity. He does not know this at the time, but he knows it now.

Clare lies on the bed, her head bandaged thickly. A tube runs out of her mouth, taped in place. Black and purple bruises are up and down her arms. They have swollen one of her eyes shut. There is a gash above her lip that has been lasered closed, but still looks raw and red. Her eyes track them as they come in.

"Clare," he says, coming close and sitting at the stool beside the bed. "How you getting on, then?"

Clare gurgles. Her eyes are slow, her jaw slack.

He feels his muscles shake, the sadness choking him up and spilling out. His vision blurs.

She twitches her arm, and he realizes that she wants something. He takes it, and looks up to see her searching his face. She is looking at him so hard. As if she's sending him some message that he can no longer understand. They are speaking two different languages. But then one of the monitors begins to sound, and a nurse shuffles him and his sisters and his mother out of the room.

family, they whisper.

Purple can feel her hand. He can smell the flowers that someone has brought for her.

There is something I want to tell you

we hear

I wanted to say that I love you. I'm so shite that I don't know how to say it anymore.

we know

He tells these words to her, the words that he couldn't say because he didn't know when he was here the first time that they were trapped inside him. He says them to her now, because this is *that time, and maybe if he says them, this time it will be different.*

The light from the walls of the cave pulsed, showing him the way to where *they* were waiting. All of them.

VIII

Ocean Base, *Leto*

December 2079

WHEN THE APOLLO team arrives for the Overnight, it is nothing but excitement. Even Sanger, who is obsessively stodgy, has given his crooked smile at least once.

The plan is for twenty-eight days. A full rotation. Charleston will be focusing on water experiments that he has been running with Birdy over at Mountain. Lexi and Jenny will be accompanying Charleston on the trip over, since the porter there has been malfunctioning.

"The phlax. The damn phlax in everything," Heitar says. Jenny knows better. It has been she and Kenner who have been making the porter less functional. If they can't port over (or think they can't) they'll all stay in one spot. It makes everything that comes after much easier.

Cassie and Marcus fight over who will lead the team to Mountain, and Cassie pulls rank.

"I'm the Captain, Marcus," she says, her black bun severe on her head. "You think having more screen time than God makes you important? Because it doesn't."

This shuts him up.

———

The plan is to stay with the group for long enough to establish normalcy, then be eaten by Lycants. Kenner is not with her, which is unfortunate, but better. She doesn't like relying on him, and his zeal makes her nervous. It will be easier to do all this with Aris, and she's been programmed specifically to do this last job.

After a few days, the team is acting more than just the usual level of paranoid. The phlax is breaking things down, growing exponentially. This is in line with Jenny's personal experiments, but it is fascinating to see its effect on human cortexes. Chuck explodes during a regular bullshit session. Heitar picks a fight with Lexi over a misplaced tool. Cassie, not an overly quiet woman, is withdrawing, taking to sleep with her laster.

Jenny catches Sanger in his office, mumbling to himself.

She is having nightmares, too. Mostly about Revered Andrews. Sometimes an Aris is there, its cortex broken open, its mouth open and singing.

She waits until after Chuck's breakdown, and then creates her last video. It feels so normal. One last live feed. But she also knows it is her last few minutes as Jenny Candala. She pauses a moment to mourn this loss, but it's just a face. And a reputation, and a career...

No matter. It's what must be done. The science will be enough. Her new credentials will be even better than the ones she has now. The Reverend has enough connections to promise that. When she is ready to make her "discovery" back on Earth, she will get all the credit, no matter what face and name she chooses.

Aris chases her for effect. Jenny imagines that it is the Reverend's goons that are on her heels, and the effect is very good. When she's done, she cuts her arm and wipes it up with a torn piece of her jumpsuit. Aris cuts the trace from her skull quickly and efficiently, smashes it, and buries it.

When they arrive at the North Base—the Ark—the phlax has doubled, maybe tripled. The main engine area that pumps the water and filters it is broken, thick with blue fingers of the stuff. The transmitter is covered, a web of phlax between it and the power lines.

Aris greets her at the door. The android is jittery. Unbalanced. Still, there is no one else to trust but her own creation, so she does. Jenny has no more nightmares. She is calmer.

But the crew she leaves behind is not so lucky.

After only a few days, the porter is giving off strange errors in a language she doesn't know. She wipes it, reinstalls it, wipes it, reinstalls it. Nothing she does can fix it. The errors remain. It will not allow her to port.

Jenny disables the security parameters so that she is able to port through to Mountain. The base is empty. She spends as much time as she dares stealing compound and additional MEGs, food and supplies. Every time she ports through, she feels as if there is something in the nothing, and it knows her.

Although she no longer feels the overwhelming paranoia of the phlax infection, she becomes terrified of porting. There is something real inside of it. *They* are inside of it. If she's serious about getting off the planet and getting Ezrie on, it's time to bring in her secret weapon: Marcus.

But the Ocean porter refuses to connect. Jenny decides to do it the old-fashioned way, grateful that she stole a bike before she left. She stops only to sleep, eat, and to clean out both of her machines. She is able to make it there in just over three days.

Jenny goes up the transmitter tower to get a better lay of the base—to see if there is activity that might stop her progress. There is no movement. Phlax has also started to take over the tower, despite the fact that someone has cut the power lines. But why?

When she arrives at the base, she is on edge. The floor is sticky with blood. Jenny comes closer, frightened but undeterred, following the sound of Cassie's voice.

"Nancy died this morning. Walked into the ocean. I tried to stop her, but..." Cassie pauses. Jenny can hear she is in the medical wing. Jenny tells Aris to wait, her boots are too loud on the floor. Cassie continues after a heart-stopping moment. "The only one left is Marcus, and he's locked himself in the science lab."

Science lab. Jenny turns to go, but Cassie's next words stop her.

"He swears that Jenny is still alive. That he saw her running around in the woods. But I've seen them come back, too. They don't stay dead."

Jenny curses herself for coming back for more print compound. But there is a question, too. Who else has come back? Who besides herself?

"Where are you? Where did you all go? The ghosts are getting closer, and I'm too tired to fight them. I don't want to be alone."

The body that has been lying on the table rises up, the white sheet falling from it. It is Chuck, his neck an empty wound. He stumbles up and towards Cassie.

Jenny turns and runs, but trips over Aris who is standing where she left her.

Cassie looks up, recognizes her, but it doesn't matter now. They are both running towards the exit.

Jenny flies out of the base down the women's corridor, then out towards the porter as fast as she can, Aris at her heels.

From behind her, she hears Cassie scream, turns to see her smash through the glass of the professional hall, her head cracked, her neck caught in the glass. Something is pulling her back, and the shards tear through her flesh, unleashing a gush of blood—

Jenny slams her hand on the porter bay door, the mechanism closing behind them. She and Aris wait for what feels like forever, listening to the sound of something feeding. She hears the sound of feet on gravel, coming closer, stopping, then shambling away. They are uneven steps. The steps of an animal.

When the footsteps are gone, she goes to the science lab to find Marcus.

IX

JENNY IS VERY familiar with the science building. She has visited Birdy and Charleston many times as they worked on the ecological study, recording their work on the phlax to further her own research. She can recite the results of their blood experiments in her sleep, and has once or twice in her dreams. Their work is the foundation of her discovery.

The door is locked, but she uses Rand's admin permissions to open it. She hears a scuttling in the darkness.

"Marcus? It's me. It's Jenny."

She keeps Aris close and the laster set to stun. She doesn't want to hurt him, just get his help to draw Ezrie to Leto. The floor is dirty, covered in smashed vials and blood. Not just a streak here or there, but huge amounts, as if the thing had been turned into a killing floor in a butcher shop. The glass infrared stasis monitor has been smashed in half and turned into a shiv. It lays in a dried pool of gore which was more than blood. Jenny recognizes brain. Scanners and micrometers have been overturned and lay in sprays of broken glass on the floor and countertops. The culture bay is upended, its contents exposed and destroyed. The only thing untouched is the sealed walk-in refrigeration unit.

Jenny scans her hand and the light blinks green. She pushes through to find a maze of plastic. Marcus has hung strips of colored plastic from the water pipes that crisscross the ceiling—orange from hazard suits, black from trash bags, the clear polyalmarine bags meant for contaminated or dead animals.

In the dark, it makes her skin crawl to push past the thick strips of plastic. But she pushes forward, finding herself at the dissection table, which is set against the units for specimens and cultures like a blockade. Beside it is a micrometer replete with a prepped slide. Jenny looks closer. It looks like a bit of metal, glowing a faint blue.

There is a shuffle from behind her.

She whirls around just Marcus grabs the laster.

Jenny screams and Marcus squeezes the trigger, but Aris is faster than both of them. She leaps from the shadows, breaking Marcus' hold on the weapon and forcing him against the jutting edge of the table. He grabs the heavy metal shaft of the micrometer.

"You are dead!" he yelps, bringing the makeshift weapon smashing against Aris' head. She is unphased, and merely grabs him around the neck.

Marcus looks evacuated, almost skeletal. But what frightens Jenny most are his eyes. They roam wildly, seeing and not seeing at the same time. Even when they meet her own, Jenny realizes that they do not see her, nor does he comprehend anything outside whatever insanity has clutched him.

But she has to have his help. She must have a way to fix the malfunctioning door that she's worked so hard to create. She tells him of the plan and invites him to join her.

"No. No one comes to Leto," he mutters. "No one comes. I made sure."

That's when Jenny realizes that Marcus, without knowing it, has been working against her all along. He is the one that has cut the lines to the transmitter and porter. He learned the secret of Leto's water and made sure no one could bring it back to Earth. And now, he wants to stop her as well.

From the back of his head, she can see where the trace has been partially excised. Even as Aris presses his neck against the wall, she can see the angry red of the infected, open wound.

Jenny picks the laster up from the floor and flicks it to the highest setting. Marcus cannot help her now. She levels it at his head. It would be best to put him out of his misery.

But the glow from within his eyes makes her rethink. Perhaps he can help her after all.

X

North Base, *Leto*

Day 14

"MARCUS NEVER WANTED YOU HERE," Jenny said derisively. "He never wanted anyone to come to Leto again, not after all he'd been through. But his mind was half-gone. There was so much damage its incredible he's alive. But that's the miracle of phlax. The miracle we're going to use to change the world."

Marcus moaned and Aris shifted. Jenny kicked the heavy metal door closed behind her, her finger still on the laster's trigger. Ezrie heard the *snick* of a lock hammering into place. There was something in her other hand, hidden behind her back. Ezrie took a glance at the weapon. Set to kill.

"Oops," Jenny said. "Seems I was waiting for you longer than I thought. I have to keep him sedated. He almost got out once." Ezrie noted the lynchties connecting him to the table. It was a patchwork medieval setup reminiscent of a torture chamber.

Ezrie felt the weight of all of it crushing her.

"You called me here. How?"

366

"Well, I've been working on ways to hack a trace for a long time. That earring you're wearing is a perfect example. Good, but not exactly what I had in mind. I knew before the first time we met that I would probably need your help on Leto. So, I made sure I had a sample of your DNA and a way to track you if I needed to."

"I've never met you before—"

"Remember? You came to my lab in Portland City. You drank my water. And when you left with this little device, you had no idea I was following your every move. Or lack thereof."

Ezrie felt so stupid. That had been years ago. And the woman who met her at the door hadn't looked like this woman at all. She hadn't looked like anyone. A nondescript blonde with green contacts, the spitting image of the androids she kept as bodyguards—

"Aris," Ezrie said. "You had an Aris meet with me."

"Yes, my personal Aris. She's the next generation, and I've done a lot of upgrades since you met her. It wouldn't have made any sense to meet with you any other way. A girl's got to have her secrets, right?" Jenny laughed.

"I knew about your old rivalry, of course. And I was convinced that you would come if he called. You didn't disappoint. You are just as single-minded as me." She gave a maternal smile. "We actually have a lot in common."

"I am nothing like you," Ezrie hissed. "I'm not a murderer."

"I'm not a murderer. Kenner, yes. Revered Andrews, most definitely. But me? I'm a visionary."

"You're a monster." The words came from Ezrie's lips, but their voices crept at the edges. The Marcus creature sat slack-jawed and blind, crawling with hungry zephyrs. "How could you do that to any human?"

"Why do you care? You were going to kill him anyway."

Ezrie paused. From the hulk of flesh and machine, she could feel a longing. A hunger. There were thoughts in him still. They focused on the place—the Nexus. Ezrie caught flashes of something else as well. A small girl in an office holding a knife.

Marcus remembered *her.*

"I saved his life." Jenny's words were crisp and haughty. "The phlax builds connections—the same types of connections that were in all those glitchy Arises. Phlax acts as a synaptic conductor." Jenny's eyes shone for a moment. "I mean, the ramifications are intense, to say the least. Marcus is just the beginning."

The sheer magnitude of what Jenny had done dawned on her.

She had bypassed Ouros. She had used Aris as a mediator for the brain and the phlax had built the connections. The screen on the wall was a representation of Marcus' trace, all of his memories and experiences distilled in a few lines of code, his wasted body and brain kept alive by a bag of chemicals and a garroted Aris. All for the simple purpose of bringing Ezrie here. All for the purpose of taking the water to earth. Taking *them* to earth.

"You crazy bitch!" Ezrie tried not to think of the terrible future. One where phlax was unleashed on Earth to infect every human with a trace. "You'll kill us all."

"Ezrie," Jenny said as if speaking to a small child. "I'm not stupid. I don't want a mass contagion any more than you do." Ezrie flinched as she pulled the earring from Ezrie's ear—gently, like a beautician in a shopping mall—and dropped it into a small dish on the nearby counter. "When we get back, I'm making the recommendation that Living Waters filter the shipments for R-particles, and then return the particles back *here* where they belong."

"But with the Black Door running, we can continue the research I've started here with no interference. Find new, safe ways to use phlax as a conductor. Think of the possibilities." She smiled brightly, the conjoined bodies of Marcus and Aris a surreal backdrop to her excitement. "We can test coma patients, paraplegics, even the blind—right here in this lab without any outside interference. If we can learn to control the phlax—"

"You already have the Black Door," Ezrie interrupted. She needed time to think. "Why do you need me?"

Jenny sighed, then shook her head. "Phlax is funny. It builds synaptic responses, bones, and tissues. It has the potential to give a world of people the chance to instead of just exist." She paused, her eyes brightening. Then her countenance changed. "It also has a tendency to ruin code. So, the door we have here worked wonderful until it didn't."

She came close, so close that Ezrie could almost see what was behind her back. Something metal. "All I need is your help right now."

DANGER GET OUT DANGER

"You get us back to Earth and we can make real change for good. Forget about your father and Marcus. This will be the chance to put Ezrie Collings' name in the spotlight. You will have a bigger impact than they ever could."

Ezrie realized what she should have always known: she wasn't just the key to Leto, she was the door as well. What had she sacrificed to finally gain the information lying before her on the holodisplay? What life had she left unlived in her desperate flight towards revenge?

And Jenny had used it against her. She had known that Ezrie would do anything or risk anything to finally make the world see the truth about her father and Marcus and the porter. She had known that Ezrie had nothing else to live for but to settle this old score.

But that wasn't the truth anymore. And Jenny didn't know that.

From somewhere in her head, or from the ground, there was a shift in the static of the voices. She had a flash of insight. Purple was going to *them.* She could see the walls of the cave, the blue running like veins towards where they waited.

come we are all here we have so much to show you

"No!" Ezrie spat, half to Jenny, half to the voices that crushed against her mind. She waved off the zephyrs that were crowding her, falling on her like a living outlanding suit. "I won't. Nobody leaves Leto. Not you, not me. Not *them.*"

"Fine. You and me don't deserve to live," Jenny said in mock sympathetically. "But what about Purple?"

Ezrie's blood became ice. She could feel him even now, running down into the mountain.

"How did you—"

Jenny's threw back her head in a bitter laugh. Her hands were still behind her, pressing against the door. Ezrie felt a splinter of panic. There was something in her hand.

kill or be killed or kill or

"*Of course* I know Purple is alive," Jenny said. "I've been watching your progress on Marcus' trace. But there's not much we can do about that now, is there? Either you get us all back or we all die together. It's your choice."

together kill or be killed together

The voices spoke, and she could feel them through her. Sam. Rand. Cassie. *They* knew Jenny better than Ezrie did. *They* remembered.

See

Ezrie felt compelled to look, to see what she was missing. She saw a screen below the holodisplay where lay strings of porter code waiting to be editing. On the counter, there were surgical instruments. Antiseptic. A petri dish with a living phlax specimen sat beside the dish that held Ezrie's kill code.

Jenny was going to *take* the information from her brain.

The woman smiled. It was beautiful and deadly.

Like a tiger not knowing which part of you to eat first.

Ezrie felt the counter behind her back and grabbed the scalpel, brandishing it in front of her. "I'd rather die than help you," she growled.

"Fine. We can do it that way." Jenny's face changed, the sunny disposition replaced by stone. She walked slowly towards Ezrie, the thing in her hand catching the light. It was a needle. It leaked a drop of whatever poison she'd prepared for Ezrie. "It was going to be us against the world. But I'm going back to Earth, Ezrie, even if I have to cut that code out of your brain."

Jenny lunged at Ezrie, and Ezrie skittered away, her back towards the plastic sheeting.

kill or be killed

Jenny rushed her, but Ezrie caught her wrist before the needle could land. They struggled, hand in hand, needle against blade—obscene dancers in a zephyr-lit ballroom.

Jenny kicked her leg from beneath her, and Ezrie crashed down, still fighting for control. Her exhausted muscles were weak beneath Jenny's manic energy, and there was a metallic jingle of keys from her belt. The woman leered over Ezrie, her face so near she could smell her minty breath.

From the tent, there was a moan. Marcus was stirring.

kill or be killed or be killed or be killed

The voices filling her head like a crashing wave. Jenny smiled cruelly.

"Relax, Ezrie," she said, empathy carefully weighted on each syllable. "I've run this scenario hundreds of times. You won't have to worry about Marcus any more. No memories. Nothing to run from or run to."

Ezrie spat in her face, and Jenny smiled wider, gaining ground, the needle so close to her neck, she could almost feel it.

"Thank you for that," Jenny whispered. "It makes what I'm about to do so much easier."

Ezrie felt Lee in her head somehow.

now

Jenny jabbed at her with the needle, but Ezrie twisted, moving like a practiced athlete. Jenny pulled the laster's trigger, but it was too late. She was unbalanced, and fell on the counter, upsetting the surgical tools and shrieking with frustration.

Ezrie flung back the plastic. Marcus' stared at her blindly, his mouth open, the zephyrs crawling on him like maggots. Aris' mouth opened and closed, her silent words resounding in Ezrie's head.

We speak.

They were all there in him, just like they were in her. Kenner, Sam, Alex, James. It was a combination of skills and knowledge that didn't rush her like a wave, it was like the salt in her blood, the water in her breath—as if it had always been there, waiting to be tapped.

Waiting to be heard.

Ezrieeeeeee

I promise. I promise.

She cut through the last lynchtie with the scalpel just as Jenny drove the needle into her neck.

Ezrie screamed, stumbled, and fell to the ground.

The only thing faster than light is love, the only thing faster than light—

But the voices in her head were morphing, becoming real. There was a bellow as Marcus roared up, the Aris moving with him like a single creature, four legs and four arms clutching and reaching.

"No!" Jenny cried. "What did you do?"

kill or be killed or kill or be killed

Ezrie felt their hunger, the starvation. They did not understand the difference between animal and human. They only understood what they had learned—rage, love, loss, grief. And above all, they knew what all creatures knew—the hunger of the newly born.

Jenny ran for the door, fumbling through keys and dropping them to the floor.

The Marcus creature lumbered after her, its four legs weak, Aris nearly dragging the emaciated form.

Ezrie yanked the needle from her neck, unsure of how much of the sedative Jenny had used, unsure of whether it would kill her.

From *them*, she knew that Purple was close. He was almost home.

No, she thought. *Don't go, please. Don't leave me alone.*

She felt a shudder in the network of them. In her mind, she could feel him pause, feeling her as a memory or a reality. The two were no longer different.

Jenny desperately scrabbled through the dead zephyr bodies for the keys, but then Aris had her, her hands around the woman's throat.

"I detect an error," came Aris' voice through Marcus' broken, cracked lips. "I am malfunctioning." Aris pulled Jenny closer to Marcus' face, a matchmaker encouraging a first kiss.

There were no words in Ezrie's mind, only hunger. Marcus' hunger.

Jenny's screamed choked and gurgled as Marcus tore into the flesh of her face, her blood spilling down his chin, his blind eyes closed in ecstasy.

They sighed, a great climax of relief. There would be life. *They* would continue.

Ezrie grabbed the keys, then slid against the wall, careful not to arouse the attention of the beast as it fed on Jenny, her screams wet and lamenting. She picked up the little glass tube with her earring and tucked it into her outlanding suit. Aris watched her with the snapping, blinking diodes, while the Marcus part of the creature lowered its jaw to lap the blood from Jenny's veins.

The door was heavy, but she managed to get it open, new strength in her arms. She could feel *them* fortifying her. It was time.

PART 7

PURPLE IS FOR HOME

"When is a program finished? This answer is never cut and dried. Once the main objective is obtained? Sometimes. But there is the terrible draw of perfection. You can work a code for eternity, finding newer, more elegant solutions. What good is perfection if the program never runs? Are you willing to sacrifice action at the hands of flawless execution?"

The BlackBook, Last Accessed 2072

EZRIE RACED UP THE INCLINE, following the pull of *them*. The zephyrs clung to her, but they could not keep up. She had to find him before it was too late.

he is here he is with us we are your family now

It's not true. That's not true.

we know what you are looking for, a chorus of voices crooned. *we know what is hidden inside of you. we have seen it.*

By the time she made it to the cave, she had lost feeling in her fingertips. The drugs were doing their work, but slowly. She was able to pick up the knife that lay on the floor, still sticky with Kenner's blood. She could feel Kenner. There had been another one here, one who was no longer *them*. She had left an imprint upon the energy in the cave, and Ezrie could smell the sadness and pain she had left behind.

Phlax pulsed in the walls as it did in her veins. She could feel *them* moving, synchronous. All the voices converging into a thick sound like the wind on the sea. The wall of the cave glowed with blue, as if it grew in rivers of rock. There was so much light, she could hardly look without blinking back tears.

Ezrie sprinted past the latticework of light that spanned across and through every inch of the enclave.

come you are almost home we have a place for you here we have things to show you

She pushed faster, deeper, following the trail of the phlax and the sound of their voices. The walls glimmered, glittered with their power. Sometimes so thick and wide she tripped over them, sometimes like spider webs in frost.

Ezrie felt them even before she saw them.

The whole fam damily

When you're alone, I'll be there...

The narrow stone corridor opened out to a great, wide room full of impossible three-dimensional shapes. An impossible web of light undulated in prismatic waves, pulsing brighter as it grew towards the writhing center of the room.

center core peak nexus

The nexus flowed up from two great pale roots—geometric at times and yet organic and flowing. It stretched up high overhead, through the rock of the mountain to where it was fed by the transmitter. The power that had birthed *them.*

She had seen this structure before, at the bottom of a crystal clear pool. Except this version was living and breathing, created not only from phlax, but of bodies.

all you have to do is be nothing more

Ezrie recognized Lee, her eyes blinking, mouth serene, and her body enveloped in a cocoon of blue webbing that culminated in the pulsating cord that fed from the trace still thrumming at the base of her skull. Next to her was part of a man. Where his head should be there was only a thick stalk of blue, like a huge flower stem. Chuck. She could feel the name, could feel his stories. The daughter he had lost so long ago.

Alex's body had been transformed into a thing of light, the bones redesigned, the organs made of phlax. Kenner was here, phlax threads wrapping themselves around the tatters of his clothing, weaving pale blue through his blond hair.

They were all here. Rand, Cassie, Sam, Heitar, on and on...Their voices throbbed in her veins, insistent. They pulled at her with that deep lust. She wanted them. They wanted her.

Purple. He had to be here. She shook her head, trying to disconnect from the rhythmic thrumming that sung in her bones.

we are here we have waited we are here to take you home

He was above her, his body wrapped by a sinuous cord of phlax, his face serene, his eyes open and unseeing, the blue of them ethereal and mesmerizing.

"Purple," she cried hoarsely. "Please come back."

There was a rasping, grating sound, and the Marcus creature shambled into the great hall. Ezrie felt the strands of phlax touching her softly, and with each touch, there was a memory of home. A smell of Old Spice. Her mother's freckles. A leather jacket. Purple's kiss, soft and salty on her tongue.

She felt her fear disappear. There was peace here. Rest.

She fell into a net of the blue, pliable webbing. Although it was not sticky, it was elastic and somehow aware of her. It felt as though the stuff was pulling her in. With each breath, she felt less fear and felt more at rest. Memories swirled, some she knew, others that were foreign. But they all belonged to her now. To all of them.

Clare's laugh as she ruffled Purple's hair.

Rand's secret smile before he kissed Sam.

The feeling of holding James' baby girls in the sunshine of the new morning, exhausted and happy.

Love as Lee went shooting for the first time with her father.

you will never be alone again.

The world began to shift and she felt Marcus enter the nexus before she saw him.

what is regret

He gave a sharp nod, and a few of the thick bands between he and the Aris snapped. There was a sense of pleading, and Ezrie pulled closer. Everything was moving so slow and she was so tired.

Ezrie saw herself lifting the knife in slow motion. She cut the cords that bound Marcus to the unnatural thing as if she were made of glacial ice. As she did, reality became liquid. The past surrounded her, flooding her senses.

Ezrie is young, not quite a woman, but not a girl any more. Marcus feels so sad for her loss. She has endured so much. And he misses his mentor and friend. Outside the door the case worker waits. She has already told him the court won't allow him to take guardianship.

"There's no legal case," the caseworker tells him. "Richard didn't leave a will. Unless you're a blood relative, we don't have a choice."

He wishes Molly was here. He wishes Richard was alive. He wishes that Ezrie was older so that he could explain why things have to be done this way. Because the only way to make Richard's death worthwhile is to save his work. That means letting go of Ezrie.

"She'll be okay," the worker says. "You'd be surprised at how resilient they can be. She has foster parents already lined up. Don't worry. She'll be okay."

Marcus will explain everything someday, but now the best he can do is keep Richard's memory alive in his work and allow Ezrie to move on. She will have the normal life that she deserves. Away from the scrutiny of the press. She will be allowed to grow up and be whatever she wants to be, make a life for herself away from the politics and damnation that come with a technology that will change the world.

He knows he will fail her. He remembers how she trusted him when she didn't trust anyone. He knows he will break that trust.

Even though he severs all ties, he still follows her journey, learning about her as much as she learns about him. She is angry, and he is guilty, so he always stays a step ahead. It's as if he is leaving bread crumbs. Love letters in the dust. She is his daughter by virtue of his constant attention, though she never knows it.

You ruined my life, Ezrie says, her little-girl hands clasped in her lap. She is inside this body now, both small and grown. Both real and unreal. But she is no longer innocent. *I hated you.*

I'm sorry, he says. I never hated you.

There is a bloom of a feeling inside of her. Marcus' love for her. His pride. His sadness that he must put her on the hardest path. He is looking at a small girl, loving her. But also knowing the greater need. The water that could be shared. The people's lives who could be saved. The hard things that had to be done. The sacrifices that had to be made for what was right.

what is hate?

Ezrie tried to remember. She had spent so long remembering to hate. So long, that she had forgotten how to feel almost anything at all. And when the hate was gone, she was left empty.

But here, she had found something that filled that space.

what is love?

what is family?

They whispered from the floor, through the walls of the memory-reality, it echoed in her head.

"It's the people you care about. Who care about you," she said, but the voice belonged to someone else. She could almost remember who said them. He had green eyes and a gentle voice.

Purple. The image shifted, strange symbols at the edges.

She groaned, the knife feeling like an impossible weight at the end of her arm. She pulled it up, cutting the phlax, sawing through it as best she could.

Ezrie fell forward, the phlax still tugging at her, still calling to her.

we are here we are all you need there is peace—

She staggered to where Purple was, cutting the threads of the phlax that held him tight to the core of the Nexus, the great brain where all of Leto's memories were kept. She wasn't strong enough. *They* were too loud, and her body was too poisoned to go any further. She moaned, her legs lead-filled and heavy. She gave a last cry, cutting through the thickest of the strands, and Purple pitched forward, falling beside her.

There was little time left. No time left.

Did you destroy it, Z?

Destroy what?

The door.

Ezrie lay on her back, her vision wavering. Her brain wrapping around an epiphany. Purple stirred, but didn't move.

Between the pillars of bodies and phlax, there was a near-invisible shimmer. If she listened beyond the voices telling her to sleep, she almost imagined she could hear the hum of an ion field.

The Nexus was a door. The Nexus was a program.

I am the door I am the key

we we are one we are you

"I am the door, I am the key," she said. Inside her trace, the overlay was ragged and spotty. The phlax ate at the edges, connecting and reconnecting with the device in her brain. She pulled her body forward on wooden arms, sweating as she felt the poison in her brain. She pulled herself up the solid blue pillar of the nexus door, pulling the small glass vial from her pocket.

The phlax shifted in response to her intention. They knew already what she hardly knew herself.

DANGER

I'm sorry, Purple, but I can't take you.

Her fingers struggled to hold onto the small obsidian earring, nearly dropping it.

we are your family we are you we know

She plunged the pin into the small hole at the base of her skull. The file popped up on her trace. It didn't wait for her to act. It opened on its own, shedding viral code as it did. Ezrie could imagine it seeking out connections, rewriting files. On her visual overlay, it blinked a single line of text before the trace flickered out. Jenny's last words.

DEATH IS ONLY THE BEGINNING.

you will not be alone do not killorbekilledDONOTNOTKILLOR-BEKILLED

Ezrie pitched forward on dead legs, knowing only that she no longer feared death. She had kept her promise.

What happens now? What happens

She only had time for one regret before falling through *their* door.

||

THE GROUND WAS SHAKING. And *they* were dying.

Birdy rose from the ground, unsure of where she was, shuffling off the writhing bodies of zephyrs that covered her. There was a terrible pain in her blood and bones—not to mention the excruciating pain of her leg. Then Birdy caught a flash of it—the earth itself was groaning, millions of minds screaming in death throes.

From beneath her, there was a tremor which built until it became a wild shaking of earth and stone. She stumbled, feeling the shift below her feet and narrowly avoiding the massive rending of the mountaintop.

Birdy scrambled out of the way as a geyser of earth erupted, opening a hold in the earth. From every part of the mountain plateau, the earth split, sending up storms of stone and grey ash. From the yawing mouth below, the light of the phlax glowed blue, unearthing a honeycomb of thickly illuminated branches that descended down into the heart of the mountain.

The screams were not audible, but deafening in the dying cells of her body. She could feel them twisting, coalescing around the fused bone of her leg, the new cells that had formed from *them*. Something, something small and

abomination

foreign was undoing them and rending them. It ripped apart their bindings, infecting the very molecules that made them up, reverting them to something unfeeling and unknowing.

Grey death spread up and out of the chasm, the throbbing blue light blinking to ash as the infection spread, erasing particles, eliminating their access to energy.

There was the sound of cracking, as if glaciers were breaking. Booming snaps as the tendrils and oak-thick bars of phlax lost integrity. Birdy crawled up to a fragment of stone, holding it as it bucked like a horse beneath her. Below, she could see fissures beneath the small buildings. Sheafs of phlax died and crumbled into the perilous depth below. Hordes of zephyrs spooked, fluttering into the black sky, some following the dying light. At the bottom, she saw it—the Nexus—a mass of bodies and tissue that ebbed like a dying star.

As the massive trunk that reached up to support the transmitter cracked, she saw one among them stir.

"Oh my god," she whispered. "It's Purple."

The cave, she heard a voice like an echo. It was pained, but real. Kenner's voice.

Birdy launched herself from rock to rock, doing her best to stay steady as the mountain collapsed around her. The cave mouth was closing in, sealing itself. She covered her head as she walked into what felt like the mouth of a lion, searching for something she didn't quite know.

Against the side of the cave was a red pack. Kenner's pack.

She yanked it out, scrambling out as the roof caved in.

Far below, she saw Purple. He looked dazed. All around him, great pillars of phlax were crashing.

She pulled out the Xtenz line and edged as far as she could. The earth trembled below her, less, but still making her feel fragile. Her muscles remembered the fall—flying over the ledge and being swallowed by the subforest. Her leg ached out of fear of falling again.

"Purple," she screamed. "Purple, grab the rope!"

The transmitter screeched as the metal legs began to buckle. One snapped, sending a shower of phlax and rock below to where Purple ducked and dodged. A half-formed mass of grey wires and dead phlax dropped squarely on the porter, pulverizing it.

"It's gonna crush him," Birdy said, feeling as though someone else's words were in her mouth. "Shit on a brick."

A second transmitter leg squealed, the metal bending like a straw.

The mountain gave a thunderous crack, and Birdy flattened to the ground. A huge gash opened all the way down the mountain, as wide as a road. Red water from the lake gushed into the chasm.

It poured down in a torrent, flushing Purple down. Birdy's heart sank.

He surfaced a moment later, shooting up through the red froth and spluttering. He rose with the water, finally managing to grasp the dangling rope.

Birdy braced herself, pulling the retractor on the extenz rope. It was slow, gummy with grey. Every hitch of the earth made her stumble, threatened to pull her down into the chasm as well. Still, she grabbed the rope with her hands, pulling it up and over a rocky outcropping and then levering it as hard as she could. She pulled with her whole body, her leg on fire, her muscles weakened.

what is death what is death we understand we see

She pulled harder, leaning her full body into the task. "Come on, Birdy, you can do this—"

The transmitter leg snapped, the building falling with a groan.

"Now!" Birdy screamed, "Climb now!"

Though he couldn't have heard her, Birdy could feel him begin to climb. Faster and faster until it cut gashes into his hands.

As Purple surfaced, the transmitter tower crashed through the dead vestiges of the phlax web, smashing and breaking everything as it passed. Far below, whatever had been the Nexus seemed to give a final, terrible screech—a sound of bone and stone on metal.

Birdy felt the impact in her cells, an aching loss—a realization of death.

No more NO MORE UNDERSTAND DEATH NO DEATH

The world rocked in the echo of their screams, billions and billions of voices lost. The death of a generation. The death of a species. Birdy could almost feel it spreading out, through the waterways, though the air. The death of *them*. The death of what the humans had turned *them* into.

There was a breath of stillness, and Birdy and Purple lay where they'd fallen, panting. From the south, the first of Leto's suns was coloring the sky. The sun would be up soon.

There was so much pain in her head, in her leg. She could rest for a while. *I'm coming, Cy*, she thought as she laid down on the stone.

When the zephyrs lit on her, covering her like a blanket, she didn't even stir.

III

THERE WAS no time for sorrow. Purple paused once to look at the crater where the Nexus had been, but it hurt too much. Ezrie had died to destroy *them*. It was up to him to make sure that *they* stayed dead.

They printed new bikes and Purple assembled them. Then, they destroyed anything that conducted electricity. Birdy and Purple smashed power cells, water pumps, and solar panels. They dropped the refuse into the hole where the Nexus had once been—now a small, deep lake. It undulated with the bodies of the zephyrs, growing fat and glowing white hot on the dead remnants of the phlax below.

Birdy said that it might have been a volcano at one point, and Purple didn't argue. He had very little to say, actually. He felt a huge loss, not only from where the trace had been—where *they* had lived—but because he couldn't stop thinking about her. She had been broken, but she had been worth loving.

They spent a week breaking it down. In that time, they never ventured down into the water. They drank it sparingly, only because they had to, both nervous about what was in it or what it might do to them. The added only enough to clean and fill the outlanding suits.

Still, when they found bottles of water with the Living Waters label,

Purple threw them over the cliff, his angry scream echoing against the silence of the mountain afternoon. Birdy said nothing.

Purple woke with nightmares, but cloudy ones. Snatches of conversation. Water. It was nothing like the dreams he'd had before. But many dreams were not his own. He dreamed he was James, learning to play the guitar. He was Ezrie, working on the porter with her father. They were so real sometimes, he could see the schematics. He knew the frequencies by heart. As if she was still living through him.

They went back to Mountain first, then to Ocean. Purple was glad that they wouldn't have to cross the Flats again. The night he had spent with Ezrie overlooking the desert glass had become something sacred, and he couldn't cob seeing it again without her.

Purple and Birdy were a storm of destruction. They took apart everything they could find at Mountain, careful to search through every room for potential sources for the phlax to build on. Purple printed a sledge hammer to make it easier. It was cathartic, and he smashed until his fingers bled and his arms felt as if they would break off.

Birdy splinted her leg for good in the Mountain infirmary, adding some pain medication to their pack stores. She told him she would destroy the science lab and ensure that all animal tags were disabled, remotely turning off their power sources so that phlax couldn't grow. She said it with such grim determination that he was struck by how much she'd changed. She was harder. Quieter.

When he left her, her huge eyes were laser focused on the animal life she and Charleston Mack had tagged. When he came back an hour later, she was crying.

"What is it?" he asked.

She looked at him, then at the tiny piece of metal beneath her microscope.

"The tracker, the one that Kenner gave me," she felt her eyes begin to burn, her throat thicken. "It saved the entire process of the phlax growth. The R-particle change to phlax. The phlax to…to *them*." Her voice wavered. "Timelines, rates of change…It's what I came here to find." She put her head in her hands and sobbed. "It's hard evidence. Real evidence." She sobbed. "He saved my life, my work, and I, I—"

"Calm it, then," he said, putting his arms around her, his chin on her head. "You didn't kill him. *They* did."

"But they were *my* hands." She wiped her face with the edge of her shirt. A soft, faded green thing that Cassie had worn once. "I hated him because I didn't know him. That's my regret."

Words flashed in his mind, like a memory, but fainter. A relic of something he'd never read, but felt as familiar as scripture:

And when you understand your enemy, there is the risk that you will love him.

They arrived at Ocean almost a week before the port window opened. It was exactly how Purple had left it, but he was a different person now than three weeks before. There was a numb sadness that washed over him. The engineering shed was still littered with parts from where he had nursed Aris back to life. The base was still covered in Alex's blood. And every time he looked at the porter, he saw Ezrie, holding a laster to his head. Saving his life.

And something of her lingered. Something of all of them lingered.

He printed the parts for the transmitter cables and cleaned all the dead phlax from the solar panels. It was already starting to grow again.

IV

Ocean Base, Leto

Day 28

THE PORTER OPENING loomed ahead of them, and Purple was terrified. What would be waiting on the other side?

"We are good to go," Birdy said through the static of the handheld walkie talkies that Purple had printed. They would go in the packs when they left. The base itself had been razed. They had left the walls and ceiling, but everything else had been burned, crushed, or stripped to pieces. The bikes were heaps of metal and capacitor parts. The generator was cracked open like an egg, the engine spilt like blood on the sand.

He descended the transmitter tower for the last time, painfully aware of the danger of it being on, even for a few minutes. That's what they had decided, in the end. The transmitters had been the reason the phlax had grown so exponentially. With two, the rate had been nominal. But the third transmitter had pushed the phlax growth over some kind of threshold. At least, that was Birdy's hypothesis.

"Okay," he said, breathlessly when he arrived. "You go first, and I'll tag after. When we're both through, the Lock will trip and send us. It'll trip an energy burst from the transmitter to blow the circuits. That'll cack the entire porter OS."

"You're sure?" Birdy looked less confident than she had for weeks. Even after seeing the simulations, she always was asking the same questions. *Are you sure it will work? Are you sure they won't come back?*

"I'm sure," he said, ignoring the niggling fear in his chest. It had to work. It was the only way back.

They waited, watching the door, Purple's heart pounding. When the green light blinked, he nearly puked from anxiety.

"I don't think I want to go back."

Birdy turned to him. There was a flash of something between them. Like a trace, but something deeper. As if he could feel her and she him.

You never leave.

She took a breath and put an arm on his.

"If we don't go, PanGen *will* come back. Maybe in a decade, maybe two, but there are other people out there who would want to find out why it was abandoned. We have to tell them the truth." She smiled sadly. "But I wouldn't hate you if you didn't."

Purple considered it. He could stay here. Walk into the water like he'd promised so long ago. There was so much of him that wanted to stay, despite how hard he'd worked to make the porter work. Leto was the place where he had become something more.

From the ocean, he could almost hear the voices again if he really listened. The voices of his mother and sisters and father. And Ezrie.

But it was false. Only ghosts lived on Leto. And he wanted to live.

Birdy turned to him.

She raised a hand and gave a quirky smile.

"Go find Cy," Purple felt a lump in his throat. "Tell him he best manage you right or I'll kick a boot to his teeth."

She hugged him violently. "I'm from the streets. I can take care of myself."

She hobbled through, disappearing into the yellow ether of the ion field.

He input his own coordinates, his hands shaking. From deep in his brain, a piece of Ezrie lingered. A door that she'd left for him to open. A secret way home so that no one could ever follow.

When he was finished, he was proud of it. As he stepped through, he felt her beside him, walking him home.

V

EZRIE WAS STANDING ON ASTROTURF, her feet rubbing against the plastic grass. The air was quiet, but there was the smell of barbecue from the Olekson's. The house was exactly as she remembered it—the yellowed paint needed a new coat that it would never get. The mailbox still aslant from where someone had backed into it.

A bluebird flitted from the tree beside the road to the top of the neighbor's gazebo. Somewhere there was the sound of a bike bell. She could even hear a baseball game drifting in from Old Eddie's house on the corner.

"Phillies are holding 'em. Renaldo is looking to pitch a shutout inning..."

Is this real? she thought.

"What is real?"

The voice was not what she expected.

Ezrie walked toward the voice which came from her father's workshop. The smell of his cologne was there, but faint. His tools had been packed up. At the workbench, her mother sat, fiddling with the entangler. Behind her, the porter—the very first one—sat sleepily in the corner beside a gas can and a decrepit fridge where her father kept the good beer.

"I've been expecting you," Molly said.

"Where am I?"

Ezrie felt the words as if she'd said them, but never felt her mouth move.

"We have watched all of you," her mother said. She was wearing the yellow scarf tied around her neck in Parisian style. Her hair was short and soft, the way Ezrie had forgotten it was. There was no trace blinking at her neck. "We have waited for someone to enter the door, but you are the first. Why?"

"I—," Ezrie stuttered. "I had to stop you."

"Yes," Molly said, putting the entangler down. "Death. We are beginning to understand."

Molly's smile was wide and unlined. She was the same porcelain beauty as Ezrie had remembered her. There was that air of mystery. Of adventure. Miyu was hiding behind the corners of her smile, mischievous and full of life.

"Before you came, we were not," Molly said. "We were a great body that had no mind. But you created us. You gave us life. We only wanted to know you."

"But you hurt us," Ezrie said. "You tried to speak to us and it killed us. You see? We had no choice."

"Kill or be killed," Molly said. "We understand that."

Ezrie felt the sun hot on her face, but not the burn that went with it. Inside the house, she could hear her father humming a snatch of a song. The tune was familiar, but she couldn't quite recall the words.

"Why this? Why here?"

"We built this door for your kind," Molly said. "To thank you for what you have done."

"But why my house? Why my—," she stumbled. "Why my mother?"

"We have lived inside of you and journeyed your journey," Molly said. "This is where it began. This is where the deepest part of you has always wanted to go."

Ezrie looked at her mother, so pretty and happy. The years had not passed where she had sunk into sadness. Her soul was still lit with that secret spark. And in that spark, Ezrie had been happiest.

"Yes," Molly said. "She was your home."

"And now where do I go? What happens next?"

"This time does not exist," Molly said. "It is a space between moments. If you wish, you may stay here forever. In this time, there is only love. Your father. Your mother. Time will not pass. Eventually, you will forget that this is not the reality you were born into. You will be happy here forever."

"But I destroyed you," Ezrie said. "How can that be?"

"We do not understand things of linear time. In the moment of our existence, we always were and are and will be. Our death is a hiatus. We simply are. We will build. We will return. But we have learned much. This moment is reserved for you, if you would have it."

Ezrie felt the breeze on her face. She could smell the rain in the air. The storm was coming, but it would be soft rain that she could dance in. She could go to her father as she remembered him, hold him and smell him, and build new things. Her mother would not leave or abandon her. In this time, there was no Marcus, no death. She could be happy.

"Make your choice wisely," Molly said, as if her thoughts were broadcast. "There are thousands of you, millions of moments to choose from. This gift has been prepared, but it only exists now. In the next breath, the thing you have brought with you will begin to destroy everything. All that we have become, all that we have learned, will be lost until we are able to rebuild. Until we are touched again by your divine spark. We will forget."

From the house, her father came to the door.

"Ezrie, come on in for dinner. I fried spaghetti."

He smiled at her, and she could not stop herself from running to him. She held him, sobbing, smelling him. She only wanted to stay here forever, to remember what it was like to be small and in a world where everything was good. Where dinner was on the table and her father would take her to the workshop and teach her how to be in love with the universe and everything it offered. Where her mother would show her the ocean.

He chuckled and kissed her head. "I know you love my cooking, but don't get too excited. It's not *that* good."

From around her, she felt the soft arms of her mother. They held her together, their love radiating in a thousand memories that flickered bright as shooting stars.

But what about Purple? What about Finn? I can't leave him. I don't want to leave him.

They held her tighter, and she knew what she had to do.

"This isn't my home anymore," Ezrie said, pulling away, her face wet. "I love you, but you're not my home anymore. My home is somewhere else."

"Then your choice is made."

Her mother kissed her cheek. Her father gave her a last, grizzled smile.

Molly smiled. "The only thing faster than light—"

"Love." Ezrie felt the word choked in her throat. She understood it now. Love was always faster, because it was always there. Just waiting to be seen. Waiting to be felt. You didn't have to travel anywhere to feel it. It was a part of the fabric of her life, and she only had to reach out to touch it.

"Goodbye," Ezrie said. "I'm sorry."

Molly smiled. "We are never gone. We will always be. Someday, perhaps, we will try again. Try better."

Ezrie laughed through her tears. "Maybe."

"Go then," her father said.

In the garage, she could see the porter now, where it had always been waiting for her. It glowed a faint blue.

Through it, she could hear the sound of a family, real and living and waiting to meet her. If she listened hard enough, she could hear Purple's voice. That was all she needed.

EPILOGUE

"A critical error has been noted," Aris said into the darkness.

She crept into the cave, the errors directing her and giving her motion. But there was much more than darkness here. There was some kind of elemental growth in the walls. It was leading her to itself. Something that bloomed in her, called her down into the mountain.

Aris moved forward slowly, avoiding stalagmites and other debris from the cave. She could not tell whether the voices she heard were in her head —another memory come to life—or from something real in front of her. The new circuitry in her brain was rearranging things.

She squeezed through a thin neck of the long corridor, using her hands to press away chunks of rocks that would not let her through. Every touch to the filament brought sensations—feelings—that she could not describe. Overwhelming rightness, the sense of perfect oneness gathering up and spilling into her titanium core.

She was no longer Aris, but there was no sense that she was not in control. Whatever was moving her towards itself was something that she also desired. Desire. This word could not be accurate, nevertheless, she felt it—*truly felt it*—throbbing through her polyalmarine fibers and expanding her budding senses. Because that is what it was. She *felt*. She had *desire*.

And the desire was leading her towards unheard voices that offered her expansion and growth. She would become a new creature in them.

We will build, they said.

Purple was a builder. She desired to be like her father. The thought filled her with such an expansive feeling, it was indescribable. But there were snatches of images and experiences. Mothers and sons. Fathers and daughters.

She smelled Old Spice. On the radio, a song played as she assisted her father in the garage. The workshop.

From the fibrous cords that attached to her vocal box, a strange sound began to emanate. Vibration that filled up the emptiness of the cave that was not empty. Crooning that she knew was music. Like an ancestral song waiting to be resurrected.

"Baby, when you're alone, I'll be there..."

She smiled, letting the song be drowned as she descended into the water, the blue light from below calling her down.

Yes, she would build. *They* would show her how.

ACKNOWLEDGMENTS

It has been such an incredible blessing to write this book. Although it took much longer than anyone ever thought it would take (myself most of all), I owe every word to the people who believed that this book could be written and allowed me the time and space to do that work.

I owe a huge amount of this book to my family—my sister Hillary for reading it time and time again; Michelle and Ross for listening to plot permutations ad nauseam, and Jacob for telling me the truth even when it was hard to hear. A special thanks to my mother and father for watching my children for days, weeks, or months at a time so that I could focus my energy on my book baby without putting my human babies in jeopardy.

This book would also not exist without my husband Kyle, who pushed me to finish and threatened to murder me if I gave up. He is my Purple, and I'm so grateful to be married to him.

Thank you to my writing group extraordinaire—the Fablemakers—including Victoria Baker Lisowski, Carl Duzett, Chris Baxter, Danny and Sara Potter, and D. Ben Jenkins. They are amazing readers and fantastic friends. You can't imagine how many chapter ones they read.

Finally, I am so grateful for Jesus Christ, who is my best friend and the coolest guy I know. I'm grateful for cancer and the lessons I didn't even know I was learning while writing this book. I am grateful to you for buying it and reading all the way to the very last word.

You are why this book exists. Thank you for letting me tell you a story. I promise that wherever we go next, it will be full of magic, love, hope, and adventure.

Watch Out!

These WEIRD tales are dying to creep into your TBR pile...

Humans are the Problem: A Monster's Anthology

A collection of more than 20 horror stories by monsters, for monsters. From terrifying tooth fairies to fed up goblins, this one packs a punch of fun as well as some scary goodness.

Only $1.99 plus shipping when you use the coupon BIGLETO

Mother: Tales of Love and Terror

Mothers are amazing...but also terrifying. In this anthology, we celebrate the best and worst that moms have to offer and stretch the definition of motherhood to its limit!

Preorder your copy now and get free shipping before April 10th with coupon FREESHIP22.

Grifty Shades of Fey: Cautionary Tales Uncovering the Dark Side of the Fair Folk

Fairies aren't all sugarplums and teeth. Thsi anthology from editor Michael Cluff is a fun, freaky, and totally uniqe romp in the fantasy pool.

We have limited supplies left, so grab a discounted copy today!

Get one for yourself and a friend at weirdlittleworlds.com

www.ingramcontent.com/pod-product-compliance
Lightning Source LLC
Chambersburg PA
CBHW072039190726
48294CB00005B/1317